NOW YOU SEE US

Balli Kaur Jaswal is the author of five novels, including *Erotic Stories for Punjabi Widows* which was a Reese Witherspoon's Book Club pick in 2018. Born in Singapore and raised in Japan, Russia and the Philippines, Jaswal studied creative writing in the United States and worked as an English teacher in Australia and Turkey. She has held fellowships at the University of East Anglia and Nanyang Technological University, where she also completed her PhD in South Asian diaspora writing. Jaswal's non-fiction has appeared in the *New York Times*, *Harper's Bazaar India*, Refinery29 and Salon.com, among other publications.

@ballijaswal
@balli_jaswal
@ballikaurjaswal
www.ballijaswal.com

Also by Balli Kaur Jaswal

Inheritance
Sugarbread
Erotic Stories for Punjabi Widows
The Unlikely Adventures of the Shergill Sisters

NOW YOU SEE US

BALLI KAUR JASWAL

HarperCollins*Publishers*

HarperCollins*Publishers* Ltd
1 London Bridge Street,
London SE1 9GF

www.harpercollins.co.uk

HarperCollins*Publishers*
Macken House, 39/40 Mayor Street Upper
Dublin 1, D01 C9W8
Ireland

First published by HarperCollins*Publishers* 2023
1

A catalogue record for this book is available from the British Library

ISBN: 978-0-00-843374-1 (HB)
ISBN: 978-0-00-843375-8 (TPB)
ISBN: 978-0-00-843378-9 (PB)

Set in Bell MT Std by Palimpsest Book Production Limited, Falkirk, Stirlingshire

Printed and bound in the UK using 100% Renewable Electricity by CPI Group (UK) Ltd

This book is produced from independently certified FSC™ paper
to ensure responsible forest management.

For more information visit: www.harpercollins.co.uk/green

For H.

Breaking News:

A woman was found dead in her home in the east of Singapore on Sunday evening. Police received a call for assistance from a member of the woman's family between 6.30 and 7.00 p.m. They classified the death as "unnatural" but declined to provide further details on the cause of death.

Neighbours of the victim say that they saw police arresting a woman near the crime scene. Police have confirmed that a person of interest connected with the case is in custody and that she is a domestic worker from the Philippines.

Investigations are ongoing.

Chapter One

One month earlier . . .

From the way Corazon Bautista is clutching her rosary beads, she could be mistaken for a religious woman. Every other person in the waiting room of Merry Maids Employment Agency is peering into their phone screens or staring straight ahead, but Cora – with her eyes closed and her lips moving – appears to be having a spiritual moment.

The truth: she is only holding the beads because she discovered a rip in the lining of her purse, and doesn't want them falling in there. She lost a gold earring that way once. Prayer is the last thing on her mind. Sitting in a hard plastic chair along with all the other Merry Maids, she is making up a grocery list and ticking the items off each rosary bead. *Rice, vegetable oil, eggs, milk* . . . It has been a week since she arrived in Singapore, and Ma'am Elizabeth hasn't asked her to cook a thing.

The rosary beads slip through Cora's fingers like water. *Onions, garlic, ginger, soy sauce* . . . The waiting room is full of women – Ma'ams and their maids, sitting on the plastic chairs joined in rows to face a long reception counter which is partitioned into cubicles. A blue sky is painted on all four walls, with words like *Happiness* and *Service* floating in white clouds. The wall behind the reception counter is a gallery of framed photographs. *Our Merriest Maids!* The title is made from cut-out birthday party letters that dance over pictures of maids clipping pieces of laundry to bamboo poles and running vacuum cleaners over Oriental rugs. There are young maids dutifully wiping ketchup off the faces of small children and helping elderly men into their wheelchairs. One grinning maid wearing a *kerudung* holds her broom at her side like it's her best friend. Printed under each photo is a description of the woman's nationality and marketable qualities:

The Filipina maid is a favourite among Singaporeans because of her ability to speak English, and her friendly demeanour. Good with children, the elderly and pets. Suggested monthly wage: $580-$750, public holidays and Sundays off.

Indonesians can handle all household chores, including deep cleaning of floors and windows. They will cook a variety of dishes but may not be able to handle pork for religious reasons. Suggested monthly wage: $580-$650. Some public holidays and alternate Sundays off.

NEW! The Myanmar maid: she will need some training, especially about living in high-rise apartments and other aspects of city life, but if you are on a budget, the Myanmar girl is a cost-effective option. Suggested monthly wage: Please enquire.

Cora supposes Merry Maids has a friendlier environment than those agencies on the first floor of this quiet shopping plaza. In brightly lit storefront windows, the maids on the first floor perform their skills for potential passing clients. They run cordless irons over men's office shirts, and wipe counters in the same circular motion all afternoon. There is a model kitchen outfitted with a fridge and a sink where one maid is stationed, rinsing dishes under an imaginary flow of water. Every surface is already as glossy as a pamphlet, and a slick-haired woman, wearing a fitted black blazer, struts between the maids, nodding her approval.

As Cora and Ma'am Elizabeth passed one of those agencies on their way upstairs, Ma'am Elizabeth muttered, 'There's no need to be so *literal*,' and twitched her shawl over her shoulders. Cora nodded, and then wondered if that was too much agreement – maybe Ma'am was trying to test her? Who was Cora to criticize the way the agencies advertised their services? So she shook her head as if this action would neutralize her response, except then it looked as though she was disagreeing with her Ma'am.

'Are you all right, Cora?' Ma'am Elizabeth asked.

Cora brought her hand to the back of her neck. 'Just having stiff neck, ma'am,' she said, and right away she wondered if this sounded like a complaint about the pillows in her room, which were comfortably firm. Luckily, Ma'am Elizabeth didn't seem to notice as she became preoccupied with searching her purse for her buzzing phone.

'You go on, Cora. I'm on my way,' she said. Riding the escalator up, Cora watched two maids in the window of the first-floor agency pantomiming a scene of a nanny feeding a child. The maid dressed as the child wore a Paw Patrol bib and clapped as the nanny scooped air out of a plastic bowl and brought it to her mouth.

Plain flour, rice flour, salad dressing, sugar, sliced cheese, breakfast cereal . . . Does Ma'am Elizabeth have allergies? These are things Cora will have to guess, or wait for Ma'am Elizabeth to reveal. Hopefully it won't take long. Some employers' preferences and habits remain shrouded in mystery and contradiction for years; others are prepared with long lists of dislikes.

Ma'am Elizabeth has been chatty since Cora's arrival, though not in ways that are relevant to Cora's grocery list. Cora knows about her daughters: Jacqueline, a banker who lives in River Valley with her Swiss fiancé, and Cecilia, who is at university in New York (she's on a six-year under-graduate track, Ma'am Elizabeth said with an eyebrow raised).

'Do you have children?' Ma'am Elizabeth asked, and Cora thought about the picture on her phone of her nephew Raymond in the restaurant where they celebrated her birthday. He died later that night and she has not been able to look at that picture since.

'No children,' she said.

Ma'am Elizabeth's late husband was Harold Lee, the founder of Lee's Kopi, who passed away two years ago in a tragic car accident. 'I helped him here and there with the business but for the most part I've been . . .' She paused and slipped Cora a smile as if there was some joke between them. 'I've been Mrs Lee,' she said.

That was several days ago and Ma'am Elizabeth still hasn't told Cora yet what her job will entail. Not that Cora needs a detailed job description – she knows the general needs of a household: cooking meals, making the beds, dusting, scrubbing the toilets, hosing the grit off the cars in the driveway, lighting the mosquito coil, changing the light bulbs. Et cetera, et cetera. But so far, every time Cora tries to do any work, Ma'am Elizabeth asks her to stop.

'Oh Cora, don't bother with that,' she says, looking embarrassed at the sight of Cora dusting the banisters or picking the laundry off the line in the back yard. And the fridge! The shelves are completely empty except for a packet of spinach leaves, a jar of ginger paste, and takeaway containers of leftover *bistek Tagalog* from Tuesday night, when Ma'am Elizabeth insisted on ordering takeaway from a Filipino restaurant because Cora must be homesick.

(For the record, the *bistek* was quite good, although Cora would have let the meat braise low and slow rather than try to rush the process with a meat tenderizer as the restaurant clearly did, and it was clear that they used lemons instead of *calamansi* because the marinade wasn't as tangy as it should be . . .)

'I want to speak to a manager immediately!'

The voice that breaks Cora's thoughts comes from the back of the room. Spines straighten automatically as the reprimand sweeps through the rows. A middle-aged Chinese woman with a frowning, heavily made-up face, and hair shellacked into a stiff, short bob marches down the aisle of the waiting room. With each stab of the woman's heels into the floor, the receptionist shrinks into her seat, until she is nearly on the floor herself. Another man behind the desk grabs a stack of papers and hurries to the photocopier, which is in the front corner of the room, near Cora's seat. She can see that the papers going in and coming out are totally blank.

As the shouting woman advances on the front desk, there is only one staff member left there. Through the young woman's round gold-framed glasses, Cora can see her fear magnified a thousand times. Her decision to gather resolve is visible – she grits her teeth, then crosses her arms over her chest, then uncrosses them. The shouting woman demands again to see a manager.

'Mrs Fann, you need to take a number,' the girl says firmly, adjusting her glasses on her nose. 'We will attend to you as soon as—'

'I want a refund,' Mrs Fann says. 'I want to return my maid.'

Return her to where? As though there's a storage room full of maids, stacked like mannequins and waiting to be chosen. Then again, seeing that first-floor agency with the maids on display, Cora can see where Mrs Fann got that idea.

'Cooking? Terrible. Ironing? Clothes still crumpled. Cleaning? Sloppy – I can see the soap marks on the tiles. What is this "happiness" and "service" you people claim to provide? Each new maid is worse than the one before.'

'I understand, Mrs Fann, but there is a procedure,' the girl with the glasses insists. 'We told you this the last time you came here.'

'Last time I came here, Belinda Quek still ran this agency efficiently. She's a church friend of mine, and she was very understanding. Now I don't know who is running the place. I tried calling several times this morning and got no response. Who is answering the phones?'

Accusatory looks shoot between the staff members. Glasses Girl straightens her posture and tries an official approach: 'If you want to transfer your maid, there are government protocols to follow. You will have to contact the Ministry of Manpower first—'

'I called them on my way here,' Mrs Fann interrupted. 'Automated system, press one for this, press two for that. I waited to speak to an actual customer service representative and they put me on hold for so long, the call timed out.' Cora suspects that the whole of Singapore recognizes Mrs Fann's voice and goes into hiding when she approaches. She looks around for the maid in question, but Mrs Fann hasn't brought her along. 'Just let me know who the manager is here, so I can speak with them.'

The argument continues, with Mrs Fann waving her hands around, and Glasses Girl trying to calm her down. They have switched from speaking in English to Mandarin. A handbag hangs from the crook of Mrs Fann's bent elbow. It's a solid case of deep navy leather, with gold buckles that clatter like bangles, and a silk scarf knotted at the handles. Cora expects a dog to pop its head out from the bag – something with pointy ears and a sharp bark to punctuate Mrs Fann's accusations.

Somehow Glasses Girl convinces Mrs Fann to take a seat. She casts a disdainful glance over the waiting room. There is an empty seat in the front row, next to Cora, but Mrs Fann doesn't take it – she walks back down the aisle and settles in a seat near another Ma'am. Moments later, Cora can hear her fuming, this time to the woman next to her.

'How can they send me a maid who can't do anything properly? And then she wants one day off a week. I tell her, you're a fresh maid, you are here for experience. You're lucky to have any work at all. In their country, there are no jobs – even teachers and nurses are only making two hundred dollars a month. Here she gets free lodging and food in my flat – I mean, my *house* – and she's earning in Singapore dollars, and she still complains?'

Thank goodness Cora was hired directly, through Ma'am Elizabeth's network of friends. They are only using the agency to complete her work permit paperwork. If the agency employed her, she wouldn't see her salary for months until she paid off her placement debt. Cora's former employer from years ago, Ma'am Anne-Marie Gomez, didn't ask any questions when Cora got in touch out of the blue to ask if there were jobs in Singapore and recommended her to Ma'am Elizabeth without hesitation.

'She's very nice,' Ma'am Annie assured Cora, who, in her short time with Ma'am Elizabeth, already knows this to be true. Ma'am Elizabeth makes a point of saying each of her neighbours' names when she greets them. The GrabFood delivery boys always receive a generous tip from her. On the drive over here, she pulled over when she noticed a stray cat wandering along the main road. Cora watched from the passenger seat as Ma'am Elizabeth picked up the cat and walked all the way to the grassy lot at the end of the street, where the cat leaped out of her arms and scrambled off into the bushes.

However, no employer can be so nice as to simply pay Cora to live in her huge house and not expect her to do any work. This morning, Cora woke up with the uneasy feeling that Ma'am Elizabeth had changed her mind and the trip to Merry Maids was her polite way of cancelling her work permit. Then, as they entered this shopping mall, Ma'am Elizabeth glanced at the arrow sign for the supermarket and said, 'We'll do some shopping later. Maybe you can make lunch today?'

What a relief! Cora's idle fingers have been worrying away at her rosary since she arrived in Singapore and now she can put them to some use. While Mrs Fann continues to fume, Cora concentrates on adding to her list. She can do a hearty chicken Caesar salad with crispy bacon, and a special dressing if Cold Storage has those bottled anchovies that she used to buy for the Calverts, her American employers in Manila.

Now that the agency workers have settled back into their seats, they begin clacking on their keyboards and answering phones again. Nervous tension thrums in the air as Mrs Fann continues her complaints.

'At least the previous maid was good in character,' she says. 'Not that I can prove this maid has done anything wrong, but just look at her, give her *one look*, and you'll know what type she is, and what she'll be doing on her days off.'

Cora doesn't turn around but it sounds as if Mrs Fann is showing a picture on her phone to the woman next to her, who murmurs her agreement.

'Corazon Bautista?' the man at the front desk calls, shuffling some paperwork on his desk.

'Yes,' Cora says, raising her hand and glancing over her shoulder at the door. Where is Ma'am Elizabeth? Cora takes out her phone to send a quick text: *Ma'am, they are calling me. Are you coming?* The second sentence looks a bit aggressive and she deletes it. Then she changes Ma'am to Ma'am Elizabeth, but her thumb hovers over the backspace. Is it necessary? Obviously she's referring to Ma'am Elizabeth. She adds 'Dear' before 'Ma'am Elizabeth'.

Dear Ma'am Elizabeth. They are calling me. I hope to see you soon. With Warmest Regards, Corazon Bautista.

What is this, a love letter? The man calls her name again, louder this time.

Cora's thumb slips and lands on the emoji menu. She presses delete several times, erasing the whole message and replacing it with emojis.

'No!' she cries, shooting out of her chair.

The man looks confused. 'You are not Corazon Bautista?'

To her horror, she realizes she has sent Ma'am Elizabeth a row of salsa dancing girls and a cow.

'I am Corazon,' she says, approaching the counter. 'My ma'am is coming.' She settles in the seat across from him, still staring in dismay at her phone.

'Your passport and employment forms please,' he says. His confusion is gone, replaced by a grimace that makes him look more like that angry Mrs Fann. Cora takes the plastic folder from her bag and shakes out her passport. 'The forms are with my ma'am,' Cora says.

He opens up her passport and types the details into his computer system. Cora wonders if the scan of her old passport is still in the government database. Age has scored the corners of eyes, gravity tugging down the loose skin at her jaw. For her first passport photo ever, a twenty-four-year-old Cora had worn lipstick and crimped her shoulder-length hair with a searing iron. Flying was a bigger deal back then, even if you were going abroad to clean houses. At fifty-two, Cora's style is all about the practicalities: cotton T-shirts that don't get easily rumpled and a pageboy haircut that keeps her neck from getting sweaty.

'You worked in Singapore before?' the man asks.

'Yes sir,' Cora says. 'From 1991 until 2007.' How much information is recorded in his system? Do they know about Cora's first employers, a three-generation family who lived in a terrace house in Serangoon Gardens, where snakes some-times flitted across their doorstep? Or Mrs Motwani, who taught Cora how to cook rich korma dishes that she still smells in her dreams? Do they know about Ma'am Roberta's husband, who flung an ashtray at Cora because he was convinced she'd thrown away his parking coupon?

The man's expression betrays nothing as he continues to type. His fingers are long and slender, and there is a jade ring on his little finger. She watches the jewel catching the fluo-rescent light of the place, turning it into something softer, but she looks away when he notices her staring. It is a reminder that Cora should never let her gaze linger on anything; many people don't know the difference between admiring and coveting.

Ma'am Elizabeth finally arrives, pulling up a seat next to Cora. 'Sorry about that,' she says. She looks a bit harried. Cora wonders if the salsa dancing girls came across as an insult – who knows what any of these things mean? She only learned recently what the aubergine meant and she was horrified, having sent it several times to Maddy Calvert to let her know she was making her favourite vegetarian lasagne.

Ma'am Elizabeth pulls the forms from her bag and slides them across the table. The man fans out the documents and, on each signature line, he makes an X. He taps the pen impatiently at Cora. All other questions about her are directed to Ma'am Elizabeth.

'She's done her medicals? No health problems? No disease? X-rays clear, AIDS test negative?'

'She's under the age of sixty?'

'She was employed directly from the Philippines?'

Yes, yes, yes, Ma'am Elizabeth answers to everything, but then comes a question about Cora's previous employer.

'She was under a contract from her previous employer in the Philippines. Where is the letter of release?' the man asks.

Cora freezes. 'Letter of release?' she repeats. She did not think it would matter how she left the Calverts, as long as she left the country altogether. They had returned to America for the summer holidays when Cora decided to go, and there was no time to request a letter in any case. She had simply packed her bags and left a note: *Sir Jack and Ma'am Patricia, I'm very sorry I must leave for personal reasons. Madison, Sierra and Bennett, I will miss you so much.* She had pressed her single gold earring into the security guard's palm so he would stall the men if they returned for her.

'Yes, letter of release,' the man says slowly, as if Cora cannot understand English. 'We need to provide this to the ministry, in case there are any questions about your employment pass and previous work experience.'

Cora searches her mind for an explanation, but she finds it crowded with groceries. *Iceberg lettuce, ranch dressing, garlic. There were two brands of bottled anchovies but Mrs Calvert preferred the one with the gold lettering on the label, what was it called?*

'We don't need the letter immediately though, do we?' Ma'am Elizabeth asks, glancing at the silver chain-linked watch on her wrist. 'She's a good worker. My friend recommended her to me. I'm sure there won't be any issues.'

'I can make Caesar salad.' Words spurt out of Cora like from a rusty tap, as if she has been holding her breath for days. She wonders if this is why Ma'am Elizabeth hasn't asked much of her so far.

The man gives her a strange look before he resumes typing, and then he pauses to peer at the screen. His face is knotted in concentration and, for a moment, Cora fears that he has found out everything. It's not possible, her name was not in the news, but her heart is pounding so loudly, she is sure that every Merry Maid and Ma'am on the island can hear it. What if they cancel her work permit? What if they put her on a plane this afternoon and send her straight back to Manila? She crushes the rosary beads into her palm.

'That's fine then,' he mutters, stacking the papers into a yellow cardboard folder.

'We're done?' Ma'am Elizabeth says. 'Thank you very much.' She gathers her bag and tugs at the edges of her shawl so it covers her slender shoulders. The cold air streaming from the air-conditioning vents makes the hairs on Cora's arms stand up.

As they walk out of the agency, Cora realizes she has probably raised a few questions in Ma'am Elizabeth's mind. She's still clutching the rosary beads, and they are biting into her skin. *Please don't let her ask me about what happened in Manila,* Cora pleads with a God who stopped listening to her the day Raymond died. She doesn't want to lie to this kind-hearted Ma'am, but she will have to if it means avoiding being sent home.

'Elizabeth Lee?'

She and Ma'am Elizabeth both turn around to see Mrs Fann coming towards them, her arms outstretched. She is wearing the kind of smile that you give the dentist when he needs to look at every single tooth. 'It's been sooooo long! How are yooooou?' she coos, puckering the air with kisses as she approaches. Gone is the fury from before. Cora might be imagining this, but just before Mrs Fann's kisses land on her cheeks, Ma'am Elizabeth lets out a quiet groan that sounds like a shorthand version of, 'Oh no.'

'I'm well, Poh Choo,' Ma'am Elizabeth says, her lips stretched into a thin smile. 'Just needed to get some paperwork done and, halfway through filling out the forms myself, I remembered Belinda Quek's agency and figured it would be easier for them to do it. This is my new helper, Cora.'

Mrs Fann acknowledges Cora with a quick glance as she links her arm through Ma'am Elizabeth's.

'We *must* get together, it's been *so* long. How is Cecilia these days? The kids don't want to come back once they've gone abroad, do they? They like that relaxed *ang moh* lifestyle. Ha-ha! I see Jacqueline is doing well. I heard she and her fiancé closed on an apartment in Quayside Suites recently. Setting up house already, hmm, before marriage?'

For the first time, Cora notices that it's possible for Ma'am Elizabeth to be aloof. She uses the straightening of her shawl as an excuse to break away from Mrs Fann's grip, and her answers are brief. Mrs Fann doesn't catch the hint. The further Ma'am Elizabeth withdraws, the higher and louder Mrs Fann's voice becomes. They form a wobbly convoy moving towards the escalators, with Ma'am Elizabeth meandering away, Mrs Fann tugging her back and Cora falling two steps behind. Mrs Fann prattles on:

'Belinda Quek is my friend lah, okay, but this girl her agency sent me? A nightmare. You're lucky you never had to deal with this, although I don't know how you managed to maintain that big house without any help before this.'

Cora knows that the first rule of being a maid is being invisible: strive for the translucency of ghostly soup stains on *kopitiam* tabletops. Sidle from room to room and pretend to know nothing unless it is directly revealed to you. But she cannot hide her surprise at Mrs Fann's words. The Lees have never had a maid? How did they manage the cooking, the cleaning? Between the living room, the dining area and the five rooms upstairs, just washing all the curtains would take an entire day. Who swept the dried leaves from that huge back porch, or brought in the laundry at the first distant rumble of thunder? She can't imagine Ma'am Elizabeth, with all her poise and grace, on her knees scrubbing the floors. Yet the house was clean when Cora arrived, if a little bit bare in the pantry.

Mrs Fann's eyes narrow when she catches Cora paying attention. She nudges Ma'am Elizabeth and says something in Mandarin.

Ma'am Elizabeth replies in English, 'Establishing trust goes both ways, don't you think, Poh Choo?'

Her answer brings a flush to Mrs Fann's cheeks. She takes

a small step away from Ma'am Elizabeth and her tone becomes icy. 'I hope that's true. The older maids tend to be better anyway, hmm? Age slows them down, makes them more sensible maybe. There's my girl, by the way.'

Cora follows the direction of Mrs Fann's nod, and immediately she sees the problem. Dressed in a skin-hugging pink tank top and tiny white denim shorts that reveal slender legs, this girl does not look like she apologizes for anything. Her large rhinestone-studded hoop earrings wink as she tosses her hair from side to side. If Mrs Fann's husband has a wandering eye, she probably has a reason to worry.

A long time ago, Cora overheard her former employer Mrs Motwani advising a neighbour to avoid hiring pretty maids. 'Have you seen mine? Hardly a threat,' she said without bothering to keep her voice down, as if she thought Cora was deaf as well as plain. With sleek long hair and heavily-lined eyes, Mrs Fann's maid is very striking, and she appears to know it. The purse that swings from a narrow strap on her shoulder matches the cherry red gloss of her lipstick and fingernails. She is holding two Cold Storage plastic bags limply at her side, as if she wants to forget them.

Ma'am Elizabeth and Cora walk with Mrs Fann towards the supermarket and, as Mrs Fann examines the contents of the bags, Cora gives the girl an understanding smile. The girl gazes back coolly. A young man wearing jeans and sandals walks past and stares so hard at her that he collides with the cart outside Cold Storage, where a supermarket clerk is peddling a new matcha-flavoured pizza. She offers samples to Mrs Fann and Ma'am Elizabeth, who pauses to have a taste. 'It's . . . interesting,' she says to the representative, who beams like this is the highest compliment. She holds out a tray and explains the other pizza samples: red bean and corn, mango-chilli, durian-prawn and spicy-sweet pork floss. Ma'am Elizabeth reluctantly tries the mango-chilli. 'That one is a little better,' she says unconvincingly.

'Donita, I said *no breasts!*' Mrs Fann's voice booms.

Yes, we get the point, Cora is tempted to say. How many more faults will Mrs Fann find with her maid, who obviously does not understand the unwritten rules about modesty? Then she sees Mrs Fann holding up a packet of chicken fillets. 'I cannot cook with these, do you understand? I need the bones in order to make stock for the soup,' she cries. Her voice echoes off the walls. 'You see what I mean?' she asks Ma'am Elizabeth. 'Every little thing, she gets wrong. They're supposed to make our lives easier, but I'm doing more work correcting her mistakes.'

'I'm sure it's like that in the early days,' Ma'am Elizabeth says. 'Give her some time to settle in.' She offers Donita a reassuring smile but the girl's sullen expression doesn't change.

'Aiyah, Elizabeth, you are very patient,' Mrs Fann says, then she looks around conspiratorially before continuing. 'I think Belinda Quek's standards are dropping. Even her office staff are sub-par. I finally got the receptionist to tell me where she is and she said, "Myanmar recruitment trip." She used to have Merry Maids, now they are Budget Maids. To tell the truth, I was tempted to go elsewhere to hire better help but how would that look? What if it got back to her?'

As she launches into another litany of complaints about maid agencies, Cora introduces herself to Donita in Tagalog. 'I'm Corazon Bautista, from Manila.'

'I'm Donita.' Her eyes brighten at the chance to say her name. Cora feels a pang – Raymond was around the same age. If he were alive, he would be like that young man in the sandals who is lingering nearby, suffering through sample after sample of terrible pizza-flavour combinations in a bid to get a closer look at Donita.

Cora glances at Mrs Fann. 'Is she always like this?'

'So far,' Donita says. 'She doesn't give proper instructions just so she can scold me for not reading her mind.' She holds up a hand, trembling from *pasma*. 'She made me hand-wash all the laundry last night because I asked her how to use the washing machine. She said, maybe after this you will make the effort to learn.'

Donita speaks Tagalog with a strong Ilocano accent. 'You're from the north?' Cora asks.

Donita nods, and there is a flash of longing in her eyes at the mention of home. Cora recognizes this too; the first months are the hardest. She wants to tell Donita that it will get better, but she knows what a long road it can be with employers like Mrs Fann.

'Just a word of advice,' Cora says. 'If you cover up a bit more, she might give you an easier time.'

Donita's expression hardens again, and with a defiant upward tilt of her chin, she says, 'This is who I am. If she doesn't like it, that's her problem.'

Her response twists something in Cora's gut. Maybe Donita is too young and idealistic to understand that nobody cares who she is here. Cora's mind flashes back to her younger self, crimping her hair for the passport photograph, thinking surely the authorities would see her as somebody worthy of respect. Surely the family in Serangoon Gardens wouldn't make Cora continue sleeping in a tin shed outside when they had two spare bedrooms. Surely the Motwani kids would stop shouting, 'You're stupider than the maid' to each other as an insult. Surely Ma'am Roberta's husband, who was always misplacing things, would not accuse Cora of sweeping his parking coupon into the bin. As he picked up the ashtray and reared back his hand, time slowed down to accommodate her denial for one last time – *surely this is not happening to me* – before it landed with a blinding crack against the bridge of her nose.

Of course she says none of this, and soon Donita is turning her back as Mrs Fann hustles her into the supermarket to return the other grocery list items that she got wrong. 'Elizabeth, we must make a time to catch up soon, hmm?' Mrs Fann calls over her shoulder.

Ma'am Elizabeth smiles and waves back. 'Have a good day, Poh Choo. Bye-bye, Donita.' They walk in the opposite direction, towards the lift to the basement where Ma'am Elizabeth has parked her car. Cora has to hurry to keep up with Ma'am Elizabeth, who seems eager to get away. As the neon signage of Cold Storage recedes behind them, Cora doesn't remind Ma'am Elizabeth that they still need to buy groceries. She's just glad to leave Mrs Fann and Donita behind.

Chapter Two

On Sunday, Donita clutches her list from Mrs Fann and jostles with late morning shoppers in Marine Terrace market. The crates in the vegetable stalls are piled high with rippling green leaves of *kai lan* and *sawi*. The man who runs the fruit stall makes proud announcements about his crop of dragon fruits. 'Ripest in Singapore,' he declares, directing drifting shoppers to take in the blushing pink fruit and its curly green tendrils. In one swift move, he cleaves a pomegranate and prises it open to show the gemstone seeds gleaming within. Donita zigzags through the rows. If not for all these people who pause and ponder and bargain and suddenly shoot out their arms to pick up a lemon or collect their change, Donita's shopping would be quick, and she wouldn't be so worried about being late to meet Flordeliza. The market is a muggy, raucous maze, and the wet floor squelches under her black slingback wedges. After each purchase, she also must ask for a receipt, which makes the vendors scratch their heads – what receipt? This is not a supermarket – which leads her to explain: 'Just write the amount and the product on a piece of paper, please.' Some understand, and do this for her. Others, like Ah Seck the fish-monger, thinks it's a trap.

'For what?' he asks, his chin jutting out. 'No return policy, this mackerel. All sales final.'

'I do not want to return it. It is for my boss,' Donita says, but Ah Seck has already turned to another customer. Donita sighs and picks up the crinkly plastic bag of red snapper. A stiff tail pokes out of the opening and scratches her wrist. Every trip to the market is like this, and Sundays are the worst because Mrs Fann will return from church fizzing with nervous energy. She will scrutinize Donita's purchases and complain trium-phantly – a-ha! – when they don't tally up with the receipts. 'How do I know these sugar-snap peas cost three dollars? What if they actually cost two dollars fifty and you kept the fifty cents for yourself?' Mrs Fann asked last week, waving the bag at Donita. 'And these eggs? Did you really get them from the market?'

'Where else I will get them from? You see any chickens here, you idiot?' Donita replied. Although she and Mrs Fann comunicated in English, she said the last part in her language – *tanga* – and it was satisfying to see Mrs Fann stare blankly to an insult.

'Don't try to be smart with me. There was a maid in this block who used to keep the grocery money for herself and then just go around borrowing from all the other households. One cup of sugar here, a few eggs there; she managed to fool her employers. I. Will. Not. Be. Fooled. In. My. House.' Mrs Fann punctuated each word with a jab of her finger.

'Ma'am, if you think I am taking advantage, then why not you go to the market yourself and see how much is everything?' Donita retorted. Mrs Fann's nostrils flared in anger. She stalked off to the study. 'You see what kind of attitude I have to put up with?' she asked Mr Fann, before launching into a tirade in Mandarin. Donita did not understand any of it, but the shrills of Mrs Fann's voice suggested that she was urging her husband to get involved. He didn't say much, but there was nothing unusual there. Mr Fann is the quietest man Donita has ever met. She has heard his newspapers rustling more than his actual voice.

Emerging from the market, Donita takes a gulp of fresh air and looks around. She spots Flor standing at the edges of the entrance, sipping from a tall plastic cup of orange juice. Two oversized gold-hooped earrings graze her slender shoulders, and the tips of her nails are perfect white squares. Donita always felt a mix of admiration and envy for women like Flor, who came home at Christmas basking in the sheen of their overseas salaries. The first time Flor returned, her lips were buttery with a shade of maroon deeper than anything Donita had seen in real life. Long-lasting Revlon, Flor had said, flicking a tube of lipstick at her. Gifts shot from her hands just like that – Mars Bars; souvenir T-shirts wrapped in rustling plastic; a toy electric guitar for her daughter, Josephina, who wore it around her neck for days.

'Donita,' Flor says happily, squeezing her with a hug. It feels so good to hear a friend say her name. 'How are you?'

Donita shrugs and tries to brave a smile. She turns to show Flor her block. 'That's where I live,' she says, as if it will explain everything. It is strange, speaking in Ilocano about a place that she loathes calling her home. Standing at the end of this boulevard of white concrete apartment blocks, Block One breaks the sky. Even Mrs Fann doesn't seem to like it in this neighbourhood of identical government housing flats. She keeps a stack of leaflets for exclusive private condominium developments that property agents slip into the letterbox –

The Prescott! D'Azure Apartelles! Regal Living! A canal runs inland towards the tree-lined neighbourhood off East Coast Road, where Donita suspects Mrs Fann would rather live. The houses there have slanting red rooftops and green lawns, and probably enough space for Ma'ams and maids to get on with their days without constantly butting heads. Flor works there and she seems happier.

'I've got a few more things to get – the market is really crowded today,' Donita says.

'I'll help,' Flor offers. 'You look like you'll need an extra pair of hands.' It's true. The groceries are heavier today because Mrs Fann's list included one kilogram of onions, a sack of Thai red rice and two whole pumpkins for a cake she is baking for a church fundraiser. The pink plastic bag handles have already begun to stretch and turn into string.

The silver-haired butcher is friendlier than the fishmonger. He hums to the tune pouring out of his portable speakers and his smile doesn't drop when Donita gets to the front of the queue after two Singaporean women move on to another stall. 'How many grams, Miss?' he asks, and he says 'no problem' when Donita asks for a receipt.

'See? How hard is it to just be helpful?' Donita asks, shooting a scowl at the fishmonger behind her.

'Not hard at all,' Flor agrees. 'But the fish guy, he's different because his wife is around. You see her over there, watching him?'

Donita follows her gaze. Behind Ah Seck stands a small-framed woman with short hair and a clipped-back fringe. Her eyes follow his every movement. Donita realizes it then: Ah Seck might be at the front of the store, shaking buckets of crushed ice over the fish and declaring his tiger prawns the freshest catch on the island, but his wife is the real boss. Donita thinks of Mrs Fann chastising Mr Fann and demanding his attention last week. His responses whittled down to nothing and she stormed out of the study, fired up by her defeat.

Together, Donita and Flordeliza walk back out onto Marine Terrace. The sky is high and bright above the tall apartment blocks, and there is only a smear of clouds. Children in neon sneakers shriek and chase each other through the fanned shadows of palm leaves. Beyond this road is the winking blue strip of sea, where throngs of workers convened first thing this morning for their day off. The wind carried their celebratory reunion upwards into the Fanns' kitchen as Donita washed the breakfast dishes, wishing she was part of it. On weekdays, she lingers at the kitchen to peer out at the bright green belt of trees hugging the island's edges. Water laps gently at the shore and cyclists glide along the concrete East Coast Park path that leads westward to the jagged city skyline.

Donita can feel the excitement tuning her voice as she tells Flor every bit of news from home. The Tantoco family had a small accident with their truck on the farm-to-market road. Rumour had it that Junior Salangsang's new wife was a *mangkukulam* – because only a witch could manage to seduce somebody so handsome and educated – and his sisters had taken to wearing *anting-anting* and spreading salt outside their doors to reduce her powers. The sugar-cane crops were supposedly worse off due to the weather, but everyone was saying that the *basi* produced after a heatwave several years ago was the sweetest they had ever had, so who knew?

'I really miss it,' she confesses. Around them, the white apartment blocks look like bones picked clean. 'It is nothing like this.' As she turns away to fight back tears, her bag snaps. Out tumble the shallots, followed by the garlic cloves. 'Ay, this is hopeless,' Donita cries. She lowers the bags to the ground and drops there with them, sobs juddering through her shoulders.

Flor briskly gathers the ripped bags and brings them to the concrete mahjong table to consolidate the groceries, while Donita tells her about the fining system that Mrs Fann implemented after last week's chicken breast/thigh mix-up. Twenty cents for every misunderstood instruction, fifty cents for every surface still covered in dust at the end of the day, one dollar for every eye-roll or sour look from Donita. 'At this rate, your ma'am will be able to pay herself a nice bonus by the end of the year,' Flor quips.

'I can't seem to do anything right,' Donita says. She hesitates. 'Is it true that rice cookers can be possessed?'

Laughter dances in Flor's eyes. Donita swats her on the arm. 'I'm not saying I believe it, but I posted a picture of Mrs Fann's rice cooker on the East Coast Pinoy Maids Facebook group to ask for help because I kept burning the rice. And everybody offered the measurements I was already using. Then this one woman – let me find her,' Donita takes out her phone and starts scrolling. 'This woman, Luwalhati Macablo, she said: "Has there been a death in the house? Sometimes spirits can possess electrical appliances, especially the spirits of children. They are playful, but be careful not to offend".'

'So you're being extra-polite to the rice cooker now?' Flor giggles.

'I think the Fanns' son died,' says Donita.

This information wipes the smirk off Flor's face. 'He was older,' Donita says quickly, so Flor isn't reminded of the daughter she is unable to tuck into bed every night. Flor makes up for her absence in daily phone calls and gifts for Josephina. Donita visited her parents once and saw the slatted bamboo floor covered with colourful foam jigsaw tiles that

Flor had sent home to soften her daughter's falls. 'I don't know it for sure, but when Mrs Fann gave me her son's room, she said, "Weston is no longer with us, but this is still his room."' She wants to describe the slight quaver of Mrs Fann's voice, but Flor dismisses her.

'That means he's probably studying abroad,' Flor says. 'And she wanted you to know that she was being very generous, not making you sleep on the kitchen floor.'

Donita finds herself unloading all her burdens on Flor as they walk towards her building. She tells her first about the cluttered flat. In the absence of décor, there are rows of Precious Moments figurines, picture frames covered in seashells, and glass participation trophies. A pocketed wall hanging with silver embroidered elephants overflows with junk mail, and there are stacks of yellowed newspapers in Mr Fann's study. 'She's always complaining that the apartment isn't clean enough but she's the one who collects junk,' Donita tells Flor. The storeroom is piled high with bottles of paint samples, spare bicycle parts, a cracked, mouldy fish tank and old appliances. Every time Donita goes in there to get the broom and dustpan, she holds her breath to avoid choking on the dust.

'She goes to church nearly every day for meetings, but before her Sunday service, she is moodier than ever. She brushes her hair one way, then clips it back, then shakes it out and starts again. The whole flat is cloudy with hair spray. Then she starts fussing over her outfit and her jewellery.'

When Mrs Fann ran out of things to fuss about this morning, she pointed a finger at Donita's door.

'Why is it shut?' she had demanded.

'For my privacy,' Donita had replied. She saw this word register on Mrs Fann's face: privacy meant Donita was being dishonest; what was there to be private about if she had nothing to be ashamed of? Before Mrs Fann could start accusing her of hiding something, Donita had flung open the door.

'I had my lacy lavender bra and a fresh pair of blue and white polka-dotted underpants on the bed. One glimpse, and Mrs Fann was hastily rushing to shut the door,' Donita says now, her story bringing a flash of delight to Flor's face.

'She was probably terrified her husband would see it,' Flor says.

Donita screws up her face at the thought.

'Make sure you're never alone with your sir for too long,' Flor warns her.

'I think my sir is pretty harmless,' Donita says.

'Sometimes it's the quiet men that you can't be so sure about,' Flor tells Donita. 'But you also have the kind of ma'am who will accuse you of trying something if you're alone together. Trust me, you don't want any of that.' When Flor catches Donita searching her face, she smiles. 'Not me,' she says. 'Although I think my sir has someone on the side.'

'Who is it?' Donita asks.

'No idea. It's not like they tell you anything directly, right? You just pick up information here and there. There was online gossip about him sleeping with a teaching assistant at his university a few years ago – I heard that from the neighbours' maid across the street. And then, last December, my ma'am noticed a hotel key card at the bottom of the laundry basket and she asked me about it. I told her it wasn't mine and she believed me – I mean, it was the Ritz-Carlton! There was lots of angry whispering after that, and then they all packed up and went for their annual holiday.'

'Everything was OK when they returned?' Donita asks.

Flor shakes her head. 'It was really quiet around the house, sir wasn't talking to anybody, and the daughter was always moody and sniffling. They all avoided each other. I overheard my ma'am on the phone with her friend one day, crying and saying, "I cannot believe he would betray us like this."'

'Wow,' Donita says. In comparison, Mr Fann's presence is a benign shadow in the landscape. She can count on one hand the number of times he has spoken directly to her. Last Tuesday, she woke up in the middle of the night to use the bathroom and found him at the sink, tossing two white pills into his mouth. 'For sleeping,' he muttered as he passed her on the way out.

Flor's hands plunge into her tank top to retrieve a silver cigarette case. She pops it open and offers a cigarette to Donita, who hesitates.

'You don't smoke any more?' Flor asks.

'I do, but . . .' Donita looks around. 'Around here, anybody can see us, and I don't know who will report back to my ma'am.' The black windows of the apartment blocks stare back at her.

'The canal then,' Flor says. A paved jogging path and bank of trees line the canal's edges. There is a fitness corner with heavy exercise equipment bolted to the ground, and two park benches that are partially shrouded by the shadows.

Sneaking off like this brings back the thrill of skipping school with Flor in the old days. They would hitch rides on the backs of lorries and go to the market in town to buy hair clips and rings. Sometimes they found themselves undressing hastily in alleyways for boys who kissed them and made promises they never kept.

Donita checks her phone for the time and sees a notification – another private message from a stranger on Facebook. Friendship requests from men have come pouring in ever since she changed her location to Singapore. *Hi, how r u? Hey beautiful body so sexy want to b frenz? When ur off day where 2 meet u?* She blocked most of them immediately, but there is one picture that she saved last night. This one has taken care to present his personality: he is standing next to a No Smoking sign and holding his hand to his lips. A cartoon Popeye cigar has been edited onto his fingers. Donita can't help smiling.

'What do you think of this guy?' she asks Flor when they find a seat near the canal.

Flor glances at her screen and looks impressed. 'Not bad,' she says.

She opens the message and reads it aloud:

Hello! You are in Singapore just to visit or working? I'm Sanjeev Singh, doing hospitality course, always happy to make new friends.

It's not very different from the messages from the other men, but Sanjeev has made no reference to her sexiness or called her 'hotttt stuffz', which is an improvement.

'I'd send him a reply,' Flor says. 'There aren't many guys I'd say that about.'

If Flordeliza approves, it must be a big deal. 'You have a boyfriend now?' Donita asks.

Flor shrugs. 'If he feels like calling himself that.' She takes a long drag from her cigarette and looks away.

Donita scrolls quickly through Sanjeev's pictures to see if he's attractive from other angles. She finds that the No Smoking profile photo is part of a series where Sanjeev poses in front of signs doing the opposite of what they say. He's high-kicking an imaginary ball next to a No Football sign under a void deck, and he's wearing thick black glasses and peering into a book next to a No Studying sign in a café.

Flor peers over her shoulder. 'If you don't reply to him, I'm going to do it for you.' She pretends to snatch the phone from Donita, who squeals and pulls it away. 'Wait!' Donita cries. 'I need to do more research. Don't you know, I have high standards.'

She and Flor are doubled over with laughter when Mrs Fann's voice rings out suddenly from across the canal.

'*Donita!* What do you think you're doing?'

'Oh shit.' Donita tosses the cigarette into the bushes. Mrs Fann was supposed to be at church for another hour at least. That would have given Donita enough time to put all the groceries away, sweep the house, hang the clothes that she left in the machine on the bamboo poles to dry outside, and chop some vegetables for lunch.

Flordeliza is still giggling as Donita shouts her goodbyes, hurrying back to Block One. With every fervent gesture Mrs Fann makes, berating her from the other bank as she hustles to join Donita at the entrance, her brick of a purse swings from her elbow. Around the corner in the car park, Donita notices Mr Fann standing by the door of his car. He appears as if he's leaving it to come home too, but then he gets back into the driver's seat. Moments later, the car is backing out and leaving Marine Terrace.

'I send you to the market to do the shopping, not to stand downstairs and talk to your friends,' Mrs Fann says to Donita as they enter the lift. 'You were smoking, I saw you.' The rings on her fingers clatter together as she jabs the button for the seventh floor and the Door Close button. 'Hand me your phone.'

'No,' Donita says, putting her phone behind her back. If she has to put it down her trousers, she will. She doubts Mrs Fann would want to get her precious rings anywhere near Donita's crotch.

'I said, give me the phone,' Mrs Fann says. Her voice is quiet and full of menace. Donita wonders what would happen if Mrs Fann lunged at her now and snatched the phone out of her hands.

'No,' Donita repeats calmly, which infuriates Mrs Fann. The lift door opens and they crabwalk out of the door, facing each other and carrying the argument to the gate of the flat. 'You can't have my phone. My things are my things. You don't like this, you send me back to Merry Maids.'

Donita hopes her fiery stare is enough to make her point clear, but Mrs Fann takes a step towards her. 'They'll send you straight back to the Philippines.'

'I don't care,' Donita replies, but it's hard to keep the panic from rippling through her voice as she thinks about the debt she won't be able to repay the agents, who initially wanted a hefty deposit because she was inexperienced. Donita didn't understand how they could say that. She grew up shuttling between the homes of distant relatives who fed and clothed her in exchange for doing housework. In her aunt's home in Solsona and then another relative's home in Pasuquin, she had woken at dawn every morning to scrub the dirt off the *kamote* planted between the rice crops. She lit fires under a clay stove and used all her strength to crank the lever on the village well. But those are not necessary skills here.

What's necessary, is keeping her cool around Mrs Fann, who is making a show of picking up her phone and calling Merry Maids. 'Pack up your things,' Mrs Fann tells Donita. 'You will leave this afternoon.'

Will she go back to the boarding house, Donita wonders. Upon arriving in Singapore, she and seven other women crammed into a van and were shuttled there. In the dark of the next morning, they were piled into the van again and told they were to begin work. 'I didn't bring my suitcase,' she protested, and the driver said, 'You'll come back tonight.'

He drove for so long that Donita was convinced they were crossing over to Malaysia or heading even further north to Thailand. Through windows mottled with dried rain stains, Donita watched the shy pink streaks of daylight prising the sky open until the van peeled off the highway and began climbing up a long gravelly path. Fields of scraggly grass surrounded the van, followed by tamer squares of land and a loose cluster of boxy buildings. A sign said NENG TEW AGRICULTURAL INDUSTRIES. The women were led to a fetid-smelling room with high walls and only three small windows in the top corner like postage stamps. A row of blue crates lined one side next to a shallow gutter and some hoses extending from taps in the wall. The crates were piled high with mushrooms, the source of that smell of festering mud. A supervisor arrived and ordered them to wash the mushrooms in the crates. Donita opened her mouth to ask if there had been a mistake, but she shut her mouth right away when she saw that all the other women had the same question on their faces. From 6.30 a.m. till 6.30 p.m., every day for a week, they crouched over basins teeming with oversized mushrooms, alien and slippery. Donita found that at the end of each day, she could not scrub the dirt out from the ridges in her own skin, or stop the dreams of monstrous billowing white caps expanding and engulfing her.

In the evenings at the boarding house, she overheard some women saying that this type of work was illegal, that the Merry Maids people were loaning them out to factories for a profit, but who would dare complain?

'What do you mean, I will lose my security bond?' Mrs Fann's shouts into the phone bring Donita back to the present. 'You send me these kinds of lousy maids all the time and now you're saying I have to make it work?'

Donita begins gathering her things – her lipsticks, her bottle of lavender Baby Bench cologne, her hot-water bottle for period cramps, an extra box of Sutla papaya soap, a spiral-bound diary, and her razor. In the corner of the room, there is a faded built-in closet with sliding wooden doors that don't close all the way. Something is rattling back there – probably a loose roller that has fallen out at the end of the track – and it's preventing her from sliding open the door fully.

She sends Flor a message. *Looks like I'm about to be fired,* she types. *Goodbye Singapore.*

FLOR: *It's not so simple. The agency will try to transfer you to another household.*

DONITA: *I can transfer? Why didn't anybody tell me?*

FLOR: *Because it's not up to you. Your ma'am has to release you. And just so you know, they have their own way of blacklisting maids. Hopefully your new employer isn't on any of those Facebook groups.*

A couple of screenshots follow Flor's message.

> Do not trust this maid Perlita Kristine Ortega, also goes by Krissy. She is a thief. If she tries to apply for a job with you, please contact me.

> Here is a picture of our former helper, Uthpala Gunaratne. She left us and returned to Sri Lanka without any warning in January.

DONITA: *How did you come across these?*

FLOR: *A couple of us made fake profiles so we could see what they were saying.*

DONITA: *Clever. What else do they talk about?*

The bubbles of a reply in progress dance in the white space, and then a series of screenshots arrive in quick succession. *Does this maid belong to you?* shouts the header of the post from one irate woman named Anchita Chowdhury:

Was with my toddler in this playground in Tampines today when I saw this Filipina maid talking with some foreign workers, either Indian or Bangladeshi. Worse, she had a child with her! Didn't get her name, but here's a picture.

There are many more screenshots like this, taken from various Ma'am groups all over Singapore: Yummy Mummies SG, Mothers of West Coast, Singapore Parenting Community of North-East Region.

My maid is in debt and wants a salary advance again, if I say no will the loan sharks come after me??

Is it true that the Indonesian ones can use black magic? After I scolded our maid today, I heard her reciting some kind of chant, and since then my husband has had non-stop diarrhoea.

There is some sort of beauty pageant all the Filipina domestic workers are participating in this Sunday in the Ngee Ann City atrium, has anybody heard about this? They dress up by region and parade around? How come our government is allowing this? Do they have permits?

Mrs Fann is continuing to shout on the phone outside, now in Mandarin. 'I will not calm down! This is not what I signed up for.'

You and me both, Donita thinks.

When she had made the decision to apply for this job and leave the Philippines, Donita had been hopeful. On the bus ride to Laoag, she saw re-election banners for a local congressman who was known for sending off a record high number of Overseas Filipino Workers, and it felt like a good omen. Slits were cut into the canvas to withstand the wind pressure, and when the gusts swept in from the West Philippine Sea, he looked as if he was laughing. In the recruiter's office, a mounted screen on the wall played a video – music swelling over images of nipa huts turning into solid brick houses, three generations of one family at their reunion, all dressed in matching imported T-shirts provided by one woman. Donita had her eye on a poster showing a skyline of buildings against blue mountains that appeared to be carved out of sea and sky. In comparison, Pasuquin's rice paddies were waterlogged descending steps, taking her nowhere.

'Vancouver?' the recruiter asked, following her gaze. 'They want nurses, not maids.' He told her that a domestic worker needed to swallow her pride. It's what Corazon Bautista had advised her to do as well, but how? If Donita sets aside her pride, she loses something precious, and look . . . look at her life scattered across this room. How few precious things does she have to lose?

The Pokémon sticker on the closet has been stuck there for so long, it has absorbed into the wood. Donita shakes the closet door and the Pokémon stares balefully at her. She can hear the roller rattling around back there. It's useless. In anger, she smacks the door. It shudders, and there is the sound of something dropping. Donita tries to slide the door open again and, this time, it goes all the way. She crouches down and pats around the closet floor to pick up the loose roller, but she's surprised to find a long, chunky, lightning-shaped earring studded with pink and blue diamantés. Donita rolls it around in her palm, briefly considering a small way to gain Mrs Fann's favour – *look ma'am, I found this.* Then Mrs Fann's screeching voice pierces the air again and Donita knows that hell would have to freeze over before she makes any attempt to appease Mrs Fann. She tosses the earring back into the closet.

'Fine,' Mrs Fann shouts into the phone. 'I can cancel the maid's contract if she breaks the law, right?' There is a pause and then Mrs Fann's feet can be heard padding across the flat.

She appears in Donita's doorway with her phone. 'From now on, you can expect frequent spot checks,' she says. She goes on a rampage, looking through Donita's drawers, pulling the sheets off the mattress, knocking things over with fervour and spite. She is looking for evidence that Donita has stolen something. Donita can feel the rage rising within her now and she clenches her fists so hard her nails dig into the soft flesh of her palms. Mrs Fann is picking at each item hanging in the closet, knocking the hangers carelessly together and screwing up her face in disgust at some of Donita's clothes. In Donita's mind, a voice shouts, *Stop it now!*

As if Mrs Fann can read her thoughts, she freezes. She crouches down slowly and picks something up. Donita sees it glistening in her hand – the lightning bolt earring.

'Where did you find this?' Beneath the make-up, Mrs Fann's face has gone pale.

'Inside the closet,' Donita replies. Is Mrs Fann really going to accuse her of stealing one useless cheap earring?

'Did Mr Fann see it?' Mrs Fann asks.

Donita shakes her head. 'No, I find in the closet so I leave it there.'

Mrs Fann's fingers fold around the earring and she storms out of the room. The grocery bags from Donita's trip to the market are slumped at the foot of her bed. She knows the fish needs to be put in the fridge right away but, judging from the receding volume of Mrs Fann's footsteps, she is also making her way to the kitchen. Donita sits on the edge of her bed and scans the disarray of her room. All the work Mrs Fann insisted on, undone by her own hand.

From the beach, there is the sound of cheering and scattered applause, followed by thumping music. The students from the junior college on the other side of the canal are having a Sunday sports event. In the kitchen, Donita can hear the trapdoor for the rubbish chute creaking open and then slamming shut.

Did Mr Fann see it? What would be so offensive about a gaudy old earring to Mr Fann, whose face barely registers any emotions? Donita hears it now, clanging against the inner walls of each floor of its descent.

Chapter Three

I can't wait to see you tomorrow! Orchard Station, twelve o'clock?

Angel waits while her old friend Corazon Bautista answers her text, the three dots blinking as she types. The reply is a few squares and a goat emoji. Another message quickly follows: *Sorry, I was trying to give you a thumbs up!* Angel smiles, recalling the things they used to laugh about while they waited with towels in hand for their employers' children to tire of splashing in the pool in Reverie Residences, the gated condominium community where they worked.

Angel pushes Mr Vijay's wheelchair along the walking trail until she finds a shaded spot to park. She gently prises his fingers open and wraps them around the handle of the badminton racket. They will repeat this action for the next ten minutes or so until Mr Vijay grips the racket, and then Angel will show him how to swing it. One day, it will be effortless again. He had been playing badminton when the stroke seized his body. Doctors said it was an undiagnosed heart condition, but Angel believes it was grief over Mrs Vijay's death from cancer last year. It was a double tragedy, but doesn't that mean that they are due for something good to happen soon? Whenever Angel watches physiotherapy videos on YouTube, she is drawn to the suggested video clips of people rising to their feet after years of paralysis. Miracles are possible.

Angel's sister Joy is more sceptical of miracles. Last night, she sent Angel this message: *Flight for Riyadh confirmed.* Angel sank into her bed, defeated. *I will be with you wherever you go,* she finally replied to Joy after many unfinished and deleted messages.

The air is tinged with the loamy scent of wet soil from last night's downpour. A man wearing a florescent yellow vest is aiming a high-pressure hose at the drain. The water jets out in a solid white blade to blast away the dirt before it can settle. Angel exchanges a wave with Rubylyn, the new nanny from the floor above. She is walking along the trail with one napping baby slumped in a carrier on her chest, and a toddler picking apple slices off a contoured tray on his stroller.

Mr Vijay is making progress with grasping the racket. 'Good, good,' Angel says, wiping the sweat from Mr Vijay's brow. Together, they trace the racket along a low, invisible arc over the sparks of honeysuckle flowers bursting from the crouching shrubs. He allows her to guide him. It was his wife who used to grumble when Angel made her do her physio-therapy routine. Sometimes she'd swear under her breath, and they'd both break out in uncontrollable giggles. Mrs Vijay would wag her finger – *you started this.* Cora used to give Angel that look of warning too. 'Don't make me laugh,' she would say, the corners of her lips already twitching.

Cora has been on Angel's mind ever since she learned that Cora's nephew, Raymond, died. She couldn't believe it – Raymond, whom Cora returned to Manila to raise after her

brother abandoned his own child. The wife had had enough
of his drinking and had run off, and when Cora returned to
the Philippines, she found that most of the money she'd sent
home had gone towards gambling and the seeding of foolish
business ventures that never materialized. Angel was shocked
to hear that anyone under Cora's wing could suffer an untimely
death. He was nineteen years old, the same age that Angel
was when she arrived in Singapore. In those days, Cora had
soothed her homesickness with comforting words and advice,
and Angel felt safest in her care.

It was even stranger how Angel found out. A friend of
Cora's had posted a condolence message on Cora's Facebook
wall. *My condolences for your loss, Cora. May God forgive
Raymond's sins.* Moments later, Cora's Facebook profile was
gone. Angel looked up Raymond's name but couldn't find any
information on his death. All she saw were school announcements about his achievements: his scholarships and prizes, and
a small picture of him and Cora hugging at his graduation
ceremony. There was also a news article about him and a
classmate winning full scholarships to the University of the
Philippines. That boy had so much promise.

Then out of the blue this morning, Cora had sent Angel a
message. *Hello Angel, remember me? Is this still your number? It's
Corazon Bautista. I'm back in Singapore, working in Bukit Timah.
Feeling settled now. Let's catch up on your next off day.* Angel
wasn't surprised to hear from Cora. This is how it works when
you think of somebody; eventually they reappear in your life.
They haven't seen each other in over a decade, but Angel just
knows they'll pick up where they left off. Of course, Angel
won't ask Cora anything about Raymond, especially if she
doesn't want people to know. (*May God forgive Raymond's sins
– was it suicide?*)

No, Angel doesn't have to know anything. She just needs to concern herself with Mr Vijay, whose wrist is trembling slightly. 'Too heavy?' Angel asks. 'Come, we rest for a while then we start with the other hand, okay?' Mr Vijay's forearm, the muscles atrophied, is limp and soft as a bird wing. 'Okay, you've worked hard already,' she tells Mr Vijay as she kicks up the locks on the wheels of his wheelchair. They take the longer route home, passing mesh nets tethered across an adventure playground and the tiered canopies of *pulai* trees crowded with creamy whorls of new flowers.

The Vijays live in an older private apartment complex on the park's edge called Jacaranda Gardens. On the ground floor, there is a function room, a gym and a two-lane bowling alley for residents. The tennis court is covered in yellow leaves that look like tiny flames. At the gate, Hassan the security guard presses the buzzer to let Angel and Mr Vijay in. 'Hot weather today, Angel,' Hassan says, and Angel replies, 'Really hot. Hope it rains.' Sometimes Angel wants to break the pleasantries and tell Hassan that she has no hard feelings about what happened last year. She knows it was a resident who saw her walking on the treadmill in the gym and made a complaint, and that Hassan was just doing his job when he rounded up all the maids and scolded them on the building management's behalf. 'You have a nice day,' Hassan says, tipping his head towards Angel, which is probably his way of saying that there are things he cannot help.

On weekday mornings, the MRT carriage is a silent sea of pressed shirts tucked into the sharp edges of waistbands and the soapy fragrance of the freshly showered workforce. The office workers and schoolchildren peer into phone screens or listen to their earphones while staring into any slivers of white space in the crowd.

Sundays are different. Angel boards the train at Choa Chu Kang Station and feels it pick up momentum as it slices through the sun-bleached suburbs. Clouds of greenery billow beneath her feet, and she is brought to eye level with the silvery edges of apartment blocks that loom over her throughout the week. On Sundays, Angel owns the city, and she's not the only person who feels this way. A glance at the trimmed parks below shows women spreading out picnic mats, weighting the corners with tall steel pots and boom boxes. Dressed in their best clothes, they croon their favourite songs from home and serve buffets of home-cooked food, relishing the freedom of being outdoors. Angel knows she looks her best too. Her chin-length hair is brushed smooth of bobby pin dents and her small lips break into an easy smile. Watching her reflection in the train window, she turns her head from side to side to let her silver earring cuffs catch the light.

Two Burmese girls get on at Bishan Station. Their cheeks are streaked with tree-bark paste to protect their skin from the sun, and they hold onto each other as the train judders and picks up speed again. Construction workers arrive at the next stop, in checked shirts tucked into trousers, clutching their mobile phones. The carriage seems to rock to the chorus of this crowd, and Angel feels that she's part of every conversation, even the ones in Bengali and Burmese. The suburbs peel away and the train plunges into the night of the underground.

Angel spills into Orchard Station with the crowd and lets the surge carry her towards the escalators. She is early because she always tries to leave home promptly if the Vijays' younger son Raja is on Sunday duty. Raja never paid much attention to Angel when she started working for the family three years ago, but something changed at Mrs Vijay's funeral. Angel had spotted him sitting alone on the steps of the crematorium and sobbing into his long shirtsleeves, so she held his hand and told him that the pain would get more manageable over time. Her own mother had died when she was in her early twenties, only a little older than Raja. Since then, he's been lingering too close.

Police officers in bulky vests patrol the station entrance. 'No loitering,' says an officer to a cluster of Indonesian women near the ticketing machines, and the women scatter like raindrops.

Angel pats her purse instinctively. She knows where her employment pass is if she needs to produce it. After the officers move away, she takes out her phone to let Cora know exactly where she is. Back when she and Cora used to have days off together, they would wait near the station control booth until all their other friends arrived. Orchard Road was a glittery shopping district then, but now it is a wild competition of pulsing lights and frantic, churning crowds. New underground tunnels shoot like fireworks in every direction, fanning out into mammoth shopping malls.

There is a message from Joy: a picture of herself wearing a traditional Saudi abaya. The black cloak is unbuttoned and the sleeves flare like batwings. The material swallows her up. *Borrowed this from my friend Pilar who worked in Jeddah for a few years. What do you think?*

Looks like a graduation gown, Angel replies. All Joy needs is a cap with tassel, and then maybe the image will be easier to accept.

My real graduation portrait is gone, Joy writes back.

Is there anything that wasn't destroyed by the flood last year? Angel had watched the news footage while frantically exchanging messages with Joy, who assured her that she was all right, even as the murky water began to seep into her living room. Luckily all the pictures of Joy's kids survived because they were backed up online. *And your diplomas?* Angel types, but she deletes the message. No need to remind Joy of her business degree, the fact that she was running a company before disaster and debt swallowed her career.

Another wave of passengers comes crashing through the station. Angel spots a portly woman with short, silver-streaked hair, clinging to her purse. Angel waves and calls out in Tagalog, and sees recognition wash over Cora's face. 'It has changed, huh?' Angel says, after they hug.

'But you haven't changed,' Cora says warmly, stepping back to look at Angel. 'Not one bit.'

'Ay, don't lie,' Angel says. In a few years, she'll be forty, and she knows her body has become soft in places. 'All of this has come out and all of this has gone down,' she says, pointing to her tummy first, then her chest. Cora laughs and hugs her again. Angel catches a whiff of Cora's perfume and it brings her back to their days in Reverie Residences, when Cora would always leave for church first thing on Sunday mornings, while Angel preferred to sleep in and go for a later service with the younger crowd.

'Are you back at Blessed Sacrament?' Angel asks as they navigate their way out of the station and into one of the malls.

'No,' Cora says. 'I'm not really . . . I don't go to church any more.'

That's a big change. Angel doesn't attend church either, but it never felt like a place for people like her. She waits for Cora to elaborate on her reasons, but when she doesn't, Angel moves on.

'What are your ma'am and sir like?'

'Just ma'am, no sir,' Cora says. 'No other help either.'

'Thank goodness for that,' Angel says. 'You don't want to be fighting with someone all the time.' It was hard enough being hired by the Vijays after their previous maid Erni retired; Angel felt as if she was competing with a ghost. 'You're dusting the house *now?*' a bemused Mrs Vijay would ask, to suggest that Erni dusted later or earlier in the day. Their daughter Sumanthi, who had a corner in the pantry for her tubs of pea protein powder and Himalayan pink salt, once asked Angel to pick up a pack of *keen-wah* from the supermarket, and when Angel called her after pacing the aisles (was it a type of gourd? A brand of spice?), Sumanthi spelled it out for her, 'It's Q-U-I-N-O-A.' Sumanthi laughed it off, but Angel was embarrassed, knowing that Erni probably never called the Vijays on the verge of tears over a packet of grains.

'Is it a big house?' Angel asks, picturing Cora without any other help in a sprawling Bukit Timah compound.

'There's a lot to do, but my ma'am still looks embarrassed sometimes when she sees me making the beds or washing the car. I've given up counting the number of times she has apologized for not being able to cook. Every time I make a meal, her face goes red and she says sorry. And if she does have to ask me to do something, she pretends it took her by surprise. "Oh! Cora! Could you hand-wash these? Oh! Cora! Do you mind going to the shops?"'

'What happened to her previous maid?'

'She's never had one,' Cora says. 'There were nannies for her daughters, who are grown-up now, and then she just hired a weekly cleaning service and she'd spend all of Sunday at the spa while they did everything.'

Angel's mind flashes to a memory with Joy and she begins

to laugh. 'Joy and I went to one of those fish spas last year when I returned to Bulacan.'

'Where the tiny fish bite the dead skin off your feet?' Cora asks.

'It was awful,' Angel says. 'We screamed and screamed. It didn't even hurt! She just started squealing, and that set me off, and the owner came to tell us off for scaring away the other customers. We were in hysterics. We got banned from that spa for life.'

'How is your sister?'

Angel's smile fades. 'She's going to work in Saudi Arabia,' she says.

Cora hesitates. 'Good money,' she says.

'Irresistible,' Angel agrees.

Her eyes bulged out of her head when Joy first told her what her salary would be – more than twice what Angel made. Back when Angel's mother started showing the first signs of lung disease, Angel had rushed to sign up to work in Qatar but it was Joy who forbade her. There were too many news reports about domestic workers there being abused by their employers. Every couple of years, the death of a Filipino in the Middle East sent shockwaves through the Philippines, and women avoided the sweet-talking recruiters who tried to convince them it wasn't so bad. But there were enough women who needed that kind of money to send a sibling to college or pay off loans for their children's medical bills, and so they took the gamble.

Cora and Angel are still underground but now they also seem to be underwater. The domed ceiling is an animatronic aquarium. A shark sails over their heads, and neon spotlights swing to the pop beats throbbing through the walls. Cora is asking a question, but Angel can barely hear her. She points to a swatch of sunlight at an entrance on the first floor, and Cora clutches her hand as they weave their way to the escalators and stagger out onto the street. There is a rumble in the distance, but Angel isn't sure if it's from a pending storm or the giant billboard screen across the junction, where an animated robot has burst into flames that are transforming into the words *Coming Soon*. Three women are taking selfies in front of a display of luxury cars in the sparkling atrium outside Ion shopping mall, their phones angled from long wands.

'This way,' Angel says as they head towards the narrow underpass that will bring them to Lucky Plaza. Cora knows where it is; now she is the one leading the way, driven towards a place that feels like home.

Lucky Plaza is heaving with Sunday crowds of Pinoy women rummaging through clothing-store racks for pyjamas, shoes and purses. Angel and Cora make their way through a corridor of money-changer windows with green and red lights marching around the borders of their signs. Passing a souvenir shop, Angel sees a woman asking about the price of a pair of plastic camouflage toy binoculars. 'And this one?' she asks, holding up a snow globe, then a pack of scented soaps, then a silver picture frame. Her enthusiasm feels familiar. All the *pasalubong* Angel has bought over the years for her family could fill up this floor. On her first visit home, her father devoured a box of seashell-shaped milk chocolates, and her cousin shyly presented a traced outline of his right foot so she could buy him sandals that fitted. Pride bloomed in her heart, and when she returned to Singapore, she spent many Sundays collecting items for the *balikbayan* box that she would send home once it was full.

Most of the tables in the basement food court are already taken by this time, so Angel brings Cora to an eatery on the third floor. A frown comes over Cora's face as she scans her options: deep silver trays piled high with crispy rolls of *lumpia* and rich oxtail stew. 'I can't believe how much they're charging for the *galunggong*,' she says, nodding at the tray of fried mackerel. 'And eight dollars for grilled *liempo*? Look at how small those portions are.'

'Your lunch is on me,' Angel says. They squeeze their way into the restaurant. 'Don't be silly,' Cora protests. 'You're younger. I'm paying.' But Angel insists. She tells Cora to find a place to sit while she chooses their dishes and puts them on a tray and carefully navigates her way to their table.

There is a flyer on the table for BalikExpress, with a print of their signature glossy black tape stretched across the page as a banner. Cora's eyes bulge at the rates listed there too. She holds up the flyer and shakes her head slowly.

'This is a premium *balikbayan* service,' Angel assures her. 'The post office upstairs still does a good job, but BalikExpress takes less time. They have all these fancy add-ons, like they'll send you a professional video of your family receiving their gifts.' Cora is still thinking in pesos, a habit Angel falls into every time she returns to Singapore from a home visit and everything seems astoundingly expensive. She still has a stockpile of *menudo* sauce packets and Magic Sarap seasoning from her last trip home to last several more months of comfort meals.

Twirling her fork through her *pancit bihon* and watching the steam escape the fried noodles, Angel tells Cora about a Turkish drama series she's been watching online – 'even without the English subtitles, you can follow the story' – and about the soap she bought to try to lose weight: 'It's called diet soap. I saw it in an ad. It washes away your cellulite.'

'That is nonsense. You bought it?'

'I believed it! They had a whole range of products. I wondered about the bubble bath though.'

'You soak for two hours and disappear completely, is that the idea?'

Angel giggles. 'I guess so. Anyway, it didn't work. Big surprise.'

'You're looking thinner these days than I remember you.'

'I lost some weight,' Angel says. 'I had a bad break-up last year . . .' She hesitates. She could refer to Suzan as '*siya*' and then Cora wouldn't know whether she was talking about a man or a woman. Before Angel came out to Joy, she made the assumption that Angel had a boyfriend. Angel never had to correct her as long as they were speaking in Tagalog, and she could hide Suzan's identity behind a pronoun that had no gender. But it still felt like a lie, and Angel is done with hiding who she is.

'Suzan didn't see the relationship the same way I did.' Although she doesn't put any emphasis on the name of her ex, Angel hears it blasting through a loudspeaker.

Cora nods slowly. 'It was a girlfriend?' she confirms.

'Yes.' *Please don't tell me I'm confused*, Angel thinks. That was what Joy told Angel when she came out to her. *It's a phase*, she said dismissively. Maybe Cora is thinking the same thing. Maybe she is wondering about all those men that Angel pretended to have a crush on at Reverie Residences – the lifeguard, the FedEx delivery driver who sang the lyrics to the only Tagalog song he knew to any Filipino working in the building.

'I'm sorry Suzan hurt you,' Cora says finally. 'What happened?'

Angel is so relieved she could hug Cora. 'I met her around the time that I left my old employers, the Lai family, and started working for the Vijays. We were together for nearly three years,' Angel says. Her first days in the Vijay house coincided with falling madly in love with Suzan. On some mornings, standing on the wide apartment balcony, the sight of kingfishers darting between the trees still remind her of the quick flash of Suzan's grin.

'She was everything,' Angel says. 'We even talked about immigrating to another country and getting married.' She doesn't want to look at Cora when she says this. 'Then she met somebody new. A Pinoy guy who works in shipping.'

Was that the hardest betrayal to handle? Or was it when Suzan denied she was ever a lesbian? Or was it when their friends began supporting Suzan, celebrating her choice, making it clear that they never believed the love between two women could be anything other than confusion or convenience?

Suzan had loved her. Their relationship wasn't about the lack of available Filipino men or having sex without the risk of pregnancy. Angel had been with those sorts of women too, but those relationships didn't go deeper than trysts in pay-by-hour hotels or in quiet park corners. 'We talked about how we were tired of hiding. I thought she meant she wanted to come out to her family. I didn't know she was thinking of pretending to be who she wasn't.'

Cora's face brims with sympathy and then she reaches out and grips Angel's hand. 'This is your first time talking about it?'

'I told Joy about Suzan,' Angel says. A fresh wave of pain washes over her. 'She didn't understand. When I returned to Singapore after my last visit, Joy told me they didn't need me to pay her daughters' school fees any more. She said that I needed to save my money for myself, but I think it's because

I told her I was gay. She doesn't want me to influence her kids somehow.'

'It's not such a bad thing to stop sending all of that money home, Angel. Remember when you first started working here? You were standing in line at the remittance centre every week.'

'Everyone needed help,' Angel recalls.

For the first two years she was here, Angel was helping to foot her mother's medical bills but, after she passed, requests came flooding in from other family members. Her cousin Tito's motorcycle needed repairs, could she help to cover the costs? Her recently widowed aunt's farm needed petrol for the machinery, could Angel pay for that? Fees for waterproof schoolbags, a leak in a roof, a bribe for an official – Angel said yes, yes, yes until Cora had taught her to say no. 'You'll end up borrowing from loan sharks at this rate,' Cora had warned her. Cora had already been working in Singapore for ten years when Angel arrived in 2001, and she had seen other domestic workers going into debt to try to please their families back home.

Angel can't help noticing that Cora is different now, and not just because of the deep age-lines that score the corners of her eyes. She used to show up in eateries like this with fire in her eyes, ready to distribute the free weekly newsletter that she wrote for Filipino workers. Everybody was eager to read those folded pink A3 sheets for tips and useful information from a veteran worker. Around the holidays, she always included a special edition about packing *balikbayan* boxes, complete with diagrams on space saving and tips on padding breakable items like Ritz crackers and souvenir shot glasses. She advised women about resolving conflicts with employers too, and she always included all the hotline numbers for places they could call for help. In 2001, there was a famous murder:

Marisol Concepcion, a maid from Nueva Ecija who was executed in Singapore for strangling her employer and her daughter. The Philippine newspapers reported that Marisol had been framed. Most women didn't have computer access in their employers' homes, so they began filling the cybercafés to read the news online until Cora offered to consolidate the information into an extra page for no charge.

Now Cora seems diminished. Sadness drapes over her like a cloak. Angel wonders who takes care of people like Cora, who are so often depended on to take care of others. The thought of being bereft and alone unsettles her. 'Your family is well?' she asks casually.

Cora nods but after a beat she says, 'My nephew Raymond died.'

'I know,' Angel says before thinking.

Cora's face seizes with panic. 'Who told you?' she asks.

'On Facebook,' Angel says. 'Somebody commented. I saw it just before you took your profile down.'

This information seems to bring some relief, but Angel also notices that Cora has dropped her hand and now her fingers are clenched in a tight fist. *What happened?* Angel wants to ask, but the words don't form. Cora looks too fearful, as if she might spring out of her chair and run away if Angel pries. Angel's gaze settles on three women at the next table whose orders of *suman malagkit* have just arrived. 'Dessert?' Angel asks. The women peel open the banana leaves to reveal rice cakes soaked in coconut syrup. Behind them is a display case of cassava cakes and fried skewered plantains.

Cora, still lost in thought, shakes her head. 'Let's take a walk then,' Angel says, and Cora picks up her things slowly to follow her.

Outside, the sky has grown darker, and it looks as if the

sleek silver skyscrapers are icicles dripping from the low clouds. A fat raindrop plops onto Angel's head as they step out onto the boulevard. 'This way,' she tells Cora. The downpour begins as they hurry towards the awning of a hotel lobby. A procession of blue and yellow taxis threads through the front entrance. Angel and Cora dodge the slow traffic and the sudden blooming of umbrellas as thunder cracks and the clouds shed the rain in a torrential rush.

'It's freezing,' Angel squeals as they enter the lobby, where the fierce air-conditioning gives her goosebumps. Two doormen in tailored coats nod to greet them. Cora runs her fingers through her short hair. They wait and watch as the lobby begins to fill up with other escapees from the weather. Although Angel feels guilty for marvelling at any kind of storm after what happened to Joy's home in Bulacan, the chaos is comforting to view from behind these wide glass windows and red awnings. The raindrops blur the dagger-sharp edges of the towers, and lights from the buses smear across the glistening black roads.

'I need to use the toilet,' Cora says. She and Angel walk towards reception, but a desk clerk stops them. He doesn't greet them like the doormen automatically did. 'The washrooms are for hotel guests only,' he says. The women taking the selfies outside Ion mall earlier trot past them to the washroom entrance, boxy white shopping bags swinging from their wrists. Angel feels a flash of anger; they don't even hesitate, and the desk clerk doesn't give them a second glance.

'What do you think he would have said if we had told him we were guests? If we had just made up a room number?' Angel asks Cora as they step outside again.

Cora wipes the raindrops from her eyes like they are tears. 'He would have asked for more proof. Our keys. Our passports.'

'Our grandparents' names,' Angel quips. 'How much liquid we drank.'

They dodge to a sheltered bus stop, and then it's a short sprint to another haven: TANGS department store. It's a sale day, too busy for anybody to mind them. Customers flocking towards the racks are accosted by salesgirls with perfume spray bottles and invitations for free make-up trials. 'I'll be in the bra section,' Angel tells Cora, who nods and hurries to the washroom. Two saleswomen are folding bras and chatting animatedly to each other when Angel starts to look through their sports bras. 'Come girl, I take for you,' one saleswoman says. Her name tag says 'Mei'.

'What size you want?'

'Can you measure me?' Angel asks.

Mei nods and picks up her measuring tape. Her colleague smiles at Angel. 'Day off?' she asks in Tagalog. Angel nods. 'You get one a week?'

'Yeah,' Angel says. 'Where are you from?'

'Iloilo,' the saleswoman replies. 'I don't usually work on Sundays either, but we're getting overtime because of this sale.'

'Lots of customers?'

'The rain always helps to bring in the crowds. Where are you from?'

'Bulacan,' Angel says, and she watches the woman's features crumple with sympathy.

'That flood!' she says. 'I saw people living on their rooftops on the news.'

'Good thing they still had rooftops,' Angel says.

'Was your family caught up in it?'

'Not too badly,' Angel says, because this is easier to say. There is no space in small talk for describing the swirling water that inched its way up her nieces' ankles and rotted the wooden floors that her brother-in-law had laid with his own hands.

Mei steps back from Angel and writes down her measurements. She looks back and forth between them curiously. 'Relax, Mei, we're not talking about you,' the Filipino saleswoman tells her. Angel laughs. 'Anyway, best of luck. My colleague will show you some of our latest styles. It's time for my lunch break.'

Angel bids her goodbye and continues shopping. She holds up a sports bra with an adjustable racer-back strap and pictures herself wearing it on long morning runs in the park. Mei clears her throat and tucks her hair behind her ear. She gives Angel an apologetic smile. 'There's no discount on this one.'

Angel figured as much. But when Mei tries to nudge her towards a range of plain bras with flimsy cups and sizes S, M, L and XL, Angel holds onto the bra. 'I will try it on,' she says, knowing full well that she won't end up buying it. It is $89, more than half of what she earns in a week.

On her way to the fitting room, she notices a small crowd has formed near the MAC counter. Voices are rising. There is a young, pale-skinned Filipino woman with glossy black hair wearing a pair of skin-tight denim shorts that are cut to reveal the half-moons of her pert bottom. Three saleswomen have surrounded her, and Angel's first thought is that she has stolen something. Angel can only see her face in profile, but her voice rings clearly across the department store: '*I don't have to buy it!*'

The saleswomen's voices escalate as well, and one of them returns to the counter to make a call. As the Filipino woman continues arguing, she turns to reveal a heavily made-up face. It looks like she has tried every sample of every product on this floor, and the saleswomen are now pressuring her to buy something.

Angel waves Cora over when she notices her wandering back from the restroom. Another round of heated arguing catches Cora's attention. She takes one look at the Filipino woman and marches over to the counter. Do they know each other? Angel hurries over to join them.

'Donita, what is going on?' Cora asks. The girl scowls at Cora. In all those layers of foundation and bronzer and crayon-thick eyeliner, she looks like a sad, beautiful clown.

'I don't need your help,' she says. She hitches her purse on her shoulder and reaches for another tester product – a tube of concealer.

'Enough,' Cora says, gripping her wrist. Donita tries to shake her off but Cora's grip appears to be strong. Angel looks around nervously. In Cora's effort to calm things down, she has actually created a bigger scene.

'Security will be here soon,' one of the saleswomen announces. Her arms are crossed over her chest.

'Why does security need to be involved?' Angel asks. 'She doesn't want to buy something, it is not a crime.'

Donita looks at her, and Angel thinks she's going to tell her to mind her own business as well, but she nods. 'Exactly,' she says. 'I am a customer, you're not treating me like one. You let all of those other ladies try everything.'

'Donita, you do not want security to get involved,' Cora says. She looks around nervously.

'I didn't do anything wrong,' Donita replies. 'Your friend here understands it.'

'Yeah,' Angel says. 'This is unfair.'

'It doesn't matter,' Cora snaps. 'It doesn't matter who's right.'

Behind her, Angel can see the blue blur of security guards approaching. At the crackling sound of their walkie-talkies, all heads turn and the store becomes a sea of excited whispers. Then something happens that Angel will be thinking about for days. Cora flees. She bolts out of the doors as if she is being chased, and she doesn't slow down even as she gets closer to the main road. 'Cora!' Angel cries. She's only thinking of Cora's safety as she runs after her, but when she crosses the threshold of the store and the alarms start wailing, she remembers that she is still holding the expensive sports bra.

The storm has subsided to a drizzle but the concrete pavements are dark with puddles. Cora, Angel and Donita stand in a row like schoolgirls. The police had to be called, even though Angel ran right back into the store as soon as she realized her mistake. She steals a look at Cora, who returned at the wail of the alarm too, and sees her staring straight at her feet, nodding to the policeman's questions. 'Elizabeth Lee,' Cora says. 'I have been working for her for three weeks.'

'I need to see your employment passes,' the policeman says. 'All of you.'

They fumble with their purses and bring out the green plastic cards. Angel's tiny black-and-white photo looks like a mug shot. 'And you?' the policeman asks Donita. 'Where do you work?' He looks her up and down as he says it.

'Marine Parade,' Donita says, peering at the policeman from behind her thickly shadowed eyelids. 'Also new here, sir. It is my first day off.'

'You're a maid or you do some other kind of work?' the policeman asks. 'Why are you dressed like you're selling some- thing in Geylang?'

Donita stares blankly at him. She might be too new to know

that the policeman is referring to the red-light district, but Angel feels the anger swishing like dark waters within her. What can she say? The policeman's black holster gleams like his badge and polished shoes. He begins to search Donita's bag and pulls out her *kikay* kit – a small pink pouch for grooming essentials. Her comb and a pack of tissues fall out as he unzips it, and he takes no notice before turning his attention to Angel.

'Sir,' she begins for the third time since they were rounded up. Her voice trembles – is it rage, or fear? 'I can explain.'

So many people are strolling by and gawking. The roar of traffic along Orchard Road drowns out their whispers, but Angel knows they are assuming the worst. 'No need to explain. The security team is reviewing the footage. Do you know the penalty for theft? You could go to jail. Your friends here could have their employment passes cancelled right now and they can be deported.'

'I know, sir,' Angel says, bowing her head. Next to her, she can feel Cora stiffen. Donita mutters something under her breath in Tagalog about preferring to go back.

The policeman begins to quiz Angel on her identification details. Who is her employer? Where do they live? What is their phone number – he will have to call them. When she explains to him that Mr Vijay is unable to speak, he raises an eyebrow. 'Then who is in charge today? Who is there?'

Angel feels sick as she gives the policeman Raja's number. As she slowly reads out the digits from her Contacts list, she feels the pain in her palms. The strap of the bra burned her hands when security ripped it away from her once she ran back into the store. She can still feel the tight grip of the security guard's fingers around her wrists, and the way Raja brushed against her this morning on purpose.

'Excuse me,' a voice interrupts. It is Mei the saleswoman, waving at the policeman. He looks annoyed but he motions for her to approach. Mei flashes a nervous smile.

'Officer, this is all my fault,' she says. 'I was handling the purchase and forgot to take off the tag. That's why the alarm went off.' She waves a receipt. 'She bought it just now, and in all of the commotion with her friends, she wandered off before I could put it in a bag as well. Here Miss,' she says, handing Angel a TANGS department store bag made of stiff tartan-print paper. 'I'm very sorry about this.'

Angel takes the bag wordlessly. 'Let me see the receipt,' the policeman says. Mei hands it over. The policeman squints at it, and then he surveys Mei. 'Okay,' he says to Angel. 'You can go. But don't let me catch you up to any nonsense again.' He wags a finger at each of the women.

After he leaves them, Angel realizes she's been holding her breath. 'Thank you so much,' she says.

'No problem,' Mei says. 'I have to return the bra, though. I just quickly picked up another one and made the purchase when I saw what was going on.'

'Of course,' Angel says, returning the bag.

'These will be on sale in November,' Mei tells her. 'I'll put one aside for you, okay?' She smiles and returns to the store.

Cora, Donita and Angel are still standing in a line, as if waiting for permission from the policeman to unfreeze, even though he is sauntering away with his partner. Donita is the first to speak, turning to Cora. 'I'm really sorry.'

'As you should be,' Cora retorts. Angel notices she is trying to hide the shakiness in her voice. 'This is not how I was expecting to spend my day off.'

'How do you two know each other?' asks Angel.

'Our ma'ams are friends,' Donita says.

'Not quite friends,' Cora says sourly. Donita cracks a smile, and Cora's lips twitch as well. 'My ma'am couldn't get away from yours quickly enough that day.'

'She's horrid,' Donita agrees.

'Still?' Cora asks. 'I hoped she was just showing off.'

'What you saw was her *good* behaviour,' Donita says. 'Anyway, what happened to you? Why were you so scared of the security guards that you ran out of the store and gave them a real reason to call the police?'

Cora shrugs off the question. 'Just a childhood fear I guess,' she mutters, but Angel knows this can't be true. She had known Cora for years and had never seen her behave so skittishly around anybody. Where is the woman who championed the rights of her friends for so long?

Donita accepts Cora's response, but only because she is distracted by her own reflection in a sliver of mirror that frames the glass door of the department store. 'It's not too much, is it?' she asks.

'It's too much,' Angel says. 'Are you going to a nightclub in the middle of the day?'

'No, just meeting someone,' Donita says, twisting a lock of her hair in her fingers.

'Enjoy it,' Cora says drily. 'It could be the last time you have a day off if your ma'am finds out you've been up to trouble.'

'How will she know?' Donita asks. 'The policeman didn't end up calling her.'

'The videos,' Angel says. 'Did you see how many people stopped and took photos? They put them up online on their social media pages – look at these maids getting into trouble, is this your maid?'

'Shit,' Donita says. 'I'll ask Flor.'

'Who's Flor?'

'She's a friend of mine. She has an account on the Ma'am Facebook pages. I can ask her to look out for the video. Give me your numbers, I'll text you if anything comes up.'

If the videos are out there, there is nothing that they can do. But being informed is a small mercy, a courtesy that they are aware of their faces being public. Angel exchanges her number with Donita, and Cora does the same. In their small huddle on the street, they are no longer drawing anybody's attention.

From the Ma'am Facebook pages:

Elaine Yip: My helper has her own tin of Milo (the Malaysian one) but lately we have found her taking from the family tin (Australian recipe)!!! The Australian one is nearly twice the price as the Malaysian brand and better quality, more nutrients, etc, that's why I got it for the kids. We've never had problems with things going missing from the house but this is tantamount to theft. Can't be too careful nowadays. First they're helping themselves to your food, what's next?

Nurzafira Mohamed: Can you all help me with this grammatical issue? My son's primary school English teacher says 'museum' is a proper noun but my maid was looking at his worksheets and said it's incorrect. I actually think she's right. She was an English teacher in her hometown and sometimes she even helps me phrase my work emails correctly. But the teacher called me up and said, 'I'm the professional here and you should trust me.' My son said she gave the class a pointed speech about people from Third World countries trying to take jobs from Singaporeans. I think we started it with this whole grammar issue.

Chapter Four

The heavy windows of the study release a soft sweet scent of oak when Cora opens them to let in the breeze. She wraps a damp rag around her finger and runs it along the sills to pick up tiny pieces of grit. From here, Cora can see everything, from sunbirds perching in the trumpet trees to the curved border of rocks around the carp pond at the edge of the Lee property.

Another storm is coming. Cora knows Ma'am Elizabeth doesn't like the house being sealed off. When she saw Cora shutting the sliding glass doors downstairs earlier, she said, 'I'll take my coffee in the garden then.' Cora can see her stepping out barefoot to enjoy her *kopi-c* under the double-slatted timber roof of the pergola. The low outlying branch of the old *tembusu* tree jostles as a heaving gust sends its leaves fluttering to the ground. Ma'am Elizabeth once confided to Cora that she doesn't like going out much. 'I'm such a home-body,' she said. 'The other retired women like their brunches at the Intercontinental and so on, but it's so tiresome, all that dressing up and chatter.' In a button-down silk blouse and tailored loose trousers, she still looks very presentable for somebody who doesn't have anywhere to go.

Who wouldn't love to stay at home in a place like this? Cora's own fondness for it is surprising. In her experience, many big houses feel like museums; in Dasmariñas in Manila, where she worked for the Calvert family, the homes were exaggerations in every sense. Deep private roads flanked by thickets of pruned jungle to obscure the other houses, the properties so expansive that at first Cora did not notice the cluster of squat, yero-roofed buildings scattered out at the back – guardhouse, maids' quarters, boiler room, garage, gardening shed. But this home has a spirit that Cora attributes to Ma'am Elizabeth's presence. Even Mr Lee's study would find a way to breathe without Cora tending to it. The walls are adorned with framed news articles from various decades of his career: Mr Lee grasping handfuls of coffee beans in 1993; Mr Lee addressing employees in hairnets in one of his factories in 2005.

Cora was surprised when Ma'am Elizabeth told her that her family objected to her marrying Mr Lee. 'My father said, I didn't educate you in London only to marry a boy who barely finished secondary school,' she said. 'They were convinced he was after our family's wealth. He spent his whole life trying to prove to my father that he was good enough.' At this, Ma'am Elizabeth swept her hand across the living room and Cora was not sure if this meant Mr Lee succeeded by building this home, or if he never managed to measure up to the family's expectations.

The articles framed on the wall praise Mr Lee for starting his business from scratch, but Ma'am Elizabeth confided that her family eventually helped him. Cora knows this is how it works in rich families. They go to great lengths to make sure that their daughters marry within their milieu but, if those efforts fail, they groom him with tailored suits and business titles to elevate him to the role. Raymond's schoolfriend Marco Vallares comes to mind. If he continues seeing that Martell heiress, then his pathway is certain. And when that happens, Cora hopes he remembers where he came from. She hopes he remembers Raymond. In a sea of students fresh out of private schools and beachside holiday homes, they had once been a pair of scholarship kids working towards a better life.

The thought of Raymond and Marco fills Cora's mouth with a bitter taste. She can't dwell on her loss or she'll sink into despair, especially after her brush with the police at the department store last Sunday. The overwhelming urge to flee had taken her by surprise. It felt as if Raymond himself were propelling her legs forward before she could even think, and later, when Cora had to explain herself to Angel and Donita, she knew they didn't believe her. She shuts her eyes. This room suddenly feels like a reminder of everything Raymond could have had and everything he lost, from the fountain pens sitting in their leather holder, to the deep red hues in the oversized mahogany desk. Raymond was going to be a lawyer. One day, he was going to work from the grandeur of a desk like this, his office a private island. He was going to, he was going, he was. The shock of every unfinished sentence rings in Cora's ears.

Ahem.

Cora's eyes fly open. A slender woman is standing in the doorway, holding a cake box. Tucked under her other arm is a glossy black portfolio. Her charcoal pencil skirt hugs her waist, and a tiny gold teardrop pendant dangles just below her sharp collarbone. 'You must be Corazon,' she says, striding into the room with her hand outstretched. Cora eyes the portfolio. Has Merry Maids sent an agent to check on her letter of release?

'I'm Jacqueline.'

'Hello Miss Jacqueline, it's nice to meet you,' Cora says, just barely containing her relief. Ma'am Elizabeth's daughter, she can see the resemblance now. Jacqueline's long fingers clasp hers firmly. Cora can feel the cool metal of a bulging diamond ring which looks outlandishly large on Jacqueline's delicate frame.

'You have settled in all right?' Jacqueline says. Her eyes roam the study. She doesn't give Cora a chance to respond. 'My goodness, I haven't been in here in ages. I can't believe some of those old pictures are still here.' She nods at the cluster of framed family photographs that sit on the corner of the desk.

'That one is you?' Cora asks, pointing at a picture of a young couple posing in formal attire. A satin gown pools at the girl's feet, and she is waving a feather boa at the man.

'No, that's my sister Cecilia. Funny you should mistake us for each other. People generally don't think we look alike.'

Another look at the photograph reveals the differences between the sisters. Cecilia is shorter, and her curves more pronounced. She is laughing candidly, whereas Jacqueline's thin lips don't look as if they move that way.

'Have you seen my mother? I brought her some breakfast,' Jacqueline says. 'You're welcome to have some as well. Almond croissants and *kouign-amann* from Merci Marcel. Freshly baked, but they'll need a minute in the oven.'

'Yes miss, I will do that,' Cora says. 'Your mother is sitting outside.'

Jacqueline swivels soundlessly like a ballerina. Cora quickly finishes wiping down the table's surface. She is suddenly conscious of all the things that need to be done in the house to meet Jacqueline's careful surveying. Below the window, she can hear Jacqueline and Ma'am Elizabeth greeting each other. *You must have just walked past me*, says Ma'am Elizabeth. *Since when did you start sitting out here in the mornings?* Jacqueline asks. Cora can hear Ma'am Elizabeth explaining herself with the same line about wanting to be outdoors but not necessarily wanting to be around people. It sounds different now, like a defence.

Cora swishes the feather duster between the balustrades as she goes down the stairs. She takes the box that Jacqueline has left on the dining table and brings it to the kitchen. As she arranges the pastries on the toaster oven tray, she can hear that Jacqueline and Ma'am Elizabeth have moved into the living room. They are talking about her. Not her name exactly, but a whispered mention of *she*, followed by *good cook* and *keeps to herself though*. The air fills with a sweet buttery smell. She arranges the pastries on a tray and brings it out to find Ma'am Elizabeth squinting at an iPad.

'I don't see her, but it's saying she's online,' Ma'am Elizabeth says.

'Press the Call button,' Jacqueline says. 'Honestly, FaceTime is already built into the system and it works better than Skype. I don't know why you won't even try it.'

'I'd rather stick to what I know.'

Jacqueline looks up at Cora as she sets the tray down on the coffee table. 'Would you like tea also, ma'am? Or coffee?' Cora asks.

'I've already had my cup for the day, thanks,' Jacqueline says.

'Tea would be lovely, Cora. I'll have an Earl Grey,' Ma'am Elizabeth says. Cora nods and returns to the kitchen. While waiting for the kettle to boil, she checks her phone and sees that there are messages in the chat group that she, Angel and Donita set up together.

DONITA: *What's our group name?*

ANGEL: *We don't need a group name for the chat. This is not a band.*

DONITA: *Don't be boring.*

ANGEL: *Cora, any suggestions? Don't say 'Angel Donita and Corazon's Group Chat'.*

CORA: *I think that is a very straightforward name. Nothing wrong with it.*

DONITA: *Something more creative please.*

CORA: *Team Girl Power?*

DONITA: *Is this 1995?*

ANGEL: *Hahaha oh dear Cora. Girl Power? Really?*

CORA: *You young people don't know anything about what's important.*

ANGEL: *CORA CALLED ME YOUNG!*

DONITA: *Okay, forget the group chat name for now. I have asked Flor to check the Ma'ams groups. She says there are always videos of misbehaving maids floating around on Mondays and Tuesdays, after the days off. So far, there's nothing.*

ANGEL: *Please pass my thanks to her for looking out for us.*

DONITA: *She suggests that if anything does come up, we all agree on a good excuse for running out of the store like that.*

ANGEL: *Cora . . .?*

Cora imagines for a moment typing out everything that happened to Raymond in a series of text messages. Instead, she puts the phone away and takes out the bulbous little clay teapot with its matching cinnamon-coloured cups before remembering that Ma'am Elizabeth told her she only uses that one for oolong. The clay absorbs the tea with each brewing, and over time it develops a coating that enhances the flavour of that tea. 'Best not to contaminate it with any other flavours,' Ma'am Elizabeth had said. 'I've had this one going for several years now. I was devastated when my previous one broke.' Cora reaches deep into the cupboard to find a white silver-rimmed porcelain tea set.

A smile blooms on Jacqueline's face as she recognizes the cups. 'This one brings back memories,' she says, holding up the cup to the window where the sunlight catches the subtle silver pattern of a leaping dragon. Her delight is a relief to Cora, who immediately wonders what else in that cabinet she could bring to the front of the house. There is an antique tiffin carrier that could be displayed after a good polishing, and some engraved silverware that has not seen the light of day in some time.

'You girls used to beg me to let you use this set for your games with your dolls,' Ma'am Elizabeth says, as Cora pours her a cup. Swirls of steam carry the bergamot scent through the living room. The iPad begins bleeping. Ma'am Elizabeth presses a button and a face fills the screen.

'Finally,' Jacqueline says. 'People have to get to work, Cecilia.'

'Happy birthday, darling!' Ma'am Elizabeth says.

'Thanks Mummy! Hello Jac! Taking precious time out of our morning, are we? How much overtime did you have to do to earn us the pleasure of your company?'

'It's called being an adult. I wouldn't expect you to grasp such a foreign concept in your fifth year of university.'

'Sixth,' Cecilia says cheerfully. Cora steals a glimpse at the screen. Cecilia's hair is a crown of glittery twists. In the background, there is laughter and hooting.

'Are you in a car?' Ma'am Elizabeth says, squinting.

'Chase ordered us a limo for the occasion. It's the first of many surprises, he says.'

Ma'am Elizabeth mouths: *Chase?* to Jacqueline, who shrugs.

'Boyfriend of the week?' she smirks.

'Jac, not all of us want to settle down and play wifey right away. How are your wedding plans going?'

'I've narrowed down a few dress boutiques. I think the best option is to get it tailored with Michele when I'm in Paris next month. I'll have the bridesmaid's dress sent to you from her New York boutique. I chose the charcoal in the end.'

'Grey bridesmaids' dresses? Why? The cantaloupe was so much more fun,' Cecilia protests.

'It's tight around the waist, Ceci. I was only thinking of you.'

'What's that supposed to mean?'

'Darker colours form a better silhouette for all body shapes, not just yours,' Jacqueline says smoothly. Ma'am Elizabeth shoots her a look and puts the iPad in front of Cora. 'Cecilia, you haven't met Cora yet, have you?'

'Hello Cora,' Cecilia says. Her glow-in-the-dark bangles clatter when she waves. Cora crouches towards the screen and waves back. 'Happy birthday to you, Miss Cecilia. May God bless you with health and happiness.'

'Thank you,' Cecilia says, kissing the air. 'How is life in Singapore?'

Cora isn't sure if this question is for her or the family. After a beat, Jacqueline says, 'The weather's been atrocious lately. It's like we're having a mid-year monsoon.'

'And New York?' Ma'am Elizabeth asks. 'Your outfit suggests that it's a warm summer.'

'Oh, that's no indication of anything,' Jacqueline says drily. 'Since when has Cecilia considered the weather when dressing up? This is the person who wore a fur stole to her outdoor prom in the Botanic Gardens.'

'Don't remind me,' Ma'am Elizabeth says. 'If there's one

argument I would like to revive with your father, it's why he bought me a dead fox to wrap around my shoulders for that winter trip to Shanghai.'

'You realize that no protesters would have emerged to throw red paint on you, right? It was *China?*' Jacqueline asks.

Cecilia giggles. 'Yeah Mummy, they were probably more outraged that you didn't wear a whole polar bear.'

'It's the principle of the thing,' Ma'am Elizabeth says. 'That poor animal.'

'The principle,' Cecilia repeats with mock solemnity. She and Jacqueline share a smirk. Watching the two sisters interact, Cora has the impression that making fun of their mother is their one commonality. Their teasing is gentle but Ma'am Elizabeth looks hurt. She turns to Cora and says, 'Will you redirect the air-con vents, please? The fan is cooling my tea too quickly.'

'Certainly, ma'am,' Cora says. She unclips the remote control from its holster on the wall next to the light switch and fiddles with the settings.

'Ceci, that prom picture is still in Dad's study,' Jacqueline says.

'Really?' Cecilia groans.

'I think it's a lovely picture,' Ma'am Elizabeth says. 'You and Weston look so happy, even if it didn't work out.'

Jacqueline smirks. 'Do you think his mother has a huge blown-up version in her house? Is she still hoping it will happen?' She and Cecilia titter together. Ma'am Elizabeth looks as if she is caught between wanting to chide her daughters for being rude, and wanting this moment of harmony to last. She looks at Cora and shakes her head with exaggerated dismay. 'Girls, you are not presenting yourselves in the best light,' she reminds them. 'There's no need to make fun of Fann

Poh Choo. Everybody has their flaws. Cora and I ran into her outside the supermarket and she asked after you, Cecilia, which is very civil considering you broke the boy's heart.'

'Oh Mummy, I did him a favour!' Cecilia and Jacqueline are in hysterics now over some joke that Cora doesn't understand. She keeps a benign smile on her face and begins to clear the plates, which are left with mounds of croissant flakes. Once in the kitchen again, she notices that her group chat has gone quiet. She types a message for Donita: *Your ma'am's son and my ma'am's daughter used to be a couple!* There is only one tick after her message, which means Donita's phone must be off now that Mrs Fann is home.

ANGEL: *Eww! Raja? Who would want to date him?*

CORA: *Mrs Fann's son. Not Mrs Vijay.*

ANGEL: *Okay. Makes more sense. Who broke up with who?*

CORA: *Girl broke up with boy.*

ANGEL: *Son must be like the mother then. How are Ma'am Elizabeth's daughters?*

It's hard to sum up the two girls in a text message. They take after Ma'am Elizabeth in manners – Jacqueline politely thanking Cora and Cecilia's smile beaming from a thousand miles away. But something is also absent. They are like the circle of kids who Raymond joined after his best friend Marco started dating the Martell girl. Cora begins typing but she doesn't know how to put it in a way that Angel would understand. Good manners and not spoiled exactly but . . . She thinks. There is a breeze that accompanies their mannerisms, a sense of lightness that comes with having little to lose. *They behave like their feet have never touched the ground,* Cora types to Angel.

There is that bitter taste in her mouth again. She deletes the message before sending it; she does not want to dwell.

71

Once Cecilia reaches her destination, she bids a hasty fare-well to her mother and sister, which is drowned out by resounding cheers from her friends. All of Cora's work for this morning is in the living room, but as she steps out of the kitchen she pauses. Ma'am Elizabeth and Jacqueline's voices have gone quiet again. This time, there is an edge to Ma'am Elizabeth's tone that pierces through the hush they are trying to create. If Cora lingers in the kitchen, the tall antique mirrors won't get wiped down, and the silk runners on the coffee table won't be straightened. She returns, but she starts her tasks in the furthest corner of the room, where she cannot be at risk of eavesdropping.

Only once during the conversation do Cora's ears perk up, and this is because Jacqueline says something about 'domestic workers on Sundays'. Cora inches closer to them, worried that the video from the department store has surfaced. They are speaking in normal tones again now, and Ma'am Elizabeth is leaning back in her chair, looking more relaxed. '. . . so many of them last time that they had to start another service in addition to the one they already have,' Jacqueline is saying.

With a sigh of relief, Cora realizes that they are talking about the church. 'I don't see why they can't worship with everyone else,' Ma'am Elizabeth replies. 'Whose idea was this segregation within the church anyway?'

Cora sneaks a look at Jacqueline's frowning face. 'It was my impression that the domestic workers themselves wanted it that way. They didn't feel comfortable worshipping with everyone else.'

'Maybe some people made them feel unwelcome,' Ma'am Elizabeth says. 'We know who's responsible for creating those divisions. It wasn't the workers.'

'You get so fired up about these things, Mum, but when it comes to actually speaking up, you don't do anything,' Jacqueline points out.

'I have no interest in participating in Rising Star Church activities these days. Not since the leadership's focus shifted away from community service. It used to be about helping the needy, and now all I see is a lot of people helping themselves.'

'I only mentioned Rising Star because I've been coordinating the wedding and I had to jump through so many hoops this time. They've added even more administrative levels and committees.'

'And that's why I won't get involved,' Ma'am Elizabeth says. 'You think I want to cross Fann Poh Choo? She's vying for some high position.'

'She adores you though,' Jacqueline says. 'She would listen to you, and then maybe she wouldn't be following along with this new initiative they're being so hush-hush about, whatever it is.'

'Probably another letter-writing campaign. They're all about writing letters about the latest moral outrage,' Ma'am Elizabeth says. 'I remember how they celebrated when they managed to pressure the government to cancel that Swedish heavy metal band's performance here. *A win against sin*, they called it in the newsletter. I wonder what it is this time?'

'You could find out if you participated in some social activities,' Jacqueline reminds her. 'And maybe if you left the house once in a while, you'd also see the great opportunities out there for Lee's Kopi.'

Ma'am Elizabeth stands up so abruptly that Cora feels her own head spinning. Jacqueline sighs and picks up her purse. 'I'm just saying you should think about it. It's the most sensible step, and it will bring the business into the twenty-first century.'

'Thanks, Jacqueline, but I've done enough thinking about the family business for three decades. Lee's Kopi will stay exactly where it is. It's what your father would have wanted.'

Jacqueline opens her mouth to protest, but her lips quickly come together again. Seeing the disappointment on her face, Cora realizes that Jacqueline came for a business proposal, not to visit her mother. The black portfolio sits between them on the coffee table. Ma'am Elizabeth gives it a pointed look and, with a resigned sigh, Jacqueline picks it up.

'I'm happy to discuss wedding plans with you, Jacqueline. If you still want me to call Mr Khosla at the Raffles Hotel, he'll be happy to organize a food tasting. Or the organizers at Capella? Antonia Sutanto was raving about the luxury resort atmosphere at a wedding she attended there last year. She said it felt like being in Bali without the hassle of having to travel. We could make an occasion of it, try out a few places.'

'We've already decided on the Fullerton Bay Hotel,' Jacqueline says haughtily.

Ma'am Elizabeth looks crestfallen as Jacqueline gathers her things and heads to the door. Cora can feel the sting of Jacqueline's rejection. She is surprised at the rage she feels towards Raymond, fresh as it was on the day he didn't return her calls when she needed a lift home on his moped from Dasmariñas. There was a driver strike in response to the government's plans to phase out old jeepneys, and the highway was clogged with taxis. She didn't get through to him and ended up staying overnight in the Calverts' maid quarters. The next morning, when Raymond tried calling her back, she was so spitting mad that she didn't answer the phone. It was better that he didn't hear what she had to say to him: you're spending so much time with those rich kids, you're forgetting where you came from.

But then hadn't it been Cora's dream to remove Raymond from his origins? To escape a legacy of poverty and alcoholism – wasn't that the whole point? She recognized the hypocrisy in her own anger towards him. When he had told her he was thinking about joining a volunteer programme to travel to rural provinces to teach students, Cora balked and told him that she had not spent her life cleaning other people's homes just so he could be a do-gooder. 'If you're so free, you're not studying hard enough,' Cora said, echoing the words she had heard her Singaporean employers telling their kids in the past. 'Do an internship that will lead to a job. Surely one of your new friends can connect you to somebody.'

Alone now, Ma'am Elizabeth is quiet in her chair, lost in her thoughts. Cora can't tell her one thing about Raymond without revealing everything else, but she wishes she could reassure Ma'am Elizabeth somehow. Whatever choices her daughters make, wealth will cushion them and turn any failed ventures into opportunities. Cecilia can afford to delay completing her degree – it's an adventurous detour that precedes the next stage of her life. And Jacqueline is alive. The chances of her being hunted and killed like Raymond is so unlikely in the world of the Lees that Cora could almost laugh at the absurdity.

There is a click and a shudder before the automatic gates draw slowly outwards to make way for Jacqueline's exit. As quietly as it arrived, her car purrs into gear and glides out of the driveway.

Chapter Five

If there is a polite way of saying, 'you are wasting my time', Donita wants to learn it. She has tried everything, from hinting about her curfew to remarking that they should go indoors to escape the scorching sun. Sanjeev does not get it. Was he this obtuse when they exchanged messages? Or when they met two weeks ago on Donita's first day off? She remembers telling him about her run-in with the police, and the concern on his face. She'd sidled closer to him, inviting him to comfort her with a stroke of her hand or an embrace, but he just nodded sympathetically and said, 'Please be careful on your days off.' At the end of the day, he did kiss her, and their flirty messages since then have indicated that he wants her.

He wants her. She wants him. So why the hell are they standing here looking at abandoned trains?

Beads of sweat are forming on Sanjeev's brow. 'This is the most peaceful place in Spottiswoode Park. We are right in the city, but this feels like I'm in a hill station in India. I always come here to clear my mind,' he tells her. As he launches into another lecture about the old railway station and the project to demolish it, Donita has to overcome two conflicting urges: to slap him, and to fuck him.

Maybe this is all Donita's fault. This morning, after a walk on Sentosa Island, she told him she wanted to see where he lived, but she meant that in a flirtatious way. It was supposed to lead them closer together, not to this social studies lesson. He looked thrilled to show her around his neighbourhood, a small slice of tranquility in the city. Traditional shophouses, spruced up in cheery pastels to house yoga studios and art galleries, and skyscraper luxury apartments with sky gardens and gleaming infinity pools. Plumes of smoke billow from the *roti prata* stall on the corner of the main road. A roofed walkway leads to the older concrete apartment blocks, where Sanjeev rents a room.

'Sanjeev,' Donita says, tapping his arm playfully. 'I only see you two times in one month.'

Sanjeev nods and wipes his brow. 'It is so little time, yes.'

Donita waits for him to say more, but Sanjeev turns his attention back to the old railway line. A rusted track runs like a faded scar through overgrown weeds and tangled branches, and there is an overturned bin with plastic bags skirting the rim. When they first arrived at this lookout point, there was a huddle of elderly men and women shrouded in white cotton, facing the train tracks. Their eyes were shut and they clasped their hands together in prayer. 'They are worshipping the old train?' Donita whispered to Sanjeev. She was impressed with their devotion. 'No, there used to be a Hindu temple here,' Sanjeev said. 'The government tore it down but they still consider this place holy, so they come back here.'

If Donita hadn't been so eager to rip off Sanjeev's clothes and run her tongue all over his body, she would have participated in the conversation. 'I know how they feel,' she would have said, thinking about the way she used to collect little trinkets and tell stories about how they were gifts from the parents who left her with relatives when she was too young to remember. She once stole a faded red T-shirt from the neighbour's clothing line because it had the words *Howdy!* printed in cracking raised yellow letters across the jagged shape of the state of Texas, and she could pretend that her parents had ended up there somehow.

'Sanjeev,' Donita tries again. She twists a lock of hair between her fingers. The cloying scent of jasmine incense smoke fills her nostrils. 'I don't know if I have off day next time. My ma'am is doing a project and she want my help.'

Sanjeev is supposed to understand from this that it could be a month before they see each other again. A month! Who waits that long to get down to business? She had texted Flor this question yesterday. *One day off every two weeks. How am I supposed to have a life?* She knew the answer: she wasn't supposed to have a life. Flor sent three crying-face emojis to let her know that she sympathized.

Remember to use protection, came another message from Flor afterwards. *We get tested every six months for pregnancy, and if your test comes up positive, you will be deported.*

It was better advice than the agents gave: avoid sex while working overseas. It did strike Donita earlier today that perhaps Sanjeev was abstaining. Like a religious thing? But he also told her that he's not religious. He certainly isn't like those pilgrims. His Sikh temple sits in the near distance, a plump golden dome atop a short white building. They passed it on the bus coming here, and saw turbaned men slipping off their shoes and women tugging the sequined hems of their scarfs. Sanjeev had muttered a quick prayer, but then his eyes also definitely lingered on Donita's cleavage when she leaned towards the window and squeezed her shoulders together to make her breasts bubble up to her neckline.

'What project?' Sanjeev asks.

You are an idiot, Donita wants to say. 'Something for her church,' she replies. 'Anyway, we are standing here so long, it is so hot already.'

'Sure, let's go,' Sanjeev says, nodding in the direction of the apartment blocks. 'I'll show you where I live.'

Now they're getting somewhere. Donita ignores the pinch in her toes from her patent high heels and trots along with Sanjeev. 'You go to church with your ma'am?' he asks.

She shakes her head. 'Not for worshipping. They have meetings; last Sunday I went along to help.'

The church was like nothing Donita had ever seen before: busloads of people streaming into a lobby, from where ushers directed them to different sections of a massive auditorium with plush red seats. Long spotlights swung around the stage where a 3D hologram of a cross rotated slowly. An usher handed Donita a programme and said, 'You can go to upstairs seating.' The women like Mrs Fann were being escorted to the front rows. 'She won't be joining the service,' Mrs Fann explained, before directing Donita down the hallway to a meeting room that ran deep into the end of the building. On a long mahogany table sat three cardboard boxes labelled Appeal Letter, New Member Registrations, and Envelopes. 'By the end of the service, I want all of these envelopes stuffed with one letter and one registration form each,' Mrs Fann instructed. Donita did as she was told, tapping her feet to the music throbbing from the auditorium. It was repetitive, like her work at the mushroom factory, but at least she was in an air-conditioned room and alone. For the first time, Mrs Fann actually looked impressed with her work. Three women entered the meeting room with her and filled canvas tote bags with the sealed envelopes. They talked excitedly about 'starting a movement' and 'having a strong presence on the big day.'

Mrs Fann returned to her usual self on Thursday when she hosted Bible study. She was very anxious in the hours leading up to it, scolding Donita multiple times. She had to reschedule the meeting from two days before because the council had announced an extra round of cockroach fumigation due to unusually humid conditions. After the monthly fogging, there were always large-winged roaches attempting to escape the poisonous fumes. They sometimes climbed up the rubbish chute and died in the kitchen, which was what happened on Tuesday, prompting Mrs Fann to call the council to ask them to please wash away the cockroach corpses from downstairs immediately. When it didn't happen, she sent Donita down with a can of Baygon to finish off the survivors, and a broom to sweep them into the gutter.

The leader of Mrs Fann's church group was a woman named Dr Lena Teo, who sat at the head of the table and commanded everyone's attention. Donita didn't catch the other women's names, but she noticed that everybody deferred to anything Dr Lena Teo said.

'Poh Choo, you are a living example of good,' she said. 'You have volunteered so much of your time to this project, and you readily opened up your home when the rest of us couldn't.' Donita caught a few quick looks and smiles passing between the other women, but Mrs Fann beamed like God himself had touched her hand.

'Have you all heard that Swee Lin's son, Justin, is engaged?' one woman asked as Donita went around the table pouring tea.

'To that Eurasian girlfriend of his from junior college days? What was her name?'

'I don't remember her, but this girl's name is Juli. Juli Ashraf.'

There was a chorus of tea cups clattering to saucers. Donita stepped in to wipe a few drops that had spilled on the table. Even serene Dr Lena Teo looked perturbed. 'She's Muslim?'

The woman who announced the news took a sip of her tea. The pitying frown on her face could not hide the glee from her voice. 'Swee Lin was beside herself. He's converting to Islam. He says it's more compatible with living a moral life.'

As the women continued talking about the choices that children make, Mrs Fann's demeanour began to change and her body seemed to shrink into her chair. 'These boys, they just think in the short-term about everything, especially when hormones and pretty girls cloud their judgement,' somebody said. Donita remembered Cora's titbit of gossip that Weston Fann and Ma'am Elizabeth's daughter had been a couple.

'Speaking of falling in love, how was the media launch for Come Home?'

'Spectacular. It's already getting some buzz online. The You-Know-Whos are finding fault with it, as usual. They say we're co-opting their flag, as if they have sole ownership over the colour pink.'

'What do you think of it, Poh Choo?' Dr Lena Teo asked.

The women turned to look at Mrs Fann. A smile cracked across her face. 'It was very good,' she said.

'Has your son seen it?'

Mrs Fann shook her head. 'You know how busy our children are,' she said apologetically. The women exchanged glances again, and this time Mrs Fann was aware of them. Donita felt the slightest bit sorry for her, until she snapped, 'Donita, *where* are the lemon biscuits?'

Donita hurried to the kitchen and shook the box of lemon biscuits onto a rectangular plate. She brought it out and Mrs Fann began offering them fervently to the women. 'Shall we return to the task at hand?' she asked. 'We don't have much time till the election.'

After the women left, Mrs Fann cornered Donita with a list of things that she had done wrong. 'The biscuits were soggy. Didn't you store them in an airtight container? And did you have to put on the washing machine while they were here? So loud, they had to raise their voices to talk like we were in a hawker centre. If you managed your time properly, you would have finished all of this work early in the morning.'

By the time Donita has finished telling Sanjeev all of this, they have reached his apartment block. It sits on the end of the neighbourhood, adjacent to other identical towers that form a loose horseshoe opposite Keppel Shipyard. The land is tiered, and three lengths of stairs are built into the hill so they can descend to the road. Brawny container ships nest on the glassy surface of the sea. The sun hasn't begun to set yet but the ship lights are blinking, or maybe they just appear to twinkle because of the shimmering water.

'Your home is that way,' Sanjeev says, reading her mind. She was just wondering how long it would take to walk along the shore from Marine Terrace and reach here. One hour? Two? A tiny black cable car moves across the sky like a cursor between the sheer afternoon clouds. The deep green hills remind her of home, but only from a distance. This morning, she was disappointed to find that the man-made Sentosa Island was nothing like her province. The sandy beaches were cut out as if from paper, and a monorail packed with noisy tourists glided above the rooftops of resorts and restaurants.

'You have this view from your flat?' Donita asks. 'From your bedroom?'

Sanjeev nods. 'But we are eight people sharing one flat, so somebody is always blocking the window,' he jokes.

'Oh,' Donita says. 'Even now, everybody is there?'

'A few. Some are working today; some have their day off so they're out.'

The pilgrims from earlier are wandering across the park between the blocks. They look like a drifting cloud. Does everything move this slowly on Sundays in this neighbourhood? Even the stray cats are spilling like liquid across the first-floor steps. Sanjeev's face is turned towards the sea and, as he takes in a deep, calming breath, Donita decides she has to be direct.

'Sanjeev, can we go upstairs to your flat so we can be closer together?' she asks.

Sanjeev opens his eyes and smiles. 'Aren't we getting closer all the time? Aren't we close now?'

'Yes, but . . .' Donita shakes her head. 'Sanjeev,' she says firmly. 'I want to be alone with you.'

Sanjeev looks around and Donita follows his gaze. There aren't any people around except the shrouded pilgrims shuffling across the walkway now. 'This is so much more peaceful than my flat, believe me,' he says.

'SANJEEV I WANT TO HAVE SEX WITH YOU.' Donita's announcement reverberates across the void deck, bouncing from lift to stairs to concrete mah-jong table to the wall of steel letterboxes. The pilgrims all look up, aghast, and they hurry away. Sanjeev begins sweating profusely.

'You do?' he asks.

'Yes!' Donita cries. 'Why we go this building, that building, you show me Singapore whole history – for what?'

'I didn't want to . . .' Sanjeev throws his hands up and seems to be making a shape in the air. Donita stares at him. 'The first time we talked, you said you liked my message. The other men were all sending you messages about your body.'

'Yeah, of course I want to have respect first. But now I want to have sex.'

'Okay,' Sanjeev says. He swallows. 'I also would like to have sex.'

'In your room?'

'No, no,' he says, and then when Donita puffs her cheeks in exasperation, he says, 'I can bring us somewhere better.'

'We must be quick,' Donita says. 'My curfew is seven p.m.' It is now almost five p.m. Sanjeev springs into action. He takes Donita's hand and leads her down the stairs onto the empty, tree-lined road that divides the neighbourhood from the high-ways and harbour. The taxis parked along the kerb have their green lights on to signal they're available, but the first driver in the line refuses to take them. 'Uncle, I have money,' Sanjeev says, prising apart the mouth of his wallet to display his dollar bills.

'I'm not going there,' the driver says, winding up the window. They have not even told him where they're going.

'Then we give our money to somebody else,' Donita says. Behind him, there is a driver leaning against his car and finishing a cigarette. He nods and tosses his cigarette into the grass when Donita waves at him.

As they pull away from the kerb, Sanjeev tells him they want to go to the nearest Hotel 81, and the driver says, 'Nearest is Chinatown but sometimes on Sunday fully booked.' He grins sheepishly. 'People tell me ah, I never go inside one.'

'Okay, then where?' Donita asks.

'Got some hotels in Jalan Besar, but not so safe place,' the driver warns.

'It's okay, uncle, I will protect her,' Sanjeev says firmly. He puts an arm around Donita and she feels the heat coursing through her body. 'Not safe?' she asks after the driver revs up the engine and his radio begins playing. 'What place in Singapore is not safe?'

'I think he means it's old, that's all. And a lot of foreigners like us.'

Donita has come to understand that there's old and charming, like those preserved shophouses in Spottiswoode Park, with their original wooden shutters and intricate flower-design tiles bordering the porches; cafés with complicated machinery and people tapping away at their laptops on high benches. There's new and filled with foreigners, like Marina Bay Sands, a boat suspended in the clouds between three dizzyingly tall buildings; the technicolour fireworks of electric super-trees and financial buildings raised like swords. Then there's old and filled with *foreigners like us*, like these lanes they are starting to enter, with pavements shaved to ledges and used Fanta bottles and plastic bags strewn in the street corners. The disorder would repel the Mrs Fanns of the country. Even so, there are families milling around and entering restaurants and women holding up apples and mangos at a street stall. Sanjeev tells her that his friends arrange cricket games in these lanes sometimes. On one wall, a mural of a woman peering from her headscarf watches over the crowded junction.

As they scoot out of the cab, the driver winks at Sanjeev and says, 'Good luck!', which makes Sanjeev's cheeks turn red. Donita feels a throb of tenderness that grows as she watches him ask the front desk manager about the rates, and hands over his identification. The front desk manager is a woman wearing a navy blazer that is too tight around the shoulders. The tips of her long side-swept fringe are dyed the colour of milky coffee. She gives Donita only the quickest glance before handing over the key card to Sanjeev.

The bed fills up the tiny room, scarcely furnished but clean, with white sheets, white walls. Sanjeev looks sheepish. Maybe it's because he works in some classy hotels, and has been inside the ones where you can stand over the bay and hold the entire city in your hands. 'If you don't like this place . . .' he says. His words trail off as he watches Donita's face. He thinks she's having second thoughts, or she's disappointed, but actually she's surprised by her emotions. *I like any place where you are*, she thinks before they tumble onto the bed together.

Donita has some awareness of how much time has passed, and she knows she should leave in the next few minutes if she wants to make it home by curfew, but it's so hard to part with the cool air and the crisp sheets, and Sanjeev's bare body next to hers. Both of them are bathed in a sheen of sweat, and Sanjeev's chest is still heaving, as if he cannot believe what just happened. It is not the time to invoke Mrs Fann, but she pops into Donita's head nonetheless. This morning, before Donita left the house, Mrs Fann made her stand with her legs and arms spread as she ran her hands up and down to check if Donita had taken anything from the house. With a hard jab at Donita's inner thighs, she asked her to spread her legs wider, and then she rummaged through Donita's bag.

Sanjeev's touch healed all the places that Mrs Fann pawed at, but now, as their time together is whittling to its last minutes, dread mounts in Donita's stomach. If only she could buy time somehow, the way they bought the hour in this hotel, and she could learn more about Sanjeev in those whispered, lingering conversations that only happen in bed. His eyes follow her naked body as she picks up her clothes. She steals a bit of time for this, picking up her bra and tracing her fingers along the front hooks, giving him a chance to savour the sight of her breasts before pulling the cups close like shutters. Bending to pick up her shorts, she is aware that his vision is filled with the curves of her bottom. It is the opposite of a striptease, and it's riveting to Sanjeev, who smiles as if they are speaking a secret language. When Donita is finally fully clothed, she picks up her phone and checks the time. 'Okay, I really have to go now,' she says. If she leaves now by bus, she'll be able to get home on time.

Sanjeev is sitting at the edge of the bed, and his arms are resting on each side of her waist in a loose embrace. 'Don't go yet,' Sanjeev says, drawing her back to bed. 'Never mind your curfew. Tell your boss you got stuck in traffic.'

'Hah!' Donita says, pushing Sanjeev away. 'Mrs Fann doesn't believe anything I say, even when I tell the truth.'

'Then just tell the truth,' Sanjeev says. Mischief twinkles in his eyes. 'Tell her what you were really doing.'

Donita mimics putting her phone to her ear. 'Hello, Mrs Fann? I am late because I am having fun in a hotel room with my boyfriend.'

The word 'boyfriend' falls out of her mouth and hangs in the air between them. It startles Sanjeev a little bit – Donita could see the jolt in his shoulders and the way his mouth suddenly twitched as if he wanted to say, 'Boyfriend?' She can feel the flush rising in her cheeks. 'Just as an example,' she mutters, swiping her purse off the nightstand. 'I don't say it seriously.'

'Boyfriend is fine,' Sanjeev says. 'But I don't see you very often.'

'That's why when we see each other you don't take me on tour of Singapore,' Donita snaps. She's angry all over again at how much useless information about the railroad she had to learn today.

'Okay, okay.' Sanjeev puts up his hands. 'Maybe we just have to plan better. I want to keep seeing you.'

'But you don't want anything serious? I understand,' Donita scoffs, trying to hide her hurt.

Sanjeev pushes himself off the bed and wraps his arms around her. She falls into his chest, bare and slightly damp. 'Stay here with me a few more minutes. I'll call you a taxi to go home.'

Donita shuts her eyes. She has never felt this safe with anybody before, and she can feel her whole body go limp against his. 'Okay,' she whispers, and time doesn't matter any more. The moments stretch and shrink when she is as far away as possible from Mrs Fann's flat.

There are no windows in the room, so when Donita and Sanjeev step out of the hotel an hour after entering it, they are surprised that the island is roaring with rain. The potholes are overflowing with puddles, and storm water gushes along the gutters. The rain pelts Donita's bare legs, and a rush of wind sprays Sanjeev in the face. Getting a taxi will be impossible now, even if Sanjeev tries to book it.

'This way,' Sanjeev calls over the crash of thunder. They duck into a back lane, past a row of motorcycles slumped against a kerb, and they huddle under an air-conditioning unit jutting out under a window. Other people are seeking shelter

– under the awnings over fruit stands, and at the entrances of *thosai* shops. The wind punches the plastic sheets draped over the newspaper racks. Donita peers at Sanjeev's phone and sees him frowning: there is a cab available but the asking price has tripled 'due to inclement weather'. He hesitates, but presses the green button to book it.

Everything has become blurry and indistinct. A mural of roses blooming across the cracked wall of one shophouse has now turned a muddy imitation of pink, and the cars are wobbly shadows. Donita checks the time again: 6.43 p.m. She sighs and accepts that she will get into trouble for missing her curfew. The walls of the Marine Terrace flat will rock with Mrs Fann's fury and she will probably check Donita again, poking and gripping her flesh just to humiliate her. Could she run away? Donita takes a peek around the corner at the cramped lanes and the strings of vegetable vendors and garment shops. For a moment, she pictures herself stepping behind a mannequin wearing a sari and disappearing.

A flash of colour draws Donita's attention back to the main road. She is not the only person who notices it: a bright yellow umbrella. Three chuckling teenaged boys sharing a plastic sheet see it too, and an elderly woman holding a newspaper over her thinning scalp pauses to watch as the umbrella bobs along in the storm. But Donita is the only one who recognizes the familiar shape beneath it. She squints through the sheets of rain while everyone else returns to their huddle. Flordeliza. She is alone and stepping gingerly around the puddles, and there is something about her slow, careful walk in all this chaos that makes Donita hesitate before calling her name. A black leather backpack hangs from her shoulders.

'Flor!' Donita shouts, waving. Flordeliza keeps walking, gripping her umbrella. Donita calls her again and again, and finally she looks up but in the wrong direction. The wind must be carrying Donita's voice and distorting it. *'Flordeliza!'* She hears the strain in her voice and the futility of shouting in this kind of storm. Flordeliza cocks her head, and turns her face to the sky. There is a look of complete despair in her expression, and it comes through so clearly that Donita stops shouting. Flordeliza continues onwards and disappears around the corner. On the main road, a passing double-decker bus smashes into a puddle and the huge splash can be seen from the lane. Donita thinks about Flor's painstaking steps, and wonders if she bothered leaping out of the way.

The lights are off in the flat when Donita gets home, save for the one in Mr Fann's study. He is sitting on his rattan chair, flipping through the newspaper. A couple of private property brochures are scattered on the floor in the doorway. 'Sir, I am sorry,' Donita says. 'The traffic, the rain is very bad.' The storm seemed to follow her across the highway.

Mr Fann just nods. 'Mrs Fann is also held up at her church meeting. Don't know what is going on out there.' He points out of the window and that is when Donita sees it for the first time. In the neighbourhood with the houses, a crowd has formed. It's probably an otter-family sighting. People flock from all over the neighbourhood to take pictures every time the otters swim inland from Marina Bay.

Donita picks up the loose brochures and places them on Mr Fann's desk. He is staring out through the window in the other direction, towards the sea. His stern face looks soft and woeful in the bluish evening light. When he turns to look at her, it is to say, 'You can throw those away.' Donita hesitates. Mrs Fann told her to keep the brochures last week when Mr Fann made the same request. 'Pastor says motivation is important. That's how you start getting back on your feet, building confidence, going for a promotion. Not from sitting down and brooding all day,' she told him. It was the first time Donita heard anything like pleading in Mrs Fann's voice.

'Sir, what you like to eat for dinner tonight?' Donita asks.

'Just get me some chicken rice from downstairs,' Mr Fann says. He reaches into his wallet and hands her a stack of coins. There is enough money just for one packet.

'And Mrs Fann?' Donita asks.

Mr Fann shakes his head. Donita checks the fridge and sees leftover porridge and some Teochew noodles from yesterday, just enough for Mrs Fann. There aren't even packs of instant noodles in the pantry because the Fanns don't consider that Donita also needs to eat.

'Okay, I go down now,' Donita says. She'll have to use her own money to buy herself a packet of something. Mrs Fann does this strategically, she knows. 'You want Sunday's off, you must pay for all of your own things on Sundays,' Mrs Fann told her on her first day off. Even though she's been back on the clock since returning home, she's still somehow responsible for her own dinner.

Outside, the rain has subsided and the air is cool. Joggers pump their way down the pathway along the canal, which is so full that the water is sloshing along the walls with a powerful current. Behind Donita, the waves on the sea must be crashing onto the sand as well. She smiles at the memory of walking on the beach in Sentosa this afternoon with Sanjeev, the water tickling their toes.

The crowd across the road looks bigger from down here,

and although it's in the wrong direction of the food stalls, Donita makes her way towards the park. Later, she'll wonder why she did this – did some instinct tell her? Some current pushing her along like the water surging through the canal? A short detour won't throw her off time, and she can always tell Mr Fann that there was a long queue at the food stall.

As Donita approaches, she notices that there are many people gathered, but the buzz of conversation is low and the air is tense. Something is going on in one of the houses along the row. Through a crack in the crowd, Donita sees a parked ambulance, and the lights of a police car on the other side of the house. Then a hush falls over the crowd, and a girl shrieks. Another person collapses, and the crowd folds in to help them up. There are loud, ragged sobs as two grim-faced medics carry out a stretcher. The body on it is completely covered with a white sheet.

The sobs turn to howls, and from the whispering around her, Donita pieces together that the police were called after somebody heard a girl screaming. It must be this girl that two men in uniform are helping to prop up. Her legs have given way beneath her and her cries have become hoarse. 'Mum! Mummy! Mum! No! No!' The crowd rustles with excitement and some people turn away. 'This is terrible. She was killed in her own home,' one woman says, her face pale with shock. Her husband ushers her away.

Donita watches the couple as they leave, her heart thumping. A murder? That would explain all the police. The girl's gut-wrenching screams for her mother are making her feel queasy, and her ears are ringing. Around her, people begin to gasp and cry out once more. Donita turns around, expecting to see another body, but what she sees instead knocks the wind out of her.

Flor, in handcuffs.

Donita pushes back into the crowd, elbowing past the people who are clamouring to get a look at this woman. She can hear the roaring of a gathering storm but it's only a flash, a glimpse, and then Flor vanishes into the police car.

East Coast Murder – Filipina Maid Arrested

A foreign domestic worker from the Philippines has been taken into police custody for the alleged murder of her employer.

Mrs Carolyn Hong's body was found in her Oldham Walk home on Sunday evening. Her husband, Dr Peter Hong and their daughter were not at home at the time.

Police found no signs of forced entry, but noted that a robbery was in progress, as Mrs Hong's jewellery box had been ransacked. There had also been multiple attempts to enter her safe.

The 51-year-old marketing executive's death has been ruled a murder due to injuries to her skull. Police have not commented on the weapons found at the scene.

Flordeliza Martinez, a domestic worker from the Philippines, is said to have been the only person on the property when the attack occurred around 6.30 p.m. If charged with murder, Martinez could face the death penalty. The Embassy of the Philippines has not given any comment on the case.

For more updates, subscribe to The Straits Times.

Chapter Six

Angel sinks into bed and cups her lotion-scented hands to her nose. She inhales the sweet floral smell and squeezes her eyes shut. A thousand roses burst into bloom and swirl through her consciousness. On the bedside table, her phone will not stop buzzing. She should leave these group chats altogether – she hasn't spoken to her old friends since Suzan broke up with her. But everybody has a theory about the East Coast murder, and Angel can't resist another scroll.

Her ma'am probably worked her too hard. This is what it came to!

I think she was stealing. These Ilocano are all kuripot, they see money and have to take it.

What does this have to do with Ilocos? My mother is from there, she says they are much more honourable than you metro people.

We don't know much yet, but if the Singapore police have caught her, they must have a good reason.

How come it takes them so long to arrest their own people when they abuse us? Remember that girl from Myanmar who was beaten and starved by her employers? Took five years to convict them, and then they only got three years in jail!

This morning, hearing from this group chat that a murder had taken place off East Coast Road, Angel's first fear was that Donita had finally snapped at Mrs Fann and gone after her with a meat cleaver. Even though the linked article clarified that the victim's name was Carolyn Hong, Angel immediately sent Donita a message on their group chat saying: *Donita are you okay? That murder happened around your neighbourhood.* Two ticks next to her message indicated that Donita received her message, but there was no reply until just an hour ago, after Angel put Mr Vijay to bed.

DONITA: *This is my friend Flor! The one who was looking out for us on the Ma'am pages!*

Angel stared at the message for a while to let the information sink in. She went back to the article and read the woman's name again. Flordeliza Martinez. Flor. That was when Angel retreated to her room.

ANGEL: *Oh my God, Donita. This is awful. Were her employers really horrible?*

DONITA: *She didn't do it! I know it.*

ANGEL: *You must be in shock. Please take care of yourself.*

DONITA: *You don't understand. I saw her.*

ANGEL: *Where?*

DONITA: *Around Jalan Besar at 6.43 p.m. The murder happened at 6.30. It would have taken her at least thirty minutes to get home in yesterday's storm. She couldn't have done it.*

ANGEL: *You're sure?*

DONITA: *I'm positive. I know I saw her. They're accusing her wrongly.*

ANGEL: *Who did it then??*

There was a pause and then Donita sent Angel the link to

a university website. Under the title Dr Peter Hong, Dean of Mechanical Engineering, a man's headshot filled the screen. He was looking past the camera with a small smile, but his eyes were steely, and his squared shoulders made Angel feel small.

DONITA: *This is the husband. Flor told me he was having an affair. Who do you think killed the wife?*

ANGEL: *There has to be evidence though. They can't just arrest someone for murder if they don't have any proof.*

DONITA: *What about the way the police rounded us up the other day? What if that saleswoman hadn't come out to cover for you? They can do whatever they want.*

Sitting in her bed now and breathing in the scent of a rose garden, Angel wants to think of Singapore as a place where these things don't happen – where powerful men can't get away with murder just because they sit in boardrooms and live in big houses. But she also remembers Marisol Concepcion, the Filipino maid accused of murder in 2001, and the trial that dominated the news. Angel's employers became nervous around her, and started locking their bedroom door at night. During Sunday gatherings, Angel became acutely aware of the divisions among her friends of those who believed in Marisol's innocence and those who insisted she was guilty and were upset with her for ruining the image of Pinoy workers. In 2001, Angel was new to Singapore and she had not known what to think until Cora had printed a special edition of her newsletter. 'It could be you or me,' Cora had said as she slid the double-sided pink sheet across the table. 'Any one of us could come home to find that we're a murder suspect.' After Marisol Concepcion was sentenced to death, the sound of that lock clicking into place felt personal.

Cora hasn't chimed in on the conversation between Donita and Angel, and thoughts of Marisol make Angel realize how much Cora has changed since that time. Is it age? Mrs Vijay used to tell her that, as she got older, she became more accepting of the things she could not change. But Mrs Vijay was never a fighter, not like Cora.

As Angel ponders Cora, she watches her old group chat blink with new messages and her stomach twists every time she sees Suzan's name come up. They don't talk to each other any more. Angel was the one who went silent — after Suzan broke up with her, this felt like a way of regaining her pride: *see, I don't need you after all* — and she stopped showing up to Sunday gatherings with their friends. Sometimes she regrets doing this, and she stays in the chat group in hopes that they will reach out to her. Leaving this chat group feels too final; it's the last space she and Suzan still share.

I heard she's got a daughter back home.

Poor little girl! What's the news in the Philippines saying?

Nothing yet.

Cowards. Probably don't want a diplomatic incident. At least the embassy should issue a statement?

You think they care that much about us? They're not interested in our welfare unless we're pumping money into our provinces.

A sudden knocking on Angel's room door startles her. 'Hold on,' she calls, pushing herself off her bed. She opens the door to see Raja standing in the hallway. Canned laughter rises from the television in the living room, where Sumanthi and her boyfriend Anand are camped out with a Vietnamese take-away. The Vijay's two shih-tzu terriers, Coco and Toffee, are curled up on the sofa next to them.

'Hey,' says Raja. He is holding two bottles of Sprite, the lemon-flavoured kind that Angel keeps in the fridge.

Angel straightens her shoulders. *What do you want?* she thinks, but she says, 'Yes?'

'I just wanted to see how you were doing. You seemed a bit upset yesterday.'

Upset? Angel wants to snort. She was livid. Raja, who was supposed to assume caretaking duties for Mr Vijay at ten a.m. on Sundays, slept in until noon. By the time he took over, Angel had missed her lunch with Cora. 'I'm fine,' Angel says curtly.

'How was your day off?' Raja asks. She is not imagining it, he is saying it pointedly. 'Must be nice to have a rest day.'

'I spent the whole day walking here and there,' Angel informs him. She had to make up for lost time in various queues. First, at the bank, which had special opening hours on Sundays for domestic workers. She was only there to reset her internet banking password, but it took nearly an hour to get to the counter. Afterwards she stood in a crowded train, determined to get to Tai Seng where there was a CHARLES & KEITH warehouse sale. Cora had joined her for that one. In front of her, there had been two women who suddenly grew quiet when Cora arrived and she started speaking in Tagalog with Angel. 'You want to go or not,' one of them whispered to the other. 'This must be one damn cheapo sale if the maids are all lining up.' They hurried away, which meant Angel got the last pair of sandals that she had really wanted.

'I just wanted to say sorry about yesterday,' Raja says. 'It won't happen again.' He holds out the Sprite. 'Peace?'

'Thank you, apology accepted, but I don't have sugary drinks at night,' Angel says. She steps back and starts to shut her door when Raja begins speaking again.

'I don't know if my sister has told you that she's looking into hiring a nurse?'

'She is?' Angel asks. Sumanthi hasn't mentioned it. There has always been an agreement that Angel, despite her lack of home nurse experience, would stay and acquire the skills needed to take care of Mr Vijay.

'I mean, I wouldn't want you to leave,' Raja says, stepping closer past the threshold so his feet are planted in her room. Angel wonders what would happen if she shouted. Sumanthi and Anand are just down the hall, so Raja wouldn't try anything, but how would they react if she marched out right now and complained that he was harassing her? Sumanthi grumbles about Raja not doing his share of the work, and she scolds him for leaving his shoes scattered in the doorway, but she doesn't see Raja doing this kind of thing. Neither does Mr Vijay. Raja knows it is easy to hide; even now, he waits for the television noise to drown his voice and he smiles conspiratorially at Angel, as if they are both in on a little secret.

'Thank you for letting me know,' Angel says. 'I'll talk about it with Miss Sumanthi. She is the one who handles all matters related to my employment.' *You are not my boss. You have no power.* Angel wants to get this across to Raja somehow, but a smirk plays on his lips. He has no fear. As he turns to leave, Angel says, 'Please throw away your drink in the rubbish bin when you are finished.'

After Raja walks away, Angel wonders if this was going too far. She has never told anybody to clean up after himself in his own home. This is her only coping tactic – pretending that Raja is a guest, easing her discomfort with the knowledge that he lives in his university dorm for most of the week. She feels particularly unsafe on the nights when he returns because she keeps her bedroom door ajar to listen for Mr Vijay.

She reaches for her phone and sees there's still nothing from Cora.

ANGEL: *How was your day?*

Cora comes online. *So she is there*, Angel thinks. She wonders if she should ask Cora what she thinks about this East Coast murder, but before she can type, Cora replies: *It was okay. Ma'am wanted to know where I got my shoes.*

ANGEL: *She was suspicious?*

CORA: *She wanted to know where to get her own pair!*

ANGEL: *Hahaha should have invited her to take the place of those women in front of us.*

CORA: *How are you today? Spoke to Joy?*

It's another thing weighing on Angel's mind. Last week, her sister bade farewell to her husband and children and took a bus to the training centre. 'I am thinking of you,' Angel had written to her, but she was glad she hadn't been anywhere near as their relatives peeled Joy's wailing daughters off her. In their brief phone call last night, Joy hadn't wanted to talk about the departure. Instead she told Angel that the training for work in Saudi Arabia would be quite different from what she expected. There were lessons on ironing, washing and basic cooking, which Joy had no trouble with, but also lessons on basic Arabic phrases and Islamic culture. A trainer had taught them how to manoeuvre a mop without getting their abayas wet, and told them to always wash the family cars before sunrise to avoid heatstroke.

ANGEL: *She's keeping busy. Just have to hope she has fair employers.*

CORA: *That's all we can do, no?*

I should have . . . Angel begins typing. She can't complete the sentence. It's what she shouldn't have done that haunts her. Why did she have to tell Joy about Suzan? Things haven't been the same between them since.

ANGEL: *Hey . . . this East Coast murder is making me think about 2001? Remember that?*

CORA: *Not really.*

ANGEL: *Oh come on, Cora. Marisol Concepcion? You don't remember how everybody became scared of us? It looks like it's going to happen again.*

Cora doesn't reply. Angel wants to talk to her about Donita's messages as well. She sees that Cora is still online and has read her messages but she is not typing anything. After staring at the screen for another ten minutes, Angel gives up. It's quiet in the living room now. She steps out into the corridor and can hear Mr Vijay's gentle snoring from his bedroom across the hall. The walls of the corridor are lined with framed photos of the family – Sumanthi in cap and gown; Raja in his National Service uniform; a faded wedding photograph of Mr and Mrs Vijay, resplendent in their wedding garments against a waterfall backdrop.

The television is paused and Anand is sitting at the edge of the couch where Sumanthi is stretched out, fast asleep. On her bare feet are tattoos that crawl up her ankles, which she covers up by wearing long trousers and high-top shoes to work. Anand gently takes Sumanthi's glasses off her face and folds them before placing them on the coffee table.

'Will you wake her up later?' Anand whispers. 'I have to go. I don't think she should spend the whole night on the couch like this.'

'Before I go to sleep, I'll wake her up,' Angel replies. Never mind the yawn escaping from her mouth as she says this. It's close to ten, and she has been on her feet all day. Today, Mr Vijay was stubborn. He did not even want to grip the badminton racquet. 'You are being naughty,' Angel chided him. Mr Vijay avoided her stare and Angel felt overcome with pity.

'Ay, sir,' she sighed, smoothing a wrinkle in his shirt. 'You used to do everything by yourself, now I have to make you practise this simple child's game. I also would be frustrated.'

After Anand leaves, Angel brings her phone to the balcony and sits on the deckchair, watching the lights twinkling in the neighbouring buildings, and the nature reserve, reduced to a hulking shadow in the night. The baby in the apartment upstairs is fussing and Angel can hear Rubylyn on the balcony, singing 'Sa Ugoy ng Duyan' to soothe him. She flicks two black ants away from the table. They must be coming out from that crack in the wall again; Angel needs to sprinkle repellent powder here. The tennis court downstairs will stay lit all night, and in the adjacent apartment complex, the pool ripples softly. The Vijays' apartment is on the fourth floor, low enough that Angel can see the television screen flickering in the security guard station. During school holidays, Hassan's grandson follows him to work, dragging a trolley bag full of books from the library and reading them under that long fluorescent bulb. Hassan leans out of the window and waves to Anand's car before returning to his seat and recording the departure in his logbook.

The island appears like a silent movie at this time of the night, but Angel's group chats tell her otherwise. The comment about that poor girl from Myanmar has gained momentum, and everybody is contributing their own example of outrage. What about the woman who endured third-degree burns from having a kettle of boiled water thrown at her? What about the two sisters from Indonesia who were forced to slap each other for each of their mistakes? What about the woman whose sir made her take off her nightgown, mop the floor with it, and then wear the filthy sopping clothes to bed? Those were just the cases that made it to the news. So many more cruelties go unpunished, and the thought makes Angel feel ill.

Joy is on her way to a place where there are even fewer laws to protect maids.

Another message pings on Angel's phone, this one from Suzan's WhatsApp group, the one she never left:

Listen, I know we all want to defend this woman but we don't know her motives. My cousin in Tacloban has a friend in Singapore who knows the nanny for a kid who lives on the same street as Flor. She heard that Flor was supposed to meet with her friends for a picnic near Dhoby Ghaut Station but she never showed up. Why would she do that? If she was innocent, she'd have at least told her friends.

Someone else types: *I'm hearing some rumours about her too. She sleeps around. She has a daughter back home but nobody knows who the father is. Better not to claim to be friends with her, or even friends of a friend.*

A third person adds: *Yeah, stay away. What if they come around to question everyone she knew?*

Maybe there are things we don't know yet, Angel types angrily.

She's not just saying it because of Donita's sighting. It's the way the conversation has turned so easily to smearing Flordeliza. She knows why they are eager to disassociate themselves from the case; there is more peace of mind in not asking questions. Isn't that what they did to Angel after her break-up because the truth was too uncomfortable? She presses Send and feels queasy doing it; it has been so long since she spoke up in any of these chat groups that the other women probably think she left Singapore. Or they have forgotten she ever existed.

Then her phone buzzes. Joy? No, and when she sees who it's from, her heart goes still.

SUZAN: *Hey! Been thinking about you. How are you doing?*

The phone suddenly feels like the whole world to Angel,

and everything else in the periphery dissolves. Is it really Suzan? The phone number is hers, and her face fills the circle next to her name. Angel has managed to avoid looking at pictures of Suzan since Christmas, and even though this profile picture is tiny, the sight of Suzan's arched eyebrows and impish smile makes her stomach twist with both longing and anger. She reads the message over and over again, assigning meaning to each word and considering the implications. *Hey* . . . It's like they've just brushed past each other in the street. *How are you?* – it's a little formal and open-ended. How to respond? What does Suzan expect? – a run-down of all her complicated feelings? Or a nonchalant, *Hey, I'm good. How about you?* to see where the conversation goes?

And *been thinking about you.* Angel puts the phone down and paces across the balcony. *What do you mean?* she wants to ask; the message is glowing from her phone screen. It is hard to keep her mind from getting carried away, but soon she is lost in the hope of this message, the sign that Suzan might be reaching out tentatively. For a moment, she dares to be as honest as she's ever been. *I've missed you so much. I think about you all the time. I wish there were some way I could change your mind about us, because you're the only person I want to be with.*

Angel's heart pounds in the hollow of her chest as she types her reply. *Good to hear from you* ☺ *How are you?* The moment she presses Send, she regrets it, but she doesn't try to retract the message. Time passes slowly before the words 'typing . . .' appear under Suzan's name. Angel's stomach somersaults and the jitters travel to her fingers, which begin to pinch the hollow of flesh between her knuckles. Another black ant scrambles across the table.

The message, when it finally arrives, is so simple and cruel that it cuts off Angel's breath: *Sorry, wrong number.* Angel feels as if her insides have been scooped out. Her first instinct is to take the phone and fling it off the balcony – she imagines how it would feel to watch it soar and get swallowed up by the night sky. What she does, what she knows she must do now, is much less satisfying. She blocks Suzan and exits the group chat. There is no subtle way to do this; everyone will see that she has finally gone.

As Angel sets her phone down, the glowing screen highlights a dark line running across the table. Ants. She follows their squirming trail with her phone's light until she reaches the source – an opened Sprite bottle on its side in a pool of thick liquid. A punishment: Raja tipped it over on purpose.

She trains her eyes in the distance and waits for the anger to seep away. Where does it go? Does it swirl into the atmosphere to take the shape of the island's gnarled branches and hunkering shrubs? Does it settle as fine dust on eyelashes and windshields? Or does it build in your fingertips, in your heart, seizing upon a moment where everything collides and your body becomes an engine of rage? Donita claims she saw Flordeliza Martinez at the time of the murder, but Angel would understand if Donita's imagination was working overtime. She knows that it's all the little things that add up to make you really want to hurt a person.

From the Ma'am Facebook pages:

Yu Fang Ong: We want to send our maid to classes to learn some conversational Mandarin so she can communicate better with my in-laws. She is refusing because the classes are on Sundays. So choosy! I told her it's only two hours and she said she has other things to do. Of course I'm not going to send her on weekdays or Saturdays because she has responsibilities in our household. So lazy and unmotivated, that's why you're only a maid! We sacrifice so much for them and they turn around and backstab us. This is what happened to that poor Carolyn Hong.

MK Ng: Maid wants our Wi-Fi password so she can talk to her children. OK with me, but my husband asked her to just use her mobile data. He told her, this is like me asking my boss to send me to work via hired taxi every day because the MRT is too crowded. Not the same thing lah, but he say must draw a line otherwise these women will climb on our heads. As long as she dun climb into our bed and try to steal my husband I'm okay lah, otherwise one day kena bludgeon to death like that East Coast lady then how?

Chapter Seven

Don't get involved!

Cora sent this message to Angel and Donita in their group chat last night, but they continued sharing snippets of information about the Flordeliza Martinez case. Angel posted screenshots of comments she found on the original news article, while Donita contemplated making an anonymous tip to the police. Cora wanted to march over to both their homes and knock some sense into them. The last thing any maid could afford to do in a time like this was get into trouble – despite what she said to Angel, Cora vividly remembers how it felt to have all the employers looking sideways at the help after Marisol Concepcion, as though one false move would make them pounce. To stem her anxious memories, Cora has been working overtime, polishing every bit of silverware in the back cupboards and re-filing the loose sheets jutting out from Ma'am Elizabeth's neglected recipe folder.

The sun is a boiling yolk over the island, and even the outstretched tree branches are unable to keep the concrete driveway from baking. Ma'am Elizabeth is perusing the recipe folder now, with her feet curled up under her on the verandah, a small bowl of cubed honeydew melon at her side. Occasionally, she shifts on her lounge chair. From the carport, Cora keeps her in the corner of her vision. *Cora, there's no need to be outside in this heat,* Ma'am Elizabeth would say if she spotted her washing the car, and then she would implore Cora to come inside and have an iced drink. Yesterday, she asked Cora if she wanted to install a television in her room. 'Is that something you might like to keep you entertained? You're welcome to watch TV in the living room, of course.' Cora shook her head so vigorously that her neck felt sore afterwards. What next? Ma'am Elizabeth giving her the keys to her BMW and encouraging her to take a joyride? There are lines that cannot be crossed, and if Ma'am Elizabeth tells her one more time to sit and have tea with her, or offers to lend her a silk scarf to match her Sunday clothes, Cora might have to say something.

One allowance that Cora does concede to, though, is the Samsung speaker that Ma'am Elizabeth bought her after noticing that she liked listening to music while cleaning the dishes. Cora objected at first, but when Ma'am Elizabeth demonstrated how much clearer and deeper the sound was with the speakers rather than her phone, Cora accepted it graciously. It is sitting on the front porch now, thrumming through a playlist of songs that remind her of home. She can't help singing along with Lolita Carbon's husky tones. The sound of Freddy Aguilar's voice stirs memories of seeing hundreds of thousands of protestors singing 'Bayan Ko' in Manila during the People Power Revolution in 1986.

She dunks the washrag into a soapy bucket of water and wipes off the flecks of dirt that splattered the car's windows during last night's storm. Heat shimmers off the hood of the car, and Cora fights to keep her sluggishness at bay. Last night, the rapid-fire raindrops hammering the roof made Cora sit upright in her bed, clutching the sheets to her chest in terror. She had turned on her music to soothe herself back to sleep but she was too alert, and the force of the storm still unnerved her. That was when she scrolled through the news articles and studied Flordeliza Martinez's picture – a heart-shaped face with arched eyebrows and lips painted red. She looked like Donita.

Cora indulged in reading a few comments under the news article. Most people had no doubt that Flordeliza had killed her boss. *Filipinos can't be trusted. Thieves and liars, now murderers,* said one commenter. Another one wrote: *Send her back to get executed in her own country. No need to waste taxpayer dollars here, we are* always *supporting these foreigners with our hard-earned money and they turn around and stab us in the back!!*

There were lots of replies to that one, people expressing their general dissatisfaction with the government and going off the topic of Flordeliza Martinez altogether. There were comments about the Philippines too.

Their own government is so corrupt, what to expect? Good thing Duterte has come into power. I see he is setting things straight in the Philippines. You have to pull out these bad weeds or they'll infect the whole society.

Setting things straight. She couldn't blame people here for thinking it was so straightforward. She too was impressed with Rodrigo Duterte when he ran for president in 2016. With his promises to bring down crime rates in the whole country, he could be forgiven for speaking crudely sometimes. She paid little attention to the reports of his death squads, or to the *tsismis* around her neighbourhood about vigilantes gunning down suspected drug dealers.

She continued scrolling past the derogatory comments until she found an interesting comment.

UNILASS007: Obviously the husband did it and this is just a cover-up. Peter Hong is known among students as Peter the Cheater!

Cora clicked on the user's profile, but no useful information came up. She searched for the name of Carolyn Hong's husband, and immediately the page was filled with search results and photographs of Dr Peter Hong, the dean at a local university. The pictures of him sitting at his stately desk reminded Cora of Mr Lee, but this man stared directly at the camera. His lips were set in the same stern expression in every picture, and he didn't look like the kind of boss that Cora wanted. What kind of husband was he, she wondered?

Further down the thread, there was another comment from Unilass007.

Peter Hong presided over a case that involved a tutor named Merissa Fang and my friend Priyanka. The tutor plagiarized Priyanka's essay for an article on her wellness blog but denied it completely. Peter Hong didn't bother investigating and threatened Priyanka with suspension for going public with the matter on social media. Why was he protecting some part-time tutor?

There were a few replies to this one.

If a university official can cover up something that is so blatant, imagine what else he was hiding.

That's Peter the Cheater! We also call him Petty Peter.

Does anyone know where Merissa Fang was that day? How do we know she didn't kill Carolyn Hong? Must have slept with the dean for the job in the first place, next 'promotion' is wife status.

She was on holiday in Bintan. Look at her Instagram. She was doing 'daily blinks for positivity.' She's dumb but she has an alibi.

Angel and Donita also discovered this story about Peter Hong. Within minutes of sending links about Peter Hong over the group chat, they were convinced he was the murderer, and that some huge cover-up was at play. Their excitement was apparent in their rapid, overlapping messages, which all but forgot Cora's existence in the group chat. Cora returned to the profile of Peter Hong and read about him. Graduate degrees from top universities in England, government scholarships all the way. A Young Achiever award that kick-started his academic career. A long time ago, these milestones were rungs on a ladder of achievement that she used to plan her nephew's future. Now she saw them as a fence that protects powerful people from facing consequences. Her hand travelled to the soft flesh of her earlobe – a lingering habit even though she never got to wear those gold earrings that Raymond bought her.

After Raymond died, she tried calling her younger brother – Raymond's father – to notify him, but the number had been disconnected. The last time she'd tried to involve him, when Raymond had been graduating from high school and was going to UP on a full scholarship, it had taken her weeks just to track her brother down to let him know that his son was making a success of himself. Her brother had muttered 'congratulations' and hung up before Cora could tell him that it would mean the world to Raymond if he came to the ceremony. Now that Raymond had died, not only was there no time to find her brother, but there seemed very little point.

'Cora,' Ma'am Elizabeth calls, tugging Cora out of her thoughts. 'I wouldn't bother cleaning the car. It's supposed to rain again today.'

Ma'am Elizabeth is far enough away that Cora can pretend not to hear her. The same swollen clouds from yesterday hang over them, but if they relied on the weather to decide on a car-cleaning schedule, Cora would never get her work done. She's halfway finished now, anyway. The music continues to pulse. A food delivery motorcycle pulls up to the house across the road. The driver dismounts and unzips his cooler bag to produce a stack of plastic containers from the local North Indian restaurant.

'Cora,' Ma'am Elizabeth calls again a moment later. She has appeared in the doorway with a glass of iced water. 'If you must do this now, take some breaks please. It's scorching today.'

'Ma'am, the weather is like this every day,' Cora says. She can't hide the note of exasperation in her voice. *Just let me do my job*, she wants to say. Next thing she knows, Ma'am Elizabeth will be rolling up the cuffs of her tailored linen trousers and scrubbing the floors to keep her company.

'It's unrelenting,' Ma'am Elizabeth says. She flaps her hands at her collarbone. 'Just make sure you stay hydrated. Oh hello, Reilly!' The yellow Labrador from next door pokes his leathery black nose through a gap where some bricks in the adjoining walls were knocked out by a stubborn tree root. Ma'am Elizabeth walks over to him to give him a pat. Tucked under her arm is the folder of recipes. When Ma'am Elizabeth spotted it on the counter this morning, an expression crossed her face that gave Cora a flash of panic. Was she not supposed to touch them? Were they private? Ma'am Elizabeth had shown her the messy folder last week and said, 'You're welcome to look through this for some inspiration', but perhaps she should have waited? Ma'am Elizabeth has that same look on her face now. 'Thank you so much for this,' she remarks.

'No problem, ma'am. I just straightened them up.'

'You did more than that,' Ma'am Elizabeth says, and yes,

it's true. Cora arranged the recipes from the scraps of yellowed paper filled with scribbles to the magazine cut-outs and printed emails. Initially, she thought there was a categorization process she could follow, because many of the initial pages had Cantonese/Hakka/Teochew written in the top corner and highlighted pink, green and yellow respectively. But the labels stopped about a third of the way through, so she just went alphabetical and focused on keeping the folder tidy.

'I'm thinking of compiling these recipes into a book. It would be a nice wedding present for Jacqueline. What do you think?'

'Good idea, ma'am.'

'I could type them up. Some are really old. I scribbled a few from memory and conversations with my mother and aunties when I first got married. I'm not sure this recipe for jellied pig trotter is salvageable, for example,' Ma'am Elizabeth says, holding up a brittle yellowed foolscap sheet. 'But it wouldn't be practical for a busy woman like Jacqueline to spend hours by the stove brewing the stock anyway. I could prepare the more popular dishes and get a photographer to take high-quality pictures.'

'I can cook them,' Cora offers quickly, because she doesn't want Ma'am Elizabeth getting in the way in the kitchen.

Ma'am Elizabeth clasps her hands together. 'That would be wonderful. We could even include some of your recipes; what are some things from your culture that Jacqueline might be interested in eating?'

'I think there are enough recipes from your family,' Cora says gently. Draw the line. Imagine Jacqueline opening the book to find Cora's grandmother's specialty: blood stew. Thankfully, Ma'am Elizabeth doesn't force the issue. She leans against the garden wall, flipping through the folder.

'These dumplings were the highlight of fifth month festival when I was a child,' Ma'am Elizabeth says, holding up a picture of pyramids of sticky rice wrapped in bamboo leaves. 'I have a nephew whose team won the dragon boat races last year and he credited the family *bak zhang* recipe in the press for giving him the strength. It was probably Red Bull and all those years of rigorous rowing training, but he scored well with the family for mentioning our traditions. Our version is stuffed with minced pork, wild mushrooms and water chestnuts, but I prefer the Peranakan-style ones. I had a neighbour growing up who blended her own five-spice mix and added it to braised pork and candied watermelon. The flavours were incredible. And if you use jasmine rice, the subtle sweetness adds even more depth. I'll have to track down her recipe to add to the book.'

Cora nods to show that she is listening as she unspools the garden hose to connect it to the tap. She can hear Reilly panting in excitement as Ma'am Elizabeth rubs his ears. 'You're a happy little guy,' she coos. 'You're so happy. Cora, have we got anything to give him?'

'Yes, ma'am, some leftover roast chicken in—'

A gunshot rips through the air then, knocking the words out of her mouth.

The garden hose flies out of Cora's hands, and she is dropping to the ground. Her knees hit the ground first and then a sharp pain rips through her scalp. She is vaguely aware of warm liquid pooling near her ribs. The last thing she hears is Reilly's frantic barking before she blacks out.

Cora's eyes flutter open to darkness. Pain flashes brightly through her skull and she has a sense of hurtling through a dark passageway. She croaks a question but it cannot be heard.

There are voices, and a hazy figure in front of her sits stoically with arms outstretched, saying nothing. Then, without warning, the blinding white light of day floods her consciousness. The awareness settles slowly. The voices are coming from the news on the radio. That figure is Ma'am Elizabeth, gripping the steering wheel and speeding through the tunnel. They have emerged now onto the expressway. Mammoth rain trees clip past the window and rain has begun to speckle the windshield.

Cora brings a hand to her head and winces when she grazes the tender bump. She remembers the ground rushing towards her before she blacked out. There is a wet patch on her clothes. The garden hose. Ma'am Elizabeth must have dragged her into the car and buckled her in the back seat.

'Ma'am,' Cora croaks.

'Oh Cora,' Ma'am Elizabeth gasps. 'Oh, thank goodness. The delivery boy's motorcycle backfired across the road and you just dropped to the ground. You knocked your head on one of the garden stones. You're going to be all right, okay? Just stay still, and we'll be there in no time.'

Where is *there*? Cora has trouble formulating the question, but it doesn't matter because soon the car is slowing down and turning off onto a private road leading to a white building set on a hill overlooking pristine gardens. The only sign to Cora that this is a hospital and not a resort, is the ambulance quietly waiting at the entrance.

'This isn't necessary, ma'am,' Cora says immediately as a valet comes bounding to the window. 'We might need a wheelchair,' Ma'am Elizabeth says after handing him the keys.

'No,' Cora says, and to demonstrate that she is just fine, she flings open the door and takes a step. The ground wobbles beneath her. Two attendants appear at her side and she is lowered onto a seat and ushered through the sliding glass doors. The warm lighting and faint tinkling of classical music make the waiting room feel like a place where high tea will soon be served.

'Ma'am,' Cora tries one more time after Ma'am Elizabeth hands her the registration forms. 'I don't have concussion; I am not dizzy or having any vomiting. We can go home.' How much will this cost? She knows Ma'am Elizabeth won't take it out of her pay cheque but that's even worse somehow.

'Cora, this could be serious. I saw the way you fell, and you blacked out – that's not something we can just neglect,' Ma'am Elizabeth says. Her tone is firm and Cora knows she has lost the battle. She takes the clipboard from Ma'am Elizabeth and finds comfort in the fact that it is a cheap plastic thing, with a hospital ballpoint pen chained to the metal clasp.

'Elizabeth Lee, is that you?'

'Oh, hello Audrey,' Ma'am Elizabeth says to the woman who has approached them. Her navy blazer is tapered at her waist, and her hair is pulled back into a round bun. A gleaming leather briefcase is tucked under one arm.

'Everything all right?' Audrey asks.

'Everything's fine, thanks. This is my helper, Cora. We're just here for a check-up.'

'Ah, those six-monthly checks?' Audrey asks. She doesn't bother acknowledging Cora. 'They've got their own clinics for that, you know? We send our maids to the one down the road and they're in and out in half an hour. The ministry only needs to know that they're not pregnant.'

Ma'am Elizabeth's smile is thin. 'Thank you, I didn't know. Maybe next time we'll go there.'

'We're here because somebody couldn't resist going for a swim before his cast was taken off,' Audrey says, rolling her eyes towards a young boy of about eleven or twelve, transfixed on his iPad. 'Gregory was furious at the condo staff for letting a boy just jump into the pool on his own without any supervision, but we don't have lifeguards on duty at ours. I'm writing to the management about it. The cast seemed fine for a few days, and we thought maybe he managed to keep it dry. He got *that* injury from playing football, by the way. Anyway, now he's telling me it itches.'

'Poor little thing,' Ma'am Elizabeth says to the boy, who flashes her a grin. Stronger than the throbbing in her head is the ache in Cora's chest. She is embarrassed to feel her eyes burning with tears. Raymond, Raymond, Raymond, in the face of every boy. 'Maybe a day off school is all you really wanted, hmm?' Ma'am Elizabeth teases.

'We can't afford to miss any more school with exams coming up soon,' Audrey says. 'He missed one day for getting the cast on and they covered an entire new unit on photosynthesis in Science. He's still catching up.'

'I'm sure he'll get into a good secondary school,' Ma'am Elizabeth replies. 'Are you still hoping for Anglo-Chinese School?'

'Fingers crossed. St Joseph's International is our back-up. I've doubled up on his weekend tutoring, but then look at what happens when he has five minutes to spare. It's like he's destined to derail his academic future somehow.' Audrey shakes her head in exasperation.

Cora can't help thinking about how many times she's heard parents in Singapore talk in these same breathless, panicked tones about their children's educations. She remembers how Ma'am Roberta would tutor the twins after school with towers of assessment workbooks and stock her kitchen fridge with herbal broths and fish oil capsules. She often sent Cora out to the neighbourhood's traditional medicine hall to pick up the tonics customized for each daughter's needs. Years later, when Raymond began studying for the scholarship exams in the Philippines, Cora took regular trips to a small Chinese supermarket near her *barangay* for wolfberry and snow fungus to add to chicken soups to support his growing brain.

The receptionist calls Cora's name and Ma'am Elizabeth and Audrey say their goodbyes. Dr Gopalan is looking at Cora's file when she takes a cautious step past the door to his office. 'Come in, have a seat,' he drones, but when he looks up, his tone changes. 'Mrs Lee, hello!' he says. Shoulders straighten and a smile appears. 'I didn't know I was expecting you.'

'I'm not the patient. This is my helper, Corazon Bautista. I'll be outside,' Ma'am Elizabeth says. 'Unless you need me to be here, Cora?'

'It's okay, ma'am,' Cora says. She can't help remembering her visit to the hospital after Ma'am Roberta's husband threw the ashtray at her. Cora's nose had been swollen for three days before her ma'am had said, 'We'd better go to the doctor.' The doctor took one look at Cora and said, 'How did this happen?' He did not ask Cora; he asked Ma'am Roberta, who shifted in her seat and mumbled an excuse about slippery floors. The doctor then asked Ma'am Roberta to leave the room and then he asked Cora to tell him everything. She begged him not to report it. 'They will fire me,' she said. 'I need my job. I support my family.'

Dr Gopalan asks Cora questions about her fall too, but there is no suspicion in his tone. He sounds bored. Maybe it's because Cora's bruise does really look accidental, or maybe the cause of the injury makes no difference to him.

Cora is relieved at the lack of concern. *Just ignore me*, she kept praying as she entered this private hospital. *Don't ask any questions.* Dr Gopalan declares that he has no major concerns, but if she has any symptoms of a concussion, please go to the emergency room. He pronounces the words 'dizziness' and 'vomiting' slowly and loudly. Then he remarks, 'I suppose you'll want a few days off then?' Cora's face burns. She did not try to give herself a concussion to get out of work, if that is what he is implying, but the way he sighs, it's as if she has admitted to the ploy. She sits there for a few moments, her cheeks flushed with indignation, and then she gets up and walks out.

On the drive home, they cross an intersection under a pedestrian bridge that is laced with spiralling branches of pink bougainvillea flowers, soft as kisses against the hard concrete. The hospital recedes behind them as they return to Bukit Timah, where walls of tropical trees flank the highway, and the houses behind them are only visible in snatches of red brick and white concrete, and the occasional icy flash of swimming pools. Cora wants to say something about the doctor to Ma'am Elizabeth, but what if it's not appropriate? She has no gauge for how to behave with her boss, or maybe she has just lost her sense of how to interact with people altogether.

Years ago, after the polyclinic doctor had taken pity on Cora, she had been transferred to a public hospital for X-rays and treatment. Cora had found out later that the doctor had threatened to report Ma'am Roberta to the police. The compromise had been a peaceful and uneventful transfer to the Gomez family, family friends of the doctor's. Cora had started her newsletter after that. She composed many of her articles in her mind while doing housework, and each night, the words poured onto the pages of her notebook. Disbursing advice to other domestic workers had given her a sense of control over her fate, until her feckless brother's disappearance threw everything up in the air once more, and she had returned to the Philippines to care for Raymond who was in primary school.

The sudden blast of Ma'am Elizabeth's ringtone through her phone speakers makes Cora sit up straighter. 'Mum?' Jacqueline's anxious voice crackles.

Ma'am Elizabeth turns up the volume and leans closer to her speakers, even though it makes no difference. 'Hello darling, I'm driving now. Is everything okay?'

'I should be asking you that. I heard you were at the hospital today?'

'Goodness, this island is too small,' Ma'am Elizabeth laughs. 'How did Audrey Chow-Broadley get to you so quickly? I thought she'd use whatever free time she had to teach her son a fourth language.'

'I happened to call her about the property – she's looking over some contracts for us – and she told me that she had just seen you. What happened?'

'Nothing, Jacqueline. I was just there because Cora had a fall.'

'Is she okay? I've always told you that our kitchen floors get too slippery; it's a hazard when anything spills on those light tiles because you can't even see the puddle.'

'She's fine, it wasn't in the kitchen. Just a small scare, that's all.' Ma'am Elizabeth gives Cora a sideways glimpse. 'We don't need to talk about it now. I'm touched by your concern though.'

'I just wanted to make sure it wasn't another relapse. The doctors said—'

'Jacqueline, this traffic is making it hard to concentrate on two things at once.' Ma'am Elizabeth cuts off Jacqueline. 'I will call you back when I get home.'

The rest of the drive is silent. At one junction, Ma'am Elizabeth mentions brightly that it's a nice day to be outside. Cora nods, and then immediately wishes she hadn't, because it's all the permission Ma'am Elizabeth needs to keep driving straight on, chattering away about an Italian restaurant that she hasn't been to in ages. 'Maybe you can drop me at home first?' Cora asks. 'I haven't cleaned the upstairs bathrooms.'

'The bathrooms can wait,' Ma'am Elizabeth says. 'You've had a difficult day. Let's have some lunch. You can see them making the pasta from scratch through a little window. It's mesmerizing.' She pulls into a car park outside a row of delis and florists.

Cora bites her lip. Her head had stopped aching a while ago, but now a mild pain has returned and is pulsing behind her eyes. It is as if there is too much light on her, which is how she feels every time she and Ma'am Elizabeth go out together. It's not being in public together that Cora objects to – it's the confusion in other people's expressions. The waiter at the restaurant now, for example, is looking back and forth between Ma'am Elizabeth and Cora as he rattles off a list of today's specials. As if his eyes have lost their sense of focus, his gaze is darting around, and Cora is getting dizzy just watching him try to process their relationship. Is this your maid, or your friend? Will she be eating with you? Who is she, to be sitting across from you like this in a restaurant, wining and dining on her work hours?

And then, when the menu comes, Cora cannot help looking at the prices. As always, she searches for the cheapest thing on the menu, and she insists on only having tap water even when the waiter says they only serve bottled, and asks her to choose between sparkling or still. 'I will have the garden salad,'

Cora says, pointing at an appetizer that costs thirty-four dollars.

'Just that? Cora, you must be starving. Have some pasta. You eat shellfish, right? Their shrimp fettucine alfredo is amazing. The cream sauce is better than anything I've had in Italy,' Ma'am Elizabeth says.

'No, thank you,' Cora says. 'I will just have the garden salad.'

The waiter accepts their orders and retreats to the kitchen. It is a small, elegant restaurant with starched napkins that sit upright next to wine glasses. Through the viewing window, Cora sees long noodles powdered with flour splayed across a marble counter. The cook calls something over his shoulder but his voice is muted. Cora avoids Ma'am Elizabeth's curious gaze.

A message alert pings on Ma'am Elizabeth's phone. She looks at the screen and sighs. 'Jacqueline worries about me,' Ma'am Elizabeth says, not looking up. 'I haven't told you this, Cora, but I was very sick last year.'

'Sorry to hear that, ma'am,' Cora says. She rolls the corner of the tablecloth between her fingers to keep them busy.

'I didn't tell my daughters about it for a while because I didn't want them to worry, and then when the doctors started bandying about words like "metastasized" and "advanced", I thought my days were numbered. I finally told Jacqueline and Cecilia, and they were understandably upset when they found out I'd been going to chemotherapy. They had only lost their father the year before. They were furious with me for keeping it from them until it got serious. Jacqueline started dropping in all the time. It drove me crazy to be supervised like that, so I conceded to having them hire somebody, even though I'd been given the all-clear.'

So this is where Cora came into Ma'am Elizabeth's life.

'Ma'am, it is very nice of them to be concerned. This is only natural for daughters to do. I supported my parents too.'

'Did your siblings help you?' Ma'am Elizabeth asks. 'I think Jacqueline feels the pressures of doing it all on her own because Cecilia . . . well, she's a free spirit, that one.'

'No,' Cora says. 'I had four brothers. I did everything.' There was a time when she used to lament that her brothers relied on her too much, but the bitterness is gone. Too much has happened to make her feel hostile towards anybody in her family.

Ma'am Elizabeth's smoked salmon and artichoke risotto arrives in a huge white plate trailing a cloud of steam. Next to it, Cora's salad is a limp arrangement of leaves, and her stomach really is starting to growl after catching a whiff of the risotto, but she still refuses when Ma'am Elizabeth offers to share. When Ma'am Elizabeth scoops a couple of spoonfuls onto a side plate and puts it in the middle of the table, Cora looks away. She stabs her fork into the salad and chews her way through it.

'Mr Lee and I could never decide on a place to eat together,' Ma'am Elizabeth comments. 'We always ended up at hawker centres, even on special occasions, because there were so many stalls to choose from. I remember spending our wedding anniversary in Lau Pa Sat after we wandered around the city for ages – he had satay and I had *char kway teow* and we called it a night.'

It's funny to imagine a couple so dignified, and dressed to the nines, eventually finding themselves in that whirlpool of hawker stalls in the heart of the business district. 'Ma'am, I think you prefer more simple things,' Cora says. This is the impression that Ma'am Elizabeth always tries to give her, at least. So why are they here? If she wanted to take Cora out to lunch, why not take her to one of those hawker stalls in

Newton Food Centre where skinned ducks and chickens hang from hooks in the window, and a meal would only cost four dollars?

'I do,' Ma'am Elizabeth says, nodding deeply. 'Before I married Mr Lee though, I didn't really know about life in Singapore. My family dined in hotel restaurants like the Shangri-La or Raffles. I was wrapped in cotton wool, as they say. Then Mr Lee came along and showed me a different life.' Her eyes are glossy with reminiscence.

'You must be missing Mr Lee very much,' Cora says.

There is a distant look in Ma'am Elizabeth's eyes, and then she takes another scoop of risotto. 'Have you ever been married, Cora?'

'A long time ago,' Cora says. She instantly regrets it, and wishes she had just said no to Ma'am Elizabeth, who is looking at her curiously. 'We couldn't have children, so I gave my husband my blessings to find somebody else.'

'I'm sorry,' Ma'am Elizabeth says.

'It was a long time ago,' Cora repeats. It was not altogether a terrible thing to have no children. Enough responsibilities were heaped on her after she went abroad to work, without the worry of mothering *in absentia.*

'I can't imagine how those women do it, the ones who have to leave their children behind,' Ma'am Elizabeth says, unconsciously following her train of thought. 'Of course, it's not easy for any of you.'

'It's okay, ma'am,' Cora says. 'Our lives are different from yours but—'

'Cora, I know why you dropped to the ground like that,' Ma'am Elizabeth says quietly. 'We should talk about it.'

Cora's fork is suspended between her plate and her lips when Ma'am Elizabeth says this. She pushes it into her mouth and chews carefully, looking down at her plate. Her heart begins to thump wildly.

How does Ma'am Elizabeth know about the shooting? Did she send somebody to investigate Cora's background? She must know everything then – about the way Cora had to flee after she tried to get justice for Raymond and those men had trailed her to Dasmariñas, their guns gleaming in their belts. She must have contacted the Calverts and found out about Cora leaving in the middle of the night. She must know about the deal Cora made with the Calverts' security guard so he would give her a head start. Cora feels her legs getting weak and she is thankful to be sitting down. 'Ma'am, please understand . . .' she whispers.

Ma'am Elizabeth's eyes widen and she reaches across the table. 'Oh Cora, of course I understand,' she says, squeezing her hand. 'It was inexcusable.'

'This doesn't affect my job, ma'am? I don't want to go back to Manila right now.'

'Of course not! It was his fault, not yours.'

At this, Cora pulls her hands away and stares at Ma'am Elizabeth. 'Raymond didn't do anything wrong.'

'He absolutely did,' Ma'am Elizabeth says firmly.

Cora's voice gets louder as she repeats herself. 'My nephew did not deserve this.'

'Nephew?' Ma'am Elizabeth looks at her, confusion wrinkling her features. 'Cora, we must be talking about different things. I thought you were having a reaction because of the abuse you suffered in your previous employer's house.'

Cora doesn't know whether she feels more relieved or angry. 'You think I jumped to the ground because somebody threw an ashtray at me?' she asks, and she doesn't realize she's speaking in Tagalog. It's the language for first reactions, and for complete disbelief. Ma'am Elizabeth shakes her head slightly.

Cora wants to ask the question again in English, but what comes out instead is a build-up of all her frustrations. The red and white chequered tablecloth, the waiter pulling out the chair for Ma'am Elizabeth and coolly ignoring Cora, the doctor's assumption that Cora would injure herself in order to get time off. 'Ma'am, you don't understand anything,' Cora says. 'And you keep taking me to all these places as if I am your friend, and you think we are the same, but we are not the same. Ask the Starbucks barista, ask the neighbours, ask anybody who sees us together. They know I am your maid. Why you must pretend it is not like that? And why you must pretend you know one thing happened to me long time ago, this must be the reason for all of my problems?'

By the end of her rant, Cora is breathless. The colour has drained from Ma'am Elizabeth's face and she looks mortified. 'Cora,' she starts, and then she can't continue. 'I don't know what to say.'

'Just take me home,' Cora pleads. 'I just want to do my job, not go out and share my life with you.'

Ma'am Elizabeth's hand trembles slightly as she runs her spoon through her risotto. The other people in the restaurant have dissolved into the background, and it is just the two of them. Cora's mouth feels dry, and the salad goes down her throat with difficulty. Ma'am Elizabeth gestures for the waiter to bring the bill. Moments later, they are hurrying out of the restaurant and into the car. Ma'am Elizabeth lets Cora open the door herself, and she turns on the radio to fill the silence between them.

As the car merges onto the main road that cuts through the abundantly green land, Cora sneaks looks at Ma'am Elizabeth. She appears to be concentrating very hard on her driving, leaning slightly forward and squinting like a person pretending to drive. Cora is still annoyed with her, but also feels a bit guilty for her harsh tone. Ma'am Elizabeth has never scolded her, or spoken to her with anything but kindness.

'Ma'am, maybe Miss Jacqueline is right,' Cora says gently. 'You should go out more with your friends. You stay at home all the time and I am the only person you talk to. It's not appropriate, ma'am.'

Ma'am Elizabeth grips the steering wheel. 'I really don't want you to feel uncomfortable. I know you've had a hard time with employers in the past, and I just wanted to make sure that you were being treated well.'

'You treat me well,' Cora assures her. 'But sitting in the restaurant, going to your private hospital – you think you are being generous, but the other people think I am taking advantage. I get funny looks from them, and they say things to me. There must be a line between us.'

'Okay,' Ma'am Elizabeth says. 'Okay. I'm very sorry, Cora. I meant well.'

'I know it, ma'am,' Cora says.

'I won't compel you to keep me company like that any more. I had no idea how uncomfortable it was making you. But if you get injured again, or ill, I insist on getting you the best care. That's my responsibility as your employer.'

'Thank you, ma'am,' Cora replies. 'It is difficult, I know. When somebody close with you dies, there is a lot of loneliness and things you wish you could say.' She feels her throat becoming thick with tears. If Raymond were here, she'd tell him that she was always proud of him, even in her angriest moments over his new wealthy friends. 'You must be missing Mr Lee very much,' Cora says.

'I do,' Ma'am Elizabeth says. 'Every day.' She takes a deep breath. 'I missed him even after I found out about . . . Cora, can I tell you this? One last thing, I promise. I need to tell somebody.'

The pain on her face is clear. 'Okay ma'am,' Cora says.

'There was a woman in the passenger seat next to my husband when he died.'

'Oh,' Cora says. She realizes that this is something Ma'am Elizabeth really wants to talk about, so she asks. 'Who was she?'

'She was Loretta Kwok. In her late forties, a divorcee with three children. That was how I knew it wasn't a silly, lust-driven fling; it wasn't some Hong Kong debutante. He was committed to her. It hurt so much more, knowing that they were carrying on together like that, going out to nice dinners. And the papers didn't report it. They didn't want to tarnish the name of a success story like Mr Lee with any speculation that he was having an affair.'

'I'm so sorry,' Cora says. 'I did not know.'

'Neither did I,' Ma'am Elizabeth says. 'I was the last to know, apparently. It turned out that all my friends had known about her. All of the women that I saw every week for coffee and in church.'

So that's why Ma'am Elizabeth has so few friends. 'You confront them, ma'am?' Cora asks. 'Ask them why they don't say anything?'

'I'm still working up the courage. I've withdrawn from most social events, though, because I feel like such a fool. My daughters didn't know about it either, but when they found out, they were . . .' She shrugs. 'Not so bothered. They tried to convince me to move on by insisting that the past is the past. We shouldn't speak ill of the dead. I felt like nobody understood me.'

What Cora knows about grief is that it comes in waves. It crashed down upon her last week when she saw a schoolboy stepping off the bus, his backpack thumping against his skinny frame. It blacks out all of her senses and makes her say and do things she might later regret.

'Ma'am, whatever you are feeling, it's the right way,' Cora says.

'Thank you, Cora,' Ma'am Elizabeth says.

As they pull up to the driveway and Ma'am Elizabeth presses her buzzer that opens the automatic gates, Cora remembers her daily trips to the Calverts' house in Dasmariñas. Immense properties cloaked in the shadows of towering hedges, gardeners dragging hoses across rambling lawns, and swimming pools glaring boldly against the heat. It was only after Raymond died that she asked the Calverts if she could take them up on their offer to live in the maid's quarters. 'I don't know how you've managed to travel to Quezon City and back every day,' said Mrs Calvert sympathetically. 'Two and a half hours, three jeepney changes, a bus and a twenty-minute walk you said? It just makes sense for you to stay with us.' But the commute, though inconvenient and draining, had never been a problem for Cora. Home was narrow streets filled with the lingering smell of grilled *isaw* from a street vendor's stove. It was the hanging vines that wound around the iron bars of her windows, and the clean, cool tiles kissing her feet. She would have spent the rest of her life in her house if the men who killed Raymond hadn't threatened her life and driven her out.

When Cora and Ma'am Elizabeth walk up, Cora spots her phone still sitting on the garden path and she picks it up to find that it has run out of power. As they enter the house, Ma'am Elizabeth turns to her and says, 'Cora, please take the rest of the day off.' She holds up her hands when Cora starts to protest. 'No, Cora. This isn't special treatment. You've had a head injury, and it's important that you take it easy. There's nothing left to do in the house that can't be done tomorrow.'

'Okay, ma'am,' Cora says. To tell the truth, she is exhausted. Thinking about Raymond can be so draining – this is what loss does as well, she wants to assure Ma'am Elizabeth, who sometimes takes long afternoon naps and wakes up looking slightly ruffled and self-conscious, guiltily confiding to Cora about the indulgence.

In her room, Cora plugs her phone into the charger and shuts her eyes. She lets her mind wander away from this strange afternoon where the past came rushing at her from all directions. The phone jolts awake and begins to update her on all she has missed.

Angel and Donita are still busily discussing Flordeliza Martinez. *What do you think, Cora?* Angel prompts a few times. In 2001, Cora had advised the other maids on how to handle the fallout from the Marisol Concepcion murder. Now is the time to be careful, she had cautioned them, but don't keep your head down too low or they will think we all have something to apologize for. At Sunday gathering spots, she had discreetly collected cash donations in a large envelope to send to the woman's family after the court ruled that she was guilty and would be executed.

That was all a long time ago – now Cora doesn't even have the words to explain to Angel and Donita why she doesn't want to be involved. All she has are flashes of regret: the single gold earring she pushed into the security guard's hands. The smirk on his face, the cold dread spreading through her chest. The way he grasped her hand tightly, just long enough to make her understand that he wasn't satisfied. 'What will I do with one earring?' he sneered, and he waved away her suggestions that it was valuable enough to pawn. He wanted her to return to the house and come back with a bigger prize. When he told her what it was and where exactly to find it, Cora knew this was a sin that no God could ever forgive, no matter how many times she prayed the rosary.

Murder Maid Has No Alibi

A foreign domestic worker from the Philippines who is accused of murdering her employer has not been able to explain her whereabouts on the day of the alleged killing, say police.

Flordeliza Martinez is the lead suspect in the murder of Carolyn Hong in Oldham Walk off East Coast Road last week. Police speculate that Ms Hong caught Miss Martinez in the middle of a theft, and Miss Martinez pushed her against a wall. Ms Hong died from injuries to her skull.

Miss Martinez was the only person reported to be at home at the time. Mrs Hong's husband, Peter Hong, was in East Coast Park training for a marathon. Their daughter, Elise, 17, discovered her mother's body.

If charged, Miss Martinez could face life in jail or execution by hanging.

For more updates, subscribe to The Straits Times.

Chapter Eight

It feels as though the Fanns might never leave the flat today, and this is a problem for Donita because something is happening across the road. Two white catering vans have come down East Coast Road and turned down the street leading to the Hongs' residence. Earlier this morning, Donita could also see a bright yellow tent being pitched outside their house. Today is one of her working Sundays, so she'll need a good excuse to go outside to get a closer look if the Fanns plan on staying in.

What do you think is going on? she asked on her group chat with Cora and Angel after sending them a blurry picture taken from her window.

Funeral wake, Angel replied. *They are setting up for it. It will be an outdoor thing, probably a few days.*

DONITA: *Are their funerals open to the public?*

ANGEL: *Nobody notices if it's a big funeral.*

Judging from the size of the equipment being unloaded from the trucks outside the residence, they are setting up for a major event. Crowds of well-wishers will pack the street and

workers will be scurrying around to keep them fed. Who will
notice Donita casually slipping in? If only Mr and Mrs Fann
would quit bickering in the living room and just leave for
church already. Last night, after the latest news article was
posted, she couldn't get the phrase 'execution by hanging' out
of her head. She needs to get closer to the house if she wants
to help Flor but she can't do it alone. Keeping an eye on the
Hong residence as it pulses with activity, Donita sends Angel
a direct message. *Want to come here?*

She hears Mrs Fann calling her name.

ANGEL: *Already on my way* 😌

Donita tosses the phone onto her bed and hurries to the
hallway just in time for Mrs Fann to bellow her name again.
'How many times must I call you?' Mrs Fann asks.

'Sorry, ma'am,' says Donita.

'There is a bag of old clothes for the *karang guni* man to
collect. Fold them neatly before putting them outside – I don't
want the neighbours to see the clothes in untidy piles.' Mrs
Fann glances at her watch. 'You ready or not?' she calls to
Mr Fann, who is still in his study.

After a long pause, Mr Fann replies. 'Go ahead without me.'

Mrs Fann takes in a breath so deep, it feels as if the pressure
of the atmosphere is changing. She picks up her purse and
marches out of the flat.

Donita crouches to sort through the faded, musty-smelling
clothes for donation. She can hear Mr Fann shuffling around,
the way he does in the middle of the night when he can't
sleep. This morning, she heard Mrs Fann telling him,
'Depression is a problem of the spirit, just like Weston's weak-
ness. Pastor Ong says he'll talk to you.'

Mr Fann comes out of the study just as Donita is holding
up a blue T-shirt with the words St Lawrence Secondary

School Track and Field printed in white letters across the back. 'Mrs Fann told you to get rid of these?'

Donita nods.

'I'll keep that one,' he says. It looks much too small for him, but Donita hands it over. Could that T-shirt have belonged to Weston? Mr Fann clutches it tightly with both hands.

'Sir?' She should ask if he wants to look through the box for any more clothes. Those words clog her throat; she doesn't know how to talk to Mr Fann.

'Do you need something?' Mr Fann asks. There is something in his voice, a type of softness, that Donita seizes upon.

'Uhh . . . I need to go out,' she says. What is the one excuse that guarantees a man will ask no further questions? 'Period, sir. Very heavy flow. Need extra sanitary pads.'

'Okay.' Mr Fann's permission comes so easily that Donita instantly regrets divulging such personal details. She could have probably said 'female problems' and he would have understood, but maybe it's best to keep him uncomfortable so he won't ask any questions.

On her way out the door, Donita sees a message from Angel: *On the 36 bus, just passed Parkway Parade.* Perfect, she's only five minutes away.

Donita arrives on East Coast Road just as the neon green bus is pulling up. She sees Angel tapping her fare card and then gesturing urgently at somebody else behind her. Donita squints – through the tinted doors, she recognizes Cora. They both step onto the kerb, Angel flashing Donita a grin, and Cora making a visor of her hands to shield her eyes from the sun's angry glare.

'This is the wrong stop,' Cora says. 'I thought we were going to the airport?'

'Come along, Cora,' Angel says, briskly falling in step with Donita.

'You told her you were taking her to the airport?' Donita whispers.

'I couldn't tell her we were going to a murder house, could I?'

'Why the airport though?'

Behind them, Cora is calling out, 'Do we need to change buses?'

'She hasn't been to Jewel yet. She didn't believe there was a rainforest and a waterfall in the middle of the airport.'

Donita wouldn't have believed it either. The first time she saw a video of the water gushing through that enormous glass domed roof, she thought she was witnessing a grand flood. Then she saw the shuttle trains weaving through the thicket of tropical trees, and the camera panned over the little balcony lookouts and restaurants nestled in an indoor forest. Behind them were the winking storefront banners for handbag boutiques and gadget stores.

They are turning down the road when Cora calls for them to stop. 'Tell me what's going on right now,' Cora commands. 'Where are we . . .?' Mid-sentence, she appears to realize where Angel and Donita are headed.

'I don't understand why you had to bring her,' Donita mutters to Angel as they turn to face Cora.

'She will be helpful,' Angel whispers back. She turns to Cora. 'Donita saw Flordeliza that evening, Cora. We know these homes better than most people do. Maybe there's something that the police missed when they were investigating.'

'Then why not tell the police?' Cora asks.

'Do you remember the way they spoke to us the other day? They probably have my name on record. If I tell them I knew

Flordeliza, they will probably pin somebody else's murder on me,' Donita says.

'Shhh,' Angel says, even though they've been speaking in Tagalog. Still, the word for murder strikes the air like a match.

'This isn't right,' Cora says. 'I'm going home. I'm not getting involved. I'll take a walk on the beach.'

'Flordeliza is innocent,' Donita insists. 'Can you live with yourself knowing that an innocent person was executed?'

Those words do something to Cora. Donita sees it in the way her eyes grow cloudy, her mind retreating into another place. It's like the expression that overtook Mr Fann's face earlier when he saw Donita holding that T-shirt.

'We can have a look from across the road,' Cora says finally. 'I'm not going anywhere near the house.'

'Okay,' Donita and Angel say in unison. They briskly make their way towards the Hong residence, a double-storey terrace house with wide windows and a red-tiled roof. The iron gates are spread open like wings, and white plastic chairs have been set up in the driveway. Metal scaffolding extends across the outside area and forms the outline of a tent.

There is nothing to see from out here, but in her mind, Donita begins to search for clues in Flordeliza's daily path. The walk to the wet market; the cleaning of each room of the house; the dinner preparations.

Upstairs, the windows are closed and shades are drawn. Donita edges along the pavement, obeying Cora's instructions to only observe the house from a distance. The main door is propped open and there is a clear line of vision into the living room and kitchen. She pictures Flordeliza returning home that Sunday after Donita saw her. Was the house empty and strangely silent? Did she know right away that something was off?

'This wake is going to be a big affair,' Angel observes as two men edge their way onto the property carrying a long wooden table. 'They will probably cremate her body privately, but this ceremony will be for everybody to attend.'

The wreaths have already started piling up, trails of satin ribbon and stiff, bulky hoops of flowers. Donita watches one of the workers at the top of a ladder, adjusting the tarp. The thick silver bangle on his wrist looks like the one Sanjeev wears for religious reasons. Yesterday, when she was trying to piece together the timeline of Carolyn Hong's murder and her encounter with Flordeliza, she messaged Sanjeev: *On Sunday, the place we went to, what is it called?* He replied: *Baby, we were in HEAVEN.* Not the answer she was looking for, but it did make her giggle.

'Do they have surveillance cameras?' Cora asks.

'If they had caught somebody else on camera, Flordeliza wouldn't be a suspect,' Angel points out. 'If they had camera footage, Flordeliza would be able to prove she was out of the house when the murder happened.'

There is a twitch in Donita's feet, and she notices Angel shifting her weight as well. The hot pavement is beginning to burn through the worn soles of Donita's rubber sandals, but it's impatience too, because there isn't much time before she is due home. 'We'd have better chances of seeing what's inside if we went closer to the house,' Donita suggests.

'She's right, Cora,' Angel says. 'We look more suspicious just standing here like this.'

Cora sighs, relenting as Donita leads them across the road. The edges of the driveway are piled with workers' equipment – folded tables, ladders resting on their sides, thick spools of black cables. A portable toilet for workers has been set up in the garden, even though, just a few feet away, there is a bathroom next to the gaping open main door of the house. Donita knows this because she sees a teenager coming out, wiping her hands on her jeans. In a flash, she crosses the living room and disappears from view.

'The daughter?' Angel asks.

Donita nods. Elise Hong, the girl whose devastating cries for her mother parted the crowd that Sunday evening. From here, Donita notices an alleyway hugging the side of the house. It leads to a paved courtyard out the back where laundry lines hang between two poles and three mountain bikes are slumped against the wall. She glances at Cora. 'I guess there's nothing to see here,' she says, although she is eyeing the back door. It has been left open for the caterers, whose stoves are connected to the gas lines.

'Told you,' Cora says. 'Let's just go to Jewel now, please.'

'Fine,' Donita sighs. 'There's a short cut to the bus stop this way.'

Cora and Angel follow her. It's true that cutting through the access lane between the houses will shave a minute or two off their journey back to the bus stop on the main road, so they don't sense Donita's plans until she makes a sharp left turn onto the alley that leads to the Hong house's back yard.

Behind her, Angel lets out a noise of protest, but follows Donita as she hurries down the alley and makes for the back door. Cora hisses, 'Stop it, this is crazy.' She reaches out to tug Donita's hand, and in the excitement of entering the house, Donita grabs Cora's wrist and pulls her inside.

They are frozen for a moment: the air here is cooler and tinged with the lemony scent of dish detergent. Copper frying pans hang from a row of hooks above their heads. Cora makes a move to run back outside, but Donita and Angel tumble past her, accidentally pushing her further in, and then suddenly they are scattering frantically around a marble kitchen island. They scan the kitchen to take in everything they can. Here is a faintly humming stainless-steel fridge and a floating shelf of cookbooks. Here is a bowl teeming with kiwis and overripe bananas and a single glass bowl with a dessert spoon lying in the sink. What did the killer touch? What did he see?

Finally, Cora breaks past them and makes for the back door. Donita registers movement as a shadow approaches the open kitchen door; they all freeze with fear. Thankfully, somebody in the hallway calls out and the shadow retreats. Angel's palms are flat and her hands are hovering in a limp version of the surrender position, just to let everybody know that she is not touching anything. The women are completely silent, until the sole of Cora's sandal squeaks against the floor, and she lurches forward, falling to her knees.

In that same moment, they hear heavy footsteps descending from above. 'Go, go, go,' Angel whispers urgently, and they scramble out through the door. Donita feels her heart leaping into her throat. Laughter, the hysterical kind overcharged by sheer fear, begins bubbling up from her stomach as soon as she is outside. She is stumbling across the courtyard when Angel grabs her arm. *Cora*, she whispers. Her eyes are wide and full of terror.

Cora is still inside the kitchen, slowly pushing herself to standing, when those feet become visible on the stairs. Donita returns to the doorway to beckon her urgently, but she is a split second too late – if Cora is seen racing out of the house, she will look more suspicious. Donita and Angel crouch by the door, their bodies flat against the brick exterior of the house. Cora freezes. They all watch as the stairs reveal the body like an image gradually downloading: legs in a pair of black trousers, then a grey polo shirt, then a face that Donita has only seen in that headshot online. Peter Hong.

They have left Cora inside the house with a murderer.

The thought brings a chill to Donita's bones. Seeing that Mr Hong is busy tapping on his phone, she waves to get Cora's attention, to let her know she should escape now. But for some reason, Cora goes deeper into the kitchen.

'What is she doing?' Angel asks.

Donita shakes her head. This is very bad. They should run. But she cannot leave Cora there, even though her whole body is burning for an easy escape. Angel grips her arm and Donita feels the same thoughts charging through her. They must stand by their friend.

Cora turns her back on them but stays within view. She picks up a washcloth near the sink and begins wiping the counter vigorously. The movement catches Mr Hong's attention. He snaps his head up and stares at Cora.

'Good afternoon, sir!' Cora chirps. The enthusiasm and pitch to her voice are new to Donita, who presses closer to the open door to see what is happening.

Mr Hong's stare is unnerving. Remember this, Donita thinks as she trains her eyes on the scene. If he hurts Cora in any way, Donita and Angel will be witnesses, but they must know all the details, or the police won't believe them. Donita takes in the details of the kitchen: the little black flecks on the marble flooring, the names of each fruit on the bowl on the counter. On the side of the fridge, a clip magnet has slid down from the weight of the papers fastened to it.

'Who are you?' Mr Hong asks.

Cora is still grinning and swiping the countertops with her washcloth when she says, 'Lucy Marie Gonzalez, sir, from Lucky Lucy's Cleaning Agency.'

Donita feels Angel take in a sharp breath.

'Excuse me?' Mr Hong asks. 'What are you doing here?'

'Sir, you booked me to do the cleaning?' Cora says. Her eyes are round like a doll's.

'I did not book you.'

Cora's face crumples from confusion. 'Oh, you booked Rainy then? Rainy sometimes does the Sunday shifts.'

Through gritted teeth, Mr Hong says, 'I did not book anybody.'

What is she doing? Donita wonders. She glances at Angel, who looks just as perplexed.

Cora has stopped wiping the table, and she's reaching into her pocket for her phone. 'Sir, maybe there has been a mix-up,' she says. Before taking out her phone, she squints at Mr Hong. 'This is 86 Oldham Drive, yes?'

'No,' Mr Hong says. His shoulders relax a little bit. 'This is Oldham Walk. I don't know where Oldham Drive is.'

'Ay!' Cora cries. 'I'm so stupid, sir. I go to the wrong house!' In a frenzy, she picks up the washcloth and brings it to the sink. 'I must call the ma'am and explain, ayayayay! I'm so sorry, sir.'

Mr Hong stares after Cora as she makes a play of collecting some things in order to depart. The phone is pressed to her ear and she's grovelling to nobody at the other end. Donita and Angel jump to their feet and race up the alley. Breathless and giggling as they turn the corner onto the access lane, Angel says, 'You see? *That* is why we need Cora.'

'I didn't recognize her,' Donita gasps. She takes in a gulp of air.

When Cora comes around the corner, the sunlight is illuminating her hair and she looks as if she is on fire. 'I'm going to kill you both,' she growls. Angel gives Cora a hug.

'Did you see anything?' Donita asks.

'She was too focused on pretending to be a cleaner to take on any more spy work,' Angel says, laughing. 'Isn't that right, Cora? You were wiping that counter so hard I thought Mr Hong was going to give you a job in the end.'

'I don't think a job was what he was planning on giving me,' Cora says. 'I'm lucky I got out of there.'

They are walking through the park that leads to the main road when Angel speaks up. 'When I was in the kitchen, I noticed a few pictures of Flordeliza – I recognized her from the news report. There was a mug from Universal Studios with a photograph of Flordeliza and the Hong girl on a roller coaster.'

So? Donita almost asks, and Angel must see it in her expression because she says, 'I just don't think a maid who is so included in the family would suddenly betray them like that.'

Cora bites her lip and doesn't say anything. 'It's hard to know,' she says. Donita and Angel exchange a look. 'People are capable of anything when they're desperate.'

'You think Flordeliza was really trying to get into the safe to steal something?' Angel asks.

'Not steal. I don't think she had money problems.'

'She didn't,' Donita says. 'She regularly sent money home to her family.'

'And she used a premium *balikbayan* service too,' Cora says. 'BalikExpress. I saw a roll of their complimentary packing tape on the kitchen counter.'

'Did her employers keep her passport?' Angel asks. 'They usually keep those in a safe. Maybe she was just trying to get to it, and then she and her ma'am got into a fight.'

'But I saw her,' Donita says, exasperated that her friends are ignoring this detail. 'I saw her, I know I did.' What will it take for everybody to believe her? Even Sanjeev, when she clarified her question about where exactly they had been that Sunday, replied, 'But are you sure you saw her? It was raining so heavily. Could have been anyone.'

Angel and Cora exchange a look. Donita sees that Cora is still panting slightly from the run, and the adrenaline no doubt, and Angel's cheeks are flushed.

'Donita, what we did was really dangerous,' Angel says. 'I know she's your friend, but . . .'

'But what?' Donita snaps. 'I should just wait for them to execute her for murder? Why did you come here if you didn't want to find out the truth?'

'I was curious,' Angel says. She glances back at the house. 'But that man looks dangerous. I don't want to get mixed up with him.'

'You're probably too young to remember that something similar happened to a Pinoy woman here almost twenty years ago,' Cora says.

'Marisol Concepcion?' Donita asks. 'Of course I remember.' But perhaps 'remember' is not the right word. Marisol Concepcion was a spectre who haunted every family across the Philippines that had daughters and wives working over-seas. A movie about her life had screened at the outdoor cinema in Pasuquin a few years later, and some people who watched it declared they would never go to Singapore. Over time, those sentiments faded, but nobody forgot a story like that, especially not the women.

'The police here said Marisol strangled her employer, but there were experts in the Philippines who said that somebody with her small frame couldn't possibly have overpowered that woman,' Angel says. 'The media back home also revealed that the employer was having an affair, which the news barely mentioned here. It could have been her jealous husband or lover. Right, Cora?'

'What Angel is saying is that if you want to investigate, Donita, you could get yourself into some serious trouble,' says Cora. 'Let's say you found some evidence in the house, but the police didn't believe you? The husband could come after you. You live so nearby.'

All Donita hears is 'evidence'. 'I'm not afraid of anyone,' she says to Angel and Cora and, before they can argue, she turns around and heads straight back up the path. The wind is rushing in her ears but she imagines Cora and Angel are calling out for her. By the time she reaches the back gate, her hands have stopped shaking. She steps through the threshold, thinking only of Flor.

The back yard of the Hong residence is a cluttered plot of overgrown weeds and discarded items like a rusted barbecue grill and some cracked clay pots. The small window with iron grills – probably the maid's room – faces this area, but it's too high to see into. Donita's sights land on the breezeblocks holding up the mini slide set that Elise Hong clearly outgrew a long time ago. Donita tugs at one block but it barely budges. She notices something brown and leathery curling around the corner of the slide and she recoils quickly. A snake? She squints, peers closely, and sees the gleaming curve of a buckle. It's a bag. A leather purse backpack, exactly like the one Flor was wearing that day.

There are voices approaching – workers, speaking in a language Donita doesn't understand. Donita ducks for cover and crawls towards the slide, tucking herself under and out of sight. She pops open the bag's buckle and begins rifling through the contents: a tube of lipstick, a mirror, and a small black compact. There is also a fistful of cash: two fifty-dollar bills and a few loose notes crumpled like old tissues at the bottom of the bag. Donita reaches into her pocket for her phone to take a picture, but when she hears a girl's voice, she hurries to pack everything back into the bag and place it back under the slide. She stays crouched there, her heart pounding in her ears.

'It's just so hard.'

Donita takes a cautious peek at Elise Hong talking on her phone. 'The funeral, all these people. I can't believe it.' She bites her lower lip as a fresh stream of tears pours down her face. Donita wishes she could comfort this girl. She was too young to mourn her parents when they left but, when she was a teenager, she found places to hide and cry for the mother she never knew.

'It would be easier if you were here,' Elise continues, and then she nods quickly. 'I know, I know, but I'm just saying, I wish you were around.' Another pause as she listens to the person on the line. She takes in a deep, shaky breath and exhales loudly. 'Like that?' she asks. 'It helps a little bit, but the middle of the night is hardest for me. I feel so scared.' Then she lowers her head and begins to whisper. Donita leans out as far as she can without being seen. She scans the back yard. Would it be possible, if Elise keeps her head down, for Donita to belly-crawl her way to that slouching sack of soil and old tiles? They are piled high enough to hide Donita even better than this slide, and she'll be able to eavesdrop.

Suddenly, Elise stops and hangs up without a goodbye. Around the corner, a shadow darkens the concrete pathway.

'Elise! What are you doing out here?' a deep voice demands. It is Peter Hong. Donita squeezes back into the small space behind the slide, hoping that they don't make their way over here.

'I was just checking my messages,' Elise replies. The shadows disappear, they are moving away towards the front door. Donita eyes another hiding spot behind the rusty barbecue grill. As the voices move further away, she darts to take cover there, bringing her closer again to the Hongs.

'Messages from who?' Mr Hong is asking.

Elise replies but Donita cannot hear her exact words. What she can catch is the pitch of the girl's voice getting higher with her protestations.

'I told you, don't just talk to anybody,' Mr Hong says. His voice booms with authority. 'Any calls people want to make, any condolences, they can make them through me. Understand?'

Donita doesn't hear anything. She pictures Elise nodding. 'Give me your phone.' Elise's protests are thin. 'I said, give me your phone,' her father says.

The menacing tone in his voice, the way his daughter abruptly stops whining, sends chills down Donita's spine. She waits until their shadows recede completely before she pokes her head out from behind the barbecue grill to make sure the coast is clear. Then she scrambles out of the back gate. Racing towards the canal path, Donita sees Cora and Angel boarding the 36 bus towards Jewel. They can continue their day as if nothing happened. The white suds of a gathering wave rise and crash against the shore as Donita reaches Block One. She has to stop herself from racing across the bridge and leaping into the sea, leaving the Hong residence even further behind.

Chapter Nine

The morning passes with scrubbing. Angel scrubs the grouting between the kitchen tiles and feels an unusual dose of satisfaction when they grin back, white as teeth. With a fistful of steel wool, she scours away the film of oil that has settled in the sink. The lemony scent of Cif cream cleaner fills the house like a song. When the dogs, led by their twitching noses, approach her as she is attacking the accumulated soot and grime on the oven grills, she pauses only to scrub them too. A woman's laughter erupts from the other end of the flat: Nurul, the new nurse, started on Monday morning, and already she is acting like she and Mr Vijay are old friends.

The dogs can sense the tension in the air. They had a fight this morning and now they are avoiding each other. Coco sits on a cushion on the balcony, licking the spot on her paw where Toffee nipped her. Angel gives Toffee a scratch in her favourite spot on her ribcage. 'You tell her sorry later, okay?' Toffee wheezes and settles into a cool spot in the living room where the late morning shadows have pooled. Her heart beats furiously under a mess of fur.

'You're so loving with them.'

Raja's voice startles Angel. 'I didn't know you were home,' Angel says.

'My class was cancelled,' Raja says. 'Thinking about going somewhere quiet and far away from here. Maybe a stroll along Changi Boardwalk. Ever been there?'

Angel shrugs and goes to the kitchen. There are many remote corners of this island that she and Suzan discovered together on their Sundays off. She still has pictures on her phone of the towering granite cliffs in Little Guilin and a long-tailed monkey clinging to a tree branch in MacRitchie Reservoir. She wondered aloud if they needed their passports when they took the boat to cross the water to Pulau Ubin, an island of wild mangroves and darting mudskippers. Sand crunched beneath the rented bicycles they pedalled as chickens scattered away and mosquitos whined in their ears. Changi Beach had been one of their favourite places; there's no need for Raja to have any share in those memories.

'You could come along if you want,' Raja says. He has followed her into the kitchen and he is taking a pitcher of water out of the fridge.

'No, thank you,' Angel says. There are glasses in the cupboard next to the fridge, but whenever she is standing near the sink, Raja reaches for the dish drainer overhead so he can lean towards her. She ducks out of his way.

'Why not?' Raja asks. 'Aren't you tired of spending the whole day indoors? Now that Nurul is here, you have more spare time, right?'

'I still have many things to do,' Angel says firmly, and to illustrate her point, she opens the cupboard next to the sink and pulls out the mop and bucket. Raja lingers only for a moment, and then he leaves her alone.

The nerve of Raja to suggest that Angel sits idle just because Nurul has taken over looking after Mr Vijay. The list of tasks around here keeps growing – mould spotting the edges of the shower curtains; Sumanthi's jacket, which needs express dry-cleaning; the light bulb in the kitchen that has started flickering to warn Angel it's time for a replacement. And then there are the constant repairs. Lately she feels as if she needs to be multiplied into two people in order to get everything done.

Yet when Sumanthi told Angel about trialling a nurse for a week, Angel balked at the thought of another person coming in and interrupting her running of the household. She barely listened as Sumanthi explained, 'Nurul was very helpful to Anand's mother after her hip surgery. She's a private home nurse, and she offered to come in to see what Dad might need.' It has been three days now and Angel is ready for Nurul to leave. *She thinks she knows everything,* Angel texted Cora on Monday after Nurul breezed through the apartment, pointing out possible hazards and asking about Mr Vijay's routine. Angel had showed her how Mr Vijay was making progress with swinging the badminton racket and Nurul had said, 'There's actually a technique to make him learn it faster. I'll show him.'

As Angel runs the mop over the kitchen floor now, she recalls those days after Mr Vijay had his stroke. Angel had been working for the Vijays for three years at that point and, like the children, she was still in a fog of grief over Mrs Vijay's death when they found Mr Vijay struggling to get out of bed, his mouth twitched to one side. After his week in hospital, she and Sumanthi had toured nursing homes together. One place was acrid with the smell of antiseptic. Withered patients in pale blue pyjamas, who stared glassy-eyed at a single television screen playing a Mandarin soap opera. Angel couldn't take it.

'Miss Sumanthi, we cannot put your father here. I will take care of him.'

Taking on extra duties was nothing new to her. In the first blurry decade of working in Singapore, there were families whose faces she can barely remember now because she was so buried in correcting practice spelling tests, cleaning bird cages, defrosting breast milk, programming cable television channels – any skill that was needed, Angel became the master. The caretaking of Mr Vijay was about practice and perfection, like learning how to control the caulk gun to replace the rubber strip under the shower door, or finding the exact spot between the dogs' shoulder blades to squeeze the drops of flea prevention medication so they wouldn't be able to reach it with their tongues.

Angel's phone pings on the counter. Finally, a response from Donita on the chat group. They haven't heard from her since they parted ways on Sunday. Both Angel and Cora had sent her messages of apology for running off. *We were scared and just wanted to get away,* Angel had written. *We had no business being there in the first place,* Cora added. The single tick indicated that the messages had been sent but not received until just moments ago.

DONITA: *Mrs Fann took my phone away as punishment for going out without her permission.*

ANGEL: *She's awful! So did you find anything in the house?*

DONITA: *I found Flor's bag hidden in the back yard. It had her make-up and lipstick and some cash.*

ANGEL: *OMG! Did you take them?*

DONITA: *Are you crazy? Of course not. And while I was hiding there, Mr Hong came out and started scolding the daughter for texting her friends. I managed to sneak out, but by the time I got home Mr Fann was wondering where I had been and then later one of Mrs Fann's nosy neighbours said she saw me talking to my friends across the road.*

CORA: *Why would Flordeliza's bag be hidden in the yard?*

DONITA: *I don't know. It's the same bag I saw her wearing on the day of the killing though. Even though you don't believe that I saw her.*

Angel begins typing but doesn't know how to phrase what she wants to say – that she is sorry for making such a hasty exit. She was scared. And she was worried for Cora, whose fear radiated off her like heat.

CORA: *Donita, I believe you. I just want you to be careful. Especially with the kind of Ma'am that you have.*

ANGEL: *Will you return to the Hongs' house?*

DONITA: *Not this week. Mrs Fann is making me go to church with her for her big project. I've been running around all day taking orders from her committee. The only reason she gave me back my phone was so she could find me in this huge complex.*

CORA: *Ma'am Elizabeth mentioned Mrs Fann's church project the other day. She said, 'I don't know what they're up to now, but if Fann Poh Choo is in charge, it's not good news.'*

DONITA: *Whatever keeps her busy.*

ANGEL: *Hard to believe a woman like Mrs Fann is close to God.*

DONITA: *Can I ask you two for a favour? There's a lot of news going around about Flor. I set up an alert for her name but so many things come up, and I hardly have time to read everything. I don't always have access to my phone.*

ANGEL: *I'll read and send you the most important links.*

DONITA: *Thank you. You can send them directly to me so Cora doesn't have to read them.*

CORA: *No, send them in this group please. I don't know how to set up an alert. I want to stay informed.*

DONITA: *Even though you don't want to help me investigate?*

ANGEL: *Cora helped enough by distracting Mr Hong. That wasn't easy.*

She has some hopes that Cora will say something about wanting to help by starting another version of her newsletter. A minute passes and there are no more replies from the group.

Nurul pops her head into the kitchen. 'What time will lunch be ready?'

'Whenever I serve it,' Angel retorts. A startled Nurul opens her mouth and then simply nods and retreats.

Angel is more conscious of what and how she cooks now that Nurul is around. 'He needs more protein,' Nurul said, frowning at the porridge on Monday and the cheese sandwich on Tuesday. Angel is picking the hair-thin bones out of a raw salmon fillet when her phone trills with a notification. It must be an update about Carolyn Hong. Angel shakes the seasoning onto the salmon, washes her hands and picks up her phone.

The media has landed on every little detail of this case, and this article, naming all the other 'famous' people who live in the Hongs' neighbourhood, is a stretch. Most of them are well known only because they have been featured in the newspaper before – an heir to an antique furniture business on Joo Chiat Road; a top O-level exam student who chose to go to a poly-technic and was in a documentary about making his own choices; and a national swimmer who was injured in the ASEAN games several years ago. Under the photo of the swimmer, there are lots of Likes and comments from fans. Of all the 'famous' people in the area, he is the best-looking one, and Angel sends his picture to the group.

Message from Donita: *Guapo!*

Indeed, he is good-looking. She writes back: *Interested, Donita? It says here: 'Now retired from professional swimming, Sterling Luo runs Parkway Swimmers, a school set up to train young athletes for worldwide competitions.' That can be your next mission on your off day.*

DONITA: *I'd pay the registration fee just to watch him swim.*

ANGEL: *LOL. What about Sanjeev? You're ready to move on from him already?*

DONITA: *Nope. Sanjeev is a keeper. But I can still appreciate a good body from afar. Send Cora then. Cora, take pictures of this Sterling in his swimsuit please.*

CORA: *I could be his mother.*

DONITA: *You could be anyone, we saw your artista skills on Sunday.*

She sends a bikini emoji that makes Angel grin, and then there is a peal of laughter from Nurul, who is helping Mr Vijay into his wheelchair for his round of outside therapy. It's too late, Angel mentally notes. He should do it first thing in the morning, when the weather is still cool, but Nurul would likely give her some reason for taking him out just before lunch. The dogs are bobbing at Nurul's ankles when she emerges from the room, wheeling Mr Vijay toward the door. She gives Angel a little wave as she passes the kitchen, which Angel chooses not to reciprocate, feigning busyness by fiddling with the oven knobs. It's satisfying to hear Nurul struggling with the door, the wheelchair and the dogs. Angel waits a few beats before she goes to the door, tugging the dogs back by their collars, and holding the door wide so that Nurul can pass through.

'The sheets on his bed need replacing.'

It's how Nurul says it. She might as well snap her fingers or ring a bell to summon her. Angel lets the door slam right in her face.

She does the work though. After putting the salmon in the oven, she goes to Mr Vijay's room to strip his bed. Shaking out the new sheets and pulling them tautly over the mattress, Angel thinks of all the things she could say to Nurul to let her know that she is certainly not the boss around here, and she needs to understand that. Maybe she could write her a letter. Or send her a text message, just with bullet points of all the house rules. She could word it in such a way that Nurul thinks they are directives from Sumanthi and Raja, or from Mr Vijay himself – yes, maybe this is the way to go, to establish to Nurul that Angel and Mr Vijay have a way of communicating. It pains Angel to think of Mr Vijay struggling to express himself with his little shifts in facial expressions, and Nurul not pausing to understand. She is brisk and professional, sure, but Angel's job is the spaces in between.

Angel flounces back to her room to start making some notes for her letter. With each bullet point, Angel prompts Nurul to question whether she really knows what she's doing. Would Nurul smooth down every wrinkle on the sheets? Would she turn on the fan and open the windows to make sure fresh air circulates thoroughly through the room? Would she keep among her personal things, as Angel does, a small bottle of lavender oil to tip onto Mr Vijay's pillow to soothe and comfort him to sleep? The ideas come quickly to Angel, and she needs to write them down before she forgets. She pulls open her dresser drawer for the spiral-bound journal where she copies the occasional inspirational quote. 'Life is abundant' was the last one, written a year ago.

Then she spots the pen.

It sits in a bouquet of ballpoint pens and markers in a mug on her dresser but it's different, shinier somehow. Angel picks it up and checks it for a hotel logo – sometimes Sumanthi gives her the freebie stationery from overseas conferences, and maybe she dropped this into the mug while passing the room one day. But this pen is smooth and silver like a bullet. It is solid and heavy, and she is sure it arrived at the same time as Nurul because she would have noticed it on Monday when she wrote the grocery list for the week. It must be Nurul's pen.

So she was in this room, probably snooping around. Angel flings open her drawer and notices immediately the disarray of her clothes. Nurul was here. Nurul was definitely here. While Angel was hard at work, Nurul was rummaging through her things. What kind of person arrives in a home and feels entitled to trespass like this? Angel's door was left open, but there was nothing Nurul needed from here. She could have at least asked permission to enter the room, but of course why would she draw attention to herself if she wanted to snoop. Angel picks up the pen – it's heavier than she expected, probably expensive. This is a signal from Nurul. It was no accident that she left the pen behind. She's marking her territory.

Angel paces the hallway and the dogs pace beside her. Who the hell does Nurul think she is? She barely introduced herself before setting up her place in this flat like she has been here all along. Angel picks up her phone to tell Donita and Cora about it. They would understand.

The front door lock clicks open and Angel puts her phone away. She takes in a deep breath and prepares herself to say something to Nurul, but it's only Raja. He combs his fingers through his wet hair. 'It's drizzling out there,' he says. Angel nods and closes all the windows. A gust of wind in the wrong direction can send the rain shooting sideways and create puddles on tiled floors, slipping hazards. From the living-room window, Angel sees Nurul briskly pushing

Mr Vijay's wheelchair under the covered walkway. They disappear into the building.

Angel pretends not to hear the door opening this time and she only looks up when she hears Nurul saying, 'You're doing such a good job!' Her voice is dripping with condescension.

'It's not so difficult, closing the windows,' Angel retorts, before she realizes that Nurul is talking to Mr Vijay. He is gripping the badminton racket tightly and raising it close to his head.

'He could catch a cold,' Angel points out. 'You shouldn't bring him out in the rain like that.'

'That's why we came back,' Nurul says.

Angel brushes past her to get a towel. When she brings it to Mr Vijay, she can see that he is hardly wet at all. Just a light sheen of dew glistening in his silvery hair. He clutches the badminton racquet and waves it.

'I was trying to get him to practise with the racquet, but it's not the most effective activity for him,' Nurul says. 'He could do with some strength exercises.'

'He does just fine,' Angel says. 'You're probably not showing him how to do it properly.'

'I don't think that's the problem,' Nurul says. 'In my experience with occupational therapy patients—'

'Oh, your experience!' Angel spits.

Nurul takes a step back at this outburst. 'Did I say something . . .?'

'You're a professional. I get it. You walk into this house thinking I don't know how to do my job.'

'That's not what I think,' Nurul says. But her tone makes Angel seethe. Her words are delivered gently, as if to a small child.

'You had no right to come into my room,' Angel says.

'I didn't enter your room,' Nurul protests.

She can't even come up with an excuse! Angel shakes her head. 'Yes, you did. You left this souvenir behind.' Angel brandishes the pen. Mr Vijay's eyes follow it and he clutches his badminton racket.

'You are scaring him,' Nurul says. 'Please calm down.'

'What business do you have, coming in here and snooping around in my things? Shouldn't all of your time be spent with Mr Vijay?' Angel demands.

'Can I see the pen, please?' Nurul asks.

Angel restrains herself from throwing the pen at Nurul. She watches as the nurse takes the pen from her and says quietly, 'Angel, there is a camera in this pen.'

'What?' Angel asks, snatching the pen back. Then she looks and she sees – embedded in the button at the top of the pen is a small round lens. She presses down the button and the lens disappears. She presses again and the button pops back up, a pinpoint green light blinking once to indicate the camera is on.

It was sitting on her dresser.

The moment barely passes before Angel realizes who put the pen there. Who has been watching her? She turns and looks at Raja's closed room door and she becomes aware of the fact that he is inside, probably listening.

Nurul crosses the room and raps her knuckle on Raja's door. 'Come out,' she barks.

Angel's hands are shaking. What has Raja seen of her? Everything. Her body, completely stripped down, and her moments with herself in the sheets, with her eyes squeezed shut. She thought there was one place where she could be alone, where she could be herself without any judgement from anybody. She turns her attention to Nurul, who knocks on the door again. 'Come out!' Angel looks at Mr Vijay. His gaze is darting back and forth between her and Nurul and his grip has tightened on his badminton racquet. The veins in his arms surface.

Raja is wearing headphones when he emerges from his room. 'What's going on?' he asks casually. Angel could set him on fire with her glare, but he's not looking at her. He's regarding Nurul with a blank stare, which he maintains even when she holds up the pen.

'It's not mine,' he says with a shrug.

'There is a camera inside it,' Nurul says. 'This is illegal. She can report you for this.'

But she won't, he is thinking, and Angel can see that. He wasn't afraid when he sidled up to her in the kitchen, and he wasn't afraid when he put that pen on her dresser. In the room behind him, there is a laptop and his phone containing images of Angel. What can she do? Information travels much faster than justice; by the time she slips her feet into her shoes and walks to the neighbourhood police post to lodge a report, the videos could be circulating on the internet.

Nurul is questioning Raja now, and his responses are infuriating. He slouches against the doorframe, looking bored. He notices Mr Vijay watching him intently. 'Appa, these two are just looking for an excuse to get angry. They'll try to blackmail you next, just wait and see. I think I'm going to have to report you to the home care service, Nurul. This is not what we signed up for. And Angel, you're free to quit any time you want. You maids, you take advantage of everything and then you make accusations.'

He pushes past Nurul, who stumbles back. 'Come on, Appa. I'm going to take you out.'

'It's raining,' Angel croaks. It's the only thing she can think of to say.

'I don't care,' Raja says. 'We are getting away from the two of you. Appa, we should make a police report against them, hmm? What do you think?'

Raja leans towards Mr Vijay as he says this. He doesn't see what Angel sees, that Mr Vijay has clenched his fist around his badminton racquet. He is raising it above his head. Before Raja can respond, Mr Vijay is slamming it against his head. *Whack!* The sound reverberates through the flat – a perfect hit.

Big Island Weekly

Sponsors Pull Out of Influencer's Event After 'Shockingly Insensitive' Parody of East Coast Murder Case

Versus Productions, a major corporate sponsor for Unique Monique's Boutique Show has withdrawn support after influencer Monique Leow (who goes by the moniker @UniqueMo) released a video mocking a pending murder case in East Coast Road.

In the video posted on @UniqueMo's Instagram page, and viewed 58,000 times, she alternates between two characters. The title of the video is SHOULD WE TRUST MAIDS? It features Leow as slain employer Carolyn Hong, speaking very kindly to her maid who is off camera.

'Oh, you want Saturday off too? Of course. I understand. Take the whole week. Here, wear my clothes. Go into my closet, borrow whatever you want. Make sure you clean it — ah, wait, is that prejudiced of me to say? Never mind, just bring it back; dirty also never mind. We trust you 100 per cent not to bring home any foreign smells,' the character says, before the camera

cuts to Leow again, this time dressed as a maid bedecked in her employer's jewellery.

In one scene, the maid – whose long hair and mole on her cheek bear close resemblance to the accused foreign domestic worker, Flordeliza Martinez – is saying, 'Excuse me' but, in her accent, it sounds like she is saying 'Accuse me! Accuse me!'

The sponsor's statement slammed the insensitivity of the video. 'We do not wish to align ourselves with somebody who would mock a violent death, and vilify our foreign domestic workers,' says Vice President of Versus Productions, Barry De Cruz, who is a Singapore permanent resident from the Philippines.

This isn't the influencer's first controversy. Last year, she was dropped as a SingaPride spokesperson after joking on Twitter about the term 'Pansexual', followed by a photo of her seductively licking a frying pan. 'Kitchen utensils can have genders too these days!' she was quoted as saying. Leow rose to notoriety on social media in 2014 after a heated spat with MediaCorp actress Kavita Pillai, who complained on Facebook that Halloween decorations were encroaching on the annual Deepavali decorations in shopping malls. Leow's proposed solution, a Facebook event page called 'Dress like an Indian for Halloween' was eventually taken down after police reports were lodged against Pillai for stirring up racial animosity.

Chapter Ten

Are there surveillance cameras in Ma'am Elizabeth's house?

The compact black dome perched above the iron gates is probably a necessary security measure for recording trespassers. That is the only obvious camera that Cora has seen. Angel's messages about finding a hidden camera in her room make Cora search more closely for gadgets. Of course, what Raja did was not about checking Angel's work – he put the camera in her room to peep at her. But the idea of any watchful eyes scares her. She recalls her first day working for the Calverts, who were upfront about their indoor surveillance. In Mr Calvert's study, a camera peered from a bracket just above the air-conditioning unit. 'If you're wiping the top of the A/C, please be careful,' Mrs Calvert told Cora. 'Use a sturdy stepladder and make sure you don't knock the camera out of place. The previous housekeeper nudged the camera so many times that by the time we checked the footage, it was only recording the curtains.' Whether this was accidental or not, Mrs Calvert didn't say, but it did give Cora an idea when she had to run away.

Cora can't help thinking of Mrs Calvert now, when she sees Jacqueline standing before her at the top of the stairs. A broad window in the hallway frames her like a museum portrait. 'I need to speak with you,' she says gravely. *She knows what I did*, Cora thinks, her heart leaping into her throat. She remembers the prayer that she uttered as she scrambled up the stairs in her last moments in the Calverts' home; those holy words that never came to her the same way again.

Then Jacqueline smiles. The late morning light makes her silk blouse shimmer slightly, and the diamond ring on her hand winks. Her fingers pinch the edges of a cream envelope that she presents to Cora like an award. 'This is for you,' Jacqueline says. Cora accepts the envelope, and they face each other awkwardly for a moment before Cora opens it.

On thick card stock, there is an invitation to Jacqueline's wedding. Cora resists running her fingers over the raised lettering announcing the occasion. Her full name is written in calligraphy pen, the brushstrokes both bold and feathery. 'Miss Jacqueline, you will be a beautiful bride,' Cora says.

'So you will join us then,' Jacqueline says. 'As a guest.'

Cora studies the invitation again. Tea ceremony, church wedding, reception dinner, cocktails. She will have to dress the part many times over as a friend of the family. She cannot help thinking of those wealthy Manila elite friends of Raymond's and Marco's, and she has a brief moment of horror – what if the Martell girl is invited? These rich families have friends all over the world and they travel from country to country to network at occasions like these. 'I will think about it,' Cora says.

'I understand,' Jacqueline says. 'Cora, my mother considers you a family member. And I can't thank you enough for what you've done to our home.' She nods appreciatively at the squat hand-painted *gansu* cabinet in the hallway. The brass handles had been tarnished for so long that they appeared to melt into the warm cherry wood. All it took was a rag soaked in a mixture of baking soda and white vinegar, and the handles now glow in the morning light. Earlier, Cora also overheard Jacqueline commenting on the pot-bellied ginger jars that Cora had rescued from their hiding place behind the curved legs of an imperial altar console table in the foyer. The ginger jars were antiques, like the brass tiffin carrier in the kitchen cabinet that had started all of this. She had been chopping lotus roots for one of Ma'am Elizabeth's recipe book soups when Ma'am Elizabeth suggested taking a photograph of the process.

'Let me find something to put in the background,' Cora had said, and she picked the tiffin. After a round of polishing, it glinted behind the slices of eyelet-covered lotus root.

'It's my pleasure, Miss Jacqueline,' Cora says. It's true, she has enjoyed reviving this home. It started as something to do for the recipe book, but it has become a project of its own. Sometimes she pats the ginger jars as if they are shy children, or pauses to admire the scenes painted onto the porcelain: a trail of swallows in flight, three men in flowing robes conversing on a bridge between misty mountains. She notices that Jacqueline has stepped closer to her now though, and she is leaning towards her. For a brief, frightening moment, Cora thinks they are about to hug. Then Jacqueline says, 'Cora, I have a favour to ask of you. As you probably already know, I've been trying to get my mother to agree to expand my father's business into a chain of contemporary cafés. An updated twist to the *kopitiams* of his generation.'

Cora has heard the conversations and, just last week, Ma'am Elizabeth had grumbled about it in the car on their way to

Marina Bay Sands to get her Piaget watch serviced. 'Why are people lining up for eight-dollar cold brew coffee these days, as if we haven't been buying canned Pokka from minimarts and vending machines all these years?'

'My mother isn't exactly sold on the idea,' Jacqueline continues. 'She's never been good at letting go. But it's important to keep up with the times, isn't it? Look at how you've revived all these old things. You gave them a new life. And perhaps you can talk to my mother about doing the same with the café.'

'Talk to her?' Cora asks.

'Just a gentle push. She knows I have a vested interest, but you could suggest to her that she needs a project. Or you could tell her that a café that looks like a Starbucks but serves local coffee would be welcoming to you and your friends on Sundays. She certainly trusts you.'

What does she mean by that? Cora doesn't want to read too much into anything Jacqueline says, but she lingered on the word 'trusts'. As she reaches into her purse, Cora's stomach flips. Jacqueline produces a hundred-dollar bill, so fresh it crackles.

'I don't expect this to be a problem.'

Jacqueline could be referring to the task or the amount she is paying. Cora doesn't know if she is actually being treated like a family member or an agent for Jacqueline's business agenda. These things don't seem separate for wealthy people. Friendship, loyalty, transactions, debts. She says nothing, which Jacqueline clearly sees as agreement, before returning downstairs to the pergola where Ma'am Elizabeth is having her tea.

I am not loyal, Cora wants to say. If only Jacqueline knew. People have this idea that Cora is somebody to confide in.

On her first day in Dasmariñas, Mrs Calvert told her that she feared that there was something fundamentally unlikeable about her. If not, why did the staff keep quitting?

'The last gardener lasted a month in our home. Our cook? Two weeks and he left in the middle of the night. So I'm only looking for a day housekeeper.'

Cora figured out all the reasons within days of working there. The two *yayas*, brimming with resentment over a long-standing personal feud, would barely look at each other while tending to the children's needs. The gardener and one of the housemaids had a tumultuous romance that involved more *tampuhan* and tears than a telenovela. The *mayordoma* of the residence was a malicious gossip. Foreigners made the mistake of assuming that all house help would get along, but there were hierarchies and histories that didn't occur to the Calverts.

The live-out arrangement suited Cora, but when the cook quit in a fury after a housemaid tried to give him orders, the Calverts were left suddenly without meals. Cora stepped in to work overtime. She had cooked for entire families before, and it was a nice change from the endless mopping and dusting.

One morning Paolo, the security guard, saw Mrs Calvert handing Cora a few bills to compensate her for the extra duties.

'*Sipsip sa boss*,' Paolo commented. Paolo's contempt could be felt in tremors just beneath his calm demeanour. It was best to ignore his accusations that she was sucking up to the boss. His smirk vanished to be replaced by a benign expression when Mrs Calvert turned to address him and the other guard, Jun.

'I will need one of you to oversee the traffic coming in on Saturday. We have a couple of guests, and they'll need to be directed to their parking spaces.'

The guards turned to each other and, with straight faces,

began joking in Tagalog about who would take Mrs Calvert to bed.

'I'll go first. I'll get her warmed up,' Jun said. He raised his hand to appear to be volunteering.

'Don't make her too tired,' Paolo replied. 'I want her saving all her special tricks for me.'

Cora felt a rush of protectiveness towards Mrs Calvert, who had been nothing but kind to her. After Mrs Calvert nodded and said, 'You two figure it out and let me know,' Cora marched up to the sniggering men. 'You are both disgraceful.'

Paolo glared at her. 'Your ma'am is no angel.'

Later, one of the *yayas* filled Cora in on what had happened: Mrs Calvert had fired one of the drivers for arriving late to pick up her teenaged daughter from football practice. She had chastised him publicly at the entrance of the international school, where all the other drivers and *yayas* waited. *Hiya* was another thing that Mrs Calvert did not understand – the shame spread to Paolo, because the driver was his cousin. After that, Cora avoided Paolo. It made her nervous to know a man like that, with his simmering resentment, had a gun.

Now, alone in the hallway of the Lee residence, Cora stares at the hundred-dollar bill in her hands. Across from her, there is a mirror framed by the slatted wooden shutters of a Peranakan window. She sees herself holding the money, and thinks about all the times she has found herself holding valuable things in other people's homes. There was always a sense of unease: the object gaining heat in her hands the longer she held it. Does Ma'am Elizabeth have cameras in the house? If she does, then this exchange in the hallway would be recorded; if she doesn't, and Jacqueline is dissatisfied with her work, she could accuse Cora of stealing the money.

Cora wipes down the altar table and rearranges the

ornaments. Two lacquer, egg-shaped containers sit in the corner of the table; they used to hold little odds and ends like paper clips and pen caps, but Cora found better places for those stray things. Now she wonders if she should have just kept the Lee's home tidy, without interfering with these antiques. She has made Jacqueline think of her as the type of maid who wants to be involved in the family's affairs.

For lunch, Cora has plans to make another Hokkien dish from the recipe folder – *lor ark*. The whole duck that Cora bought from the market and stuffed with blue ginger and garlic has been marinating in the fridge since yesterday. Returning to the kitchen, she listens out for Jacqueline and Ma'am Elizabeth's conversation while mixing the ingredients of the sauce: rock sugar, five-spice powder, star anise, cloves, and a stick of cinnamon stirred into dark soy sauce. She gradually thins out the marinade with water and stirs until it is smooth before turning her attention to blanching the duck. The mention of Lee's Kopi comes up while she is transferring the duck into the wok and brushing the mixture evenly over it.

'But we'll lose investors if you keep delaying your decision,' Jacqueline says. Cora's ears prick up. 'These are people with their finger on the pulse, Mummy. New food and beverage concepts crop up every minute in this city—'

'I don't want Lee's Kopi to go the way of so many one-off businesses. There's a legacy to consider.'

'You're worrying too much about how things will look.'

'Am I?' Ma'am Elizabeth sounds amused. 'I seem to remember a different conversation about keeping up appearances after your father's death.'

'It wasn't a matter of covering up for Daddy,' Jacqueline says smoothly. 'I understand why you saw it that way, but the whole thing was very complicated.'

'What's so complicated about your father and his mistresses? Please enlighten me,' Ma'am Elizabeth asks.

'The fallout, Mummy. The things people would say about our family.'

'But they all knew.'

'Not all of them,' Jacqueline corrects her. 'We managed to keep the information fairly contained. You have me to thank for that. I know you think I was only protecting his reputation, but I was concerned about all of us. What if word had got out beyond your Bukit Timah ladies' lunch circle?'

'What if it had?' The exasperation is clear in Ma'am Elizabeth's voice.

'You're forgetting about how vicious that clique at the church can be.'

'What, Dr Lena Teo and all of them? They're just gossips, everybody knows that.'

'But people listen and they believe them too. You know, when Fann Poh Choo was trying to get into their circle, there was no limit to what she would have told them to gain currency. I'm certain she's the one who spread those rumours about Cecilia after she broke up with Weston.'

'But she was always going on about how they should get together,' Ma'am Elizabeth said.

'To your face, yes. It's a way to protect herself, isn't it, considering what everybody found out about Weston last year. Dr Lena and her crew saw it as an opportunity to test out their Come Home programme on him, and look at what happened. He's never coming back.'

'Poh Choo's good friends with that lot now,' Ma'am Elizabeth says. 'I saw them having high tea in Marina Bay Sands the other day.'

Cora remembers. It was while they were waiting for Ma'am

Elizabeth's watch to be serviced. The indoor streets of the mall were quiet under a glass domed roof. They walked along the replica of a Venetian canal, cutting a path between the luxury stores. A gondola skimmed the bright blue water and the chlorine scent stung Cora's nostrils. Ma'am Elizabeth had paused outside an ornate golden tea salon. Glazed tarts and cake slices preened on marble slabs behind a glass case, and the tinkling of teaspoons against fine bone china rang a soft harmony. Ma'am Elizabeth was selecting macaroons to take away when, suddenly, her expression froze.

'Oh goodness, let's just come back later,' she said, hurrying Cora away. Cora spotted Mrs Fann and a bevy of middle-aged women wearing blazers and piled-high hair. A European waiter in a pressed white shirt was lowering a three-tiered dessert stand onto their table.

'Quite frankly, I think those women are using Poh Choo for their project,' says Jacqueline now. 'I hear it's got something to do with the sex education programmes in the schools now.'

'With all the time they spend claiming our young people are being corrupted by Western ideals, you'd think they'd recognize the irony of modelling their programmes after those American megachurches. I could barely find my way around the Rising Star complex the last time I went.'

'Anyway, we don't need to concern ourselves with what Fann Poh Choo is up to these days,' Jacqueline says. Cora peeps from the doorway to see Jacqueline nudging the black leather portfolio across the table.

'I'll go through this in my own time,' Ma'am Elizabeth says.

Jacqueline sighs and looks disappointed. Cora returns to the kitchen counter and begins taking out the *tau kwa* and *tau pok* to add to the dish once the duck is finished cooking. In a separate pot, she boils four eggs that she will arrange around the sliced duck along with squares of firm tofu, which will be glazed in the leftover marinade.

The rest of the conversation between Ma'am Elizabeth and Jacqueline is about Jacqueline's upcoming wedding. Jacqueline's voice becomes lighter when she talks about table settings and guest lists, although Cora senses tension again when Ma'am Elizabeth asks her about her fiancé. 'Does Hans want to come over one of these evenings? It's been so long. I hardly ever get to see my future son-in-law.'

'He's very busy,' Jacqueline says. 'Every other week, another trip. They're still pressuring him to join the London team. He's told them now isn't the time.'

Cora slices up the duck and arranges the pieces artfully on the plate, along with the peeled boiled eggs. She sprinkles a few sprigs of parsley on top of the dish and carries it out to the dining table to Ma'am Elizabeth's oohs and aahs. The sauce is fragrant with the lingering scents of spices.

'This is what a home should smell like,' Ma'am Elizabeth says.

Even though Cora still isn't sure that Ma'am Elizabeth needs to invest in the café, there is an opportunity here to persuade her. It is not because of the hundred-dollar note that she will do this; it's because of Jacqueline. She could have handed her five dollars, and the task would be just as important. Cora has worked as a maid for long enough to know the difference between a request and a command. She also knows what it's like to press something into a person's hands and wish for fate to change its course.

She waits until lunch is over, and Jacqueline leaves. She washes the dishes and when she looks at her phone to check in on Angel, she sees a message from Donita: *PERVERT! CUT OFF HIS BALLS!* She has clearly only just caught up on Angel's update about Raja and his hidden camera. Her next message: *Have you seen the article about the influencer? Nice to see there's some support out there.*

Don't get your hopes up, Cora thinks. She doesn't know who Barry De Cruz is but she is wary of upper class Filipinos making public statements of unity when they otherwise take great pains to distance themselves from domestic workers. She has seen too much to think that this would change anything.

When she goes back to clear the table, the portfolio has been left open at a two-page-spread mock-up of the new and improved Lee's Kopi Cafés, and Cora exaggerates her lean over the table to look, as though trying not to be caught snooping. A sample menu runs down the page on a vertical panel, featuring desserts like *gula melaka* ganache, and an *ondeh-ondeh* mousse.

'What do you think, Cora?'

Cora pretends to be startled. 'Sorry, ma'am,' she says.

'No, please, have a look. Tell me what you think, honestly.'

'It looks nice.'

She is glad not to be lying about this. The café looks like something that would be popular. Of course she thinks of Raymond. She sees him in the faces of students crowding around tables in The Coffee Bean in Holland Village, textbooks piled higher than their iced blended drinks. Raymond had always studied at home, next to the desk lamp on the kitchen table that Cora cleared for him, and when his head began to droop, or he rubbed his eyes, Cora would encourage him with the same proverb her own parents had used. *Kung may itinanim may aanihin.* 'If something is planted, there is a harvest.'

Ma'am Elizabeth flips through the portfolio. After the glossy pictures and taglines, there are pages of columns and numbers and percentages and graphs. The wiring of a slick business, hidden in the background.

'It is a nice way to continue your husband's business, ma'am,' Cora says. 'Also a good way to continue your relationship with your daughters.'

'You mean if I open this café, Jacqueline will actually come over to talk to me and ask how I'm doing, instead of trying to get me to sign paperwork to expand the family empire?' Ma'am Elizabeth says. 'You see it, don't you, Cora? The way my children are more attached to things than people. All of this . . .' She waves her hands around the vast dining room, the wrought-iron balustrades that line the stairs, the columns of cascading curtains flanking the sliding glass doors to the garden outside. 'It's who they are. Who we are, I should say. I never shied away from material things when they were growing up. It was only when my husband started straying that I realized that meaning is more important than material.'

'Ma'am, you knew about his affairs? Even before the accident?'

'I always knew,' Ma'am Elizabeth says. 'Mavis Yuen from Taipei was his first mistress. She accompanied her husband to Singapore on business trips, and we would meet them at the country club. Her husband worked late, so it would just be Mavis and it became clear pretty quickly that I was the third wheel. I began excusing myself from going because the children needed me at bedtime. I didn't want the nannies to be hustling them from the dinner table, to their baths and story time, because then I'd only see them in the morning. That was the reason I told myself for leaving Mavis and Harold together, anyway.'

Cora pictures a young Ma'am Elizabeth, even more elegant and beautiful than she is now, walking up that long driveway all alone. Leaving her husband behind to continue his night with another woman, and doing it over and over again for years.

'But your daughters had all those moments with you,' Cora says. She knows there is no consolation for betrayal, but feels she has to say something. It's so terribly unfair.

'Sometimes the women bought them things,' Ma'am Elizabeth says. 'I remember when Cecilia turned thirteen. I invited all her school friends to brunch by the pool at the Intercontinental and she said to me, "This was the best birthday party." Then her father sprang a surprise: a trip to Bangkok. I knew he was seeing a woman there, an heiress to a property empire. Cecilia was thrilled at the thought of having two birthday parties and so I couldn't stop her. When she came home, I had to bite my lip as she showed me all of her new things – shoes, jewellery, a branded handbag. "Daddy has the best taste," she said, and it broke my heart. It was obvious to me that his mistress had chosen them. I didn't make a fuss though. Sometimes I even convinced myself that he was being generous, better than all those other men who leave their wives and humiliate them publicly. Mine was at least still a family man.'

'You did not want to leave him?' Cora asks. *Careful,* a voice warns her. This is the kind of personal territory that Cora has been trying to avoid. But she thinks about the end of her own marriage, the way her husband exhaled like a deflating balloon when she proposed they part ways. It was as if he had been holding his breath throughout their marriage, afraid to be the one to hurt her.

'Oh, I had fantasies of leaving. Sometimes in bed at night, when I woke up and discovered that it was three in the morning and he still wasn't home, I rehearsed all the things I would say to him: "I won't be treated like this. I sacrificed everything for you." But that was also how I knew I couldn't leave him. I had sacrificed everything. My relationship with my parents, who had warned me about this kind of thing, who had finally accepted him despite all of their initial reservations. If I left, there would be so many questions to answer. I even called SAGE at one point. That's an organization that advocates for women's equality – they have a counselling hotline. I felt so ashamed taking up their time – they were there for women who were beaten by their husbands, women who lived on the fringes of society, and here I was, Elizabeth Lee, calling them about a problem I already had the answer to.'

No wonder Ma'am Elizabeth doesn't care for Jacqueline's expansion project. Everything contained within this black portfolio is designed to continue making a great man of Mr Lee. The new updated cafés, the glossy publicity opportunities – they bring him back to life and say, look at him, always here for you.

Cora remembers then that she is supposed to be talking up the café. Her mouth feels dry, and she doesn't know how to suggest to Ma'am Elizabeth why it would be a good idea. Instead she says, 'Ma'am, back home we have this coffee called *kapeng barako*.'

'Kapeng?'

'*Kapeng barako*,' Cora says again, feeling a jolt of joy at uttering Tagalog words in this home. 'The Spanish brought it.'

'It's popular? Like *kopi* here?'

'The older generation like to drink it. It is bitter and thick. For my grandparents, it was the only coffee they knew. Then there was coffee rust, which destroyed the crops. We thought it would be gone forever. But nowadays, young people like to drink it again.'

Ma'am Elizabeth is watching Cora intently now. 'The thing I'm trying to say, Ma'am . . . you like the way your home smells when I make your grandmother's dishes? Maybe people want to go to a place that can feel like home as well. You can't change the past but you can bring it back and make it different. Make it your own.'

She can tell that Ma'am Elizabeth is considering her words, and guilt floods her body.

If Cora followed her own advice, she wouldn't be awake every night tracing her way through the path that Raymond took in life, imagining herself changing the route to lead him to a different outcome.

On some nights, she just has to blink to be transported back to that evening when Raymond gave her that pair of gold earrings. He had presented the box to her over a table at a restaurant with exposed brick walls and an espresso machine hissing in the background.

'Thank you for everything, Tita,' Raymond said.

'You're spending too much money,' Cora said, staring at the earrings encased in a tiny velvet pillow. Raymond assured her that they were made from recycled gold. 'It's ethical fashion, Sabrina Martell tells me.'

Cora refrained from saying that there wasn't much about Manila's elite that struck her as ethical. It must have been written all over her face, because Raymond piped up to defend his friends.

'Just because they're rich, it doesn't mean they're bad people,' Raymond said. 'Sabrina's father got me this internship. He is connected to every legal firm in the country. You said I should be using my connections—'

'I'm not saying they're bad people,' Cora interjected. *But they're not like us*, she thought. She couldn't say this to Raymond, not after spending a lifetime coaching him to excel in school to join the ranks of the upper classes so his future would be ensured. 'Just remember that there are things they can get away with,' she said.

'Like what?'

Murder, Cora was tempted to say. A few days ago, two men wearing white polo shirts tucked into pressed khaki trousers had gone from door to door in Dasmariñas with flyers. *Sorry to disturb you*, they told Mrs Calvert. *We are required to inform all residents about the new drug laws.* They were thugs contracted by the government to ensure compliance with the new rules, yet Cora was struck by their politeness. In the *barangays*, the warnings came by way of gunshots. Bodies of accused *shabu* dealers were left in the street with PUSHER written across their chests.

Their dinner passed in silence. A cupcake with a single candle arrived and Raymond sang 'Happy Birthday' and trained his phone camera on Cora's face. She finally offered a terse smile for the photo and then batted him away.

In the jeepney on the way home, they sat shoulder to shoulder with other passengers. Raymond fell asleep in the rocking vehicle. The occasional wash of streetlights illuminated his face, as open and pure as when he was a little boy. Cora felt seized by a sense of longing and terror – maternal love, she told herself, although this felt stronger.

Hours later, Cora understood those unsettling feelings as a premonition. Three policemen arrived at her doorstep. 'He was with me the whole night,' she tried to shout over them as they barked at Raymond to admit that he had been supplying drugs in a Makati nightclub that evening.

'Your name came up several times when we raided Flux,' an officer told him. Cora still remembers seeing the whites of Raymond's eyes as he stared at the officer in shock.

Did he realize then that his friends had sold him out? 'I wasn't at the club,' Raymond protested. 'You must be thinking of somebody else.'

'Who?' the policeman taunted. 'They told us all about you. Scholarship kid trying to make a bit of extra money.'

Raymond shook his head. 'You've got the wrong person.'

'Who was it then?' the policeman asked. He seemed to be challenging Raymond to accuse somebody else.

Marco Vallares, Cora thought. She knew the name was on Raymond's mind as well but he couldn't be sure. In that moment, Cora was tempted to blurt it out, just to give the men pause. They would see that it was a case of mistaken identity, and leave Raymond alone.

Except they wouldn't, not after bursting into her home like this, full of confidence in their righteousness. And what if it hadn't been Marco? Those rich kids could get their hands on *shabu* from any anonymous dealer, but when pressed for a name, they gave up the person most likely to be a suspect.

'Let me just make a phone call,' Raymond begged. 'I'll sort this out.' Cora wrapped her arms around him and felt the fear pulsing through his body.

The police shook her off and dragged Raymond out onto the street. Cora fell to the ground but reached for the leg of one of the officers who swung her off with one swift kick. Cora scrambled to her feet and chased after the officer, who was gripping Raymond by the back of his neck. By then, crowds of neighbours had been awakened by the commotion and they gathered, some gasping and crying, others stoic witnesses. The officer shoved Raymond to his knees before the crowd of neighbours.

'Don't hurt him!' Cora cried. 'He's a good boy.' Raymond

knelt on the ground, his eyes searching wildly. The officer cleared his throat and addressed the crowd.

'Not only is this boy a drug pusher, he has been corrupting the sons and daughters of good Filipino families for months.'

'That's a lie!' Raymond shouted. He began to scramble to his feet.

The officer drew his gun, and Cora saw it as if in slow motion. She started forward, her mouth opening in a scream.

He shot Raymond twice in the chest.

'I can see this is important to you,' Ma'am Elizabeth says now, and suddenly Cora is back in this house with its soaring ceilings and high garden walls draped with liana vines. She realizes her breathing has quickened, and Ma'am Elizabeth is looking at her with concern. 'Holding on to heritage, that kind of thing, I mean,' Ma'am Elizabeth says. 'I'll think about it. Thank you for bringing it up.'

Cora swallows, pushes away the dark street and her nephew's final gasps. Sometimes she wakes up to a distant ringing in her head, as if some version of her is still slumped over Raymond's body, begging him to live. Her screams echo against the petrified silence of her neighbours, who retreated to their houses and watched from their windows.

'You're most welcome, ma'am,' she forces herself to say.

From the Ma'am Facebook pages:

Tabitha Daud: My maid says that the man who lives upstairs keeps cornering her in the lift and asking her to be his new wife. Few weeks ago, another man saw her at the bus stop and told her he wanted to buy her gifts. Then she says some schoolboys took her photo. I am considering firing her. I don't need somebody who attracts this kind of attention. I have a pre-teen daughter you know, what if these perverts follow the maid one day and try to come into my house? They're saying that this is what possibly happened to that poor family in East Coast Road also. The wife was killed by the maid's lover.

Gyanpreet Bajaj: The bus auntie for my son's school bus is claiming that we are ten dollars short on our payment. I put the money in an envelope and gave to our helper. She is generally trustworthy and I don't think she would try to steal, but after this whole East Coast Road murder . . . I really don't know what to think. My husband thinks the bus auntie is trying to get more money from us and blaming the helper for stealing. Now it's the bus auntie's word against hers. What should I do?

Chapter Eleven

Sanjeev finds them a table near the giant glass windows that fade into a boardwalk overlooking the twinkling sea. 'Like a postcard,' he tells Donita, nodding at Sentosa in the near distance. Construction cranes crisscross the blue skies, and little red flags wave from the castle spires at the theme park's entrance. Donita has no use for the view because she is too busy staring at the stall menus advertising teeming bowls of stir-fried noodles, grilled marinated meats, Vietnamese pork rolls and platters of mixed vegetables. After Sanjeev tells her she can order whatever she wants, she wants to sweep her hand over the food court and turn it into a personal buffet.

The food court is built to look like Singapore's streets in olden times. Thatched awnings stretch over the stalls and the tables are made of heavy wood. Donita chooses the *char kway teow* with two side dishes of fried chicken and curry puffs. The dark flat noodles arrive, steaming and glossy with oil. Sanjeev orders a pyramid of yellow rice with curries and pickled vegetables surrounding the base. As Donita eats, she feels the void in her stomach asking for more. 'Is there dessert?' she asks, picking up a slice of sweet roasted pork with her chopsticks. Sanjeev points to an auntie pushing a cart and peddling shaved ice desserts and lychee jelly puddings through the fake yester-year laneways. 'Call her over now,' Donita says.

As they cross the overhead bridge to the bus stop afterwards, Donita explains to Sanjeev that Mrs Fann doesn't leave her enough food at the end of each meal, and since she's hardly allowed to go out on her own these days, she never knows when she can take a break to buy herself a snack.

Sanjeev frowns and shakes his head. 'Your boss is not treating you well.' Traffic roars on the flyover, drowning out Donita's other complaints. Mrs Fann made her stay up late last night to clear out the storeroom in the hallway. The dust made Donita's eyes burn, and when she sneezed, she was scolded for spreading germs in the flat. Mrs Fann checked her purse thoroughly again before she left the flat today to make sure she wasn't stealing, and then she made Donita raise her arms and spread her legs so she could also check if she was concealing anything. Her fingers dug into Donita's inner thighs and made her want to scream.

'She told me, "I have to do this. You people cannot be trusted. Carolyn Hong caught her maid stealing on her day off, and you see what happened when she confronted her?"'

'She knows you are friends with Flordeliza?' Sanjeev asks.

Donita shakes her head. 'If she finds out, she will probably get the police to arrest me just for knowing her.'

It is unusual to discuss Flor with Sanjeev. After Donita told him about sneaking around behind the Hong residence and finding the backpack, she was surprised at his reaction. 'Are you crazy? Something could have happened to you,' he said. 'Just let the police do their work. If she is innocent, the truth will come out.' Donita had bristled at the word 'if'. 'I know she is innocent, and don't call me crazy again,' she snapped, and the conversation stalled there. Later Sanjeev explained that a couple of years ago, there had been a riot in Little India over a Bangladeshi construction worker who was accidentally run over by a bus. 'Now the police are even more careful about any misbehaviour or protest from people like us.' Will anybody burn down buildings over Flor, though? Donita doubts it. On the domestic worker Facebook groups, women warn each other not to talk about it because their comments can be reported. Everybody is better off minding their own business.

The bus stop is on a crowded footpath on the edge of a busy highway. Donita's head begins to hurt from the roar of traffic, the dust and the hot exhaust from the buses that have crawled to a stop and lined up at the kerb. As they push through the crowd to get to the double-decker bus at the end of the line, Sanjeev grips Donita's hand but, as soon as they board, he drops it to pat his pockets, as though looking for his transit card.

'You're holding it,' Donita says. Sanjeev glances at his other hand awkwardly and doesn't say anything. He doesn't look her in the eye, and when the bus suddenly lurches, he doesn't reach out to catch Donita the way he does on the MRT, one arm hooked protectively around her waist. Donita scans the bus and, within seconds, she spots them – a man wearing a white turban and a woman whose thick line of scalp pokes out behind her scarf. Their pinched expressions and hard staring make Donita want to straddle Sanjeev and kiss him passionately, just to scandalize them even further, but he has inched so far away from her now, he can't even hear her muttering, 'Why can't they mind their own business?'

The more truthful question Donita wants to ask Sanjeev is, 'What are you so afraid of?' It gets stuck in her throat every time they go out in public and have to separate because he sees people from his community. Even when they're not on a bus that is on the route to the Sikh temple, Sanjeev tells her it's better to sit separately.

'You say people take pictures of maids on their days off with their boyfriends and post them on Facebook,' Sanjeev explained. 'If we're sitting together on the bus, they post the pictures and make up all sorts of stories about us. I don't want your ma'am to come across these photos.'

Is Donita supposed to think him brave for the few times they have been so wrapped up in each other and their bubble of conversation that he forgot to jump apart for the Mrs Fanns of the country? Or that he pretends to keep them apart in public for her sake? She can't bring herself to talk to Sanjeev about this, though, or about any aspect of their relationship. It feels like a conversation that would take days. She wants to spend what little time they have together luxuriating in the feel of someone who makes her feel fully herself. Around Sanjeev, Donita is both sexy and sharp. He gives her his rapt attention with his eyes, and in his arms she feels both tenderly appreciated and protected. Nobody has been so many things in Donita's life before.

In the apartment, Sanjeev tells Donita that he confirmed with his roommates that they would be out for the afternoon. 'I asked them to give me a few hours.'

'Hours,' Donita says, raising her eyebrow at Sanjeev. Redness creeps into his cheeks and makes Donita *kilig* – that fluttery feeling that overcomes her every time Sanjeev gets shy. She gives him a playful nudge to let him know she was just joking, but if he has the stamina for a couple of hours, they should make the most of it. Over the past few days they have been sending each other messages about all the things they want to do with each other, and Donita pictured this afternoon to be one long session of continuous pleasure.

Perhaps Donita had also allowed her imagination to roam too far. She pictured satin sheets and plush, heart-shaped pillows, maybe some rose petals strewn across the bed. Instead, the walls of the room are covered in textured paint that resembles dried oatmeal. Sanjeev's single bed is adjacent to a built-in wardrobe with paint flaking off the silver knobs. It is nice being alone together, though, and when she closes her eyes and feels Sanjeev's body pressing against hers, all the other details disappear. Yet, after an hour or so of breathless tumbling in the sheets, she also just wants to talk. Every conversation with Sanjeev is a discovery.

'Who is that?' Donita asks. She points at a picture tucked into the frame of a standing mirror.

'My friend Armeet's family. His mother, father and two younger brothers.'

'Why do you have his family's picture in your room?'

'I told you, this is not a hundred per cent my room,' Sanjeev explains patiently. 'Only like . . . twenty per cent. We share it. The room next door has two bunk beds. A few more sleep in the living room.'

'The bed is yours?' Donita asks.

'Some days,' Sanjeev says. 'Like now.'

Obviously. Donita squirms. She doesn't like the thought of sharing this bed with so many other people, but then how different is it from going to another pay-by-the-hour hotel?

'You wash the sheets?' Donita asks, poking at a threadbare corner of the striped blue and white bedsheets.

'Of course,' Sanjeev says.

At least this room has traces of Sanjeev's daily life, like his baseball cap sitting atop a pile of spiral-bound books from his hospitality course, and the laptop charger plugged into the wall. On the back of the door, there are shirts hanging from a row of hooks meant for handbags, and a crushed ball of receipts and tickets slowly unfurling across the dresser. But maybe none of those things are his. This thought makes Donita shift uncomfortably again. This time, Sanjeev notices.

'What's wrong?' he asks. He moves to give her space.

'Sanjeev, do you ever think about us together . . . next time?' Donita asks. She avoids scaring him with the word 'future', even though sometimes the only thing getting her through a tough day is fantasizing about a future with him.

'You mean your next day off?' Sanjeev asks. 'Will your ma'am let you have any public holidays off?'

Donita sighs. She doesn't really feel ready to broach the topic of where her relationship is going, but it also bothers her that there is nowhere to go. Not just on Sundays, where they have to fight for space with all the other foreign workers, in tiny public spaces and the even fewer private spaces they are allowed to inhabit. Officially, they cannot have a life together. The work permit rules are such that Donita will never be able to live in Singapore as anything but a domestic worker, or migrate here on other terms. So then, where do they go?

'The next holiday is in November,' she says. Mrs Fann doesn't give her public holidays off anyway.

Donita was even afraid Mrs Fann would make her work today because she had been going on about 'the big day coming up'. She'd spent most of last night's dinner flipping through a pile of photocopied registration forms with the heading SAGE on top. She seemed oblivious to Donita's presence, or the fact that Donita had to stand to attention and wait until she finished her dinner before she could have her own.

The best thing about Sanjeev's room is the sky. It fills half a window; the other half of the window gives a partial view of an adjacent apartment block. Sitting up in the bed, Donita can see the afternoon unfurling for the other residents. Their movements are languid; it is a day of rest, after all. Sometimes she feels like Sunday for maids is not a day for relaxation, but a chance to do everything she cannot do in Mrs Fann's presence. It's burdensome, cramming all her acts of freedom into the hours before her curfew – she smokes more cigarettes than she usually would, she hikes up her skirt so the hem barely covers her bottom, she searches for another condom in the box so she and Sanjeev can have another round to last them for the next two weeks. He looks as if he is perishing from their last hour, and Donita feels tired too.

'It's called Diwali,' Sanjeev says.

'Hmm?' Donita asks, preoccupied.

'The November holiday. My family, I miss them more during *rakhi*,' Sanjeev says. 'On Diwali, it's mostly eating food, but those other occasions are more special.'

'What do you do?' Donita asks.

'On *rakhi*, the girls tie strings around their brother's wrists, and their brothers give them money. It's to show appreciation for your sisters, all the things they do for you.'

'You don't have sisters,' Donita says.

'I do,' Sanjeev says. He reaches to the floor and picks his phone out of his trousers pocket. 'Cousin-sisters. And family friends. All considered sisters.' He scrolls through his camera gallery and shows her a picture of three smiling girls. 'Every time I leave home, I miss them the most.'

Three girls with manes of thick dark hair stare into the camera. Laughter shines in their kohl-lined eyes, and behind them are small hints of Sanjeev's homeland – a fence, a patch of pavement, a car parked on the road's edge. Donita can imagine these sisters crowding around Sanjeev whenever he returns. She can picture him teasing them and also protecting them. 'You think they would like me?' Donita asks. She feels her heart skipping as soon as she asks the question. Too soon, too much. 'I mean . . .' she starts to say, but Sanjeev gently takes her hand.

'They would like you,' he says. His words bring a wave of relief coursing through her. She smiles.

'What time do we need to leave?' Donita asks.

'Not yet,' Sanjeev says.

'Maybe we go out for a walk first,' Donita suggests. On their way into the neighbourhood, they had passed a corridor of low-slung shophouses with carved shutters where Donita wants a photograph of herself taken. For all her curiosity about where and how Sanjeev lives, Donita realizes she doesn't want to be stuck indoors.

Sanjeev nods and draws her close to him. A slow smile spreads across his face. 'Let's take a shower first,' he says. A giggle escapes Donita's lips as he wraps her in the sheets and carries her like a bride across the threshold of the master bathroom.

Yesterday, when Donita told Cora and Angel that she was going to attend a poetry reading with Sanjeev because one of his friends was performing, Angel replied immediately. 'The Migrant Workers' Poetry Competition? I submitted so many poems to them and they didn't choose a single one. Tell me if the winners' poems are any good, okay?'

Not waiting for an invitation, Angel also sent a few of her poems to the chat group. Cora replied right away: *Bless you Angel, you have such a big heart.* Donita wasn't sure what a good or bad poem looked like. 'I'll let you know,' she wrote to Angel anyway. She looked through Angel's poems and found that they were all about her break-up. One was titled 'SUZAN YOU ARE A FUCKER I WISH YOU GET A DISEASE'. Maybe the judges didn't want to know about her heartbreak.

As they arrive at the Esplanade now for the reading, Sanjeev looks as if he might launch into a guided-tour speech about the Esplanade architecture if Donita asks him about it, so she tells him that she looked it up before they got here. It was not quite what she was expecting. It's certainly a landmark building, surrounded by financial towers and a boathouse restaurant on the banks of the gleaming river, but its hunched spiky dome doesn't look very inviting.

Inside the lobby of the Esplanade a blast of air-conditioning and soft amber spotlights welcome Donita. There is an installation of delicate silver wind chimes hanging from the ceiling, and at the slightest movement or whisper on the ground, sound waves travel to create an orchestra of harmonious tunes. A grand piano overlooks the crowd from a marble platform.

'So in this country the people do have music, but only inside the correct buildings,' Donita says. Her remark reverberates through the wind chimes, which produce a tinkling melody to match. Sanjeev laughs.

Donita feels Flor's presence strongly because she woke up this morning with her mind still tangled in a dream of that Sunday when they met at Marine Terrace market. On their walk towards the canal, they heard a cheer erupting from a group heading across the road to the beach, followed by thumping bass beats. Flor told her: 'If you don't hear any music, it means somebody has made a complaint.'

'They don't allow music on the beach?' Donita had asked incredulously.

'Oh, they are fine with it,' Flor replied. 'Your ma'am makes music all the time, no? Yelling, banging things? They just don't like us doing it.'

Here, at least, it looks as if people wouldn't mind the kind of music Donita is hearing. Gathered on the stairs and gravitating in groups towards a live free concert on the mezzanine, there are other Pinoy women.

'They are all here for poetry?' Donita asks, wondering if she should have worn something a little more formal. Her hair is still damp at the ends from their shower together.

'Maybe, maybe not,' Sanjeev says. 'A lot of people come here on weekends.'

They make their way towards the stage, where a man with dreadlocks is playing bongos. Donita's shoulders begin to bounce to the rhythm. The man makes eye contact with her and thumps the heels of his hands against the taut skin of the instrument. The beats travel right through Donita's body and she begins to shake her hips. 'Come on,' she says to Sanjeev, pulling him in before he can decline. The crowd gives them space to move together, and they begin a call and response song with the bongo player. Sanjeev's feet are quick to catch the rhythms. His hands grip Donita at her waist, secure, and for a moment, she feels as if everybody else disappears. They are two people, dancing together, their bodies carried by a song from another continent. Her laughter rings in the air as the song fades to an end, the width of her smile matched by Sanjeev's.

Laughing and catching their breath, they move away from the crowd, hand in hand, and go up the escalator to a gallery on the third floor. There are people milling about here too, but they chat in low voices and laugh politely. Some are clearly artists, like that woman wearing a slick purple wig and white go-go boots who is staring intently at a framed black-and-white photograph on the wall. A couple of teenage girls carrying grainy white tote bags huddle together, peeking furtively around the room. Behind them, there is a long table with plates of sliced fruit, bottled water and cheese.

While Sanjeev says hello to his friends, Donita makes her way to the table. She fills a small plate with slices of cheese, papaya and grapes. One of the teenage girls glances at Donita, and she freezes, wondering if she was supposed to pay. There is no sign or cash register, but maybe there are things that people just know about art events. Did everybody get an email beforehand about wearing these shapeless linen dresses and gigantic black-framed glasses? There is a man standing near the window who definitely looks like he is in costume.

Another young woman smiles at Donita, calming her nerves. She notices another crowd gathering at the back, a group of Filipino and Indonesian domestic workers in separate cliques, and they have kept away from the fruit table. When the host of the event calls out to everybody to take their seats, those women hang back and gravitate towards the seats in the back row. Donita wants to shout at them: 'It's Sunday! We can sit wherever we want!' But she gets nervous too, holding her fruit plate and hovering by the front row with all the other people. Sanjeev gives her a wave from where he's still standing with his group, and she waves back and points at where she's saved him a seat. He nods.

The woman who smiled at Donita is carrying a tote bag with SAGE printed across it. That's the same name on Mrs Fann's forms, the ones she instructed Donita to help to cross-check against the list on her laptop yesterday. As they settle into their seats, Donita asks the woman, 'What is this place, SAGE?'

'It's an organization for women,' the woman says. 'Society for the Advancement of Gender Equality.'

'Oh,' Donita says. 'I think my ma'am is joining you, very busy becoming members with all her friends.' Although . . . gender equality doesn't sound like something Mrs Fann would champion. What she knows is that Mrs Fann doesn't like the way this SAGE place has been running sex education programmes in schools. 'They're saying it's okay to be gay,' Mrs Fann told Donita. 'You come from a Catholic country so you understand. They don't allow this in the Philippines, right? Singapore is becoming too liberal. It's time to get some sensible leaders in there.'

Donita looks at Sanjeev, hoping that he will call her over and introduce her to his friends, but they only look at her briefly and offer smiles and waves from a distance when Sanjeev breaks away to join her.

The host of the event is a bespectacled man who goes by the name Syncopate. He is dressed head to toe in loose black garments and even though he has a microphone, his voice is a whisper. He frowns. 'Testing?' he says.

'It's like a funeral,' Donita whispers to Sanjeev.

'I think it will be more fun than that,' he says.

'You sure? Look at him. He looks like he's going to jump into the Singapore River afterwards.'

Sanjeev chuckles and Donita nudges him back. They lace their fingers together. 'Later, when I meet your friends, I have a lot of questions about you,' she says, touching the threads on his wrist. She might just be imagining it, but Sanjeev's body suddenly tenses.

'Don't need to mention too much,' Sanjeev says.

'Mention what? All the things we did this afternoon? You think I am going to give them a full report?' She laughs. 'I was just going to ask them, "Is Sanjeev really so nice to his sisters that they give him so many threads?"' Sanjeev returns her teasing nudge, but his laugh is hollow.

Syncopate has been given a new microphone now and he is introducing the poets. Sanjeev's poet friend has a moustache that has been so finely sculpted with wax, it looks like a drawing. There are also two men from Bangladesh wearing long kurtas over their jeans. A Filipino woman in a frayed dark denim skirt and a ruffled blouse sits next to Syncopate. She keeps smiling at her friends in the back row and then biting her lips, as if she's afraid she'll start laughing. The Indonesian woman next to her is less reserved. She waves with both hands and blows kisses to the back row.

'For this year's edition of the Migrant Workers' Poetry Competition, one winner, two runners-up and three honourable mentions were awarded to poems that captured the foreign worker experience in Singapore. There are many talented writers in our midst. To think that they just started writing poetry a few years ago!'

At this, one of the Bangladeshi men frowns and whispers to the other one, who nods. 'Sir,' he says, tapping on the microphone in front of him. 'Sorry for interruption.'

Syncopate looks slightly ruffled but he allows it.

'Sir, many of us already knowing poetry long before coming to Singapore.'

'Of course, of course,' Syncopate says, nodding. He holds up his notes. 'As I was saying—'

'No, sir, something the Singapore people must understand,' the man continues. 'In Bangladesh, we all read Ravindranath Tagore, the Nobel Prize winner. Even the poorest children also can recite famous Tagore poems. My father used to read Jibanananda Das to me. You know the writer Mohammad Rafiq? I wanted to study with him. Everybody in my country is a poet.'

'I see you're ready to take the stage, Abhi,' Syncopate says with a tight smile. 'Will you read us your poem?'

Abhi reads in his native language. Like most people in the room, Donita doesn't understand a word, but the words are like a wave softly swishing over her bare skin. She feels like closing her eyes, but she's afraid she will look ridiculous. When Syncopate reads the English translation, all of the hairs on Donita's arms begin to rise.

> *'This is what I do for you.'*
> *My father says these words*
> *as I pack my bags for a land*
> *hungry for buildings. The trees here*
> *are steel against the wind; the rain*
> *does not replenish soil, but makes*
> *the rivers swell to their limits.*
> *Here my fortunes will rise like the rivers*
> *in my hometown. They will seep into*
> *the soil and the roots will stretch far*
> *so my father can forget*
> *our wealth of sweet mud and emerald fields*
> *Reduced to white paper, signed scrawl.*
> *Debt gawps like a canyon and makes my*
> *father ill. My days are compacted into*
> *dormitory solitude*
> *mobile phone screen*
> *measured steps along bamboo scaffolding*
> *One day, I will have enough to leave,*

And then I will watch this island grow
tiny under my soaring body. The buildings
shrinking, the trains scrawling
like signatures and I will say:
'Singapore, this is what I do for you.'

The audience members sigh and hmm collectively. Donita hears her voice among theirs, and she's surprised at this involuntary response.

'Tell us about your poem, Abhi,' Syncopate says.

'This one is about sacrifices,' Abhi says. 'We migrant workers, our family give up so much so we can come here. My father sell his land to pay the agent so I can come here, make money. He say, "Abhi, when you go to Singapore, first thing you must do is pray." But when I come to this country, first thing I try to find is poetry.'

'The participants were given a prompt,' Syncopate explains to the audience. '"Convey the migrant worker experience to Singaporeans". Every year we also have a theme. For this year, the theme was Returning. All the winning entries explored this theme with depth and complexity. Siti Hadiyah from Indonesia wrote about how she returned to her Islamic faith in Singapore and started wearing the hijab as a way to cope with a difficult work situation when she first arrived.'

'Yes, thank you for the introduction, sir,' says the Indonesian woman. Her round face beams like the sun. Syncopate invites her to read her poem, which is written in Bahasa, a language that crackles like applause. Donita picks up some words that this language shares with Tagalog: *lima, anak, saket.* When Siti Hadiyah says the word *mahal,* she pauses to ask the audience in English: 'Do you know what this means?'

'Love! Expensive! Love! Expensive!' The audience calls out.

Syncopate rises from his chair and makes a 'lower your volume' gesture with two flat hands that nobody heeds. Siti Hadiyah smiles. 'In Tagalog and Bahasa, one word meaning two things. Love and expensive. Which one will it be?' She repeats this phrase in Bahasa, and when she finishes, her friends cheer loudly, and she begins to cry and fan her face in embarrassment.

'Sorry,' she gasps. Donita feels as though she might start to cry as well. There are times when Mrs Fann berates her so relentlessly that Donita can feel the tears in the corners of her eyes but she blinks them back. To cry would be to let Mrs Fann win. Sometimes Donita even digs her fingernails deep into her palms to distract herself from her despair. Sanjeev noticed the little half-moon dents in her skin while they were showering today. They were small ridges and the water made them shine. 'You going to tell me my future?' she teased, and he said, 'Your future is with me.' She happily put aside all her questions.

Now his friend is taking the stage. Sanjeev sits up a bit straighter. 'I'd like to welcome Ranvir Singh to read his poem. Ranvir, will you be reading the English version? He translated it himself.'

'No sir, I only want to read the Punjabi version.'

'Then I can read out the translation,' Syncopate says.

Ranvir shakes his head. 'No need, sir. My English translation is not so accurate – the rhythm is wrong. I will just read the Punjabi version; afterwards, if anybody want to know what it is about, they can ask me.'

Syncopate grips his notes. He looks as if he might have a heart attack.

'Go Ranvir!' Sanjeev calls, as if this is a football game. Syncopate shoots him a dirty look.

Before Ranvir reads, he takes in a deep breath and looks at

Sanjeev. 'This one is about something very close to all of us,' he says, and then he reads. The lines of the poem sound like brushstrokes, one and then another. Donita has no way of knowing what he is saying, but she notices it's having an effect on Sanjeev. He leans closer to the stage, his face turned up and eyes closed, as if there is a breeze coming through an open window. At the end, he sighs.

'Very nice,' Syncopate says, and he moves on to the other poets. Donita sneaks a glance at Sanjeev and finds that he is looking off into the distance. He has also let go of her hand.

After the poetry readings, there is a reception and, once again, Donita does not understand the currency. The poets sit at one end of a long table, where Syncopate's books are proudly displayed, along with a collection of migrant workers' poems. There are price tags on Syncopate's books, but a donation box for the collection, and Donita wonders if the money will go to the poets. If so, she needs to work out how to write poetry because it could be a good side business.

Flor enters her mind then. It is impossible for Donita to cast her out of her thoughts – there she is, between the lines of all the poems, sitting in a cell and saying nothing about where she was that day. *Why won't you tell them?* The question keeps Donita up some nights, and it is making her see things. Last night, before going to bed, Donita looked out of the window and saw a woman who resembled Flor sitting by the canal, flicking the ashes from her cigarette onto the ground. The night shadows obscured her face and she was only a faint outline between the trees, maybe not even there at all; Flor's ghost, come to haunt Donita and beg for her help. Donita eyes the microphone on the stage and an image flashes in her mind: she is marching up there and calling for everybody's attention. *I want to tell you all about something important. My friend is Flordeliza Martinez and I know she is innocent.* And then what? Where is the proof? Everything sounds like speculation – the stormy look in Peter Hong's eyes as he loomed over his daughter; the glimpse of Flor walking slowly through the torrid rain. Donita knows what she saw, but sometimes doubt singes the edges of her memories. Sometimes she shuts her eyes to picture Flor and she sees a stranger.

There is another problem now. Sanjeev still has not introduced Donita to Ranvir. In fact, every time she tries to wander over to them, Sanjeev turns his shoulder slightly to close the circle.

'That guy is your lover or what?' Donita asks, irritated, when they leave the Esplanade. 'He read his poem, you pay so close attention until you drop my hand. Then you don't even introduce me.'

'No, no,' Sanjeev says. 'Nothing like that.'

'What was his poem about?' Donita asks.

'Something a bit difficult to explain,' Sanjeev says.

According to Sanjeev, anything in Punjabi is difficult to explain. Sometimes he views videos on his phone, grainy and shaky squares of people talking straight into the camera or animated in skits with other characters. His shoulders shake with laughter, but when Donita asks him what's so funny, he shrugs and tells her there is no translation.

'You can at least give me a summary. Don't be like that Stinko-Face, cannot explain anything.'

'Who?'

'The host just now.'

'Syncopate,' Sanjeev says.

'Whatever,' Donita says, losing patience. What is this

argument even about? She's annoyed with Sanjeev and she can't figure out why, exactly. She just thought that this afternoon would be more about meeting his friends and getting to know them. Maybe they'd all go out in a group afterwards, and they'd bring their girlfriends too. But since Ranvir read that poem, Sanjeev has been in a wistful mood and he's hiding something.

They walk together in an uncomfortable silence along the boulevard outside the Esplanade. The sea is silver and still. Everything in this city looks designed for permanence, yet Donita always feels as if she's on a rickety bridge. Last night, after seeing the ghost of Flor from her window, she felt as if nothing was real. As if maybe she died back in the Philippines, and Singapore was some strange afterlife. The rules are always changing, or do not exist at all. These are things she cannot quite explain to Sanjeev – she doesn't have the words for them in any language.

A long double railing divides the land from the river, and along one section of steel grids, tiny pieces of coloured paper are attached. As Donita and Sanjeev approach, she sees that they are actually small padlocks, some painted in vibrant pinks and yellows.

'Why are they locking the bridge?' she asks.

'It's something the teenagers do,' Sanjeev says. 'They put their initials on the padlocks and then lock them onto the bridge to symbolize their love.'

'What is the point of putting it here?' Donita asks. 'The padlock is forever?'

'I guess so,' Sanjeev says.

'So you will buy me one?' It comes out more forcefully than the light teasing that she intended.

Sanjeev looks at her. 'Donita . . . I'm sorry about my friends.

I thought they would be more welcoming. I invited you because I wanted to introduce you to them, but I became afraid of what they would say.'

'Why don't they like me?'

Sanjeev sighs and rubs his face in his hands. They are standing on the bridge, surrounded by couples. 'That poem that Ranvir read is about having two lives. One here, and one back home. Different expectations.'

'So what does that mean?' Donita asks.

'Ranvir's poem was a letter to his past self in Punjab, warning that he would change once he came to Singapore. He would start to walk differently, talk differently and even . . .'

'Even?'

'Love differently,' Sanjeev says. His voice is barely a whisper. Donita sees the shape of the word 'love' on his lips and wishes this wasn't the way she had to hear it the first time. 'I didn't know about any of this, but Ranvir had a girlfriend here, and they were together for two years. He kept it a secret,' he continues. 'Then he went back to India for a holiday and he was going to tell his family that he was marrying this girl – she was Filipino, so he knew they would have a hard time accepting her, but he was determined.'

'What happened?'

'His mother fainted.'

Donita snickers. 'Serves her right. Racist lady.'

'It's not funny, Donita,' Sanjeev says. 'Ranvir's whole family was grieving.'

'Why? She died?' Donita retorts. 'All this drama because she cannot accept Filipino daughter-in-law.'

'Ranvir wrote his poem about his struggle. He broke up with the girl, and he told me to be prepared for things to be very different if I wanted to be with a Filipino girl in the long term.'

'Just because he cannot say no to his mother, does not mean you are like that.'

'Our families are very important to us.'

Donita understands what he's saying now. 'Even your family?' she asks.

'I don't think my mother will faint, but she certainly will be upset if I bring home a foreign girl.'

'Then what is the point? Just sex?' Donita asks.

'No,' Sanjeev says. 'That is not all we're doing together. We are also talking, and sharing our lives. I want you to be in my life. That is why it's so difficult. Because this feels like a relationship.'

'It *is* a relationship,' Donita says.

'And it can go on,' Sanjeev says. 'But it will end.'

'When?' Donita asks. 'When they expect you to go home and get married?'

Sanjeev bites his lip. 'This is why I wanted us to get to know each other as friends first,' he says.

'Friends?' Donita asks incredulously. What they did together this afternoon was certainly not the exchange of *friends*. 'If you are using me, why don't you say so?'

'I am not using you,' Sanjeev insists. 'I just want—'

'What do you want?' Donita asks. 'Sex with me but real love from somebody your family will choose for you?'

'No, Donita,' Sanjeev says. His voice is full of sorrow but Donita is too hurt to buy it. The bile rises in her throat – this is what anger does to her.

'Then what?' she asks. 'In the shower, you said I was your future. Your future what? Future story you can share like Ranvir, so you can win some poetry contest?'

'I want to take things slow.'

'Take things slow? Everything else you do very fast!' Donita points at Sanjeev's crotch to make her point clear. His cheeks go red as Donita spins on her heels and storms off in the opposite direction. He doesn't follow.

She finds herself back in the comfort of the Esplanade. Her stomach is churning and she wonders if it's from the excessive food today – the double desserts and the cheese at the poetry gathering – or being so upset. She can feel a sob rising in her throat and she makes it into a bathroom just in time to throw up everything she has eaten.

Donita's sobs come quickly and loudly then and they echo across the bathroom. She flushes the toilet and steps out of the stall to see the Filipino poet standing near the sink, her face full of concern. 'Are you in trouble?' she asks quietly, handing Donita a tissue.

One glance in the mirror shows Donita how she must look to the woman. She has been throwing up and sobbing. 'No,' Donita says, braving a smile. 'Not like that.' She and Sanjeev are always very careful because she would be deported if she tested positive for pregnancy at her six-monthly check-up.

The woman doesn't look convinced. 'Listen, there are places to go if you need to . . . you know. They take cash, no records.'

Donita shakes her head. 'I am fine,' she insists, but she also realizes she doesn't know this for sure. What if she's pregnant? Her last period *was* a long time ago but stress always throws off her cycle. Fresh tears spring to her eyes. How did her only day away from Mrs Fann manage to bring her so much misery?

The woman scribbles down a phone number and an address for Donita. 'But listen – don't tell anybody about this place, okay? The people who work there . . . they'll be in huge trouble if the government finds out. You don't want them coming after you.'

Donita takes the piece of paper from her. It doesn't sound like a place she ever wants to go to, but if she needs to take care of matters, it's the only option. She can't just go to any clinic to get an abortion without them alerting the ministry. She stuffs the paper into her purse and wills away this problem, at least for a little while.

On the bus going home, Donita watches the buildings gathered at the edge of the silvery sea. The bus climbs a ramp to a flyover and the city falls at her feet – a spray of red-roofed resort-style apartment buildings and green parks carved around the water. The bus pulls up to her stop on Marine Parade Road far too early. There are still two hours left till curfew and she is not going to waste them inside Mrs Fann's flat where she will be confined for another two weeks. Donita follows the smell of salt and sea and crosses the pedestrian bridge to the beach. The sound of her footsteps pounding down the ramp drown out the question in her mind. *What if, what if, what if?*

Picnic blankets and tents cover the grassy parkland. A roller-blading couple zip around Donita as she crosses the running track onto the sand. All of the barbecue areas are overflowing with opened bags of chips, soft drink bottles, music and laughter. Donita finds a stone bench and sits watching the waves crash against the sand. There are families swimming and picking up seashells, and of course she wonders about the parents she never knew. By the time she was Donita's age, she had already given birth to a child, but was that when her life began to end as well? Donita looks up to see that a group of Pinoy women at a nearby barbecue party are looking over at her, and she understands why – it's strange to be alone like this on a Sunday. Everybody has company, but she landed straight into Sanjeev's arms when she arrived, and her other friend has been arrested for murder. Angel and Cora had invited her on their trek through Clementi Forest today, but she wanted to spend time with Sanjeev.

What if she is pregnant? That will be the end of her time in Singapore, which means starting from the beginning again, with even less than she had. There will be debts to pay to her agent and she will have nothing to show for her time away, not even a modest *balikbayan* box. She tries counting to her last period, but her round-the-clock work makes the dates blur together.

She takes out the piece of paper and types the address into her phone. The hushed fear in the Filipino poet's voice makes Donita feel nervous herself as the map appears on her screen. She hunches over it, noticing first that the address is in a very small side street – so small that it juts out like a ledge. All the other streets in this area are tiny veins.

Donita shrinks the map with her thumb and forefinger and sees where it is in relation to Chinatown, the Singapore river, and Sanjeev's apartment. A long straight line before a dive into back streets.

Her heart begins to thrum.

She pinches the screen and spreads her fingers apart. The lanes widen and signs expand. Donita travels through the neighbourhood with her fingers, a sense of gnawing familiarity growing stronger as the back lanes bring her to the hotel where she and Sanjeev stayed that first afternoon. With a flick of her finger, Donita is on the main road opposite the fruit stand and the tea stall. She can picture the wall mural on the building labelled Shophouse 23, and she can see the little symbol for the bus stop coming into its dimensions – the bench, the roar of vehicles, the laneways sprouting from the main road.

The only thing missing from that afternoon is the rain – and Flor walking away as Donita shouted her name.

Chapter Twelve

The eggshells from this morning's breakfast are scattered around the Vijays' home. It's a funny trick, scaring the geckos away by convincing them that something larger has hatched nearby. Angel didn't think it would work the last time, but within days the walls were clear of dots of fresh droppings.

She glances at her phone. It hasn't made a sound but she checks anyway. No new messages from Donita, so she reads through their exchange from last night again.

DONITA: *I think I know where Flor was! There's a clinic in Jalan Besar where domestic workers can get abortions and morning-after pills. They pay in cash, and the clinic won't report it to the employers, so the women's work permits won't get cancelled. I saw her coming out of this lane. Look!*

ANGEL: *Oh my God!*

CORA: *How did you find out about this place?*

DONITA: *Another woman told me.*

CORA: *Are you in trouble, Donita?*

DONITA: *Don't think so. I started having my regular cramps last night. Was having some indigestion before, so I didn't notice them.*

ANGEL: *So Flordeliza thinks she's better off being charged with murder than exposing the people who run these clinics?*

CORA: *She is. If she leads the police to the abortion clinic, those guys will come after her for exposing them. These unlicensed operations have a lot of connections with gangs. If she stays quiet, there's some hope the police will find the real killer and let her go.*

DONITA: *Or maybe she'd just prefer a slower path towards death. If they charge her with this murder, she'd get the death penalty but it will take a while.*

CORA: *Maybe she told the police the truth at some point, but they can't lose face after pinning the murder on her. It's easier to close the case here. The whole country thinks Flor is guilty.*

ANGEL: *What are you going to do, Donita?*

There's been no reply since last night. Angel doesn't know if this is because Donita returned to work, or because she is plotting her next steps. What would happen if Donita went to the police? Would they believe her? Angel wondered about this after discovering the camera that Raja planted in her room. She imagined walking into a station and approaching a blue uniformed officer sitting behind a desk, and the image stopped there. The scene stayed stubbornly frozen whenever she tried returning to it.

Thankfully, Raja has been spending more time in his university dorm since his father whacked him over the head. He hasn't moved out entirely though; yesterday Angel walked past the residents' gym to find him sprinting on the treadmill. She fantasized about bursting in and knocking him off the machine. It fills her with boiling rage to know that Raja will face no further consequences for what he did. The evening she found the pen, Sumanthi knocked on Angel's door to apologize on Raja's behalf, but she spoke of his actions as an immature prank.

'He and his buddies challenge each other to do these things sometimes,' Sumanthi said. 'I've told him it's not okay.'

'It's illegal,' Angel reminded Sumanthi.

That word cast a shadow over Sumanthi's face. She bit her lip and said, 'Can we talk about it later? I have a lot on my mind right now.' So far, the conversation has not happened. This morning, when Nurul arrived, Angel noticed her and Sumanthi chatting quietly at the door and shooting glances her way.

Mr Vijay and Nurul can be seen from the balcony. She pushes his wheelchair along the walking path and guides his hands to feel the spongy coral vine leaves. Watching them interact each day, Angel feels a growing distance from Mr Vijay. She dusts each surface twice and attempts new recipes for dinner, but the work feels simple and unsatisfying. She wants to take care of a person. She never knew this until Mrs Vijay was hospitalized, and Angel was by her bedside, feeding her meals and massaging her feet between the nurse's rounds. It just made sense to take on Mr Vijay's care after his stroke, because she had a natural ability, if not the formal training.

Angel notices the dogs nudging at the half eggshell that she placed under the dining table. Reaching down to pet them, she notices chew marks on the leg of the dining-room chair. 'Which one of you did this?' she asks the dogs. Toffee yawns, revealing her plump pink tongue. Coco is the more likely culprit, with her penchant for clamping her razor-sharp teeth on anything that isn't a chew toy. They scramble into her lap, radiating the kind of warmth that makes anger impossible.

'Now I have to learn to restore furniture,' Angel jokes. Her heart wouldn't be in it though. A sense of disquiet is brewing within Angel. She could resign and find a new job but that's not all she wants.

In the evening, there is still no reply from Donita. Angel sends her another message to ask if she is all right. Only half an hour later, a quick text: *Mrs Fann made me spend the whole day in church with her. She and her friends are up to something. I think they're planning to take over this SAGE organization.*

That would certainly be interesting. Angel doesn't know much about SAGE but she remembers Raja teasing Sumanthi for carrying a water bottle with their logo on it. 'Will you stop shaving your legs next?' he asked. 'Does Anand know you're a lesbian?'

At the sound of the main door's lock sliding open, the dogs rush to the foyer and tumble over each other to greet Sumanthi. Angel pushes herself to her feet and waves hello. 'Your dinner is ready, Sumanthi. I make the *aglio olio* recipe you always like but I replace the chicken breast with salmon flakes because the fish will be better for you.' Sumanthi tried calling in sick this morning because her stomach ulcer was acting up, but her boss scolded her so loudly that Angel could hear his voice pouring down the receiver from the other end of the flat.

'Thanks Angel. Anand's coming over too,' Sumanthi says.

'There's enough pasta for him,' Angel says.

'How was Dad today during meal times?' Sumanthi asks.

'Stubborn again about food,' Angel says. 'I don't know how to make him eat.'

She had to cut his dinner into a fine porridge, and he still resisted by pressing his lips together like a child. 'Sir, you need nutrition to be strong,' Angel had insisted. She pulled her arm back and made the fork land like an airplane, making engine noises, and felt Mr Vijay's contempt rising like smoke.

'Nurul says it's only a matter of time before we have to use a feeding tube,' Sumanthi says.

'Aging is hard, Miss Sumanthi,' Angel insists. 'They have their lows. He will bounce back, don't worry.'

'I hope you're right,' Sumanthi says. 'I don't want to . . . I can't lose him.'

'I know,' Angel says. The only movement in the flat is from the dogs' tails sweeping the floor in brisk arcs. Angel used to think of loss as one huge wave – rising floodwaters that engulfed a person. But death also sucked away the sweetness that used to tinge the air of this flat: the pot bubbling with rice and milk on Pongal, overflowing for prosperity, the same week Angel started working for the Vijays three years ago. Mrs Vijay decorating the doorstep with swirls of coloured powder for good luck – it was for the sake of tradition, as there were no consequences for the harvest for them, living in this city.

When Angel met Suzan for the first time that Sunday, Suzan was carrying a tote bag with Van Gogh's Starry Night printed on it. Angel had seen reproductions of those churning clouds and deep skies across countless keychains and mugs and mobile-phone cases, but it became something new to her. For days after the Pongal decorations faded away, Angel traced the faint outlines with chalk while she gathered up the courage to ask Suzan if they could spend a Sunday alone together, hoping Suzan would know how she meant it.

Sumanthi takes a bite of her pasta and squeezes her eyes in pain. 'You want to lie down?' Angel asks.

Sumanthi shakes her head. 'I'll just have some tea and toast.'

Angel nods and goes to the kitchen. As she does, she hears Mr Vijay's snores growing louder. She doesn't know if he's having trouble breathing, but the look on Sumanthi's face tells her she's asking the same question. 'Should I check on him?' she asks.

'I'll do that,' Angel says. She pops two pieces of Gardenia bread into the toaster and switches on the kettle, and hurries to Mr Vijay's room. He is sleeping on his side with one leg thrown over the edge of the mattress. Angel takes care to move him limb by limb, inching him to the middle of the bed before gently rolling him to his back. He snorts and gasps as she does this, and she waits for his breathing to stabilize before lifting his head so she can place a pillow under him. He needs one of those reclining beds, but she knows that suggesting this to Sumanthi would just bring them both back to that depressing nursing home. 'There,' Angel says as she smooths the wrinkles out of Mr Vijay's pyjama top.

An acrid smell tickles Angel's nostrils as she walks out of the room and she realizes that the toast has burned. Sumanthi is standing over the kitchen sink and scraping off the charred layer with a butter knife. 'Never mind, I make you another one,' Angel says.

Sumanthi goes to her room. Angel knocks on the door with the toast and finds Sumanthi sitting on her bed, the bluish glow of the laptop deepening the creases around her frowning lips.

'Ay Sumanthi, forget about your work,' Angel chides. 'You are not well.'

Sumanthi shakes her head. 'I can't fall behind,' she says. 'Anyway, I'm okay sitting down and doing my work, I just can't stand up for too long or the pains start.'

'You have your medicine?' Angel asks.

Sumanthi nods and points to a row of pills encased in foil. 'I'm taking them every three hours, but the pain is still there.'

'I make for you some porridge,' Angel offers. She checks on Mr Vijay on her way back to the kitchen – he's no longer snoring but there is the unmistakable stench of urine. It rests on her list of tasks that feels insurmountable now. The people matter the most, Angel knows this, but she still needs to clear away the dried leaves and a spray of dust which have littered the balcony after strong gusts, and last night she noticed that the hinge of the dish cabinet is missing a screw so the door hangs like a loose tooth. It is as if the apartment is turning against her.

The porridge first. Angel takes a deep breath and hurries back to the kitchen. Sumanthi has followed her and plays with a notepad on the counter, avoiding Angel's eyes.

'Actually, no need to make porridge, Angel. Nurul's on her way, she's going to bring some soup.'

Angel crosses her arms over her chest. 'I thought Nurul only works for Mr Vijay? Now she is interfering with dinner time.'

'She called me after leaving tonight,' Sumanthi says with a sigh. 'Angel, you have to give her a chance to do her job.'

'Her job is over after five o'clock.'

'She's a nurse, Angel. She's coming over after hours out of goodwill because I happened to mention my reflux issues. Nurul is doing what she can—'

'Is this about Raja?' Angel asks.

Sumanthi looks startled. 'What does Raja have to do with it?'

'You want to replace me before I make a police report.'

'That's not—'

'I know how these things happen,' Angel says. 'Some people, they accuse the maid of stealing when she threatens to report them for not paying salary, or for beating her. They plant something in her suitcase when she is packing to leave, and then they call the police.'

'How is this the same thing?' Sumanthi asks.

'You are firing me because I am complaining about Raja.'

'I was communicating with Nurul long before the whole camera incident,' Sumanthi reminds her. 'She has experience. I know that what Raja did really upset you, and I can't apologize for him enough.'

'Why is he still living here?' Angel demands.

'He's family,' Sumanthi says. *And you're not*, Angel hears. Of course she isn't, she has always known that, but Sumanthi's loyalty to her brother still stings. And even though she knows that Nurul is an expert, it hurts to feel as if she is being replaced.

I quit, she practises saying silently.

She returns to Mr Vijay in the bedroom. 'Sir, I have to change you now,' she says loudly for Sumanthi's benefit. The clock radio on his bedside table is playing the last notes of a classical violin tune before the announcer reads the evening news headlines. As always, Angel keeps her ears peeled for news about Flordeliza but of course nothing has changed. She thinks about what Cora said about Donita's discovery – there is a story that everybody prefers to hear.

Angel loosens Mr Vijay's drawstrings and is hit with a stench so strong that she can't help gagging. She sees a brown stain seeping through his trousers. 'Did you know you did this?' she whispers to Mr Vijay. 'You feel it?' Mr Vijay looks past her. 'We have to wash up,' she says as she unlocks the wheels of his chair and brings him closer to the bathroom door. She has bathed Mr Vijay before, but he's never been slumped over in defeat like this. Hooking her arms under his shoulders, Angel feels his full weight as she lifts him out of the chair and onto the low plastic stool. In the mirror, she expects to see his face awash with shame the way it was when she discovered his first pee accident a few days ago, but his expression is blank. It startles the consoling thoughts right out of Angel's mind.

The intercom beeps faintly over the sound of the running shower. Sumanthi calls, 'Yeah come up.' A minute later, the dogs are shrilly alerting each other to the new arrival and Nurul's voice can be heard rising over their yips.

Angel heaves Mr Vijay onto the wheelchair after drying him off. She grunts as his weight drags her down, and he lands on the edge of the seat. Moving to the back of the wheelchair, Angel reaches down and wraps her arms around Mr Vijay's waist to pull him in. She feels him slipping and leans further. Mr Vijay continues to slide off the wheelchair, and in her panic, Angel throws out her arms and loses balance as well. Her thumb catches on the handle as she tumbles to the ground, gasping at the bolt of pain shooting up her arm.

Mr Vijay is lying on the floor when Sumanthi and Nurul come rushing into the room. Angel tries to scramble to her feet, but putting weight on her hand makes her cry out in pain and she can only manage to sit upright, cross-legged, as if she is meditating while the chaos continues around her. Watching Sumanthi and Nurul towering over Mr Vijay and working together to help him up, Angel has never felt so helpless before.

'Let me see your hand,' says Nurul after Sumanthi has wheeled Mr Vijay out of the room. She crouches over Angel and extends her own hand. Angel places her hands in Nurul's and looks away guiltily. 'He just slipped,' she says. 'I'm fine.' But her hand is tender to the touch, and her thumb has begun to swell.

'You need help getting up?' Nurul asks.

Angel nods. Nurul hoists her up the same way she did for Mr Vijay. Angel braces herself for the awkwardness of having somebody's fingers dig into her underarms, but Nurul is gentle. She guides Angel from the floor to the edge of the bed in one swift beat and then inspects her hand. 'It's not sprained. After the swelling goes down, you'll have a bruise, but you don't need a bandage. Do you have ice packs here?'

'There are some frozen peas in the fridge.'

'I'll get them,' Nurul says. Angel feels the mattress sinking beneath her, and her hand throbbing and a rising tide of tears she's not sure she can stem. *I quit,* she thinks again, and this time she is ready to say the words out loud.

From the Ma'am Facebook pages:

Sapna J. Patel: Maid just started working with us and she is claiming her husband died and she needs to go back to the Philippines tomorrow. She's only been with us for nine days. I told her I cannot take time off work on such short notice to take care of the kids but she wants to leave anyway. I can't believe it! Why are they like this?

Denise Siau: I am trying to counsel my mother's helper but she is refusing to listen. Last November, one of my neighbours spotted her walking in Telok Kurau park with an ang moh guy. I asked her about him, and she said he's her boyfriend and they're very much in love. I tried to explain to her that white men only go after girls from poor countries for one thing, and she should be cautious. She's still with him as far as I know. It cannot be a serious relationship. He's from New Zealand. He is an engineer and he lives in an exclusive private property in Bayshore. A good-looking guy, wealthy, nice body, no kids or previous marriage, how can he end up with a maid? I have had my own share of heartbreak with these types of men. In fact,

I only date ang moh men and it's always the same story. One minute they promise you the moon, next minute they say you are too needy (always after sleeping with you). I am just trying to help her. Any advice?

Chapter Thirteen

The trilling sound that Cora initially mistook for a bird is actually Cecilia Lee, standing in the foyer between Ma'am Elizabeth and a hard-shell suitcase. 'Just look at this place,' Cecilia gushes, surveying the living room admiringly. 'I've been cooped up in my apartment for far too long.'

'Look who decided to surprise us,' Ma'am Elizabeth says to Cora. 'Cecilia, say hello to Cora.'

'Hello!' Cecilia cries, throwing her arms around Cora. 'It's nice to finally meet you.'

'Oh, thank you, ma'am. And you also, nice to meet you,' Cora blusters. Although she has encountered the bubbly Cecilia on video calls with Ma'am Elizabeth, she wasn't expecting such a warm greeting. Cecilia has Jacqueline's arched eyebrows and sharp chin, but there is some roundness to her face, like baby fat that she never outgrew, that makes her seem less threatening.

Cora takes the suitcase from Cecilia. 'Miss Cecilia, I will unpack this after I prepare your room,' she says.

'Sure,' Cecilia says. 'I'd like to sleep in the guest bedroom next to the study, please.'

'Not your old room?' Ma'am Elizabeth asks. 'Surely you miss sitting in that window seat facing the Botanic Gardens. The Sutanto family across the road is planning on building up, so who knows how much longer that view will be available?'

'No thank you,' Cecilia says. 'I want to stay in the guest room and feel like I'm on holiday, otherwise I'll never leave.'

'We can't have that,' Ma'am Elizabeth jokes. She turns to Cora. 'Cecilia decided at the last minute to visit and help with her sister's wedding preparations.'

'I needed a break,' Cecilia says. 'Nobody is in New York over the summer. It's so depressing.'

Upstairs, Cora gets to work setting up the guest bedroom. She shakes out the pressed lavender pure cotton sateen sheets from their Rivolta Camignani storage case. The cosy room is tucked away in the corner of the second floor. A framed portrait of lilies sits above the low dresser beside two tiny coned ceramic ring holders. Cora draws the curtains. The view of the neighbours' outdoor water feature is not as scenic as the Botanic Gardens, but the rhythm of cascading water absorbs the faint drone of morning traffic on the main road.

The clothes in Cecilia's suitcase are in disarray, matching the ebbs and flows of her voice floating up the stairs. 'Cora's done wonders with the house,' she marvels. As Cora sorts through Cecilia's clothes and makes a neat stack of folded blouses, she hears Cecilia commenting on the polished carved teak divider at the kitchen entrance. Ma'am Elizabeth's words aren't so easy to discern, but Cecilia's ring out like a bell. 'Of course Jacqueline would say that. She thinks clutter is crass. Everything has to be neat lines or it's the end of the world.'

When Cora comes downstairs again to announce that the room is ready, Cecilia is scrolling through her phone and saying, 'Everyone's talking about it. I have the news article right here.' Cora's heart catches in her throat – please don't let it be something about Flordeliza. She doesn't want to be standing here if they discuss the murder. So far, Ma'am Elizabeth has not mentioned it to Cora at all, except on Saturday when they were in the car and a radio announcer said that a member of Parliament recommended more thorough background checks on domestic workers to ascertain their mental stability.

'Oh that reminds me,' Ma'am Elizabeth had said, turning down the volume. 'I'm sorry it has to be brought up like this, but the Merry Maids agency still needs your letter of release. They called to ask about it.'

Cora froze.

'I told them it was ridiculous,' Ma'am Elizabeth continued. 'You've been working for me for how many months now? I've had no problems. I told them to focus on making sure their employers are treating their helpers properly. They could be a little more selective about their clientele for sure, weed out the Fann Poh Choos of the world.' Ma'am Elizabeth clicked her tongue and turned up the radio before Cora could say anything.

Busying herself with straightening the table runners, Cora feels that same sense of climbing dread now as Cecilia says, 'Here it is,' and begins reading a news article. '"SAGE Ousting Leaves Former Leaders Reeling",' Cecilia reads. Ma'am Elizabeth leans towards Cecilia with full attention, but Cora loses interest immediately. Local news – their budget updates, celebrity marriages and spats between political parties – is of no interest to her, and when they mention the Philippines on Asia News Network, it's always the kind of headline that knots Cora's stomach. Things like: 'War on Drugs Working, Says PH

President' and 'Extra-Judicial Action Necessary for Clean-Up'. The articles use the same picture of President Duterte at a podium, looking smug and triumphant, but all Cora sees is Raymond – his eyes closed in that jeepney on their way home from the restaurant, the shadows striking his face as he slept.

The conversation between Ma'am Elizabeth and Cecilia becomes a buzz of background noise as Cora retreats to the back yard to pick the laundry off the line. It is a humid afternoon and the air feels denser than usual, which means it will rain. She swats away a dragonfly that skitters along the clothesline, but when it circles back, she lets it hover there for a while. Sunlight filters through the latticework of its shuddering wings. She picks up the laundry basket and turns back towards the house to find Ma'am Elizabeth approaching her with one finger over her lip.

'Tomorrow,' Ma'am Elizabeth says when she's close enough for conversation, 'Cecilia and I will have a mother-daughter day – manicures, a swim at the club, maybe afternoon tea at the Goodwood Hotel to keep her busy and help fight off the jet lag before we go to the Fullerton Bay Hotel for a private food tasting. I'd like you to come along in the evening.'

'Ma'am, I think I will be busy here,' Cora says.

Ma'am Elizabeth takes a peek over her shoulder to the house, where Cecilia is still lying on the couch. 'I need you to help me get through this,' she says. 'That hotel . . . that's where some of those women have dinner together.'

'Mrs Fann?' Cora asks.

'Oh God no, if Fann Poh Choo starts showing up at hotels, there goes Singapore's tourism industry. I'm talking about the women that my husband used to have his flings with. If I run into them, your presence would be comforting.'

'Ma'am,' Cora says before faltering. She has no reason to

decline Ma'am Elizabeth's request for moral support. There simply isn't anything to do tomorrow evening, especially if Ma'am Elizabeth will be out all day.

Ma'am Elizabeth looks pleadingly at Cora.

'I will find something to wear,' Cora says finally. A smile breaks across Ma'am Elizabeth's face. She gives Cora a warm and tight hug that makes a lump rise in her throat.

The glass hotel is perched like a spectacular jewel on the corner of Marina Bay, where sweeping spectres of colour and bursting fountains are starting up the evening light and water show. Cora follows Ma'am Elizabeth and Cecilia through a grand lobby of glossy blond-wood floors and dark furniture, where her eyes first land on a European tour group looking woefully underdressed in their sandals and cargo pants. The edges of their leader's voice are softened by the lightly perfumed air. Cora huddles closer to Cecilia when a man in a black suit approaches them.

'Miss Lee,' he drawls, clasping her hands. 'How nice of you to come all this way.'

'Just doing my sisterly duty,' Cecilia says, returning his smile.

The man's teeth are as white as tiles and his eyes skim past Cora. He greets Ma'am Elizabeth with a kiss on each cheek, and tells her he hasn't seen her very much lately. 'My social activities clash with your high tea schedule, I'm afraid,' she says.

'I'll take you to the Banquet Room. The bride is already waiting.' He turns to Cora. 'It will be about an hour. You can enjoy the free light show from the deck,' he says to her, nodding in the direction of the crowds that are gathered outside.

'Oh, how rude of me,' Ma'am Elizabeth says. 'Gabriel, meet

Cora. She's a family friend and she'll be joining us for the food tasting.'

Gabriel squints at Cora like she is a blurry vision that must be corrected. His wide smile appears again. 'Ah, I see,' he says.

'Nice to meet you,' Cora says.

'Right,' he says stiffly. 'Come this way, ladies.'

As soon as his back is turned, Cecilia makes a face. 'Pompous fart,' she whispers. 'His real name is Ting Tee Wee. I once saw him swearing in Hokkien as he stumbled out of a midnight massage parlour in Duxton.'

Cora is more conscious of the eyes on her as they cross the lobby. A pair of ornate heavy wooden doors open out to an expansive banquet room with carpeted floors and chandeliers dripping with iridescent lights. To her relief, the food tasting is a private event and there are no other guests besides themselves. Jacqueline is towering over two uniformed waitresses. 'I don't understand why it wasn't prepared earlier,' she says icily. The waitresses look at each other and back at her. One of them mumbles an excuse that does nothing to reassure Jacqueline, who crosses her arms over her chest and hisses something at the waitresses, who nod fervently. She only acknowledges Cecilia and Ma'am Elizabeth with a glance.

'Uh-oh, someone's in a mood,' Cecilia mutters. Cora tries not to be concerned with the dark look that Jacqueline has thrown in her direction. Did Ma'am Elizabeth not tell her that Cora would be joining them?

'Nice to see you again, Miss Jacqueline,' Cora says. She ignores Gabriel's smirk at her accent. She wants to channel Donita's attitude, drawing her shoulders back and walking with ease through this palatial hotel, but discomfort presses on her chest as Jacqueline unleashes another round of commands for the waitresses. They both skitter away, leaving Cora and the Lee family waiting for Gabriel to seat them around the banquet table bordering a hardwood dance floor. Cora takes her seat at the edge of the row next to Ma'am Elizabeth. Propped up next to the dining plate is a sleek card with embossed lettering. She opens it to find a long list of course choices printed on both sides. One waitress returns to lay the napkin like a blanket across Cora's lap, and smiles at her as she does this. 'Anything to drink, ma'am?' she asks.

'Water, please,' Cora says.

'Still or sparkling?'

'Just tap water,' Cora says.

'I'll have the same,' Ma'am Elizabeth says. The waitress nods and approaches Cecilia and Jacqueline. 'It's bright in here, isn't it?' Ma'am Elizabeth murmurs to Cora. 'The lighting could be a bit dimmer.'

Cora agrees. The room is garishly bright and it gives her a slight headache. From the look on Jacqueline's face, she can tell it's not the only thing that's wrong.

'I thought I made it very clear . . .' she says between gritted teeth to one of the waitresses who has bravely returned with a pad for note-taking.

Ma'am Elizabeth leans closer to Cora. 'Her fiancé was supposed to take time off work but can't make it. I think she's feeling stressed.'

'And how are you feeling, ma'am?' Cora asks.

Ma'am Elizabeth looks around. 'Fine,' she says. 'Pleasant memories so far. We brought the girls swimming at the older Fullerton across the road during their school holidays. I had forgotten about that. Whenever Mr Lee and I went to the symphony at Victoria Concert Hall, we treated ourselves to a suite. The view of the city from up there is divine.'

Divine. These old European buildings with their domed roofs and high pillars are layered like wedding cakes. As she passed the tour guide in the lobby earlier, she heard him say that this was the landing point for Singapore's forefathers. It is no wonder that Tee Wee Gabriel gave her that look, as if she was there to single-handedly ruin his country's history. 'It's a beautiful place, ma'am,' Cora says. 'I'm glad it brings some good memories for you—'

'Mummy,' Cecilia interrupts. 'Was it the Fullerton or the Raffles Hotel where we had Po Po's eightieth birthday?'

'Raffles,' Ma'am Elizabeth says. 'And your eighteenth was at the Shangri-La. Come to think of it, we've never had a major celebration in our own home.'

'Of course not,' Jacqueline says irritably. 'Garden parties are for small-scale events. All of our celebrations have involved lots of guests.'

'Not everything has to be a networking opportunity, Jac,' Cecilia says.

Ma'am Elizabeth gives her a warning nudge. Cora runs her fingers along the starched edges of the napkin as the waitresses return with a platter. 'The appetizers, Miss Lee,' Gabriel says, beaming. His smile begins to quiver when Jacqueline takes a bite of the oyster and pronounces it 'adequate'. The same goes for the shrimp pâté with truffle oil and gold flakes. 'It's overwhelmingly garlicky,' Jacqueline complains. 'People don't want bad breath at a wedding.'

'Noted,' Gabriel says. 'Maybe you'd like to combine the Chinese and Western options? Some couples are doing that these days. We had a wedding last month where we served abalone soup with five-spiced pork belly along with a seared salmon in a lemon chive beurre blanc. A real hit. Everybody was happy.'

Jacqueline scowls at him. '*Something for everybody* is gauche.

We wanted to streamline the menu, keep it elegant. The only alternatives I asked for were vegetarian offerings, but I see nothing besides the mushroom duxelles in the appetizer section. Are my vegetarian guests supposed to munch on chopped mushrooms all night like scavengers? And what is this? You've spelled "mousseline" incorrectly.'

'That's why they call her Mousse-a-lini,' Cecilia stage-whispers to Cora.

'I'm very sorry about this, Ms Lee,' Gabriel says. He looks over his shoulder. 'There will be a ten-minute wait before the next course.'

Jacqueline sniffs. 'Thank you, I'll be counting down.'

As Gabriel hurries away, Jacqueline turns to Cecilia and says, 'Behave yourself.'

Cecilia pouts and takes another sip. 'I'm fine,' she says. 'I'm just in a celebratory mood. You could lighten up.'

'Let's talk about something else,' Ma'am Elizabeth interjects. 'Cecilia, you caught up with some old friends this morning, didn't you? How's Dominic Shen doing?'

'He started a company,' Cecilia says. 'One of those themed office share space things. It's super exclusive, though; you have to go through a rigorous selection process just to get in. They have a chef and barista who make customized meals for all the clients. Oh, and his family's private *getai* performance is going to be huge this year.'

'Bigger than last year? I can still hear those high *erhu* notes.'

'They're pulling out all the stops because they're in competition with his uncle's family in Taiwan,' Cecilia says. 'Cora, have you ever been to a *getai* performance? They have these outdoor singing performances in the middle of Hungry Ghost Festival to please the spirits.'

'I've seen them,' Cora says. She has walked past the make-shift stages and the long rows of red chairs, singers in puffy tulle skirts and sequined bodices crooning along with the band. The first time she ever saw one, she thought it was an outdoor wedding and she wondered why the front row of seats was empty. 'Don't stare,' an elderly man warned her. 'That is where the ghosts are sitting.'

'I don't know if Dominic was kidding, but he said his father was thinking of paying to invent and patent a particular mooncake flavour. Adzuki beans and dark chocolate, with rose essence. It doesn't sound bad. Do you know about the Mooncake Festival, Cora?' Cecilia asks.

'Of course she does,' Jacqueline interrupts. 'She lived here for years, didn't you, Cora?'

Cora nods. She doesn't understand why Jacqueline's question sounds so pointed.

'That's right, I forgot,' says Cecilia. 'You worked for the Gomezes. Why did I think you're fresh from the Philippines?'

'She took a long break,' Jacqueline says before Cora can answer. 'We hired her straight from Manila.'

Ma'am Elizabeth is oblivious to the change in mood at the table, and to Cora's trembling hands. She continues speculating about Cecilia's friend. 'Surely his father is bankrolling a portion of his start-up, if not the whole thing. He bought Dominic's sister an apartment in The Hamilton, didn't he?'

'How did you know that? I thought you don't really hang around with them.'

'I read about it in the paper,' Ma'am Elizabeth said. 'It was a record bid. That's the building on Scotts Road where you drive your car into an elevator. It brings your car up to your apartment so you can keep an eye on it from behind a glass wall.'

'Clever invention,' Cecilia says, sarcastically. 'People must have an eye on their Porsches at all times for security reasons.'

'That building has more security than an airport,' Ma'am Elizabeth replies. 'People want to drool over their Porsches instead of talking to their families.'

'Excuse me, what is that?' Jacqueline's voice snaps everybody to attention again. Cora looks up from her napkin to see a screen descending from the ceiling. Gabriel hustles back to the table. Despite the air-conditioning, a sheen of sweat makes the bright lights reflect off his forehead.

'The screen, Miss Lee.'

'Yes, I'm aware it's a screen. What is it doing here? Are we broadcasting my nuptials live? Is this the World Cup?'

'I had a conversation with our in-house wedding planning consultant, who said you might want to show some childhood videos of the two of you. A background slideshow will tie the whole theme together,' Gabriel says.

'The theme,' Jacqueline repeats. The word makes razor blades of her lips. 'And what exactly is this *theme*?'

'Eternal love?' Gabriel squeaks.

Cecilia is hiding her face in her hands, but she cannot fully muffle her laughter. Ma'am Elizabeth begins to say some soothing words to Jacqueline, but the damage only gets worse. Gabriel, fumbling with the remote control to retract the screen, instead triggers a loop of automatic channel flipping. The screen turns from black to blue to the ear-splitting roar of the No Signal channel.

'Just turn it off,' Jacqueline says through gritted teeth.

'I'm trying,' Gabriel says. He mutes the speakers. Now a silent drama is flashing across the screen involving a sword fight and a half-naked woman on a horse. 'Oh, goody, I haven't seen this season yet,' Cecilia chirps.

Jacqueline pushes her chair out and storms out of the banquet hall. 'Let her go,' Ma'am Elizabeth says, grabbing Cecilia's elbow as she rises to follow Jacqueline. 'She can get some fresh air on the terrace and start over. And stop being so flippant, will you? This is important to your sister.'

'You're always taking her side,' Cecilia says with a pout.

'That's not true.'

'You didn't say anything when she told me off this afternoon for gaining too much weight for the bridesmaid's dress.'

'Cecilia, I can't get between your squabbles. You aren't children any more.'

Cora decides this is a good time to excuse herself to go to the bathroom. Walking across the banquet hall, she feels the chill of the air-conditioning raising the hairs on her arms. It was a mistake to come here, to accept the wedding invitation at all. She wonders if she can pretend to be ill and take a taxi home, but the thought of Ma'am Elizabeth's concerned face makes her feel too guilty.

Then Cecilia shrieks. It is such a piercing sound that Cora is convinced that Jacqueline has returned to tackle her to the ground, but as she turns around, her eye catches on the huge screen and she gasps. On a news channel, filling up an entire wall of this glittering banquet room, is Mrs Fann Poh Choo.

Dressed in a navy-blue blazer, she appears more official, more frightening, than Cora remembers. The caption at the bottom of the screen reads: BREAKING NEWS: SAGE New Leadership Are Members of Singapore Megachurch.

'What the hell?' Cecilia is saying. Ma'am Elizabeth looks a little pale as well. Another caption flashes across the screen: Fann Poh Choo, New President, Outlines New Plans for Organization. Gabriel dives to the floor and belly-crawls behind the screen. It looks as if he is trying to hide behind Mrs Fann's gigantic head, but Cora sees him yanking a cord and, a moment later, there is a pop and the screen goes blank.

As Cecilia and Elizabeth explode with chatter, Cora hurries away to the bathroom. In a stall, she tries to process what she just saw. She pulls out her phone and sends Donita a message: *Just saw your ma'am on the news!!* There is no reply from Donita but she can't expect one. If Mrs Fann has a new title, Cora can only imagine what Donita must be tasked with. Cora looks up SAGE online. The headlines pop up like thought bubbles.

Will Original SAGE Leaders Fight Back?

Society for the Advancement of Gender Equality Was Taking Singapore Astray, New Leadership Says.

Sex Education Programme to Undergo 'Significant Revisions': Fann Poh Choo, New SAGE President.

Cora taps the last link to open the article. Mrs Fann stares, unsmiling. A gold cross glints against her skin.

The Society for the Advancement of Gender Equality will no longer run its comprehensive sex education programme in schools, says the new leadership.

The decision was announced in a press conference with new President Fann Poh Choo and Vice President Dr Lena Teo. The women were elected for the first time in the SAGE annual general meeting on Tuesday evening, which saw a surge in new members just before the election.

During the conference, the new leadership downplayed accusations that they had orchestrated a coup to bring their religious views into an organization that has been secular and accessible to all women in Singapore since its founding in 1989. Although all members of the new leadership have been identified as members of the Rising Star Church on East Coast Road, Fann repeatedly stated: 'This is not some kind of hijacking. We are doing this out of love and concern for our young people.'

Fann outlined the committee's plans for a new sex education plan that 'removes condoning of homosexuality or gender fluidity, as many Singaporean parents have concerns about these elements indoctrinating our children.' SAGE's current sex education programme describes same-sex relationships as 'healthy and normal like heterosexual relationships, as long as they are consensual'. Facilitators have also been known to ask students for their gender pronouns at the start of their sessions.

'We cannot be complacent about the corruption of our Asian way of life,' Fann said. 'This is a battle we are fighting for morality and for the sake of our family values.'

Former SAGE President Nadya Hashim and Vice President Ang Jia Ying have released a statement about their shocking ousting. 'The church carried out a covert membership drive to bring in voters to sway the election in their favour. It's clear that there is an agenda to corrupt our children's education with their religious teachings. What else will they do?'

There has been no word on whether the former committee would contest the election, but Hashim says: 'Our lawyers are looking into the legalities of the matter.'

Meanwhile, the new SAGE leaders are acting quickly. A newsletter explaining SAGE's new mission was sent to educators who previously participated in the sex education workshop, urging them to discard old materials, which included guides on condom usage and a cartoon map called 'Is it consensual?' They will be replaced by materials from Family Matters, a Texas publisher which promotes abstinence-based sex education.

Cora is so absorbed in reading the news that she doesn't at first register the sounds outside the door – the clip of stilettos, the water running. Those shoes, seen through the gap under the door, are Jacqueline's. She drops her phone back into her purse and flushes the toilet to collect herself before coming out of the stall.

Jacqueline is prodding at the skin beneath her eyes with her index and middle fingers. Whatever bags she's trying to annihilate don't exist anyway – her skin is flawless, and under these softer lights in the bathroom, her sternness is diminished.

'What a terrible mess this food tasting is,' Jacqueline says.

A mess? This hotel is a fortress of gleaming silverware and dizzyingly high ceilings. The platters were filled with dishes so exquisitely rich and beautiful that they could be jewels.

'It will be okay, Miss Jacqueline,' Cora says. 'There's still time to make all the changes you want.'

Jacqueline pinches the bridge of her nose and takes a deep breath. 'Time – people always think we can just wait, wait, wait and, miraculously, everything falls into place.' She turns to face Cora. 'Life doesn't work like that. Somebody has to be making sure of things. Doing the legwork. Making sure instructions are properly followed through.'

'Of course, Miss Jacqueline, but also you must try to enjoy—'

'Do you need to be managed, Cora?'

Taken aback, Cora stares at Jacqueline to try to understand what she's saying. 'Excuse me?'

'Does my mother follow you around the house telling you to do things?'

'Never,' Cora says. 'I take initiative.'

'I've noticed,' Jacqueline says. 'You've had a lot of *initiatives* around the house lately. Changing the décor, reviving the old dishes. I see you've really brought the place to life.'

Is she drunk, Cora wonders as Jacqueline steps towards her. 'Miss Jacqueline,' she begins. Jacqueline's appraisal of Cora is cold and steely.

'I thought we had an agreement,' Jacqueline says. 'I asked you to talk to my mother about the family business. To put it in her mind, make her think it's a good idea. *Her* idea. What have you done instead, Cora? Made our house more comfortable so she can stay a hermit for ever?'

'Whatever Ma'am Elizabeth wants is her choice. I cannot make her do anything,' Cora says. Her voice trembles.

'Of course you can. Be convincing. I paid you, didn't I? She values your opinion. You're behaving like a helpless maid now, but look at this.' Jacqueline makes a long sweep in the air from Cora's head to her toes. 'All dressed up, sitting at the table. It comes with responsibility, you understand? You don't just get to play dress-up and come to our parties without doing the work.'

Cora wishes she had her wedding invitation so she could hand it back to Jacqueline. *I didn't ask for this*, she thinks. 'Miss Jacqueline, if you feel I don't belong here, I can leave,' she says. She prides herself in staring Jacqueline squarely in the eyes as she says this. It has an effect. A ripple of uncertainty crosses Jacqueline's face as Cora sweeps past her, tucking her purse under her arm.

'I've spoken to your previous employers,' Jacqueline says.

Cora freezes in the wide powder-room foyer. She sees her startled reflection in the mirror and Jacqueline behind her, arms crossed over her chest.

'The Calverts,' Jacqueline continues. 'I believe the Merry Maids agency got in touch with my mother as well but she wasn't very responsive, so Belinda Quek asked me about it in church last Sunday. She has to keep her paperwork in order these days since some girl from Myanmar complained that she was forced to work in the family's catering business.'

Cora swallows. 'Ma'am, I can explain,' she says. In front of her are two plump velvet chaises, facing each other. She imagines the absurdity of sitting down with Jacqueline in this hotel bathroom so she can detail her escape from Manila.

Jacqueline takes a compact out of her purse and takes her time patting her cheekbones, turning to her own mirror as she does this. Cora turns around to watch and wait. 'All they said was that you betrayed their trust. I suppose they wanted to be gracious so they didn't say much more.'

Cora's breath catches. She feels relief and guilt at the same time. Gracious, yes – the Calverts could have told Jacqueline what Cora did. But it would have been embarrassing for them too.

Jacqueline, Cora realizes, is not waiting for an explanation. She snaps her compact shut and slips it back into her purse. 'I'm guessing you took something from them, yes? Something valuable? What was it? A silk? An antique?'

Of course, to Jacqueline, the only thing of value that can be stolen is expensive. Cora says nothing.

'What Mrs Calvert did tell me was that there was some issue with your nephew. She found out after you left that he was into drugs, so the situation must have been desperate, for whatever you did.'

Cora closes her eyes. 'Mrs Calvert said this?'

'She said some men showed up looking for you. They waited outside the gates of the Calverts' community and approached her when she was on her way to an appointment. Your actions have consequences, Cora. You have to remember that. Now who were they?'

Cora's whole body is shaking now. Jacqueline crosses her arms over her chest. 'Who were they? Come on. Don't lie, I can find out easily. A private investigator in Manila costs nothing. God knows my mother still has a whole legion of detectives on retainer after chasing my father around Asia on his indiscretions.'

Tears fill Cora's eyes. If the men came after the Calverts, were they safe? How about the children? Their school had high security too, but Madison liked to walk to High Street for doughnuts at Krispy Kreme with her friends after soccer practice. How many lives did Cora ruin in order to save her own?

'Out with it then. Who were they? What did they want?'

'Police,' Cora whispers finally. Plain-clothes officers. Or thugs. Same difference after the election. She knows she could lie and say 'loan sharks' or 'some gang members' but what does that make her? A person who gets involved with those types of people? She'd rather tell the truth.

Jacqueline's eyes widen. 'So you're running from the law? Now that's very serious. That could get you into a lot of trouble here.'

'I can explain,' Cora pleads. 'My nephew didn't do anything wrong.'

Jacqueline takes a step towards Cora and puts a hand on her shoulder. Her expression remains as hard as a fist. 'I am sorry for what you went through,' she says. 'You understand, don't you, what this could do for our family's image?'

Cora nods and wipes the tears from her cheeks. 'Miss Jacqueline, please,' she says again. She doesn't know what she's pleading for. Jacqueline pops open her clutch and takes out a tissue. Its lavender scent makes Cora feel nauseated.

'My mother takes these for anxiety,' Jacqueline says, holding up a small white bottle. She hands it to Cora. 'She needs an extra dose sometimes to help her really relax.'

'I am not going to feed drugs to your mother,' Cora says.

'Yes you are,' Jacqueline says calmly. 'You can crush them into your fabulous Teochew porridge. She won't know the difference.'

Cora shakes her head vehemently. Jacqueline grabs her hand and pushes the bottle roughly into it. She wraps Cora's fingers around the bottle and squeezes it tight.

'You get my mother to sign those papers, and all is forgiven,' Jacqueline says before walking out.

From the Ma'am Facebook pages:

Nikola Herber: Hi ladies! With Hungry Ghost Festival around, please remind your domestic workers that the food offerings are not for them. If you recall last year there was a case where a construction worker in Pasir Ris mistook some packets of rice for a donation meal, and it attracted a lot of ugly comments about migrant workers. If you see something like that happening, just gently remind them. There's no need to take photos and publicize it over social media.

Jovina Sim: LOL I was away on a business trip in Tokyo last year and missed this news entirely. Did somebody truly think that the food left on the ground was for him to eat? Obviously it's for dead ancestors, cannot be so stupid right?

Nikola Herber: Here's the news link about it from Big Island Weekly. It was an honest mistake. There was a retiree in that block who often bought packet food to treat the workers. The offering of chicken rice was in the same type of Styrofoam container, so the worker thought it was for him. There's no need to call them stupid.

Jovina Sim: I wasn't calling the worker stupid. I was calling you stupid.

Nikola Herber: That's uncalled for. Moderators, please remove this member.

Peiying Chen: Maybe he got possessed. That could be the reason the picture went around, not because people wanted to shame a migrant worker.

Nikola Herber: Possessed by what? The chicken?

Peiying Chen: Now you are the one being offensive. It is a known fact that messing with offerings can incur the wrath of the spirits. The offerings are for making peace with our ancestors.

Nikola Herber: A known FACT? Proven by science? And empirical studies? Are you seriously so dense?

Mia Ganesan: If you don't like this country and its customs, why are you here?

Nikola Herber: Go to hell. Or I should say, 'Go and join your ancestors.'

MESSAGE FROM MODERATORS: Singapore is a multicultural country and as such, we must respect the cultural and religious views of others. This group has a zero-tolerance policy against inflammatory language. Comments have been closed on this thread and the member who wrote the original post has been removed from the group.

Chapter Fourteen

This afternoon, it's a pair of beige underpants with a lacy trim along the waistband. Last Tuesday, it was a single athletic sock, and a few weeks ago, a striped towel with frayed edges. Mrs Mok, who lives upstairs, always arrives at their door with apologies and the same excuse for her laundry snapping off her bamboo pole and landing on the Fanns'. 'It's the wind, lah. Very strong nowadays,' she tells Donita when she comes to retrieve her fallen items.

Later, Donita sees her again as she is shuffling into the lift with Mrs Fann and her church boxes. Mrs Mok is getting out of the lift ahead of them. 'God bless you,' Mrs Mok says to Mrs Fann. She even offers to help, but Mrs Fann says, 'No, thank you, that's what my maid is for.'

'Anything you need, you just let me know,' Mrs Mok tells Mrs Fann. She slides her gold-rimmed glasses up her nose. 'What you're doing is very brave. You are a good woman.' Just for that, Donita vows to toss all her clothes off the pole next time, let the Moks' underwear fly all over Marine Parade. She can blame the wind.

Mrs Fann beams and graciously returns the blessings. These days, she walks around wearing a lanyard which dangles below her prominent cross necklace. People glance at it to confirm that she is really Fann Poh Choo, the woman who has been in the news, the new president of SAGE. 'Have to keep it on, even if it puts me in danger,' Mrs Fann told Donita. 'I need my supporters to know that I am on the ground. Then if any you-know-whos try to make trouble with me, people won't hesitate to rush to my defence.'

The compliment from Mrs Mok keeps Mrs Fann afloat while Donita struggles to maintain her grip on the cardboard box full of pamphlets. 'Sex Education Programme' is printed in stern official font across each one. Mrs Fann picked them up from the printers yesterday but forgot to take the keys to the church office with her so she had to bring them all home. Now she needs them loaded into the car so she can take them to the SAGE office which, according to Google Maps, is a twenty-minute drive away on the west side of the island. Twenty minutes there, twenty minutes back. Maybe she'll spend some time in the office, maybe not.

Her schedule has become unpredictable since she and her church friends took over SAGE, but Donita just needs an hour to go to the clinic in Jalan Besar. That's where all of the answers about Flordeliza will be.

'Gently,' Mrs Fann barks as Donita lowers the box into the boot, as if it holds precious crystal instead of pamphlets about abstinence. Yesterday, Donita opened one to find a long red list of DON'Ts, followed by a hotline number for the church.

*If you are feeling romantic urges, **DO** the following things instead: Talk to a friend. Watch a parentally approved movie. Take a walk or play a sport. Remember that urges pass. Intimacy is for married adults.*

If she were still talking to Sanjeev, she'd take a picture and send it to him with a dirty message about all the ways they could rebel against these suggestions. They haven't spoken since their fight outside the Esplanade. If Sanjeev has tried to contact Donita, she isn't aware of it because she blocked his number.

Under the glaring sun in the open-air car park, Mrs Fann rattles off a list of things she wants finished by the time she returns. Sweep the floors, mop them, clean the blades of the fans, replace the dehumidifiers, unhook the curtains and wash them. 'The news crew is coming next week but I want you to start keeping the house clean now,' Mrs Fann says. Donita's mind plays a reel of fantasy revenge scenes: leaving the rubbish chute wide open so the news crew walks into a living room filled with the stench of rotting food. Or replacing Mrs Fann's whitening deodorant with black shoe polish so when she raises her arms, the tarry streaks on her armpits make her look like somebody who doesn't bathe. Or taking down the notices for insect fumigation so Mrs Fann invites the news crew on the wrong day, and they arrive just as the last surviving roaches are juddering their wings and flying in frantic circles to escape the poison, and the whole country's first view of Mrs Fann is of dying cockroaches.

'Aiyah,' Mrs Fann says as she opens the car door. 'Forgot my phone upstairs. Go and get it, Donita. It's on the dining table.'

Donita does another calculation as she enters the lift and presses the button. A round-trip journey to the clinic by taxi would take much less time, and if Mrs Fann is out for, say, two hours, she'll be able to do some investigating. Donita could say she needs to know what time to expect Mrs Fann to be home so she can serve her dinner warm. Mrs Fann was just complaining the other day that the reheated leftovers always had cold spots in the centre.

A pungent smell hits Donita as she steps out of the lift, but she doesn't realize it's coming from the Fanns' flat until she gets closer to the gate. By then it's overpowering, the stench of fish guts and entrails which are strewn through the alcove. Somebody has flung them through the grilles of the gate in the few minutes they've been downstairs. Donita gags and steps back into the lift. As she descends towards Mrs Fann to tell her what's happened, she knows already she's going to be blamed for it.

'Ma'am, somebody throw fish at the gate.'

Mrs Fann's eyes widen. 'Who would do that? One of your friends, is it? Loan sharks? Who was it?'

'I don't know, ma'am. You must come up and see.'

Mrs Fann follows her up to the flat and shrieks when she sees it. 'Donita, who did this?'

Her voice bounces across the walls. Donita's eyes follow the tiny beige tiles and scan the trunks of pipes that run up the walls in the landing between Mrs Fann and her neighbours. She unlocks the gate and steps gingerly into the stinking alcove. About to open the door, her eye catches a flash of white in the shadows near the shoe rack. A postcard, thrown so far through the grilles that it almost disappeared between a pair of Mr Fann's black flip-flops. She picks it up and, as she turns to hand it to Mrs Fann, she sees the message written in stark capitals:

YOU DO NOT SPEAK FOR ALL WOMEN.
STEP DOWN FROM SAGE.

The colour drains from Mrs Fann's cheeks as she reads the postcard. Beneath her heavy make-up, Donita can see her bare fear. What does she expect? Each time Mrs Fann replayed her television unveiling on her phone, she stopped the video just before the camera cut to the former president and vice president of the organization, whose voices were hoarse with shock and anger. Donita watched the whole thing in her room last night.

'I don't know how these women can walk in and tear down three decades of advocacy work for gender equality,' a woman named Nadya Hashim said. 'Are these new leaders qualified to handle the calls from domestic violence victims on our hotline? Or are they going to tell them to be better wives? Why are they doing this? They can't even say the word "feminist" and they refer to members of the LGBTQ community as "you-know-whos", as if this identity is so shameful that it needs to be erased.'

They both jump at the sound of the door of the opposite flat opening. The neighbour, a sprightly retired woman named Doris who also congratulated Mrs Fann when they crossed paths yesterday, is talking on her phone and barely notices them.

Her appearance seems to break the spell, and Mrs Fann straightens her back and regards Donita, her eyes full of contempt.

'Why are you just standing there? Get my phone,' she says. 'And use the heavy duty Jif under the cabinet to scrub the floors. Throw out the welcome mat, I'll buy a new one. Wash all of the shoes.'

It's got nothing to do with me, Donita wants to say again, just to remind Mrs Fann that she has invited her own troubles, that she is not immune to this kind of ugliness. But what's the point? She still has to clean up the mess. There is no way Donita will be able to go to the clinic now that Mrs Fann is watching her so closely.

Donita is finally done with her work for the day, and the Fanns are asleep. The night is quiet and the air smells like burning.

It is the season of the Hungry Ghost, the month where the gates of hell open and spirits roam the island to feast on offerings from the living. The pavements are littered with scraps of charred paper money. Black rings scar the grass next to offerings of pillowy *kuehs* and joss sticks glowing at the tips. Whenever Donita looks out through her window at night, she sees flames lurching from the gaping mouths of metal barrels.

She is almost unsurprised to see that same ghostly figure near the canal when she looks down. In the shadows, it could be mistaken for a young tree, but then it floats across a pale pool of moonlight and Donita sees shoulder-length hair and the outline of a dress. *Is it you, Flor? What have they done to you?* Donita whispers. It is impossible to see the woman's face, but the way her head is tipped up, it looks as if she is staring right at Donita. Then, as if a spell has broken, the ghost is gone, moving swiftly in the direction of the beach. Donita watches her leave and wishes she could escape with her.

Donita's fingers smell like bleach, her skin is gritty from the Jif, and the chemical lemony smell has seeped into her pores from cleaning this morning. Mrs Fann was only away from the flat for a few hours before she returned, agitated and shouting in Mandarin to Mr Fann. The two of them spent some time inspecting the alcove, and Donita stayed at the other end of the flat, arranging the items in Mrs Fann's vanity cabinet. As she reached into the back, she came across a glittering piece of costume jewellery. It looked a lot like the one that Mrs Fann had taken from her and thrown down the rubbish chute, but it was star-shaped and dotted with emerald rhinestones.

Now, Donita trains her gaze on the sawtooth rows of rooftops off East Coast Road. *What happened to Flor?* The question is as constant as the quickening of her heartbeat when she found Flordeliza's backpack in the Hongs' back yard that Sunday afternoon. The only way to find answers is to leave this flat. It is too risky to go poking around the back lanes of Jalan Besar at night, but if she can get into the Hong property and climb into Flordeliza's room, maybe there will be some evidence of her innocence. She rummages through her closet and picks the darkest clothes she can find – a black blouse and long black drawstring trousers to help her blend with the night.

Donita opens her room door carefully, knowing the precise amount of pressure she needs to keep the hinges from creaking. Reaching the main door, her heart begins to slam in her chest, but it's from exhilaration rather than fear. She opens it carefully, slips on her shoes, shuts the door slowly behind her, and works her key gently into the lock. Stepping past the gate and into the lift, Donita lets out a long breath that she didn't realize she was holding.

Crossing to Flordeliza's neighbourhood only takes two minutes. It is close to midnight so the path along the canal is bare, but a flash of night cyclists makes Donita freeze. Luckily they are too absorbed in their ride towards the beach to notice her. From the tide of crashing waves, the wind carries the sharp smell of salt. She hurries away from the sea until she arrives at the path behind the Hongs' house. The windows and curtains are shut, and the gate is closed. She looks around quickly before gripping the gate, hoping it's unlocked. It creaks but doesn't budge. 'Shit,' she says under her breath. Stepping back from the gate, she considers the steps she would need to take to scale it. The windows of the Hongs' house are dark save for a faint light glowing in the high window of what must be a bathroom.

The sudden clap of footsteps sends Donita diving to the ground. She crawls on her belly along the pebbled ground until she is safely crouching behind a row of hedges lining the property. Joss sticks form a spiky border on the edge of the grass, where the breeze is stirring a mound of fine ashes from a paper money offering.

She hears low chatter, a young woman's voice. Donita squeezes her knees to her chest and keeps her head down but her ears perked. A man's voice overlaps with the woman's now, and they stop walking. Donita raises her head just slightly to see them standing a few paces away from the back gate of the Hongs' home. The woman flicks her hair and Donita sees a flash of a high ponytail. It's Carolyn Hong's daughter, Elise. Parting the branches carefully, Donita is able to see her silhouette, but the man's shape is unfamiliar – a wide and boxy frame towering over the girl. Donita's heart clenches. Is the girl in danger? 'Please,' the man says. 'I just want you back. We had such a good thing together.' He takes Elise's hands and draws her to him. She leans away stiffly and says, 'That was before everything. I promised my Dad I would never see you again.' The man whispers something to Elise and she shakes her head. 'I can't,' she insists. 'I only came out tonight to tell you to stop. It's over.'

A rustle in the bushes gives Donita a jolt. Something is moving in here – just a bird, Donita hopes, or a cat slinking low to the ground. Just don't let it be a rat. Since the hungry ghost offerings started, Donita has seen them from her window, scurrying between open containers of braised pork and broiled cabbage. She has joked bitterly on her group chat with Angel and Cora that the island's rodents and dead ancestors are getting better meals than her.

A sharp squeak. Donita's hairs stand. She shifts back a little bit but she is too exposed, and as she rises onto her feet to inch back into the bushes, something – a tail, a claw – scrapes against Donita's bare ankle. She manages to swallow her scream, but she loses balance and falls to the ground. The movement catches the couple's attention and the man's footsteps rapidly approach. Instinct tells Donita to curl up her fingers like claws.

'What happened?' the man asks, with his hand extended, and she realizes he's helping her up.

'Who is it?' Elise calls uncertainly, her voice still low.

'You live around here?' The man is looking intently at Donita as she straightens and brushes the dust off her trousers. She tries not to stare back, but it's difficult because she recognizes his squared jaw and broad shoulders. It is the handsome swimming champion from the article that Angel sent her a few weeks back.

'Sterling?' Elise asks. 'Who is it?'

Sterling, that's his name. He glances nervously between Donita and Elise and clears his throat. 'Anyway, I just wanted to pass you the uhh . . . schedule for the next training session,' he says briskly. 'I'll see you in the pool tomorrow, Elise. Don't be late.'

You were once a couple, Donita thinks. *He wants to get back together.* This information doesn't hit her as strange until she remembers more facts about Sterling Luo from the article. *You're married. You're an adult; she's a teenager.* She stares after his shadow receding into the distance. Elise is watching her closely.

'I haven't seen you around here before,' Elise says.

Donita stares back at Elise but doesn't say anything. In her chest, her heart thrums.

'Where did you come from?' Elise asks.

Run. She doesn't owe Elise any answers, and she can leave without getting into further trouble. 'Sorry, I have to go,' Donita mumbles and, as she turns away, she sees it. Flordeliza's leather backpack, on Elise's back.

'Why are you carrying that bag?'

'It's mine,' Elise says. She bites her lower lip. 'Where did you come from?' she repeats. There is a slight quiver in her voice.

Donita ignores her question. 'All the things inside it are also yours?' she asks. 'The lipstick, the cash?'

Those details startle Elise. 'Who are you?' Elise's gaze lands on the bush where Donita was crouching earlier. There is an altar there with an open packet of sweets that attracted the rat that spooked Donita, awaiting the hunger of a roaming ghost.

A ghost like me, Donita thinks. She sees herself through Elise's fearful eyes – her long hair hanging from her shoulders because – in her haste to leave the house – she forgot to tie it up. Her loose black trousers and the billowing black blouse she wore to blend in with the night. The smudged ashes on her black clothes must be on her face and in her hair as well.

'You know where I came from,' Donita says, nodding towards the bush. The altar glows. Surrounded by darkness, she feels her courage building. 'Flordeliza told me everything.'

Elise shakes her head. 'This is ridiculous,' she mutters, making for the gate. 'You're not real.'

Donita steps in front of her to block her way but they both freeze when a light comes on. Elise is the first one to duck quickly, followed by Donita, who sees that the light is coming from a second-floor window. Crouching on the ground, she can see Mr Hong's silhouette in the window.

'He doesn't know that you were out with Sterling tonight, right?' Donita asks. Another detail occurs to her – the Ritz-Carlton hotel key that Flordeliza had mentioned Mrs Hong finding. It was evidence of an affair, but not Peter Hong's. 'The hotel room key. That was yours?'

Elise's eyes widen.

'I saw it,' Donita says. 'I saw your mother crying.' She recalls the words that Flordeliza overheard Carolyn saying on the phone to her friend. *How can he betray our trust?* Flordeliza mistook the conflict for a husband cheating on a wife, but it was actually Sterling Luo, whom they had entrusted with coaching their daughter in swimming. Had Elise's mother found out that they were still seeing each other? Did Carolyn threaten to report Sterling to the police?

'You pushed her,' Donita whispers. 'I saw it too.'

Elise sucks in her breath. 'I didn't do it.'

'Then who?'

'Flordeliza,' Elise says. 'She was trying to get into my parents' safe. Everybody knows that's what happened.'

'Everybody *thinks* that is what happened,' Donita says. 'Do not lie to me, I can keep coming back.' She can see the suggestion sending a ripple of fear through Elise. 'I'm the spirit of a falsely accused maid, and I am very angry,' she says. The wind makes the loose black trousers flap against her hips. 'What did you want from the safe? Money? Jewellery?'

Elise swallows but stays frozen, a rabbit in the headlights.

Donita continues, 'So your mother caught you and you pushed her?'

'I didn't push her,' Elise whimpers. 'Please, don't punish me for this.'

'Tell me who did it then.'

Elise shakes her head.

'I will follow you into the house,' Donita says. 'I will be there when you wake up. Whenever the lights go off, you'll see my face.'

Elise begins to cry. She sinks to the ground and buries her face in her hands. 'You confess to me,' Donita whispers. 'And I'll make sure no spirits bother you. Otherwise, we will all come to get the truth from you.' She has no idea if this is in fact what ghosts do, but she likes the idea.

'We were just trying to get my passport, okay? She wasn't supposed to be home.'

'Who is we?' Donita says. 'You and Sterling were going to run away?'

'She lunged at him first,' Elise says. 'She was shouting about how she was going to have him arrested, I was a minor, all that bullshit. She was in such a rage. Sterling was defending himself. He doesn't know his own strength.' In a small voice, she says, 'I didn't mean for Flordeliza to get caught up in all of this.'

'She is innocent,' Donita says. 'You have ruined her life.'

'Why won't she say where she was then? The police assumed it was her right away. Sterling and I thought I could buy enough time to leave, but when she didn't produce an alibi, we . . . we saw it as a chance, okay? I know it's not right, but Flor was clearly doing something she wasn't supposed to do either.'

'But not like this. Not murder,' Donita says. 'If she gets executed, it is your fault. It will haunt you for ever.'

It is satisfying to see Elise wincing at this prospect. 'Please leave me alone. It was an accident. Things just got carried away. After Sterling sneaked out of the house that day, I wanted to call the police and report him. I picked up the phone and looked at my mother lying on the floor and something came over me. I started screaming. I couldn't stop. Everything happened so quickly after that. I . . . I have these dreams about my mother, these awful nightmares. My father barely speaks to me.'

So Peter Hong is part of this cover-up. Better to dispose of the innocent maid than his daughter. She remembers the conversation she overheard between them – who were you talking to? He sounded like a father trying to control what his daughter said to outsiders. He must have sensed Elise's desperate need to confess to somebody.

Donita bores her eyes into Elise's. The girl shrinks with fear. 'Please,' she whispers. 'I have to live with this for the rest of my life.'

The back gate creaks open and Elise scrambles to her feet, while Donita shrinks back towards the shadows. Mr Hong's figure is even more imposing from her vantage point on the ground. 'Daddy,' Elise cries, running towards him.

'What are you doing out here?' he asks Elise, grabbing her by the shoulders.

'I heard something,' she tells him. Mr Hong's eyes dart quickly to her backpack.

'Get inside,' he says through gritted teeth and, sensing his distraction, Donita jumps to her feet and runs.

She prays that Mr Hong isn't giving chase as she sprints across the empty road and along the canal. The sea invites her back with a roaring breeze, and on the dark horizon, the hulking shadows of shipping containers grow as she approaches the Fanns' apartment block. The lights in the lift pulse with stark whiteness.

Slowly, slowly, Donita thinks as she concentrates on pushing the key into the lock and turning it. The gate opens with a deafening shrieking sound that makes Donita scream and drop to her knees. A second later, Mrs Fann is at the gate, dragging Donita inside by her wrist, shouting over the sound of the alarm. 'I knew it!' she shouts, tossing Donita back as she releases her wrists. Donita's head narrowly misses the edge of the alcove wall. 'I knew you were running around at night! You cannot be trusted.'

When did she install an alarm, Donita wonders in her stunned state as Mrs Fann leads her to the storeroom. That must have been what she and Mr Fann were doing at the gate this afternoon, after the fish incident. Mrs Fann opens the storeroom door and points to the floor.

'From now on, you will be sleeping there,' she says. There is a naked thin foam mattress, but the room is so narrow that the mattress is curved like a bowl between the walls.

'You want a pillow and bedding, you have to earn it back,' Mrs Fann continues. 'I will keep your phone.'

With an ache, Donita realizes that she left it in her room in her haste to leave. She didn't even have a chance to fight for it.

She won't give Mrs Fann the satisfaction of watching her beg for forgiveness. Instead she crosses her arms over her chest and stares at the woman, as if to say, 'I'll never be afraid of you.'

After Mrs Fann leaves, Donita stands in the storeroom, watching the darkness and waiting for her eyes to adjust to the shapes. Her mind swirls with everything she's learned about Carolyn Hong's murder – she whispers the details into the dark because she does not know when or how she will get to tell the story of Flor's innocence now. She resolves to remain upright for as long as possible, to fall asleep standing if it means she won't have to lie on the floor, on that pallet that even a dog would reject. But exhaustion eventually takes over, and in the middle of the night she wakes up, scrunched on the floor, muscles so stiff that she wonders if she is still alive.

Chapter Fifteen

There was a Ferrari burning in the middle of the street when Angel walked to the MRT station this morning.

The replica was about one third the size of an actual car, but the bright red paint and slanted windows were so lifelike that Angel joined a gathering of neighbours to watch the flames engulf it. The cardboard took time to crack and succumb to the fire, and the black twists of rising smoke made her eyes sting. There is a store up the road that sells the biggest paper replicas to send into the afterlife: towering mansions, pressed shirts, iPhones, model kitchens and laptops. Angel once saw a Louis Vuitton handbag – detailed to the last buckle and logo – that she was tempted to buy and send to Joy: 'more affordable than the real thing, just don't try to wash or put anything inside it.' She took a picture instead and sent it with the comment because she knew Joy would chide her for wasting money over a joke.

She arrives at Tiong Bahru Station and crosses the main intersection to find her way to Moh Guan Terrace. The quiet neighbourhood is filled with charming low-slung apartment blocks and breakfast cafés. Angel stops to take in the wall murals of old Singapore – a sari-clad woman reaching into her woven straw basket for money to purchase vegetables from a vendor's bicycle; four sitting men in white singlets peering at wooden bird cages. The apartment she's looking for is a brick-covered walk-up opposite a bookstore painted with a rainbow and the sign LOVE IS LOVE. The gate and door are open. 'Come in,' calls Zamir, whose voice Angel recognizes from the phone call.

He is swaying from side to side to calm the newborn strapped to his chest. 'It's like a bomb went off in here,' he jokes. Angel's gaze sweeps over the table scattered with breast-pump parts and packets of wet wipes, past the swing chair and the play gym and half-assembled bouncer. 'Don't worry, sir. It's the same for all new parents,' she says. It's not the mess Angel is worried about – it's all the possible places for hidden cameras.

Before shortlisting potential employers, Angel did some research online and found that cameras could be nestled in any household object. There are light fixtures sold with tiny embedded cameras, books that blend in with libraries with beady little eyes watching everything. She even came across a framed image of *The Starry Night* – Suzan's favourite painting. A bulky gilded frame hiding the camera fought for attention with the whorls of wind and clouds reprinted in an unnatural hue.

Once the baby's mewling settles, the wife, Shu-yen, tiptoes out of the bedroom. 'Sorry,' she whispers. 'We are trying to train Lin to sleep on somebody other than me. It only works when I'm out of the room.' She peers at the baby and adjusts the moss-green fabric wrap keeping the baby bound to her husband's chest. 'My maternity leave ends in three weeks,' she tells Angel. 'So of course your main duty will be Lin. You've taken care of infants before?'

'Yes ma'am.' In her third job, she was expected to stay up all night with a shrieking colicky infant named Rushani. The flat overlooked the Old Airport Road food centre, which was open twenty-four hours, and watching the people downstairs go about their lives at two in the morning made Angel forget her fatigue. Rushani's parents also required that Angel keep a logbook detailing their child's every bowel movement, time of feeding (quantity, duration), nap time and disposition.

Will this be a similarly round-the-clock job? It's hard to say, but Zamir and Shu-yen seem more reasonable.

'I'll show you around,' says Shu-yen. She takes Angel through a narrow corridor to the kitchen first, where she points out the second freezer for storing breast milk and the area of the kitchen they have cleared for her. 'You'll get a weekly allowance to buy your own food,' Shu-yen says, before leading Angel through the rest of the apartment. A wide window in the master bedroom looks out over the community gardens, where plump tomatoes blush between tall vines and wooden stakes.

Angel tells the couple she will think about it, and at the door, Zamir says, 'I'm sure you have your pick of jobs. That was an impressive advertisement your employer posted.'

Angel bows her head deferentially to suggest the compliment is too good for her. She knows he is right.

This morning, she interviewed with a ma'am in a Toast Box outlet in Buona Vista who said she chose a mutual public place for the first meeting because she wanted Angel to feel safe and able to leave at any time. After that, Angel inched her way east to a red-brick apartment block where a cheerful teenaged boy tried to practise his Tagalog with her. 'I've been learning from an app,' he said proudly. And there is a German expat family in Mount Sophia who offered such a high salary over the phone that she almost accepted the job without meeting them.

In each interview, Angel dutifully recited a list of skills, but her mind lingered on what she would miss about her life in the Vijays' home – the smell of wet leaves after a night rainfall and orioles shooting like stars between tree branches; the dogs lolling in the hallway and the occasional shudder from the fridge. The everyday things. This morning, she ran into Rubylyn, the helper from upstairs, who commented that she looked nice.

'Interviews,' Angel said, feeling a pang of sadness as she explained that she would be moving on from the Vijays' home.

'I'll see if there's anything in this area,' Rubylyn told Angel. 'It would be nice if you didn't have to leave.' They exchanged numbers for the first time.

Angel goes down the stairs and watches the neighbourhood from under the shelter of the rounded balcony. Could she work here? Could she live here? The thought of starting afresh fills her with hope and trepidation. Every household is its own world, with its rules and rhythms, and Angel knows that the decision she makes now will impact how she lives her life for the next few years.

Tables are being set up on the pavement outside a café and a young woman is standing against a mural in the wide alley between shops, posing for a professional photograph. The morning is unfurling, and Angel is looking for a new place to call home.

The high cast-iron gates of the Botanic Gardens tower over Cora's lone figure. Angel hasn't spent a Sunday here since she came for a picnic with Suzan, and they managed to find a shaded private spot in a gazebo to watch turtles stretch their necks on the black rocks sprouting along the edges of the shallow pond. Tourists pour from the nearby MRT station and crowd at the entrance, the brims of their hats casting shadowy bands over their eyes. With the greenery of the park frothing behind them, the air is so thick with moisture that Angel could almost scoop it up with her hands.

'Am I late?' she asks, because Cora looks stricken. It's probably only a grimace against the stinging sunlight.

'No,' Cora says. 'Let's talk inside.'

They shuffle along with the crowd and, as soon as they enter, it is like walking into the outstretched arms of a relative. The gardens, abundant and serene, the electric chirps of crickets. Two little boys wearing identical bucket hats prance around the shaggy shrubs where a monitor lizard is taking deliberate steps. 'Dinosaur,' they whisper, enthralled.

'You live so near and you still wanted to come here on your day off?' Angel jokes. Cora returns a weak smile. Something is wrong now, Angel can tell. They come to a fork in the path; one path runs under the shade of a long trellis, while the other drops away to a rolling green field, so bright that Angel has to make a visor of her palm to shield her eyes from the sun.

'I wanted to see you.' Cora has her arms crossed tightly around her chest. It is as if she is holding pieces of herself together. 'I need to tell somebody . . .' she manages to say before the sobs take over her body.

'Cora, what happened?' Angel asks, steering Cora to an angsana tree with wide branches drooping over a carpet of shed yellow flowers. Angel takes her hand and presses it between her two palms. Only grief can destroy a person like this. 'Raymond?' she asks softly.

At the sound of her nephew's name, Cora squeezes her eyes shut. 'He didn't do anything wrong. Why couldn't they leave him alone?'

Angel keeps Cora's hands in hers and tries to understand Cora's teary rambling. Something about Raymond, something about his university friends. When she says Ma'am Elizabeth's name, Angel knows that this is not just about mourning something from the past. 'Take a deep breath,' she says. Cora's chest heaves. Her voice halts as she unfolds the story for Angel to see: the Martells; the wealthy clique from Raymond's university; Marco Vallares; the drugs; the betrayal – Raymond's murder.

'Oh Cora,' Angel gasps. She knows the power of confession, and she can feel something like relief coursing through Cora's body as she tells this story, but she has to resist the urge to cover her ears. It was difficult enough to read about these dreadful injustices after the war on drugs was declared, but *Raymond*. Cora's boy. Angel fights back tears.

'Afterwards, the whole neighbourhood became afraid to talk to me or be seen with me. I didn't care. Every chance I had, I told people that Raymond was innocent. They knew him. They knew he wasn't capable of something like this.'

'Was it his friend, Marco?' Angel asks.

'I don't know for sure,' Cora says. 'But he was with the Martells that night in the club. There was a picture of all of them in the news the next day: "Society Girls in Drug Bust, Police Say Shabu Supplier Caught". I don't know if he gave them Raymond's name to deflect the blame from himself, or if Sabrina Martell offered Raymond's name so the police would leave them alone. I went around telling everybody that the Martell family had my Raymond's blood on their hands.'

Now Angel remembers the nasty comment that she saw on

Cora's Facebook page before it was taken down. *May God forgive Raymond's sins.* Despite the sun's hard glare on the grass, she feels a chill throughout her body. She can imagine the fiery Cora she knew from years ago, walking through the lanes of the *barangay*, pushing her way into gossip circles to correct everybody who dishonoured her late nephew's name. She knows too how dangerous this would have been. 'Did they come after you then?' Angel asks.

'Didn't take them long. Exactly a week later, they showed up at my door and warned me to stop spreading false rumours. It was three men wearing shorts and sandals and white singlets. I didn't know if they were policemen in plain clothes or hired thugs.'

'Hired by the Martells?'

'Possibly,' Cora says. 'But who knows any more? One man kicked a glass bottle through my gate. The glass smashed and scattered into the house. I was picking out glass from my shoes when I realized they would come back for me. I made up a story about road closures and asked my employers if I could stay with them in Dasmariñas.'

'Thank goodness,' Angel murmurs. Those thugs wouldn't get past security in a gated neighbourhood.

'I thought I was safe there too,' Cora says. 'But then the calls started coming, in the middle of the night, shouting at me for causing trouble. A journalist from a newspaper in Hong Kong had heard about the story, and there was an article about it. No names were mentioned, so the Calverts never made the connection: the journalists wrote about a relative going door-to-door to save a young man's reputation. It could have been anyone, in any place in the Philippines. Since the war on drugs started, there were many cases like Raymond's. But they focused on me because I blamed the Martell family.'

'So that is why you came back to Singapore,' Angel says, understanding now. Cora's quiet re-entry, her deflated demeanour, her insistence that they didn't become involved with Flordeliza's arrest when Cora used to be so outspoken: they were signs of what she had endured in her final weeks back home – a hasty escape after roaring through her *barangay*, her grief and fury spreading like a fire through its streets.

'Luckily I stayed in touch with my old employer, Ma'am Anne-Marie Gomez, all these years. She connected me with Ma'am Elizabeth,' Cora says, her voice breaking again. Angel knows she must be worrying about losing her job.

'She is very understanding,' Angel assures Cora. 'She will know it's not your fault.'

'It's not just that, though.' Cora's voice is strangled. 'It's Ma'am Elizabeth's business. My reputation could tarnish it.'

'Oh Cora.' Angel scoots closer to Cora and envelops her in a hug. There aren't any words of consolation for what Cora is going through. All she can offer is silence.

'Cora,' Angel says finally. 'It wasn't your fault. You were just trying to protect Raymond.'

Cora hesitates and gives Angel a furtive look. 'Yes,' she says finally, wiping her eyes. 'That was all I was doing.'

Is there more Cora hasn't told her? In any case, her friend was surely only doing her best.

'Cora, I know you, I'm sure you wouldn't have done anything without a good reason.'

They sit together in silence, watching the grass darken under the shadows of merging clouds. The blades prickle Angel's bare ankles. Her mind goes back to her first Sunday catch-up with Cora in Orchard Road after Cora got in touch. She should have asked Cora then about what was weighing her down, instead of letting her struggle with her grief alone for so long. Maybe she can offer Cora some advice from her own afternoon of interviews.

'Sometimes a change of scenery isn't such a bad thing,' Angel says. She thinks about the cosy atmosphere of Tiong Bahru, or the possibility of working in Mount Sophia. 'If you're interested in changing jobs, I could get you in touch with some of the families that I interviewed with today.'

Cora shakes her head. 'I can't keep running away.'

'Running away from what?' Angel asks.

Cora takes a long swig from her water bottle and doesn't reply. Angel wants to ask again, but she's afraid of pushing Cora too far. The clouds in the sky have shifted and the sun is suddenly blindingly bright.

'I need something to drink too,' Angel says, eyeing a vending machine near the visitor information centre. It's not just thirst that compels her to move; Cora's story, the injustice of it, fills Angel with adrenaline. She doesn't know what to do with this energy except to walk it off.

'I'll wait here,' Cora says.

As Angel crosses the field and finds herself on the concrete path again, her mind churns with angry thoughts about the Martells. She is also filled with admiration for Cora – only a brave or a foolish person would dare to say anything about those people. Cora is brave. Angel wants her to know that. This is what she'll say to Cora: you are brave. You don't have anything to apologize for.

Angel puts her coins into the vending machine slot and chooses a can of Pokka Jasmine Green Tea. It lands with a thunk; as she bends to pick it up, her eye catches the words Maid Mutiny? printed across a discarded copy of the free daily newspaper, *Big Island Weekly*. Somebody has left this copy on the bench next to the vending machine.

Below the headline is a picture of Mr Hong and his daughter, and a sub-header: Big Island Weekly *EXCLUSIVE! Family of Slain Woman Says Filipina Woman Lurking Behind Their Home.*

Angel picks up the newspaper and reads the rest of the article.

The Hong family has been through their share of tragedy recently. Carolyn Hong was allegedly murdered by her domestic helper during a robbery gone wrong, leaving her only daughter Elise without a mother. Now Mrs Hong's widower says that they have fallen victim to a cruel prank. A Filipina woman dressed as a ghost visited the house on Friday evening to scare Elise into declaring the alleged killer Flordeliza Martinez innocent.

'My daughter is grieving and she's very impressionable,' says Mr Hong. 'She went along with whatever that woman told her to say because she was scared. I don't know who would do a thing like this in a time when we are just looking for answers and closure.'

Police are now investigating the incident. Ms Martinez maintains her innocence. She is due to be formally charged next week.

Angel fishes out her phone. An alert came in earlier this morning, but she was so busy with her interviews that she didn't notice. There is a link to an online version of the article, which Angel skims quickly before breathing out a sigh of relief. As far as she can see, there is no description of Donita.

She races back to Cora, waving the newspaper at her. 'Have you seen this?' she asks breathlessly. 'The Hong family says they caught some woman lurking behind their house,' Angel says. 'They made a police report yesterday.'

'Who was it?' Cora asks.

'Who do you think?'

'Donita?' Panic deepens the lines on Cora's forehead.

'Possibly,' Angel says. 'Have you heard from her?'

Cora shakes her head and takes the newspaper from Angel. She reads silently but her mouth twitches as she quickly takes in the information. 'I wonder why he defended his daughter like that,' Cora says.

'What do you mean?'

'I mean, saying "my daughter was scared, she's grieving". It's like he's rushing to make an excuse for her. What did she tell Donita?'

Angel takes out her phone and scrolls through the article. In the online version, a gallery of photographs heads the page. Angel clicks through them, seeing the same pictures that have accompanied every article about the Hong murder: the two-storey house rising behind iron gates; the headshot of Carolyn Hong; a photograph of the bedroom where the murder took place. Cora's question echoes in her mind, followed by another one: what has happened to Donita? She hasn't been in touch; in fact, all of Angel's messages since Friday night have gone undelivered. That's not unusual for Donita because of how Mrs Fann controls her using her phone, but what if she is sitting in a jail cell?

Her thumb continues to swipe through the photos, a reassuring rhythmic gesture while her mind bounces from one possibility to the next. The last photo, Angel hasn't seen before – Mr Hong and his daughter sitting on a settee in the master bedroom. The caption under it says: *Looking for closure. Mr Hong found his wife's body in this room.* His daughter's stare is wide and vacant, her pale hands resting awkwardly on her lap.

Then something catches Angel's attention and, with pinched

fingers, she expands the picture. She gasps. On the dresser, there is a framed photograph of *The Starry Night.* The colours are odd. The frame, a thick gilded square, is exactly the same as the one Angel saw on the hidden camera website.

Chapter Sixteen

Cora's eyes fly open to a wide slice of warm, honeyed light stretching across her bedroom floor. It is 10.30 a.m.; she has overslept almost four hours past her usual wake-up time. She scrambles to her feet so quickly that her brain takes a moment to adjust to her movements. Once again, she is rushing through the Calverts' house, doing one last thing before she can escape.

She was up until the early hours of the morning, unable to sleep. She lay in her bed, witnessing the evening sinking into that velvety deep silence that she has only ever known in neighbourhoods like Bukit Timah and Dasmariñas, where the houses were ensconced in towering groves and hidden at the top of private roads.

Ma'am Elizabeth had noticed Cora looking slightly pale at dinner.

'Are you unwell?' she asked.

To which Cora nodded, because what else could she say? She had crushed up the pills, as she had done every night so far, and looked at them for a long time before sweeping them into the bin, as she had done every night so far. No matter what Jacqueline thought, no matter what Cora had done in her past, she wouldn't – couldn't – betray an employer again.

She rushes to the bathroom and takes a quick shower, listening for movements in the house as she pats her body down afterwards with a towel. Stepping into her standard dress code of a cotton T-shirt and a pair of loose batik shorts, Cora wonders if it was a mistake telling Angel about what happened to Raymond. It was a confession but Cora doesn't feel absolved. And then Angel made that discovery about the camera in the Hongs' home, and Cora felt so overcome with guilt that she simply couldn't tell Angel any more.

There is a chorus of voices in the living room when Cora emerges with damp hair and a prepared apology. The television, turned to Asia News Network, is louder than usual. Ma'am Elizabeth is nowhere to be seen. The screen is split three ways for an overlapping conversation between three men in black suits, sitting against backdrops of skylines and bridges. Cora only has to pay attention for a few seconds to realize that they are discussing the stock market, not Flordeliza Martinez.

She spots Ma'am Elizabeth lounging in the pergola and her heart catches in her throat. Right then, Cora wants to tell her everything that Jacqueline did, if only to untangle herself from this family once and for all. Ma'am Elizabeth is frowning at her iPad screen.

'Ma'am?' Cora says.

Ma'am Elizabeth lifts her head and gives Cora a little wave. 'Are you feeling better?' she asks as she peels herself off the chair and steps back into the house. 'I think I'm starting to come down with something as well. I could have stayed in bed all morning, but there's this news briefing about SAGE that I want to watch.'

'I'm feeling better, Ma'am,' Cora says. Her response is

automatic; anything else she needs to say dissipates. She adds: 'I'm very sorry for sleeping so late.'

'Not a problem,' Ma'am Elizabeth says. 'No need to do breakfast this morning, Cecilia stayed over at a friend's last night. Jacqueline has the day off for another dress fitting and then they'll both be here for lunch, if they don't kill each other first.'

'Yes, ma'am,' Cora says. 'Last night, I marinated the pork belly in *char siu* sauce for tonight's dinner. I can cook that for lunch instead.'

'That would be very nice, thank you. We should have some shrimp and pork mixture left over from the dumplings you made on Friday as well. Can you steam another batch? They were divine.'

Crossing the broad living room to enter the kitchen, she glimpses Jacqueline's black portfolio sitting on the dining table. It is closed, and she would not dream of opening it, but her fingers itch for a chance to flip through it to see if Ma'am Elizabeth has signed the papers yet. There isn't a hint of revelation on Ma'am Elizabeth's face. Before getting her hands covered in a paste of tapioca flour and water for the dumpling skins, Cora does a quick survey of her messages. Still nothing from Donita, which worries her, especially after the messages that Angel sent to their group last night.

ANGEL: *Ladies, this is important. I think there is some evidence that the police either have not considered, or they are ignoring. Look at the photo in the article. There is a picture frame in the background, pointing directly towards the closet. I think there's a camera inside the frame. Look at this link! I came across the same photo frame when I was searching for hidden cameras online before my interviews. The old picture is still inside the frame. Maybe Mrs Hong put it there to catch her cheating husband? Or the husband put it there to see what she was up to in the bedroom?*

ANGEL: *Hello? Donita? This is a big deal. Please tell me you're getting these messages. I was just thinking that if the camera recorded what happened in the bedroom, the video must be captured on Mrs Hong's phone right? Or her husband's? And the police would have seen it. If Flordeliza really did something, the police would have evidence and it would be all over the papers. I think the camera recorded something else.*

ANGEL: *Donita? Are you seeing these messages? Write back when you can.*

CORA: *Donita, let us know that you're okay.*

She turns up the volume on the phone so she can hear notifications when they come through. Kneading the dough for the dumpling skins takes only a little bit of time and she doesn't have to check the recipe for portions of water or flour. The dough yields to the half rotations of her fists. Light morning rain patters against the panel window above the sink. It feels like the last time she will stand here, like she just has to blink and she'll be back in Manila. Take this, she is telling Paolo, pushing the earring into his hand, and he is shaking his head slowly. *It's not enough. I want something else.*

The doorbell rings at 12.30, just as Cora is setting the table. Jacqueline and Cecilia stride through the foyer with two blocky shopping bags. 'You bite the shoes first and they won't bite you back,' Jacqueline says. 'Wasn't that what Pó Po used to say? It worked for her.'

'There's this beeswax rub you can get for your heels. It rolls on like deodorant,' Cecilia replies. 'The last thing you want is uncomfortable feet on your wedding day.'

Cora avoids the black portfolio sitting on the dining table but it becomes a centrepiece as she inches the plates and cutlery into their places. Cecilia gives her a wave before disappearing up the stairs. Jacqueline does not pay any attention to her. Her eyes are focused on the television screen.

'What a mess,' she tells Ma'am Elizabeth, nodding at the television. Two graphs with screaming red lines fill the screen. 'Hans was dealing with this all weekend.'

'I hope they still air the SAGE briefing,' Ma'am Elizabeth says. 'They're supposed to go live in a couple of minutes. We need an indication of whether we're going to be voting again to reinstate the former executive committee.'

'We?' Jacqueline asks with an eyebrow raised.

'You didn't know I was a SAGE member?' Ma'am Elizabeth asks.

'Never an active one,' Jacqueline says. 'You've been following this drama?'

'More than following. I made a few calls yesterday to make sure that Camille Cherian was assigned to the interview today. The anchor that SAGE requested, Harris Ng? He's a prominent megachurch member. It's not fair.'

'I thought we talked about getting involved with politics. It's different for our family, especially—'

Ma'am Elizabeth cuts off Jacqueline by drifting over to the dining table to inspect the dishes. 'Just wonderful, Cora. So fragrant. What's the secret ingredient you've been putting into the dumpling stuffing again?'

'Some chopped snow pea shoots,' Cora says. She casts a quick look at Jacqueline to see her face turned to stone.

'Snow pea shoots!' Ma'am Elizabeth exclaims, clasping her hands together. 'They're subtle but they add this depth to the dumplings that we never had before. Come Jacqueline, it's time to eat. Call your sister. And keep the TV on, just lower the volume. I don't want to miss the press conference.'

Jacqueline holds Cora's gaze as she crosses to the stairs. From the middle landing, she calls Cecilia's name. Cora and Ma'am Elizabeth both look at the portfolio at the same time and then Cora reaches out for it. 'I put this somewhere else, ma'am?' she asks, but Ma'am Elizabeth shakes her head. The expression on her face is unreadable.

Everybody serves herself. Cora tries to leave two chairs between her and the Lee daughters' seats but Ma'am Elizabeth beckons her to the first seat after the head of the table, where she is positioned. Directly opposite her is Jacqueline. Behind them, the television murmurs. The dumplings explode with flavour in Cora's mouth. She didn't realize until now how hungry she was, having skipped breakfast.

'I'm so blessed to have you all here today,' Ma'am Elizabeth says. 'These opportunities will become fewer after Cecilia goes back to New York and Jacqueline gets married, so thank you for making the time.'

'It's a pleasure,' Jacqueline says brightly. 'I know I've been very stressed lately, and not in the best of moods, but I hope you all understand what incredible pressure I'm under.' She straightens her back and eyes the portfolio.

'And what a fantastic eye for accessories you have when you're trying to buy my forgiveness,' Cecilia says, holding out her wrist to show off a gemstone-clad bracelet.

Ma'am Elizabeth reaches for the portfolio then and hands it to Jacqueline. 'Darling, after a great deal of consideration, I've decided to decline your offer.'

All of the air gets sucked out of the room. Jacqueline's eyes bore into Ma'am Elizabeth's. Cora puts down her chopsticks on the carved ceramic holders. Her eyes trace the fine grain lines of the table beneath the woven placemats.

'I don't understand,' Jacqueline sputters finally. 'I thought you were – I thought we were . . .' She squares her shoulders. 'We had an agreement.'

'I said I would consider it. I made no promises.'

Cora is aware that Jacqueline was addressing her. She doesn't dare look up from the table, but then she hears her name.

'Cora,' Cecilia stage-whispers. 'Perhaps you can leave us alone to discuss this private family matter?'

'Yes,' Ma'am Elizabeth says wearily. 'I'm sorry Cora, I shouldn't have brought it up at lunch with you here. Do you mind giving us a moment?'

'Sorry Cora,' Jacqueline mimics, just as Cora nods and scoots back her chair to stand. 'So many apologies, all the time, for Cora.'

'Jacqueline,' Ma'am Elizabeth warns.

'Why are you always behaving as though Cora is a house guest that you have to tiptoe around? There's so much fear around Cora's feelings, what will Cora think, what a magnificent feat Cora achieved today rearranging our antiques or adding secret ingredients to our grandmother's recipes.'

Cecilia's eyes are wide. 'Jac, that's really rude. She's right here.'

Cora remains frozen in her chair. She sees a look of dismay on Ma'am Elizabeth's face, the apology Ma'am Elizabeth wants to utter again for her daughter's outburst, and she draws in a deep breath and rises. 'Miss Jacqueline, I am not a guest in this house,' Cora says. 'A guest is somebody you treat with respect. What you asked me to do is not respectful. I can get into so much trouble, and I can hurt Ma'am Elizabeth.'

Ma'am Elizabeth looks back and forth between Jacqueline and Cora. 'What were you asked to do? Cora?'

'Oh, I just asked her to give you a little nudge about signing the papers. No need to be so dramatic, Cora,' Jacqueline says.

There is an edge of nervousness in her voice before she recovers and commands, 'Now sit down, because we need to have a chat about your previous employers.'

'I will not sit down,' Cora says. 'Ma'am Elizabeth, I am very sorry to say, I quit.'

'What?' Ma'am Elizabeth says. Cecilia lets out a small cry as well. 'Please, Cora, let's talk about this.'

Cora shakes her head. 'I never asked for anything except a job where I can do my work and have peace at the end of the day.'

'And have a place to hide,' Jacqueline says. 'A shelter in a country where the Philippines police couldn't track you down, isn't that right?'

Cora grips the edge of the table. The smooth wood feels solid in her palms. Ma'am Elizabeth blinks at her. 'The police?' she asks.

'Do you want to tell her, or should I?' Jacqueline asks Cora. 'About your illegal activity, about men coming after you, about *stealing* from the employers who took you in.'

Cora can barely get the words out. 'I will pack up my things.'

Ma'am Elizabeth is pinching the bridge of her nose. 'Cora, it's not that simple. If there's something I need to know . . .'

'Then Jacqueline will tell you. She seems to know everything.'

As she says this, Cora catches the look on Cecilia's face. It is full of admiration. A smile tickles the edges of her lips and her eyes are round with awe. Cora's vision blurs a little, from tears and some kind of giddiness that she can't quite explain. It is so strong that, for a moment, passing the television, she thinks she sees Donita on the screen, cheering her on.

In her room, Cora begins to pack her bags. She has left her phone in the kitchen, not wanting to break her exit with a detour. Her T-shirts go into the suitcase first, and then her trousers and shorts, followed by two church dresses.

Outside, a conversation is taking place in hushed whispers. She hears the scraping of chair legs against the floor at one point, and a high note from Cecilia ringing like a fork against a champagne glass, but other than that, only the low buzz of discretion. Cora opens her bedside drawer and surveys its contents. Two fat flashlight batteries roll over a clear plastic folder containing her documents. She picks out the folder and tucks it into the front pocket of her suitcase. Pushing her hand into the pocket, she is startled to feel the tiny round beads of her rosary. The last time she held it was in the waiting room of Merry Maids.

Then somebody knocks on her door.

'Cora?' It's Ma'am Elizabeth. Cora hesitates before calling out, 'Yes?' It is her first time omitting the word 'ma'am' from her response.

'Can I come in?'

Cora looks around the room. Soon it will look like she was never here. She crosses to the door and opens it. The shallow threshold frames Ma'am Elizabeth like a portrait. Her hands are clasped together at her chest as if in prayer. 'We need to talk,' she says, eyeing Cora's suitcase.

'Ma'am, I already tell you, I am leaving. I don't want to burden you.'

'Okay fine. I accept your resignation. Can we talk now? Not as employer and worker, but as friends?'

You are not my friend, Cora would have screamed at the top of her lungs earlier today, but with her feet still firmly planted in Ma'am Elizabeth's home, it is too difficult to say this. Wordlessly, she steps aside and lets Ma'am Elizabeth into the room.

'Jacqueline's gone home,' Ma'am Elizabeth says as she takes a seat on the edge of the bed. 'I am sorry that she tried to involve you in those matters.'

'It's because she thinks I have this kind of power over you,' Cora points out. 'You make her think—'

Ma'am Elizabeth holds up a palm. 'I tried very hard to draw a line between us Cora, I did. But you live here. You are part of my household. And I saw how much pride you took in the place.'

'What Miss Jacqueline tried to get me to do is . . .' She hesitates, only knowing the word for 'devious' in Tagalog. '*Masama*,' she says. 'Very wrong.'

'I'm aware of that. But it's not fair to blame me, to punish me, for treating you like a member of my family. The way Jacqueline defines family is different from how I do, do you understand?'

Ma'am Elizabeth's eyes are bright with tears. Cora feels her own throat tightening as well, and she joins Ma'am Elizabeth on the bed. They sit together, shoulder to shoulder, in a small room with two narrow windows facing the skirt of rippled zinc roof that shelters the back shed like an afterthought.

On Cora's first day in this house, Ma'am Elizabeth had knocked on her door after she had finished settling in and commented that the room was small. 'There are empty bedrooms upstairs . . .' she began to offer, trailing off when she noticed Cora recoiling. 'Have I mentioned my children? They don't live here any more,' she recovered, before launching into a breathless description of Cecilia and Jacqueline. Cora simply watched her, ignoring the twist in her gut as Ma'am Elizabeth talked about her daughters who went to university and had careers. She could not help it, even then: she had seen them as the same as the Martell girl.

'My nephew was killed,' Cora says. 'By the police. They thought he was selling drugs.'

Ma'am Elizabeth stifles a gasp of shock. 'Oh Cora,' she says, clasping her hand.

'I had to run away because I spoke out and they came after me,' she continues, gripping Ma'am Elizabeth's hand back. 'That's the short story, okay? I don't want to talk about it any more.'

'And you don't have to,' Ma'am Elizabeth says. Then a shadow of realization flickers in her eyes. 'The backfiring of the motorcycle that day?'

'I thought it was a gunshot,' Cora says.

'Cora, why did you keep this to yourself? What you've been through – it's horrific.' Ma'am Elizabeth's expression hardens. 'And Jacqueline. My goodness. She really thought that I was going to hold it against you? Whatever your nephew was involved in – and I'm sure he was innocent, Cora . . .' Ma'am Elizabeth's eyes lower quickly as she says this. 'It had nothing to do with you. I am so sorry for what my daughter put you through.'

'Ma'am, there is something else.' Cora takes in a deep breath. 'Jacqueline knew . . . Jacqueline got in touch with my former employers,' she says. 'They are not so happy with me.'

'Because those men caused some trouble for them? Yes, I know. She told me just now.'

Cora straightens her back. So Jacqueline didn't reveal everything. She didn't tell Ma'am Elizabeth about what happened in those final moments as Cora tore through the house, searching for what the guards had been sniggering about privately, what Paolo told her to find. She had never seen the pictures of Mrs Calvert until that moment when her hands pulled open the drawer. Those limbs, artfully arranged and pale against a dark backdrop, appeared one by one – arms, legs. Cora ignored the bare breasts and the smooth-shaven V between Mrs Calvert's legs, and the way she looked at the camera with her mouth slightly open. They were there but she managed not to see them, just knowing they existed.

Cora's gaze lands on her packed suitcase. Let this be a confession then. What Ma'am Elizabeth knows or doesn't know makes no difference.

'My boss had some private photographs that she took for her husband. The previous maid came across them one day, and told the guards about them after she left. I gave them to the guards.'

'Why?' Ma'am Elizabeth asks.

'To buy more time,' Cora says. 'The guards were going to tell the police where I had gone if I did not do it. They told me where to find the photos. I think they wanted to use them for bribery later on, or sell them to the correct people, the Calverts' . . . enemies?'

'Rivals,' Ma'am Elizabeth says. 'Yes, I'm familiar with that sort of thing.' She regards Cora with a bit of wariness. 'That's really serious, Cora. It can ruin a person.'

Cora nods, once again looking at her suitcase. She could ask Angel to put her in touch with the people she'd had interviews with. Cora will keep her head down, do as she is told, and be able to stay away from Manila for a few more years.

'Why did you tell me?' Ma'am Elizabeth says softly.

'Ma'am?'

'You knew Jacqueline didn't tell me about it. You told me anyway.'

Cora looks at Ma'am Elizabeth. 'You should know from me. I don't know if, later on, these things will come out, but if they do, then you need to know from me. You also need to know that I never looked through any of your personal things. I keep my employer's life separate from mine.' She rises from the bed. It's time to go. She decides that she won't tell Ma'am Elizabeth about the pills. What good would it serve? Some betrayals are better left unmentioned. She doesn't need to leave another family in ruins.

'So you're leaving then?' Ma'am Elizabeth says. 'You're really quitting?'

'I don't do these things for a show,' Cora says. 'If I continue to work for you, Jacqueline will be around.'

'She won't be,' Ma'am Elizabeth says. 'She's not coming back.'

Cora thinks she has misheard Ma'am Elizabeth. 'Ma'am, you can't kick out your daughter—'

Ma'am Elizabeth chortles. 'I didn't kick her out, Cora, don't worry. She and Hans are moving to London. He was offered a position there, but she didn't want to go. The business proposal was her final effort to have something rooting her to Singapore. Something other than me, of course. She's just told me that this was the push they needed. They leave the week after the wedding.' Ma'am Elizabeth smiles wryly.

'Ma'am, I'm sorry. I do not want to cause Jacqueline to move away.'

'It will be good for her,' Ma'am Elizabeth says, but her voice catches as she speaks. 'I always thought my daughters needed to get out of Singapore and experience life where they weren't the heiresses of Lee's Kopi. Of course, they still stay within their circles wherever they go.'

'So Jacqueline will be all right,' Cora says.

Ma'am Elizabeth's eyes shimmer with tears. 'Think about staying. Please,' she manages, before walking out through the door.

Looking around the empty room, Cora has the sensation of

being back on her first day. *What will I find here?* she asked herself at the beginning of every job, already slightly weary at the thought of tiptoeing around the things she accidentally heard and the knowledge acquired from the corners of each home where secrets were nestled. In Ma'am Elizabeth's house, it was different. She spoke to Cora and laid bare her regrets and solace. Cora felt she was being dragged into knowing what she didn't want to know, but the discoveries were inevitable: Ma'am Elizabeth didn't want any secrets.

Cora stands up and follows her but then turns for the kitchen so she can get her phone. She types quickly: *You wouldn't believe what just happened with Ma'am Elizabeth and her daughters. I need to talk . . .*

She stops. The chat is clogged with unread messages, all from Angel. *OH MY GOD* starts the first one, followed by *ARE YOU SEEING THIS???* and *IT CAN'T BE REAL* and *AM I HALLUCINATING?* The other messages are addressed directly to Donita:

HOW DID YOU DO THAT?

ARE YOU OKAY?

THE WHOLE COUNTRY IS GOING TO BE TALKING ABOUT YOU.

The next message is just a video. On the top left corner of the still is the blue-green sphere of the Asia News Network logo. At the bottom, some text is frozen in a red banner. BREAKING NEWS is all Cora is able to make out, but it hardly registers with her at the time. Because the main image, staring straight into the camera, is Donita.

Chapter Seventeen

Friday – three days earlier . . .

'Turn this off.'

Donita wakes with a start on the storeroom floor to find Mr Fann towering over her, arms extended like a zombie. She scrambles back, a scream frozen in her throat, before she sees him holding out her phone.

'Put in your password and make it stop beeping,' he says. A slice of moonlight gives his white singlet a pale blue tint. Still shaken, Donita takes the phone and does as she is told. Mr Fann takes the phone from her and shuffles back to his room without bothering to shut the storeroom door.

Donita lingers in the doorway and, moments later, she hears the faint sound of Mrs Fann's vanity cupboard door shutting. Donita shuts the storeroom door and slumps against the wall. Her mind is churning, but somehow she manages to fall asleep.

When she wakes up on Saturday morning, her muscles sore from the hard floor, she dusts figurines and dunks a mop into a bucketful of lavender-scented bubbles and watches Mr and

Mrs Fann moving around each other like chess pieces. She waits for a moment where she can sneak into their room and grab her phone to call the Ministry of Manpower hotline.

But to Donita's disappointment, Mrs Fann locks the bedroom door before leaving the flat.

'Cannot trust these maids,' Mrs Fann says as she marches past the kitchen. 'Some people will rob you blind if you let them into your house.'

Donita keeps her head down, scheming as she pushes the mop to make the living room tiles shine. Whenever she gets anywhere near the window, she shoots a quick look towards the Hongs' neighbourhood. She fantasizes chaos – the house in flames; the police surrounding the place; protesters demanding that Elise Hong admit what she did. The stillness taunts her.

Her opportunity comes later that afternoon, when Mrs Fann says loudly, 'Some people got so much free time to go visiting their boyfriends at night but can't even clean the toilet properly. Maybe in their home country they don't have these kinds of standards, that's why.'

Donita grits her teeth and says, 'I'm sorry, ma'am. I will clean the toilet.'

Mrs Fann gasps and puts a palm to her chest. 'Was I talking to you, your highness? Oh, I thought you were too good to do all of this work. Want your own bed, want days off, want freedom to roam the streets . . .'

Donita leaves Mrs Fann to her sarcastic squawking and makes a show of hurrying to the master bedroom. From the volume of Mrs Fann's monologue, she knows she is still standing in the living room.

'Think you're so much better than us?' Mrs Fann continues.

I don't think it. I know it, Donita retorts silently as she moves into the bathroom and opens the cabinet door. She picks her phone off the shelf and searches quickly for the ministry hotline number. The call goes from ringing to a voice almost immediately.

'Hello, please I am being treated badly. My name is Donita—'

'Welcome to the Ministry of Manpower hotline. For English, press one. For Chinese, press two.'

Donita presses one. She can hear Mrs Fann's voice fading as she heads back to the living room.

'Welcome to the Ministry Of Manpower. If you are an employer, press one. If you are an employee, press two. If you are calling about the status of your work permit . . .'

Where is the emergency button to press for escaping a crazy employer? She can hear Mr Fann telling Mrs Fann to calm down. She goes into her chat group to send a message to Angel and Cora, asking them to call the ministry on her behalf. But then she hears Mrs Fann approaching. Donita tosses the phone back into the cabinet but Mrs Fann catches her hastily shutting the door.

'*What are you doing?*' Mrs Fann screeches, lunging at Donita. She grabs her by the thin straps of her tank top and drags her to the hallway, where she pushes Donita so hard she almost topples. 'Edward, you see? You say don't scold her right? You say must be lenient, give her a chance. Their country is full of drug addicts and criminals, so they come here to work, then cannot even work properly. You and Weston – ungrateful for everything you've been provided.'

The mention of her son's name chills the air for a moment. Even Mrs Fann looks slightly startled to have said it. She gains composure quickly and takes hold of Donita's arm with a squeezing grip. 'I have had enough of people questioning me. Do you know who I am? What title I have now? These rich people like Elizabeth Lee, they're just jealous that the church chose me. The reporters want to question me about it on television? I'll make sure everybody knows that you don't need to be rich and pampered like Elizabeth Lee to do good. They think they can purposely pull strings to schedule that lesbian reporter to come to my house.'

Donita can barely make sense of the rant because Mrs Fann's nails are digging into her arm. With a hard shake, Mrs Fann finally lets Donita go. She feels a trickle of warmth on her arm and notices a stream of blood where Mrs Fann's nails have cut into her skin. The area around the small punctures in her arm is tender and already starting to colour. Donita returns to the bathroom to crouch over the toilet with a hard bristled brush while Mrs Fann stands over her, barking out orders. She lets the blood run down her arm and drip onto the floor before wiping it up with a tissue.

Monday morning

By Monday, exhausted from her day off, Cora is sleeping late at Elizabeth Lee's house while Donita wakes up at dawn to begin preparing the flat for the reporters. They are only due to arrive at 11 a.m., but Mrs Fann wants surfaces cleaned, and then the disinfectant smell replaced by something that smells more like a home. As she lights a scented candle called Springtime Sense in the master bathroom, another idea sprouts in Donita's mind.

The camera crew arrives with so much equipment that Donita has to duck into the kitchen to avoid getting knocked in the head by a swinging tripod. Three men in identical black T-shirts hustle through the flat looking for the best place to set up the interview. Mrs Fann trails them to point out various objects of interest in the house that they could use in the shoot – the prominent cross mounted over the television; the Bible placed on the dining-room table; the wall hanging that said, 'As for me and my house, we will serve the Lord.' The condo brochures and tacky ornamental souvenirs have been shoved into a drawer.

Another flock arrives with rolling suitcases filled with make-up and hair spray. 'We'll need a place to plug in, preferably in front of a mirror,' says a woman in skin-tight black jeans, waving a hair curler in Donita's face. Donita leads her to Mrs Fann's bedroom. 'Thanks,' she says. 'Can you bring us some water and turn on the air-con? The lights will be hot later, so she needs her body temp to be cool or she'll sweat and it will ruin the make-up, and then . . .' The woman draws a finger across her throat.

Donita thinks she is talking about Mrs Fann at first, but then another person walks in and a hush falls over the room. Donita takes a moment to recognize the television presenter Camilla Cherian, who is now life-sized and no longer a miniature figure from the news videos about Flordeliza.

'Hello,' she says, looking at Donita curiously. 'You're the Fanns' helper?'

'Hello ma'am,' Donita says.

'Call me Camille,' she replies. 'You are?'

'Donita.'

Camille Cherian's round, peering eyes are so light brown that they are almost amber. Her short bob frames a sharply pretty face. On the news clips that Donita has seen, she only appeared for a few seconds, looking stoic as she read the latest headline. But now she is peering at Donita's arm with a mother's concern.

'My goodness, what happened there?' she asks.

'Just an accident,' Donita says quickly. 'I play with the downstairs cats sometimes.'

Camille blinks. 'Okay,' she says. 'You've been working here long?'

'Few months.'

'Okay,' she says again. A cameraman appears in the doorway. 'Camille, can we do a test shot?' Before following him out through the door, she pulls a business card out of her jacket pocket and hands it to Donita. 'If you have anything to add,' she whispers.

The card remains framed between Donita's fingers even as Mrs Fann and Camille Cherian begin to discuss the interview. 'I'll start off with an introduction of you and do a quick recap of how the new leadership of SAGE was elected, just for anybody who has missed the news lately. Then we'll go into the questions.'

Donita's heart begins to thrum, and her idea begins to grow. She shoves the card into her pocket and returns to the kitchen to get some iced water for Camille. On her way back, she peers into Mr Fann's study, where the interview is to take place. The lights are indeed warm. Mr Fann slipped out of the house earlier with his newspaper, coins clinking in his trouser pockets.

As Donita offers a glass of water to Camille, they make eye contact. 'Here you go, Camille,' Donita says. A startled look crosses Mrs Fann's face as her eyes dart between them.

'Thank you, Donita,' Camille says. 'You know, Poh Choo, if you don't mind, I'd love to get some shots of you and your helper interacting. If we do a re-run of the interview this evening, it's nice to have some footage to splice in with all the conversation, or for some online content.'

'Of course,' Mrs Fann says. 'Donita would be happy to do it. Where shall we go? The kitchen?'

'I was thinking the living room. It's a cosier environment,' Camille says.

'Maybe the storeroom,' Donita says. 'Where I sleep.'

Camille Cherian's eyes bulge out of her head. Mrs Fann laughs nervously. 'She's joking of course,' she trills. 'Donita has her own bedroom.'

'Was that your son's room?' Camille says.

'Yes, he's studying in Sydney.'

'Wes Fann, correct?' Camille asks.

'Weston,' Mrs Fann corrects, leaning hard on the second syllable. 'But I don't think you need to mention him. The focus should be on SAGE, not my family.'

'Of course,' Camille murmurs before turning to Donita with a bright smile. 'Maybe you can tell us about how Mrs Fann is a champion of women.'

'Yes,' Donita says. 'Ma'am is very supportive. She always looks out for my safety. She says, don't go out on Sundays, and she keeps my phone so I won't go down a bad path.'

Camille frowns. 'Seems a bit restrictive,' she tells Mrs Fann.

'It's out of concern for her safety, as she said,' Mrs Fann says tersely.

'In this house, there is a lot of love and compassion,' Donita says. 'You can see from all the things.' Her heart pounds in her chest as she trains her eyes on Camille. *Please follow along. Please don't make this a wasted effort, because I'm going to be in a lot of trouble either way.* Donita leads Mrs Fann and Camille to the dining room, where another Psalms wall hanging went up yesterday. Behind Donita is the closed storeroom. If she took one step back, the doorknob would dig into her spine.

'So you've always been an activist then, Poh Choo?' Camille asks. 'Because one of the concerns from SAGE members, as you know, is your lack of experience.'

'Oh yes, always,' Mrs Fann says. 'I always cared about the welfare of women. I used to volunteer at Planned Parenthood.'

'With the church though, right?' Camille presses. 'You used to stand outside and distribute anti-abortion pamphlets?'

Mrs Fann glares at Camille. 'Yes, because I was concerned about our nation's *eternal welfare*. You know, Harris Ng was supposed to do this interview. Why the last-minute change?'

Camille's composure does not change. 'There was a scheduling conflict,' she says, her voice like a steady breeze.

'Nothing to do with Elizabeth Lee then? From Lee's Kopi? I heard a rumour that she made some calls.'

Camille smiles reassuringly. 'It's understandable that you're nervous, Poh Choo. There's a lot riding on this interview. If any questions make you uncomfortable, you don't have to answer them. This is your opportunity to show Singapore that you are a deserving leader in gender equality.'

Mrs Fann doesn't look convinced but she purses her lips together and says nothing else. A cameraman emerges from the study then. 'Okay set-up finished. Camille, you need to be in make-up. We're running late.'

'Okay,' Camille says. 'Excuse me, ladies.' They have to change their configuration to make room for her to inch past the dining table and into the hallway. Mrs Fann now comes to stand next to Donita. Donita catches the strong floral whiff of Mrs Fann's shampoo and feels the bruise on her arm throbbing. It is the final boost she needs.

Donita yanks open the storeroom door, nearly knocking Mrs Fann over, before Donita catches her by the shoulders. Mrs Fann's stiffly coiffed hair trembles and her mouth forms a surprised O, as Donita shoves her into the storeroom and shuts the door, locking it from the outside with a press of the doorknob button.

'*Roll the cameras!*' Camille shouts. Mrs Fann screams and bangs on the door and the make-up artists come piling out of the bedroom to check out the commotion. A cameraman reaches for the storeroom door to open it, but Camille bats him away and calls the make-up girl with tight black jeans to stand watch.

Donita scrambles to the study with Camille in tow. 'Coming to you live from the Marine Parade home of Mrs Fann Poh Choo, the new president of SAGE. In an interesting development, her domestic helper Donita would like to say a few words on her behalf.'

Shaking with exhilaration, Donita suddenly has no words. How to sum up everything that she has endured in this flat? 'I'm Mrs Fann's maid. She's . . . she hired me to work here. It's . . . it's really bad.' Camille nods encouragingly. In the background, Mrs Fann begins to wail. Donita lifts her arm to the camera. 'She did this. I've been sleeping in the storeroom since Friday night as a punishment because I went out. And she doesn't give me enough food to eat.' Once the grievances start pouring out, Donita can't stop. It sounds as if there are gasps and murmurs all over the island, but they are only coming from the crew, who are standing in the doorway. Mrs Fann's cries have reduced to whimpers. A cameraman shoots Camille a questioning look and she responds with an almost imperceptible shake of her head as if to say, 'Keep going.'

As Donita explains her life with Mrs Fann, she feels a sensation of being lifted out of her body. It is the adrenaline, surely, and the fatigue that she has been suppressing for months, rushing back to put her in this strange dream state. She sees her younger self cradled in the valley of rice terraces, her bare feet stepping with careful balance on those narrow shelves of packed earth. She is turning her face to the sky and wondering what the world has in store for her.

Monday afternoon

The car pulls off the highway and onto a wide road flanked by broad, low-levelled buildings with blue painted railings. There are women milling about on the landings and climbing the ladder-steep metal stairs between the floors. T-shirts and skirts fly like flags from wires strung between the staircase railings and the door handles. A faded sign greets Donita: Renfield Lodge Dormitory. A few women crowd together on the balcony to peer at the car but they retreat quickly.

There is a small, air-conditioned office on the first floor where Donita, with her rolling suitcase and a black tote bag, hands over her identification card. She is almost shaking with relief that the car didn't pull into a prison, which is where Mrs Fann clearly wanted her to go. 'I want her out of my house!' Mrs Fann screamed at the camera crew when they unlocked the storeroom door. She eventually repeated these instructions to the Merry Maids agent on the phone, who asked to speak to Donita only to tell her, 'You are in serious trouble.'

Serious like deportation, which is a punishment that Donita is ready to accept if she doesn't have to go to jail first. The woman at the registration desk looks bored as she registers Donita and hands her a pair of keys. Her name tag says Mariam.

'You're in Room 327. Two Indonesians and one Myanmar girl with you. Once there is a vacancy, I can change you to a room with other Filipinos. We don't have space now, so don't ask. Rules are here.' She taps at a laminated sheet taped to the desk. 'Most important: no smoking in the rooms, no boyfriends at any time, but daytime visitors can register here. You want to go anywhere, you must sign out and sign in.

Food, you buy your own, we don't have a catering service. Nearest supermarket is two bus stops away. Shared kitchen and toilets on each floor, bring your own soap and shampoo to the shower.' Mariam looks up once. 'Your agency instructed me to take your phone.'

Donita opens her mouth to protest but she is silenced by the woman's glare. She had pushed her phone to the bottom of her suitcase so Mrs Fann wouldn't be able to confiscate it on her way out. The last thing she wants is more trouble, so she reaches into her suitcase and hands it over.

Mariam screws her eyes at Donita. 'You been here before? You look familiar.'

Donita shakes her head, wondering how many people have seen the video by now. She feels Mariam's eyes on her back as she hauls her suitcase out the door and goes to find her room. The women in the balconies part to let her through. She keeps her head down, nervous to be recognized, but the whispers begin immediately and the air is boiling with conversations about Donita's TV appearance by the time she reaches her door. A foot shoots out in front of Donita as she fiddles with the keys.

'You're not staying there,' says a petite Filipino woman who looks as if she's in her forties. She nods at another woman, who takes Donita's suitcase. She follows them, unsure of what is happening. They lead her down the corridor to another room, clearly their room.

'Chitra, this is our friend from our country. Can you change places with her? Her room also has no Sri Lankans, so it's exactly the same as this one.'

A woman wearing a baggy T-shirt over long tracksuit bottoms packs up her belongings – a thin book with a Buddhist monk on the cover and a backpack of clothes – and scoots out through the door. She exchanges keys with Donita. 'Room 327,' the Filipino woman calls out after her. She turns to Donita. 'I'm Rica. This is Maybell. And Tala will come later. Her bed is on top of yours.'

'She'll probably give you her bunk,' Maybell jokes. 'I can't wait to see her face when she sees that Donita from the viral video is in this room with her.'

Donita takes a moment to take in the room. Two bunk beds with a small dresser wedged between them under a window which overlooks the car park. Cell-phone charger cords spring from a surge protector on the wall. Dusty handprints creep up the sides of the walls, and the paint on the windowsill is scabbing away, but the floors are clean and the sheets are tautly drawn across the mattresses.

The women clear a space for Donita. Rica points out where she can wedge her suitcase so she doesn't trip over it in the middle of the night. 'Take a nap,' Maybell says as she and Rica leave the room for a smoke break. 'This dorm is not much but it has to be better than whatever that ma'am of yours was putting you through.'

And that's true. Donita climbs into a bed that wobbles beneath her weight. The mattress spring digs into her back, and the clang of nearby construction pours through a window that is stuck open. She sleeps peacefully for the first time in months.

Tuesday

At dawn, the clamour of the nearby construction site brings all the women to a grumbling, half-awakened state. 'Can't they at least fix that fucking window?' Maybell asks.

'It was between that and the pest control,' Rica says.

'I'd rather have construction noise than cockroaches again,' Tala says.

For breakfast, they share slices of bread. Donita makes a mental note to buy a loaf of bread at the 7–11 later, and some cup noodles. As she makes a mental shopping list, it occurs to her that she does not know how long she will be here. Nobody from Merry Maids has got in touch.

Maybe the main office has some answers. After breakfast and brushing her teeth, Donita goes downstairs and knocks on the office door. Mariam now definitely recognizes Donita from the news video. 'Look everyone, it's Donita Tugade, big shot celebrity,' she declares.

'There is nobody else here,' Donita informs her.

Mariam scowls at Donita. 'What do you want?'

'I want to contact the Philippines embassy.'

Mariam snorts and returns to her computer. 'Think they have so much time to talk to you? Your agency will handle you.'

'When are they coming?' Donita asks.

'You want the police to hurry up for you too? Don't worry, they're on their way to question you first. Just you wait.'

Donita cannot tell if Mariam is bluffing, but when she returns to her room, she paces the narrow space between the beds, trying to quell her panic. If only she had her phone. Angel and Cora are probably trying to get in touch; she can imagine their messages: *What were you thinking?*

And what will become of Flor now? Donita can't say anything if she's locked up. She fantasizes a finger hovering over the video record button on her phone. What would happen if she broadcast a video about Sterling and Elise, about everything she knows? She would be thrown in jail for sure then.

Footsteps pound outside and seem to shake the whole

building. Through the thin walls, she can hear a girl giggling through a video call with her boyfriend. *Sanjeev*, she thinks, and her chest tightens. She would tell him it was not over, it was never over. She was scared of what she was feeling, and frustrated with the futility of being close to someone in a place that conspired to keep them apart. *Sanjeev, I miss you.*

Her heart leaps at the knock on her door. The police? She casts a glance over her things and wonders if she should just leave them behind. There is another knock, the jiggling of keys, and then the door swings open. Mariam is standing with her arms crossed. 'You have a visitor,' she says curtly before marching off.

From the balcony, Donita can see a woman standing in the courtyard and she is struck by a sense of recognition. There is a slight slouch in this woman's shoulders and the way her dress floats around her calves, exactly like the ghost of Flor that she spotted near the canal from her bedroom window. Donita feels her knees weaken, but keeps her eyes on the woman as she descends the steep metal stairs that take her past the other floors. A small group of Pinoy women knit closer together and whisper as she passes.

The woman who turns to face her is not the spirit of Flordeliza – Donita already knew that. But she is not a total stranger either. She smiles at Donita uncertainly.

'Hi. Donita?' she says.

'Yes,' Donita says.

'I'm Wes,' the woman says.

'Wes . . . ton?' Donita says. 'Mrs Fann's . . . son?'

The woman shakes her head. 'I stopped being Weston one year ago.'

There are some traces of Mrs Fann's features in Wes's face, but mostly she looks like her father. That high nose, those pillowy lips. 'You are very pretty,' Donita blurts out, because she doesn't know what else to say.

It breaks the tension. Wes smiles. 'Thank you. Could we go somewhere to talk?' Her voice is both whispery and deep, like the Sunflower Festival queens in Pasuquin.

Donita glances over her shoulder at the reception office. 'Don't worry about them. I told them I'm from the agency,' Wes says.

'Okay,' Donita says. They take a walk to the coffee shop around the corner. A soft black leather bag hangs from Wes's shoulder. Donita can see a laptop and a water bottle peeping from it. 'You are working?' she asks as they pull up the red plastic chairs.

Wes shakes her head. 'I'm an undergraduate.'

'Mrs Fann say you studying in Sydney.'

Wes shakes her head. 'I'm studying here, in Singapore. I live with my boyfriend's family in Bishan.'

'So your mother . . . she never see you?' Donita asks.

'No,' Wes says. 'She and my father didn't want me in their house after I transitioned.'

Donita can only picture Mrs Fann's frozen, screaming face. 'Your father seem like he just follow everything,' she says.

'That hasn't changed then,' Wes says. 'At one point I thought he would come through for me. He's experienced it too. He was diagnosed with depression after he lost his job, and my mother got the pastor to tell him to find God instead of taking medication.'

The pills. The nighttime visits to the common bathroom. 'He take the medicine secretly,' Donita says. 'I always see him.'

'Was he better though?' Wes asks. 'I know he works part-time now. I've . . . I've been around the place a few times.'

Donita doesn't tell Wes that she saw her from the window.

She wonders if this is why Wes has come to see her. 'He's very quiet,' she says truthfully. 'He reads his newspaper a lot. But,' she adds when Wes's face begins to fall, 'he does not like to go to church. Every Sunday, it's an argument.'

This information lights up Wes's face. 'Probably sounds a lot like the arguments I had with my mother. Especially when they rolled out that Come Home initiative.' Wes presses the heel of her palm into the space between her eyes, remembering. 'It was supposed to be a way to get young people interested in the church again, but then my mother's friends got hold of it and made it about converting gay people. They put all the funds into protesting SingaPride and hiring these homophobic preachers from megachurches in the US. My mother followed along because she wanted to prove to them that she was trying to do everything to stop me from transitioning. It didn't work, obviously, but I wonder if that's why she volunteered to be front and centre with this whole SAGE takeover.'

'I think she did not volunteer,' Donita says. She remembers the surreptitious looks the other churchwomen gave each other when Mrs Fann wasn't aware. 'I think those women put her there. They could blame her if it did not work.'

'Not surprising,' Wes says. 'My mother trusted them more than anyone.'

'Wes, your parents cannot forget you,' Donita says. She tells Wes about her bedroom, and about how Mrs Fann didn't want her staying there. 'I know it's because she thinks a maid shouldn't have her own room, but she also said that one day you would come back.'

'I can't though,' Wes says, looking down and stirring her drink. 'Not unless I change who I am. I've returned a few times, just to picture what it would be like to walk into that building again, and it's not possible.'

'Then you make your own family, okay?' Donita says.

Wes nods, her tight smile relaxing a fraction. 'Thank you. I came to see you because I wanted to know if you were okay and if there was anything I could do to help. My mother was never nice to the helpers.'

'I'm okay,' Donita says. She'll spare Wes the details of her torment, the fact that she still hears Mrs Fann's voice criticizing her when she is alone in the room. Or when she closes her eyes in the shower, she sees Mrs Fann inspecting her body, prodding at her flesh with a mix of fear and disgust. Then she remembers something. 'I also found your earring in the cabinet, near your father's pills that he takes in secret.'

Wes's face brightens. 'My father kept them?'

Just one, Donita thinks, feeling Mr Fann's loneliness and wishing he had more courage to keep more of his only child. She remembers the T-shirt too. 'Your father wanted to hold on to everything of yours.'

The cloud over Wes's expression breaks for a moment. 'Thank you for telling me,' she says.

'Can I ask you . . . how did you know I was in this dormitory?'

'This is the one Merry Maids always sends the helpers to when things don't work out,' Wes says. 'I saw enough turnovers in our house to know where they ended up. After my father lost his job from taking too many days off, my mother had to let go of our helper Lucilla. That was when she turned all her attention on me, and she found out about my life. I think, after I left home, she probably hired a helper again just to have somebody to blame for things going wrong.'

It sounds about right to Donita. 'Your mother wants people to think she is rich,' Donita says. 'She thinks maybe this is a way to be happy. Blaming your father for not working harder.'

'I'm sorry for what she put you through,' Wes says. 'Sometimes when I stood outside the building, I wondered what was going on inside. I didn't think I'd ever find out, and then you appeared on the news.'

'You were watching?' Somehow, this makes Donita sadder: the idea of Wes sitting and waiting for her mother to come onscreen in a live interview.

'I've watched that video so many times, I could probably recite the whole thing,' Wes says with a grin. 'People hire entire teams to reach the level of fame you've achieved. Everyone's asking about you.'

'Who?' Donita asks.

Wes shows Donita her phone. At first, her eyes can't adjust to the screen, filled with mentions of Donita's name in bold lettering. *Free Donita Tugade. Where is Donita Tugade? Donita is ALL of us. #DonitaTugade*

'You're all over social media,' Wes says. 'You and SAGE are the most talked-about topics in Singapore right now.'

Donita takes Wes's phone and searches for her name. She taps on the question *Where is Donita Tugade?* and sees that a few people have answered with the name of this dormitory. The responses are outraged. Amid the sea of angry rants, somebody asks the simple question: *Is she okay?*

Donita wishes she could respond to that person. *I am fine. I am away from Mrs Fann. But there is one thing that I need . . .*

'Wes, I know how you can help me,' she says.

Donita returns to the dorm to find Mariam standing outside the reception office, holding a clipboard. 'You were supposed to sign out before leaving,' she says. She taps on the clipboard and starts to say something else when she notices Wes in tow.

'I would like to sign Ms Tugade's release forms,' says

Wes. She is holding her laptop and clearing her throat in a businesslike way.

'I got a call from the agency just now saying that they will be sending her back tonight,' Mariam says, crossing her arms over her chest. 'I don't know who you are.'

'I'm her representative. Her legal representative. I'll speak directly to your boss, please – you're the receptionist from what I understand.' Wes says. It is the way she says 'legal' that makes Mariam shrink and mutter something about protocols. Wes persists. 'Return Ms Tugade her phone immediately,' she snaps. There is something of Mrs Fann in her sharp voice. Donita suppresses a smile as Mariam hurries into the office and returns with her phone. Wes continues to stare Mariam down as she speaks. 'Miss Tugade, please go upstairs and pack your things. Meanwhile, I'm going to speak to your supervisor, Miss Mariam.'

Donita nearly trips up the stairs as she scrolls through the backlog of messages on her phone. Her Facebook inbox is flooded with people asking where she is and how she is doing – complete strangers concerned about her welfare. She goes to the WhatsApp group that she shares with Angel and Cora and sees Angel's shouting messages from the moments after the interview was broadcast. She almost begins to laugh, thinking about it from Angel's perspective.

There are no messages from her aunties or relatives back home, but news from Singapore will take a while to get around to them, unless it relates directly to Flor. Donita bites her lip and scrolls through her calls list. Although she deleted Sanjeev from her address book, there was only one person she texted all the time, and she could almost recite his phone number. She unblocks his number and lets out a breath she didn't even realize she had been holding. *I'm sorry*, she writes. *I don't want to fight any more.* Back in her room, she switches between staring at the screen to see if Sanjeev is typing, and looking away because she can't bear the thought of him seeing that message and slipping his phone back in his pocket, never to speak to her again.

To distract herself, Donita reads through Angel's and Cora's messages, starting from the most recent one. Going backwards in time like this is strangely soothing. She watches Angel's messages go from questions of shock and disbelief and OMGs to regular sentences, and then one message makes her stop. It is a picture of Mr Hong and Elise, with an explanation from Angel about cameras in a print of a painting called *The Starry Night.* Donita's hands begin to shake again. It takes a few moments to steady herself and click on the link that Angel has sent her. If there was really a camera there, it captured everything. Somewhere, there is a video of the whole murder that Elise confessed to.

As she reads this, a message appears at the top of her screen. It's Sanjeev. 'I don't want to fight either. I've been so worried – call me!' Her heart swells. But she'll deal with him later.

The first thing Donita does is send a message to Merry Maids: *Hi. This is Donita. Let me break my contract or I will make a video and tell everybody about how you made me work in the mushroom factory.*

Next, Donita trains the screen on herself. Her hands are shaking. It takes her a moment to get started, just like on the news, but then the words start flowing.

'My name is Donita Tugade, and I want to thank you for your support. Today, I am here to tell you that Flordeliza Martinez is innocent.'

Police Caution Against False Accusations in Hong Murder Case

Singapore police have released a statement warning the public against jumping to conclusions in the pending murder case of Mrs Carolyn Hong. The warning came after a video circulated showing a domestic worker claiming that former Olympic swimmer Sterling Luo was responsible for the killing of Mrs Carolyn Hong, who wanted to break up his affair with her teenaged daughter. Police had alleged that the murder was carried out by Flordeliza Martinez, the Hongs' domestic worker.

In the video, which went viral on Monday evening, a friend of Ms Martinez's claims that there is recorded footage from a hidden camera in the Hongs' bedroom where the murder took place. It is unclear why investigators did not check this security footage, but the police statement suggests that it was a hidden camera, and that the police were not made aware of it.

The video prompted a flurry of online police reports against both Miss Tugade for making false statements, and calls for the police to charge Mr Luo for committing the murder. Netizens also speculate that Miss Tugade was the woman dressed as a ghost whom Mr Hong reported to the authorities. 'We want to remind people to refrain from interfering and spreading false-hoods on a pending investigation,' the police statement reads. 'This includes online comments on social media channels.'

The police have not publicized any updates to the investi-gation. Ms Martinez, who could not provide an alibi for her whereabouts on the evening of the alleged murder, is still being detained.

Chapter Eighteen

Angel hesitates for just a moment before pressing the Find Out More option. After months of ignoring the advertisements that crowded her screen every time she searched for physiotherapy videos, her instinct is still to find a way around them. But they are not pesky hurdles now; they are invitations: Become a nurse assistant! Training on Sundays for current domestic workers. High demand with excellent pay in private homes and aged care facilities. Qualifications transferable for migration to the following countries: Australia, New Zealand, Canada, United Arab Emirates and Hong Kong.

The application does not take long to complete, but there is one question that gives Angel pause. *Why do you want to work as a nurse assistant?* Angel returns to the other details to make sure they are correct. She uploads her passport photograph and puts in her credit card information for the fee before returning to this question of why, but her mind still goes blank.

It's overwhelming trying to find the words to explain how she felt when she saw Nurul marching through the flat with authority – that confidence that only came with being recognized for a professional skill set, rather than the incidental patchwork of knowledge that Angel had. Then there was the way she felt when she learned a new skill, when she did something that helped Mr Vijay's healing. There was also the bleakness of the nursing home tours that she took with Sumanthi, and her certainty that she could make improvements.

Last night, Angel finally replied to all the families she had interviewed with to say that she would consider a position only if they gave her time to undertake her studies in her training programme. The woman who had met her in Toast Box was the first to reply: *I am very disappointed that you are already asking for time off. You would be lucky to work for our family, and you are taking advantage of the situation.*

The family with the teenaged son who was learning Tagalog said that they had decided on another helper, but they wished her the best of luck with her studies. The Tiong Bahru couple with the baby only replied this morning.

Hi Angel! We have discussed it, and we're willing to work out an arrangement. Shu-yen's mother will come over twice a week to take care of the baby during the day so that you are able to do your course work. You will have all Sundays off, so you can attend your classes.

Then Angel did something she has never done before, something that made her feel both bold and foolish. *Good morning, sir,* she wrote. *I would like these terms to be put in writing please.* It only took a few minutes for him to reply, 'Yes, of course,' and this morning she opened her messages to find an attached contract. It filled her with emotion to see her duties, hours and pay typed in black ink.

The German family in Mount Sophia contacted Angel to say that none of their interviews had been successful and the position was still open. The ma'am sent Angel her list of requirements – everything from height to temperament was listed – and asked her to circulate it amongst her 'maid community'. Angel didn't reply. That ma'am is probably still trawling the Direct Hire Facebook groups in search of the perfect worker. She is likely a member of the employer groups as well, where the gossip about Donita and Flordeliza must be thriving.

On the pebbled stepping path, some elderly people are doing their morning reflexology exercises. They grip the steel railings and make a painstaking journey across the round stones that knead into their soles, driving the blood in their veins to course through their bodies. Angel notices Mr Vijay watching them and it makes her sad. It was one of her goals to teach him to walk again so he could step barefoot on those pebbles too. 'Nurul will get you walking,' Angel tells him. 'She will know how to help you.'

Mr Vijay offers Angel a small smile. 'She will,' Angel insists. She pats Mr Vijay's hands which are folded together on his lap. The clouds that merged over the park earlier have shifted, and the afternoon sun prickles her skin. Angel wheels Mr Vijay home; she sees Rubylyn, the helper from upstairs, emerging from their building. The toddler under her care is collecting the bright red beads of saga seeds that have fallen onto the ground. 'Not for eating, okay? It's not candy,' Rubylyn says. She fishes a folded paper cup from her pocket and tells him to put the seeds in there. Her face lights up when she sees Angel approaching.

'How many days left?' she asks.

'One more week,' Angel says. She is supposed to spend this week sorting out the apartment to make it easier for Sumanthi to manage when things inevitably crack or break or run out of batteries, but when Nurul called to say she was held up this morning, Angel took the opportunity to steal some time with Mr Vijay.

'You're looking forward to your new job?'

Angel nods. 'They seem like good people.'

'That's a relief.' Rubylyn lowers her voice. 'Have you heard about what's happening tonight?'

'No, what's going on?'

Rubylyn pulls out her phone and shows Angel a message: *Tonight, eight p.m., we make our voices heard. Stand at your kitchen or bedroom window and shine your phone's flashlight to show solidarity for Flordeliza Martinez.*

It's a hoax, of course. Nobody will show up. These sorts of things have circulated before, although the dates and times were not as specific. Ladies, we call for a strike this week. Refuse to wash the dishes! Don't pick up the kids from school! See what happens!

Angel stifles a smile. Rubylyn only arrived in Singapore a year ago. She doesn't realize that protests don't happen here. Ever since Donita's video was released, the comments have piled up and Angel has been keeping track. Some people suggest storming the police station or marching in the streets. It's all fanciful thinking. Angel indulges her anyway. 'I'm glad people are going to say something. Hopefully the police will listen.'

'They'd better. Imagine if we all stopped working. Imagine what would happen to this country.'

Angel has indulged in this scenario before. Those skyline centrepieces would only shine in an architect's imagination; that reclaimed land on the island's edge would remain submerged underwater. In houses, dishes would become crusty with old food stains, curtains would grow furry coats of dust and plants would shrivel into nothingness. Mustiness would replace the smell of air-freshener and clean laundry. Children would wander the streets, not knowing how to get home after school. The windows would be left open and, after storms, spider wasps would pack their conical dirt nests against the sturdy surfaces of bookcases and bedframes.

'They wouldn't know what hit them,' Angel offers.

Rubylyn giggles appreciatively. 'My ma'am is most grateful to me after an off-day. She joked the other day that she's always ready to give her children away by Sunday evening.'

Angel watches the toddler burying his face into Rubylyn's thigh, and she gives him a tickle that makes him squeal. They have never stopped to talk for this long before. Rubylyn begins to tell Angel about her sore calves from a long walk she took with friends along the rail corridor on Sunday, but mid-sentence, the toddler begins to give chase to a pigeon and she chases after him. Angel watches the way she tosses her hair and turns slightly to give Angel a view of her side profile and it occurs to her that Rubylyn has been trying to talk to her for a while.

'You can text me, you know,' Angel says. She feels as if she has forgotten how to do this. 'I mean, if you need any help.'

Rubylyn's smile is like honey.

'I know,' she says, her eyes lingering on Angel's.

At home, after Mr Vijay is settled in his chair in the balcony and the dogs have had their morning treat, Angel looks at the nurse training application again. She considers writing: 'I want to learn these skills and change my career so I can grow as a person.' Immediately, she hears Joy's teasing voice: *You want to grow? Have another* empanada. She smiles to herself. 'I want to care for others,' she finally writes. It is probably what everybody else has written, but there isn't a better way to describe her ambition. If she is honest, she wants to be cared for as well, and she knows this will come. She thinks of the way Rubylyn's smile was like sunlight glancing off the trees in the park.

It gives Angel the courage to reply to Joy. Joy's employer has finally given her phone privileges. Her husband conveyed this information to Angel last night by text, but Joy had already sent Angel several video messages by that point. 'I'm too tired to type, I'll just talk,' she began, before launching into a summary of everything she had been through since coming to Saudi Arabia. Her lips are cracking and her hair is limp in the dry, air-conditioned world of her employers' home. Even the buildings are beige here, because why bother with colour when dust storms coat every surface? The men wear white *thobes*, the women wear black *abayas*. The walls are high so nobody can see into the home, where there are different entrances for men and women. In another message, Joy describes the way the trees are fertilized, each with their own tiny irrigation system, and the swollen black dates that droop from the branches. She sets an alarm to wake her up at two a.m. so she can help her daughters with their homework questions over FaceTime before they have to go to school. Her crucifix and Bible had to stay behind in Bulacan but she worships in her heart.

In her hunger for all that she has been missing from her sister, Angel hasn't yet replied with any updates of her own. Her life is worlds away from anything Joy knows right now. Even a glimpse out of the window would reveal such different landscapes – for Angel, it is the plumes of greenery; for Joy, endless miles of sand. *There was a murder*, Angel imagines herself typing, *and I think I've helped to solve it.* This morning,

a headline came up: *Is Donita Tugade a Performance Artist?*
Angel read through the comments to find that most people
wanted to know where she was now, and if the video were a
hoax, as the newspapers were suggesting. Only Angel and
Cora know that Donita has moved to a migrant worker shelter
whose representatives picked her up from the dormitory after
a call from Wes. Her last message on the group chat was a
picture of the clean room she was sleeping in.

She starts by typing: *Dearest Joy, there is so much I want to
say to you. I have wanted to talk to you about these things for a
while now, but I've been afraid. I didn't want to ruin our relationship after things became strained already during my last visit.*

Soon, Angel's fingers can't keep up with her thoughts and
she finds herself whispering her sentiments. As her voice gets
louder and clearer, she turns on the Recording function in her
WhatsApp so she can do what Joy has been doing – a video
message. She paces her bedroom and narrates the truths of
her life to the person who knows her best, who cannot inter-
rupt her this time. 'Joy, I am a lesbian. I like women. I loved
my ex-girlfriend Suzan. She was not a replacement for something I couldn't have; she was everything I wanted to have.
You didn't believe my heartbreak was real because it was not
the kind of love that seems natural to you, but I know that
this love is like any other. You have to trust that this is true.'

It is a few minutes past eight p.m. now and, as Angel
predicted, there is no protest. The windows in the surrounding
buildings are blank as always. She continues talking to Joy:

'It took a lot of strength for me to tell you about who I
am. I wanted you to know because I needed you to accept me.
Remember that time I fell while playing *patintero* with the
older kids? You crouched next to me and told me to look up
at the sky to keep the tears from falling, and it worked. Or

the first time your husband remarked that I laughed like a hyena, and you retorted that he didn't have such a great laugh himself. That was the sister I wanted then.'

A hooting sound from outside interrupts Angel's message, and it's just as well, because her voice was beginning to catch. She takes a deep breath, vowing to get through this message without crying, when another sound pierces the air. It's a distinctly human whoop.

Angel pauses her recording and goes to the window. She sees nothing but the shadows of the trees and the nighttime landscape of glass windows but there is a tiny bright flash in one of the windows, followed by a shout: 'FREE FLORDELIZA MARTINEZ!' There is applause and cheering, and then a few more lights appear. 'WE WANT FREEDOM FOR FLORDELIZA!' somebody hollers.

The lights and cheers are scattered at first but Angel watches in disbelief as they begin to grow. Could this really be happening? She closes her eyes and listens to the protests ringing out into the night sky. The scattered shouts become chants: FLOR-DE-LI-ZA! FLOR-DE-LI-ZA! FLOR-DE-LI-ZA! Light after light after light appears and soon it feels as if the entire building has erupted in demands for Flordeliza's freedom. The lights are on in nearly every window, joining together to form one strong bolt.

Her own throat has gone dry; she wants to join in but she is stunned. The hairs on her arms stand on end. *'Freedom for Donita Tugade!'* somebody else yells, followed by a burst of cheers that reminds Angel of flocks of mynahs that lift off from the nature reserve's branches in unison at sunset. She turns on her video and scans the street with her camera so Joy will be able to see this too. 'Do you see this, Joy?' Angel asks. 'This is happening in Singapore.'

'*Free Flordeliza Martinez!*' This shout is nearby. Angel cranes her neck to see Sumanthi standing on the balcony, holding up the flashlight from her mobile phone. '*We want justice for Flordeliza and Donita!*' a man shouts back, and then he repeats the phrase in Chinese. Pots and pans clamour noisily against window rails, followed by more whoops and cheers. A bass beat starts to throb between the apartment blocks. Somebody has brought an electric guitar into this. An accompanying drumbeat begins to rattle the skies like thunder. Angel sees more pinpoints of flashlights. '*We're in our own homes!*' a woman shouts, and Angel laughs. It's brilliant. The police can't call it a public assembly if people are simply shouting out of their windows. And how would they know who to arrest? From where Angel is standing, it appears that the whole island is cheering for Flor.

Her arms are covered in goosebumps. There is a message on her phone from Rubylyn.

It's happening!

Angel will finish her message to Joy later. For now, she wants to stand at her window and watch these beams of light. It might never happen again. She closes her eyes and tips her head to the sky. A chorus of 'Amazing Grace' has started and she can hear Rubylyn's voice joining in from above.

Epilogue

Three months later . . .

In daylight, Cora can still see the strands of confetti littering the driveway. She picks a few strands of foil streamers from the hedges as she leaves the Lee residence, even though Ma'am Elizabeth added a party cleaning service to today's Sunday crew so Cora wouldn't have to do the work. For the finale of her bachelorette party, Jacqueline's bridesmaids brought her home for a night of reminiscing. Ma'am Elizabeth greeted them at the door with a knowing smile, having coordinated this with Cecilia, who ran straight from the limo to the guest bathroom to throw up.

Cora will not be attending the wedding this afternoon. She informed Ma'am Elizabeth of her decision as four barefoot bridesmaids traipsed around the garden, spraying champagne on each other. Cora could not imagine spending her Sunday off with this lot. She'd have to smile politely all day and fend off the guests' constant requests for her to refill their glasses. Ma'am Elizabeth understood and didn't ask her to reconsider.

Instead, Cora is spending her Sunday at the Botanic Gardens. It is a short walk, but she takes a longer route through the neighbourhood because she is early for her picnic with Angel. These sloping suburban streets are even quieter on Sundays. The thin branch of a young tree dips under the weight of two crooning bulbuls, and frangipani petals lay scattered on the path to the bus stop. Cora catches a flash of long legs peeking out from a miniskirt, and she almost calls out to Donita before the woman turns and she sees it is actually a teenager from the house down the street.

She has run into Donita a few times since that Japanese family in Tanglin hired her. They live with a King Charles spaniel that Donita simultaneously complains about and poses for photographs with on her social media pages. 'This silly little fool,' she posted yesterday, along with a picture of her stroking his drooping ears. Her work seems to revolve around walking, grooming, feeding and training the dog. She bakes special pies for him and takes him to play-dates with other dogs in the area.

Cora thinks it's all absurd, and sometimes she wants to remind Donita that she got lucky with that new job. Her employers give her every Sunday and public holiday off, and they pay her reasonably well. She had her pick of employers after her video about Flordeliza came out, and she has become a social media star in Singapore – the first domestic worker with a massive online following. Cora clicked on Donita's TikTok link one day and had no idea what was going on – music videos, voiceovers, filters distorting Donita's face as she talked. After coming across something called the Hot Bae Challenge, Cora decided she didn't need to understand Donita's life. What mattered was that she was thriving.

Some people are still calling for Donita's boycott, of course.

They tend to be anonymous commenters, but Cora forces herself to scroll through everything they say because she knows that Donita will not. It used to upset her, seeing all the ugly things that people said when they could hide behind pseudonyms – the continuing accusations of murder, the broad strokes with which they painted all Filipino women. One person who called herself @Flordeliza_the_Killer wrote: *They let me get away with murder! Who will be my next victim?*

The local press hasn't said much about Flordeliza Martinez since the charges were dropped. She was last publicly mentioned in a terse news article stating that she had returned to the Philippines. With the SAGE re-elections dominating the headlines – *Thousands Show Up to Suntec Convention Centre! SAGE Original Executive Committee Restored! A Win for Feminists!* – there wasn't much room left to follow Flor's story, but there was the distraction factor as well. Nobody wants to admit how poorly the investigation had gone, how Flor was presumed guilty without any concrete evidence. The headlines about SAGE gave people the confidence that justice and good sense always prevailed.

Cora finally had a chance to meet and talk to Flor one afternoon when Donita patched her and Angel in on a video call.

'She wants to thank you both for your help,' Donita said.

On the call, it was hard to ignore how diminished Flor looked, compared to the photographs of her in the newspapers, which had been taken from social media. Her face looked gaunt and her smile was thin.

'I don't have the words to tell you both how grateful I am,' she said, her voice cracking.

Later, Angel told Cora that the phone call had made her feel sad. Cora said, 'It's still early. She'll take time to heal from everything.'

They receive updates from Donita: she is back in the Philippines with her daughter. She has taken over an ailing aunt's sari-sari shop, and she has plans to go abroad again – Hong Kong, perhaps, or Qatar. So far, no agent has wanted to take her on without a huge deposit – collateral, in case she gets into trouble again.

In private, Donita rails against the unfairness of Flor's situation.

'She didn't do anything wrong, and now she is marked for ever? Why is she still paying the price for being falsely accused?' she asked Cora one afternoon when they ran into each other in the car park of the local shopping mall. Cora refrained from saying, *This is how it is.* She knew it was useless, so she gave Donita a tight hug. It surprised both of them.

'Be careful, okay?' Cora asked.

She checks Donita's videos every day. She reads the comments. She keeps watch, whether Donita wants her there or not. The best videos are the ones featuring Sanjeev. He tends to look away shyly from the camera, but there are moments when his gaze lands on Donita and anybody can see that he has trouble looking away. Cora was happy to hear from Donita that Sanjeev decided not to hide their relationship from his friends and family.

'They are still getting used to the idea, and maybe it will take them some time to accept it, but the important thing is honesty,' Donita said in a TikTok video, where she invited domestic workers to share their challenges navigating romance in Singapore. She got a huge reaction to that one. It went viral. *Donita + Sanjeev = Singapore's #1 Couple,* somebody commented on Donita's YouTube page once. *Genuine love is so nice to see,* another person agreed, and the trolls could not gain enough traction or support for their racist comments.

This is the kind of thing that gives Cora hope. It means that things could change.

The gardens are bustling because it is one of those days that only happens a handful of times in a year, when the air is cool but the sky shows no hint of an oncoming storm. Cora keeps in step with the families and walking tours at the entrance, but she breaks away to the quiet stretch leading to the pond where Angel said to meet. A large gazebo overlooks the water, and the fields stretch out on both sides. As Cora approaches, she notices two figures in the gazebo and she pauses. Rubylyn is there too. She flicks Angel's hair away from her face and says something to make her laugh.

On my way. Cora sends the message to Angel as she turns to walk in the opposite direction. It's not that she disapproves of their relationship or dislikes Rubylyn, but it's getting harder to spend time with Angel alone and she misses her friend. Angel has become completely absorbed in her relationship – just look at the way she and Rubylyn appear to be attached at the hip, their silhouettes in the gazebo melding into one double-headed figure. Cora has things to tell Angel that Rubylyn wouldn't understand: the bachelorette party and Ma'am Elizabeth's patience wearing thin as the bridesmaids overstayed their welcome; the accidental message they both received from Donita a few days ago on their group chat – a picture of her bare breasts that was surely meant for Sanjeev; the way she has started tentatively looking at old photos of Raymond, even though the pain of raw grief still terrifies her.

Cora will join the picnic later, after Angel's and Rubylyn's excitement at being alone together has worn off. It takes a few hours; Sunday mornings are charged with the giddy delight of reuniting, of skin touching skin. She ambles onto a wide main path cutting across the field and hears the thumping of music from speakers. A group of Filipinos, all identically dressed in pastel-coloured tank tops and matching shorts, are working their way through the steps of a pop song. They applaud when they finish, just as two middle-aged brisk-walking women in workout clothes come up behind Cora.

'Did you bring insecticide or not? Nice day like this, the park will be teeming with them,' one woman says to the other.

'Infested,' her friend replies. 'Government ought to charge entry fees. It gets worse every Sunday.'

Cora turns around and shoots them both a glare. The women look slightly startled and they hurry off.

The first woman audibly mutters, 'She has some nerve to look at us like that.'

'This is a public park. It is for everybody,' Cora calls out. There is a rise of applause from the dancing troupe; Cora doesn't know if they're clapping for her or for another round of choreography. It's not like her to talk back like that, but recent events have given her courage. Those women are lucky she didn't pull her phone out and start recording them. There is a website called OnlyFanns.sg where people have been uploading pictures and videos of Singapore's worst employers.

A few weeks ago, she saw Mrs Fann in the same shopping plaza where she first encountered her. The Merry Maids agency was still running, but Mrs Fann was walking out of one of those agencies on the first floor with the display windows of maids performing their daily chores. The girl with her was dressed in a blue and white uniform. She trailed behind Mrs Fann with her head bowed.

Cora watched them walking to the Cold Storage. Mrs Fann rattled off a long list of things she wanted the girl to buy, and the girl nodded fearfully. At one point, Mrs Fann spun

around to quiz her new maid: 'On Tuesday night, we'll have
. . . what?' The girl stared back. Her whispered reply was
inaudible to Cora, who began inching closer. She could see
the beginnings of an outburst building in Mrs Fann's body
– that puffed-up chest, that twisted mouth – and she wanted
to make herself seen.

Mrs Fann began to berate the maid, but when she noticed
Cora, she paused and lowered her voice, looking over her
shoulder and around the shopping mall. She stared back at
Cora as if she was about to say something, and Cora responded
with a raised eyebrow. She didn't need to say anything, or
suggest to Mrs Fann that she could film her and the video
would go viral in an instant. People were dying to know what
happened to Fann Poh Choo after she was ousted from SAGE
and shunned by her church leaders. Cora had a feeling she
was doing the same things behind closed doors to this new
maid that she had done to Donita, but at least she knew she
was being watched.

A breeze creates a ripple through the shaggy palm leaves.
Cora finds a spot in the shade and rummages through her bag
for her rosary. It is still a comfort, running those beads under
her thumb, and she has managed a few tentative prayers lately.
When she feels ready, she looks through her phone gallery
again. There he is, her clever and sweet and funny nephew, a
six-year-old grinning so hard at the camera that his eyes are
closed. She scrolls and watches him grow taller and bigger.
That picture in his high-school uniform, the tiny specks of
stubble emerging on his chin. Holding up a plate piled high
with macaroni salad at a *noche buena* meal with neighbours.
She takes in a deep breath and taps on the last photo they
ever took together in the restaurant. Until now, she has not
been able to bear to look at it, knowing that she was annoyed

that day, and that Raymond's face could not hide his disappointment.

To her surprise, the file begins to shudder and move. Either by accident, or because he was hoping for a reaction, Raymond had pressed the video recording button. Cora presses her fingertips to her lips, unable to contain her smile. *Happy birthday to you,* Raymond sings. *Happy birthday to you.* Cora shakes her head and tells him to stop, but there is laughter twitching in the corners of her lips.

Instinctively, Cora hits pause on the video. She takes in a gulping breath and waits for her grief to swell and crash down on her – this will be the one. This will be the moment that breaks her. She will howl and tear at the grass and a crowd will gather to view the spectacle. A moment passes, and then another one, and she blinks. A blade of grass tickles her ankles and the branches of the tallest trees paw at the scant clouds. Hot tears spill down her cheeks, but she is still here.

With shaking hands, she presses the play button and allows herself to return to that day. *Happy birthday, Tiya Cora,* Raymond is singing. The camera wobbles and then straightens. All this time, Cora had remembered only her ingratitude, and sure, she does not look pleased, but does Raymond know it? He is right here with her in these sprawling gardens. That easy grin, those kind and hopeful eyes. He can't even finish singing the song, he is laughing so hard.

Author's Note

When I was fifteen years old, my family moved from Singapore to Manila, Philippines. It had been three years since the execution of Flor Contemplacion, a Filipino domestic worker who was accused of murdering a child in Singapore. Being from Singapore, and only having access to one side of the story, I didn't question what I knew until I learned a different narrative in the Philippines. Although this novel is not a retelling of those specific events, it was inspired by my formative experience of traversing places and their truths.

A quarter of the world's 11.5 million migrant domestic workers are women from the Philippines. As nannies, cleaners, elder-care nurses and cooks, they keep households running while navigating life in foreign countries. Often unseen until something goes wrong, they are vulnerable to exploitation in systems that do not protect them. I wrote this novel with hope for more dignity, compassion, and recognition of women like Cora, Angel, Donita and Flordeliza.

I want to take this opportunity as well to remember the families and communities affected by extrajudicial violence in the Philippines. Since 2016, the 'war on drugs' has claimed the lives of over 12,000 Filipinos (according to Human Rights Watch statistics). The website Paalam.org pays tribute to some of the victims. Many, like Raymond, were young people.

Acknowledgements

I interviewed domestic workers and spoke to women about their experiences working in Singapore and Saudi Arabia. Many asked not to be named for privacy reasons. DS made it possible for me to write this book. A group of women I'll refer to as 3R were particularly helpful in helping me navigate and understand the complexities of being a domestic worker in Singapore.

My writing group, The Constituents, saw some early chapters of this novel and provided invaluable feedback. Thank you Ng Yi-Sheng, Prasanthi Ram, Jon Gresham, Arin Fong, Hong Yuchen, Barrie Sherwood and Gautam Joseph. As I say every time we take a group photo, 'what a bunch of clever and good-looking people.'

Thanks to Lawrence Ypil who suggested looking into the role of gossip, friendships and sexuality in domestic worker communities. Thanks to Glenn Diaz who pointed me to literary resources and scholarship about overseas domestic workers. Thanks to Tami Monsod who helped me research an important detail, and for your passionate support.

I have deep gratitude for three readers in the novel's developing stages: Jose 'Butch' Dalisay read an early draft of this novel and provided encouraging feedback. Yu-Mei Balasingamchow's thorough reading and helpful suggestions made the novel even stronger. Kate Heceta's nuanced editorial advice allowed for more cultural and linguistic accuracy in the novel.

The SAGE coup is loosely based on the events of the AWARE takeover in 2009. I was involved in guest writing an episode for a podcast called Saga about these events (and I am shamelessly plugging it here). Thanks to AWARE for inviting me to contribute. Special thanks to Kelly Leow, Jasmine Ng and Bharati Jagdish for the collaborations and conversation.

I can't mention podcasts without citing a major influence on this book and my life: the My Favourite Murder podcast and its fan community. Thanks to Karen Kilgariff and Georgia Hardstark and all Murderinos for bringing light to darkness by creating a space for storytelling, humour and solidarity. SSDGM, always.

Thanks to my agent Anna Power for her enthusiasm when I pitched this novel. I am grateful to my stellar editors Martha Ashby and Rachel Kahan at HarperCollins who championed the book from its earliest days – thank you both for your wisdom. Thanks to Chere Tricot for her sharp attention to detail in the copyediting stages.

Thanks to the National Arts Council, Singapore for providing a Creation Grant to fund my research and writing. Yale-NUS colleagues and friends – thank you for your support.

Paul, a couple of years ago I declared I was done with writing novels, but you didn't believe me. I'm glad you were right. Your patience and unwavering faith in possibility are the reasons I continue to imagine. Also, you make excellent pancakes.

Asher, you grew from a toddler to a kindergartener during the time it took to write this book, and it has been an exhilarating ride. Your curiosity and compassion make me incredibly proud to be your mother. Thank you for being exactly who you are.